T0375313

The Fabulous
Carousels

The Fabulous Carousels

Hitchhiking the American Cultural Revolution

A Historical Novel Based on a True Story

John L. Nelson

THE FABULOUS CAROUSELS
HITCHHIKING THE AMERICAN CULTURAL REVOLUTION

iUniverse books may be ordered through booksellers or by contacting:

iUniverse
1663 Liberty Drive
Bloomington, IN 47403
www.iuniverse.com
1-800-Authors (1-800-288-4677)

ISBN: 978-1-4917-3906-8 (sc)
ISBN: 978-1-4917-3907-5 (e)

Library of Congress Control Number: 2014912488

Printed in the United States of America.

iUniverse rev. date: 07/23/2014

Edited By:
Michael Foerster

Special thanks to:
Frederick B. Karl
Jennifer Frazier
Jesse Keeton
Jim Whittlesey
John Foster
Kevin Mineer
Richard Flemings
Suzanne Goebel, PhD
William "Bill" Hayward

Dedicated to Dr. Frank Edens
... for the gift of education and friendship

Contents

Prelude xiii

Chapter 1   A Pleasurable Peace Rudely Interrupted 1

Chapter 2   Birth Of A Band 5

Chapter 3   The Carousel Club 16

Chapter 4   Metamorphosis 25

Chapter 5   20th Birthday Dinner 36

Chapter 6   Rise Of The Phoenix 44

Chapter 7   The Four Freshmen 55

Chapter 8   Destiny And Dynasty 61

Chapter 9   Big Brother To The Rescue 74

Chapter 10 Kings Of The Bossier Strip 80

Chapter 11 A Professor's Wisdom 86

Chapter 12 Big Fish in a Small Pond 91

Chapter 13 First Southern Tour 96

Chapter 14 Playmate of the Year and Shotguns 105

Chapter 15 Bourbon Street 113

Chapter 16 Seeds Of Conspiracy 121

Chapter 17 Subterraneans 129

Chapter 18 Big Mama 138

Chapter 19 Black Soul 147

Chapter 20 First Northern Tour 156

Chapter 21 Finn And The Bay Of Pigs 168

Chapter 22 A Touch Of Class 175

Chapter 23 A Fool In His Folly 183

Chapter 24 Send Me An Angel...189

Chapter 25 Your Move—My Move.......................................197

Chapter 26 Derby Town..207

Chapter 27 The Show Must Go On.......................................212

Chapter 28 Earning Nashville's Respect................................221

Chapter 29 36 Tailored Tuxedos...226

Chapter 30 Blood Donors..236

Chapter 31 Transitions...242

Chapter 32 Have Trailer, Will Travel....................................251

Chapter 33 The Big Easy..257

Chapter 34 One Day Early...264

Chapter 35 A Living Legend And A Dead President................273

Chapter 36 Things Never Are What They Seem......................284

Chapter 37 Requiem..292

Chapter 38 Celebrity Hero..302

Chapter 39 North Broadway and Absinthe............................309

Chapter 40 I'm Not Your Daddy...317

Chapter 41 Bobby's Crisis...324

Chapter 42 The Scorpion and the Frog.................................330

Chapter 43 Opportunity Knocks..340

Chapter 44 Uncle Remus..348

Chapter 45 Bobby Wears Orange..355

Chapter 46 Setting the Snare...362

Chapter 47 Gargoyles Wheezed..365

Chapter 48 Pitching Zuckerman...372

Chapter 49 The Ball's in My Court......................................378

Chapter 50 Two Options...386

Chapter 51 Line in the Sand..393

Chapter 52 A Bankrupt Brotherhood...................................398

Chapter 53 Showdown in Printers Alley...............................406

Chapter 54 Mountain High—Valley Low.............................413

Chapter 55 Nauseating Paisley...419

Chapter 56 Downward Spiral...426

Chapter 57 Cocoa Beach...431

Chapter 58 Ann-Margret vs. Ghost Crab..............................440

Chapter 59 I Apologize 451
Chapter 60 Abracadabra 459
Chapter 61 Here Comes the Sun 465
Epilogue What Happened to the Cast of Characters? 471
Final Thoughts 477
Author Resume 479

Prelude

The looking glass never lies. It stares back at us in stark indifference, mirroring our lives and culture. Likewise, music never lies. It reflects our character, reveals our psyche and melodically records our culture. Music is our looking glass into the past and present.

The music we sang and danced to between 1957 and 1967 echoed the disturbing cultural undercurrents that triggered the American Cultural Revolution. Earlier events, such as Sen. Joseph McCarthy's paranoid hunt for communist sympathizers, the unpopular war in Korea, and the 1954 U.S. Supreme Court decision in *Brown vs. the Board of Education of Topeka* all foreshadowed the dramatic change that would begin at the close of the '50s.

American optimism ran high during the Eisenhower administration, when many Americans were achieving the American dream, with steady paychecks, intact families and two cars in a new garage. Yet, a lingering Cold War between America and the Soviet Union kept the threat of global nuclear war on everyone's mind. And when Sputnik blasted into space, it sent shock waves of embarrassment and anger across our country for being upstaged by the Russians.

It was left to iconoclast philosophers to fill the gulf between prosperity and disillusion. Jack Kerouac created a sensation with *On the Road*. Ayn Rand posed, "Who is John Galt?" and a former adman with a pen name of Dr. Seuss revolutionized the way kids learn to read.

For the second time in a hundred years, rumblings of civil war crept from the shadows of racial and political disparity. Still struggling to rationalize a slave-based cultural heritage, scores of aging Southerners fanned the flames of discontent. On the national stage, a younger generation pitted itself against the status quo, embracing birth control pills, free love, easy drugs, the hippie generation and Vietnam War protesters.

On the cusp of an emotional breakdown, Americans agonized over the assassination of their president, conspiracy theories, the Cold War, faux reality and societal anarchy. The only thing certain was change.

Throughout this period of turmoil, Rocky Strong was a college student and self-supporting professional musician, struggling to deal with the truth he witnessed—but sometimes refused to see—in the looking glass. Living through tectonic events in American society during the '50s and '60s, Rocky tells the story of the Fabulous Carousels, a band of six southern musicians on the road for six years, covering 30 states, 64 cities, 132 venues and 300,000 road miles.

You are invited to step through the looking glass and share their youthful dreams, hopes, fears and free love—not to mention the subterraneans, drugs, wiseguys, JFK's assassination, betrayal—and, ultimately, self-actualization. Join the Fabulous Carousels, *The Pride of Dixie*, as they pursue dreams of becoming celebrity heroes in America during the tumultuous American Cultural Revolution.

Chapter 1

MAY 1967
A PLEASURABLE PEACE RUDELY INTERRUPTED

A *drift in a dark gymnasium, my life is a puzzle, my future ambiguous.*
"Curiouser and curiouser" defines me. A man in the looking glass. Why
am I here? Where is my promised nirvana? Is any of this lunacy God's plan?
Who is Rocky Strong?

I have to reach the high bar set by my dead father—a 33rd degree Mason—
his 12 Masonic brothers and Mom's mantra, "Make your father proud." Until
my 20th birthday, I consistently hit their marks. Then escapades on the road
interrupted God's providence. But tomorrow morning …

"Freeze!"

A gruff male voice sent a chill through the air above and to my
right, shocking me from my meditation as I sat in the center balcony
of the Louisiana Tech Varsity gym, fifth seat from the aisle on the
third row, on the night of May 28, 1967.

"Put your hands where I can see them. Now!"

The voice came closer.

"Identify yourself. What are you doing here?"

Darkness had been my companion for the past hour. Now, a
flashlight's beam bore into my eyes.

"I said identify yourself!" the voice repeated, louder and more forcefully.

Blinded by the glare, but regaining my composure, I filled my lungs to capacity and shouted back, "Who the fuck are you? And turn off that goddamn flashlight!"

My anger echoed off gymnasium tiles, an important survival lesson learned on the road about when and how to display grit. If the person in the shadows was an acquiescent North Louisiana born-again Christian, Bible-thumpin' Baptist redneck, I hoped to regain the advantage.

"Okay cocksucker. If that's the way you want it, prepare for an ass whuppin'," was the reply of the shadowy figure moving down the stairs. "What name should we put on your body bag?"

Obviously, this was not your typical born-again Baptist. Be that as it may, I wasn't backing down.

"Rocky Strong," I replied, with emphasis on strong.

In a slow and deliberate motion, I stood up, stretched out my 5' 11" 180 pound frame and turned to face the threatening voice. I spread my feet apart and hoped to create a formidable image, capable of handling most anything that came my way.

The flashlight beam lowered to my waist.

That's a good sign, although I still can't see shit.

The gruff voice behind the flashlight softened, "Did you say Rocky Strong?"

"Yep. Rocky Strong. What's it to ya?"

He lowered his flashlight again, and the silhouette of a huge bear with a baseball cap on his head and a uniform trying to contain the physique of a bodybuilder began to materialize. I guessed him to weigh in at 230 pounds. He had a cherubic face that didn't match his buffed body, and ears like open doors of a taxicab. Oh, and he packed a 1911 Colt .45.

Speaking in a more normal tone, the bear said, "Rocky Strong? The only Rocky Strong I ever heard of was leader of the Fabulous Carousels. You wouldn't be that Rocky Strong?"

"One and the same. Who are you, big guy?"

"Daryl Wallace. Louisiana Tech Security Department. I'm covering the night shift at the gym.

"You look like a football player or wrestler," I said, beginning to relax tense muscles in my arms and legs.

"Starting linebacker for the Bulldogs, but got rolled up, taking out both my knees. Just lost my scholarship in December. Coach got me this gig mostly to run up and down stairs for rehabilitation. Hopefully, I'll get my scholarship back and complete my senior year, majoring in English."

"A senior in English," I said. "That's interesting."

Daryl's head bobbed, "English Literature—want to be a writer—novelist. That's all I ever wanted to do, except play football."

"What authors have you read?"

"Hemmingway, Thoreau, Steinbeck, Fitzgerald, Joyce, Tennessee Williams, Dostoyevsky."

Before I could respond, Daryl added more proof to his literary prowess.

"Arthur Miller, Sandberg, Huxley, Ayn Rand, Ginsberg, Kerouac ... among others."

"No shit. Synchronicity is alive and well in Ruston tonight."

With a quizzical smile, Daryl then asked, "What the hell are you doing here?"

"Daryl, tomorrow morning I'll sit in one of those chairs down there, waiting for my name to be called. It's taken me ten years, but I will finally walk across that stage to pick up my sheepskin. I've been sitting here reflecting on my life, particularly the Carousel years, trying to make sense of it all."

"That's a story I'd like to hear," Daryl said, now equally at ease. "You guys are living legends. Didn't you begin in North Louisiana? Escaping to follow your dreams ... that took colossal cohones."

"You got that right. We were on the road six years, covering 30 states, 64 cities, 132 venues and 300,000 miles."

"What was it like? You know, being worshiped like a god, getting laid every night, fame and fortune. And what led you back to Tech?"

"Answering your questions will take time," I replied. "And I'm not certain I can separate fact from fiction anymore."

"Rocky, I get off at six. I have all night to listen."

I've perverted truth and suppressed reality too long. Do I have the capacity to be honest with myself, let alone Daryl? On the other hand, facing my past head-on could help me solve lingering mysteries, the source of my recurring nightmares. Who is Rocky Strong?

Turning back to Daryl, I said, "Since you are an English major, you'll probably recognize a passage from Lewis Carroll's *Alice's Adventures in Wonderland: The White Rabbit put on his spectacles. 'Where shall I begin, please your Majesty?' he asked. 'Begin at the beginning,' the King said gravely, 'and go on til you come to the end: then stop.'*

Acknowledging the humor behind the quote, Daryl's expression demanded more substance.

With an accepting sigh, I said, "Daryl, it is a puzzling story that's never been told. Its roots are wrapped around tectonic shifts in American culture that took place over the past decade. American life morphed from order into anarchy. I found myself an unwilling participant in a societal earthquake that changed America from what we were into what we have become. Somewhere on the journey, my music fell victim, casting me off to search for a new identity, struggling to keep time with changing times."

I hope he's following me. Better tone it down a little.

"Like delicious gumbo, the Carousel story is spicy—perhaps too much cayenne at times, but always yummy. We were six free spirits on the merry-go-round ride of our lives. Jump on. Abandon your inhibitions; risk madness on the other side of the looking glass. The rabbit hole beckons. Are you ready?"

Daryl's head bobbed in agreement.

Daryl was ready. Was I?

Chapter 2

1957
BIRTH OF A BAND

Like many young bands, our beginning was pedestrian. In the fall of 1957, Marion "Rooster" Badcock, Ralph "Reed" Thompson, Al Higginbotham, and I played for Paul Howard and the Arkansas Cotton Pickers. Paul's claim to fame traced back to once being the frontman for the Grand Ole Opry and the Louisiana Hayride. In both gigs, an overstuffed sense of self-importance outgrew Paul's $7^{1/8}$ Stetson hatband, resulting in unceremonious dismissal. Then he parlayed his self-anointed Grand Ole Opry fame into creating the Arkansas Cotton Pickers stage show.

Every other Saturday, appearing in small towns throughout Louisiana, Texas, Arkansas, Oklahoma and Mississippi, the Arkansas Cotton Pickers drew country music devotees. Money flowed into Paul's pocket and the bank accounts of sponsoring organizations, mostly the American Legion, Elks, Moose, Lions, Civitans, and Rotary clubs.

The venues for our shows were old high school auditoriums or gymnasiums. Rarely did they offer air conditioning. Predictably, a moldy stench greeted us at every stage door. Turn on the lights and a thousand roaches scurried for safety. More often than not, torn

5

backdrops, curtains that wouldn't open and sagging boards in the hardwood stages tested our resolve. Most of the time, a handheld megaphone would have served us better than the house amplification systems.

Undaunted, we would set up, do a sound check and wait for the curtain to rise. Before the fourth tune, heat from the 1,000-watt theatrical lights would overpower our starched white shirts, transforming them into dishrags and plastering our thin black ties to our chests. Sweat soaked through our black suits, ran down our legs, and formed puddles in the insoles of our shoes, sloshing away throughout the hour-and-a-half show. But throughout, we smiled and performed our music with manufactured star-studded arrogance.

Following every show, Paul Howard and Nelrose Parker—his country singer, ticket telemarketer and skin-flute player—joined us outside the stage door to settle up—always in cash. Everyone stayed upwind of Nelrose. Her repugnant odor could gag a gnat at ten feet, thus the nickname, Smellierose. Wilted from the bright lights of short-lived fame, Smellierose's starlet persona on stage returned to a vacuous nobody. She stood to the side, bra strap drooping down to her elbow, puffing on what smelled like a marijuana cigarette.

Even in the dark alley behind the stage door, Paul had a way of consuming all the oxygen, leaving no opportunity for others to talk. His rhinestone-studded, red-and-white Western shirt mirrored his colossal self-worth. White pants pulled tight by a silver buckle the size of a dinner plate fought against a belly best suited for Santa Claus. His custom-made red-and-white boots, high enough to reach his knees, featured guitars, fiddles, piano keys and Christian crosses. With the bluster of a carnival barker, Paul handed Al Higginbotham a wad of dough, donned a white Stetson and gave us the name of the next town on our schedule.

Then he ushered Smellierose to the passenger seat of his white 1957 Cadillac Eldorado convertible and burned rubber out of the alley, destined for another derelict $25-a-week, 1920's-era motor court, two weeks of telemarketing and the next Arkansas Cotton

Pickers stage show. Al pocketed leader pay while Rooster, Reed and I got sideman wages: $25 each per show. At least it was regular.

During this time, Rooster, Reed and I lived in Ruston, attending classes at Louisiana Tech. Rooster always wanted to be an engineer. About to complete his second semester, he was smart enough, although volatile; raising questions as to whether he'd last long enough to graduate.

Reed was a sophomore chemistry major, introverted, responsible, married with child, and a so-so reed man.

Al worked at the paper mill in Jonesborough-Hodge. Once upon a time, Al dreamed of achieving fame, fortune and induction into the Country Music Hall of Fame. Unfortunately, like many wannabes, time and talent passed Al by. At this late date, Al's dreams of grandeur could only be realized by consuming a fifth of bourbon. Al was a 52-year-old sloppy drunk determined to imitate his idol, Hank Williams, including getting stinking drunk in the back seat of his 1949 Cadillac following every gig.

I was nearing the end of my freshman year in the college of engineering and played drums.

Every other Saturday we piled into Al's Caddy, inhaling its ever-present, rotten egg, paper mill stink, and navigated two-lane roads to arrive for a 7 p.m. Saturday opening with Paul Howard and the Arkansas Cotton Pickers.

Names on the city limit signs changed, but the show lineup never varied. On stage, we forced smiles and performed the same tired Grand Ole Opry show. Country fans whooped and hollered throughout. From my vantage point, the audiences looked like characters from John Steinbeck's *Grapes of Wrath*. Paul, Smellierose and Al loved it. Rooster, Reed and I hated it, but the steady work paid our bills.

When a show ended, autographs signed and pay handed out in the alley, we packed instruments into the trunk of Al's black Series 62 four-door monster. Al snuggled up with his best friend, Jack Daniels, and soon passed out in the back seat as we waved goodbye to the city limit sign for another year.

Rooster, Reed and I dreaded the grueling return trips home. One night, facing our longest trip of the year—11 hours from Texas City, Texas—the three of us developed a system to keep awake, rotating drivers every three hours. We feared falling asleep at the wheel and ending up dead in some godforsaken ditch. Drawing straws, I got lucky, driving the first leg of the all-night trek back to North Louisiana. One slept while another told stories and engaged the driver in active conversation. As I got in the driver's seat, Rooster began his assignment as the talker while Reed caught winks in the back seat next to Al and his bottle.

The search feature on the Caddy's AM radio stopped at scratchy country stations, lasting less than a minute before fading into oblivion. One powerful AM station out of Del Rio, Texas, played Mexicali music until a fire-breathing evangelist took over at midnight, promising eternal salvation for the wicked, *"...if you accept Jesus Christ as your Lord and savior."* Within 5 minutes, we gave up on salvation and the radio.

Filling seemingly endless hours with stories and conversation, we kept the driver awake—at a price. The longer the drive, the more vulnerable we became to exposing inner demons. Sure enough, the demons surfaced that night.

Rooster and I were yin and yang, except for music, where our brains and aesthetic tastes spiritually connected. We were polar opposites on all remaining subjects. Our discussions usually ended up by hurling personal attacks at each other in order to win a point. Predictably, no one ever won.

That night, Rooster began the debate with a hot topic at the time: integration.

"What do you think about Governor Faubus calling out the Arkansas National Guard to stop nine niggers from attending the all-white Central High School in Little Rock?" he asked.

"This is the beginning, not the end," I replied. "I believe Faubus will win votes, but lose in the courts. We'll all be going to school with shines in a couple of years."

Then, to egg him on, I added, "I can't wait to hear your views on this one."

"Faubus should whisper in the ears of his Arkansas National Guard KKK brothers suggesting they create an incident as justification for shooting a couple of nigger agitators," he responded. "That'll get their attention. Niggers are cowards. One picture of a dead nigger on the front page of the newspaper will stop this unnatural act in its tracks."

"Unnatural? Where did that come from?"

"Let me ask you, Rocky: would a duck fuck a chicken?"

"Nope."

"Then why would a white woman fuck a nigger? Unnatural. Unthinkable."

"Rooster, you're full of hate," I responded. "No love for mankind."

"Fuck mankind. America is turning into a race of high-yallers, dumbin' down to nigger ignorance. Integration foretells self-destruction of the white race. That's suicide."

"Your hatred blinds your vision of the inevitable," I said. "Rooster, you're a lost soul."

Rooster and I continued in this way, moving from subject to subject, each hoping to win a debate and always refusing to accept the other's point of view.

Much like actors on the silent screen, our body language rivaled Charlie Chaplin's best scenes. Verbal jabs and body blows reverberated off the headliner, prompting rotten egg stink to rise from soiled velour seats and descend from above. For the next two hours Rooster and I slugged it out, defending polar opposite views on Senator Strom Thurmond's longest filibuster in history in opposition to the Civil Rights bill and the KKK forcing Willie Edwards to jump off an Alabama bridge to his death.

The list grew as the miles ticked by: President Eisenhower sending in federal troops to protect the Little Rock Nine, Ayn Rand's *Fountainhead* and *Atlas Shrugged*, Jack Kerouac's *On the Road*, and Russia putting Sputnik into orbit. When we exhausted those topics, we verbally wrestled with other events: the FBI arresting Jimmy Hoffa for bribery; Carlos Marcello and other Mafia leaders arrested by police at the Apalachin conference; and Hurricane Audrey demolishing Cameron, Louisiana, killing 400 people.

Predictably, our relationship eroded during every road trip. However, the spirited debates did keep me awake during my three-hour shift at the wheel.

Following some babble about Al's stinky car, Rooster drifted away from current events and asked me a personal question.

"What are you most proud of, Rocky?"

"Well, joining the Presbyterian Church, achieving Boy Scout awards, making all-state orchestra, all-state band, all-state baseball and winning the AAA high school baseball championship. Of course, paying my way through Tech is near the top."

"And what are your biggest disappointments—shortcomings—failures?"

"That's a challenge." I said, reflecting before answering. "Quitting the Tech baseball team to earn a living playing music. I'll always wonder if I could have made it in the Big Show. However, I had to choose. Economics favored music at the expense of my love of baseball.

"That's it?" Rooster replied. "That's your biggest disappointment? You're telling me you never failed at anything except quitting the Tech ball club?"

"At this moment, that's all I can think of."

"That's bullshit! You're either the biggest liar in history or auditioning for the second coming of Christ. Which is it, Rocky? Are you perfect or imperfect? Admit it; you're probably going to burn in Hell with the rest of us mere mortals. You can't admit your sinful ways. That's fucked up thinking, Rocky."

"I'm far from perfect. But your sanctimonious judgment is laughable. Look in the mirror, then tell me who's gonna burn in Hell. I've had enough of your insults. Shut your pie hole!"

In silence, a half-hour passed before Rooster took his turn behind the wheel, rotating me into the talker's seat. About an inch shorter and 10 pounds lighter, Rooster adjusted the seat, his good eye twitching wildly—mumbling under his breath, "Mother Fucker!" He turned the ignition key, floored the accelerator, and we raced off into the Texas night as Rooster sought vengeance against a faceless enemy.

Rooster's butt squirmed like a dog with worms, burrowing deep into the velour seat. Muscles clenched, Rooster began punching the seat between us, at least 20 times, each blow raising a cloud of toxic dust that sent me into involuntary sneezing.

Then he attacked the steering wheel, bending the top and cracking the plastic in several places. Practically foaming at the mouth like a mad dog, Rooster spit in his palms, rubbed them together and squeezed the steering wheel so hard his knuckles turned white.

Dear God. Please let me survive this lunatic.

Finally, at 2:30 in the morning and without preface, the reason for his violence was finally revealed. Rooster began his life story. For the first and only time during our tumultuous eight-year relationship, Rooster lowered his defenses and unleashed the demons he'd buried deep in his solitary dungeon.

With rage in his voice, Rooster let me inside his childhood nightmares.

"My fuckin' ol' man beat my Mom every time he got soused, which was pretty much every night. One night when I was ten, I tried to stop the beating. My ol' man caught my right eye with a bottle of Old Crow. The bottle shattered, and my eyeball rolled out on the linoleum. Blood went everywhere. Three days later, I woke up at Charity Hospital in Shreveport. Doctors had inserted a glass eye three shades lighter than my real eye.

"The Jonesborough-Hodge and Shreveport police interviewed me in my hospital bed. That's when I learned my ol' man turned the jagged bottle on Mom, ripping out her throat. She bled out next to me on the linoleum. I swore on my mother's grave that I'd kill that son-of-a-bitch the very day he got out of jail."

Shaking clenched fists in the air for a perilous mile, the Cadillac swapped lanes at 95 miles per hour. At last, he added, "Rock, I won't find peace till he's dead by these hands."

As the Caddy veered wildly from one side of the road to the other, I wondered how I would survive the inevitable car crash.

I'll grab the wheel just before we careen off the asphalt. However, if we head for the ditches, I'll jump over the front seat and lay on the rear floorboard. Wedged between the front and back seat I might survive Rooster's insanity. If the Cadillac catches fire, I'll have to move fast. Who will I save first? Reed's first and Rooster's second. Al's so drunk he won't get hurt in the accident— limp as a used condom. Be alert. Think quick.

Finally, Rooster's hands returned to the wheel, momentarily avoiding tragedy. I might as well have been a fence post, sitting motionless in the passenger seat, saying nothing, giving Rooster and his demons a wide berth. In due course, my patience was rewarded, as Rooster gained some sense of sanity and continued his story.

"For a long, long time, murdering my ol' man consumed me. After a while, I decided to do something positive with my life. Makin' something of myself would really piss off my ol' man. I discovered that happiness lies in playing music and, of course, that beautiful warm moist spot between a woman's legs. Music and fuckin' became my pathway to sanity. I'll fuck anything from a horse collar to a Coke bottle. If it's old enough to bleed it's old enough to breed.

"As for music, I set out to learn every tune, genre, style and in every key. When it comes to 'name that tune,' I can't be beat on keyboards. And the babes love a creative musician, even one with a glass eye."

In violation of our driving pact, I sat in silence. Rooster turned on the heater, awakening the awful paper mill vapors that promptly permeated Al's car. The odor flooded my eyes with tears, and I almost threw up from the disgusting fumes.

As I reached to turn down the temperature lever, Rooster erupted in a second crazed outburst, smashing the gas pedal against the firewall. All 160 horses of the Caddy's V-8 coughed, spit, belched and groaned. Finally, the 4,000-pound behemoth lived up to its manufacturer's specifications, reaching 105 miles per hour. Twenty minutes at top speed foretold a death wish in the making.

Thankfully, as suddenly as his outburst began, Rooster began to relax, and his foot eased off the gas. The speedometer inched down to 75, and my color and sanity returned.

The first oncoming car we'd seen in an hour closed rapidly, then raced past at high speed. A County Mountie cruiser chased in hot pursuit, it's flashing red lights temporarily blinding us. Rooster made unintelligible grumbles, contorted, and then farted, forming a lethal cloud that made a paper mill smell like perfume. I lit a match, burned off the stench and checked my watch: 4:38 a.m.

Some 17 minutes later, Rooster's hypnotic fixation on an empty two-lane road leading into a black abyss hit a dead end, and the third act of Rooster's one-man tragedy began.

"I'm tired of getting fucked in the ass by bad music, bad audiences, bad money, and no time to get my pickle gnawed after the show. That brunette wanted my body—bad—but I had to get in the car with you swingin' dicks. That really sucks. This is supposed to be fun. I'd like to bang a starry-eyed virgin after a college gig, be the only man in a five-girl orgy, experience every position in the *Kama Sutra,* and play some good music for a change."

Rooster's boisterous proclamations finally awakened Reed. He leaned over the front seat and joined the conversation.

"I'm married, but I'd sure like to play some good music for a change. I've had it with country and these grueling drives back to Ruston. By the time I get home this morning, I'll be too tired to make love to Sally. Now that sucks!"

Quick on the uptake, Rooster responded, "I've seen Sally. Any time you need a stand-in just let me know."

"Asshole," replied the usually prudish Reed.

I said, "Count me in for change. Know any good musicians interested in joining us? Better yet, either of you know where we can book paying gigs? So far, playing music has been our primary source of income, and the only way we can remain at Tech. Let's make sure we get some gigs before dumping Al, Smellierose, Paul and the Arkansas Cotton Pickers."

That night, despite Rooster's maniacal driving, we reached an agreement that would lead us on a long journey in search of nirvana. Within a month we lined up three new musicians: Bobby Starr, lead vocals and drums; Lance Love, lead vocals, bass, keyboards and reeds; and Norman "Smoke" Van Dyke, guitar, bass, banjo and fiddle. Calling ourselves the Carousels, we signed five contracts for college dances before unceremoniously dumping Al, Smellierose and Paul.

Rough, but determined, our newly formed band put together enough songs to impress the high school and college audiences. Rooster even got his sausage sucked following a college gig—and we never heard the end of that story.

Two months later Reed announced he was leaving the band, in large part because of his wife's jealous paranoia. We replaced Reed with Joseph "Big Joe" Robecheaux, a bonafide Morgan City coonass and engineering student at LSU. He sang the R&B and Zydeco songbooks and played several instruments. Immediately, Big Joe raised our music to a higher standard. His expansive repertoire of music genres and abilities as a music arranger set a new course. As long as we avoided all forms of challenge to Big Joe's machismo, his 500-pound ego assumed responsibility for the Carousels' sound. Gifted musically, managing Big Joe required a velvet glove and a PhD in Psychology.

By default I was elected leader of the Carousels, principally because of my tenacity at finding, pricing and contracting gigs. Truth be known, my fear of financial collapse and dropping out of Tech was huge. I wasn't willing to trust anyone else to consistently produce steady income. With little forethought on my part, I naively accepted responsibility for the economic support of six college students, quickly realizing that leading highly creative free spirits was tougher than herding cats. Counting feathers during a pillow fight would've been easier.

Somehow the Carousels made enough money to survive, playing dances and nightclubs. With the legal drinking age set at 18 in Louisiana and all other southern states, nightclub owners were attracted to our low price, our college-age audiences and our lack of street smarts. Although dances paid more, I focused on booking club dates—infinitely easier than selling one-off dance gigs.

For the most part, I successfully juggled the demands of engineering college with my income requirements. Although good grades remained paramount, playing music satisfied my financial and creative needs. During 1957, my life was in balance.

Chapter 3

1958
THE CAROUSEL CLUB

Playing nightclubs had advantages: steady income, steady improvements in our music, and a steady supply of squeezes. Early in 1958, five of the Carousels spent more time servicing chickadees than maintaining their grades at LSU, Northeast and Tech. By mid-'58 they had dropped out of college and rented a three-bedroom, one-bath house in Monroe.

Nothing was private at the rental home. One would shit while a second brushed teeth and a third showered, all at the same time. Through it all I remained a year-round, full-time student at Tech and rarely went to the rental house, for obvious reasons.

The Carousels began playing three nights a week at an after-hour's bottle club leased by Betty Booth, a girlfriend of our frontman, Bobby Starr. Betty was a beautiful woman—once upon a time. Although still shapely, with pearly white teeth brighter than the grill of a '55 DeSoto Firedome, she was now a 40-year-old bleached blond who had been ridden hard and put up wet too many times. Betty's Dad was a big-money cotton plantation owner, and she lived to party on his money. Always up for a good time, Betty Booth loved to laugh, drink and party day and night. She also loved musicians—especially Bobby Starr.

As leader of the Carousels, I convinced Betty, without much difficulty, to name her after-midnight joint the Carousel Club. Built in the late '20s while Huey "Kingfish" Long was governor, it had been the top showpiece of North Central Louisiana—an upscale gambling house with cavernous ballroom, several back rooms for private gaming, three full bars, and featuring the finest big bands of the day. Opulent accommodations upstairs were designed for passing pleasure in the art of horizontal refreshment.

Over the years, however, the club had become a decaying monument to North Louisiana blue laws and the grayness of benign neglect. Rats scurried across the floors, undaunted by the presence of mere mortals. A colony of bats lived in the attic, sleeping by day and hunting mosquitoes by night. Bat droppings had accumulated for more than 20 years, and nothing was going to get rid of the bats or their deposits.

Adding to the dreadful odor and assorted health concerns were the residues of 50 years of cigarette smoke, alcohol-saturated carpets, faded fabric wall coverings and worn velvet drapes. Four bottles of Air Wick were set out every week, although they did little to mask the stench.

A three-tiered scalloped hardwood stage elevated the band above the drunks and provided a good defensive barrier when brawls broke out. We practiced the rapid conversion of electric piano legs into clubs to defend ourselves and instruments.

The saving grace of the old club was its massive oak dance floor—smooth as glass and considered the largest and best dance floor in North Central Louisiana. Otherwise, the building was a dump. But, it was our dump. One Sunday we painted the outside white and bribed a drunken sign painter to splash *"Carousel Club"* in huge script letters on the front.

The club opened at 11 p.m. on Thursdays and midnight on Fridays and Saturdays; closing at 3 or 4 in the morning. We entertained drunks three nights a week in a packed house in exchange for a small guarantee plus a generous percentage of the cover charge. This paid for my education and sustenance for six Carousels.

The Carousel Club gig dominated my Thursday, Friday and Saturday nights, including the nightly round-trip drive from Ruston to Monroe and back to Ruston. My 1940 Ford dutifully navigated the snaky, two-lane Highway 80 running through North Louisiana—a 50-minute, one-way drive. Sunday through Friday I attended mechanical engineering classes, studied and rested.

I knew this grueling pace could not last. But, for the moment, playing music supported my tuition, books, rent and basic needs. I was living in two worlds: days as a straight college student and nights as the devil's disciple. This duplicity tested reason. Self was always somewhere else. I began to identify with a mythological dragon.

The dragon stands at the entrance to his cave, guarding captive virgins and gold, neither of which he can use for pleasure or profit. It's all about pitting good against evil, isn't it? Sooner or later a white knight will take up his sword and slay the dragon, screw the virgins and plunder the gold. So I ask, who is good and who is evil in this battle? What am I trying to accomplish anyway?

The standard ensemble of instruments we used at the Carousel Club included keyboards (two organ manuals and one electric piano), guitar, bass, drums and reeds. Three lead singers plus three backup singers rounded out our show. Great entertainment for drunks, but open to criticism from sober audiences, the Carousel sound improved to marginally better than the average white band. In a typical set, we played songs in much the same manner as other copy bands: rock and roll, rhythm and blues, pop and country. We planned and printed set lineups ahead of time, maximizing variety, freshness and short pauses between songs.

SECOND SET LINEUP—THE CAROUSEL CLUB				
SONG	ORIG'L ARTIST	GENRE	ENSEMBLE	FEATURE
Stagger Lee	Lloyd Price	R&R	Standard Ensemble	Bobby—Vocal
Mack The Knife	Bobby Darin	Pop	Standard Ensemble	Bobby—Vocal
The 'In' Crowd	Ramsey Lewis Trio	Jazz	Standard Ensemble	Rooster—Piano
For The Good Times	Ray Price	Country	Fiddle Solo Big Joe	Lance—Vocal
Tequila	The Champs	R&R	Standard Ensemble	Big Joe—Sax
Volare	Domenico Modugno	R&R	Standard Ensemble	Bobby—Vocal
Love Letters In The Sand	Pat Boone	Pop	Standard Ensemble	Lance—Vocal
Twilight Time	The Platters	R&R	Standard Ensemble	Bobby in Falsetto & Lance & Big Joe—Vocal
Kansas City	Wilbert Harrison	Pop	Standard Ensemble	Bobby—Vocal
Venus	Frankie Avalon	R&R	Standard Ensemble	Bobby—Vocal

During our gig at the Carousel Club, Rooster became so bent he made a corkscrew appear straight. One night on break, Rooster spotted a couple seated next to the dance floor and approached their table. The woman quickly introduced Rooster to her husband, a frail man with a gimpy left arm. Rooster extended his right hand, connecting with a hand better suited for a woman than a man. Rooster's left hand went for the gimp's right shoulder, blocking the gimp's view so he couldn't see Rooster's good eye winking at the wife.

We knew Rooster had been banging the chick, unbeknownst to the husband. Rooster then sat next to the gimp and directly opposite the wife. Under the table, her warm stocking feet went straight for Rooster's crotch and did what they'd done many times before. If she thought her seductive actions were hidden from her husband, she was very mistaken. The gimp suddenly backhanded his wife with incredible force, making a sound that filled the room as she fell from her chair and slid across the full length of the highly polished hardwood dance floor. Unconscious, she crumpled like an accordion against the stage riser.

With his Arkansas toothpick drawn, the gimp grabbed a handful of his wife's hair and dragged her across the floor like a rag doll and out the door of the club.

Rooster sat in stunned silence, as did everyone else in the club.

Sooner or later, we'll have to find another keyboardist. Rooster is destined to be shot by a jealous husband for sticking his johnson where it doesn't belong.

Our weekly routine included rehearsal on Saturday afternoon, followed by supper at a local hash house. That night, Bobby Starr chose Fat Willies. Full of piss and vinegar, Bobby was our spark plug, launching rapid-fire comments and questions over barbecue. Fun to be with, Bobby kept things moving, usually toward a predetermined destination. There was never a dull moment when he was in the room.

His dinner topic of the evening was to challenge us with new opportunities way beyond our North Louisiana roots.

"Well, Elvis will be in Germany with the Army for at least two years. Now is our time to move up and get a hit record."

"Wonder if Colonel Parker is looking for a replacement?" Smoke asked, speaking with a pronounced southern accent, with shades of an English lilt.

Smoke had an opinion on most subjects. Often well-conceived, although soft spoken, his comments usually took a back seat to louder and stronger personalities in the group. Today, with no response from the guys, his pencil-thin frame visibly collapsed.

As was his habit, Big Joe abruptly changed the subject.

"Pope Pius XII's dead—Pope John XXIII is da new guy. Anyone Catholic—sep me?"

As awkward as that was, none of us wanted to offend Big Joe's clumsy conversational skills. Typically, we'd smile and nod in agreement, avoiding any verbal response that could upset his delicate emotional balance.

Getting no support from the other Carousels about expanding our band's horizons, Bobby moved on to another topic.

"Read where Shreveport native Van Cliburn won the Tchaikovsky International Competition in Moscow? Supposedly this will calm Cold War tensions, but I don't think so."

I responded, "Yeah. Van Cliburn played Tchaikovsky's Piano Concerto No. 1 and Rachmaninoff's Piano Concerto No. 3 to win. My all-time favorite piano concerto is Rachmaninoff's No. 2. Any of you familiar with it?"

No response. I wasn't surprised, although I regretted being so pompous in my reply.

Just being one of the guys is elemental. Relax and roll with it. Dancing in the intellectual hallways is one thing. On the contrary, these guys dance to a different tune. Better learn their rhythms, tempo and dance steps. Just relax and be one of the guys.

Uncharacteristically silent until now, Lance blurted out, "Wake up guys. The world's about to end and you're wasting time on Elvis and Van Cliburn. Get your heads out of your asses. Russian and American satellites are poppin' off monthly, a nuclear submarine just launched and nuclear bombs are exploding all over the world. Our own B-47's have accidentally dropped an atom bomb on South Carolina and a hydrogen bomb off the coast of Savannah. It's just a matter of time before we're all incinerated—vaporized. What's the point?"

Even my shrimp Creole turned bitter. Normally these were happy times—Saturdays at rehearsal and supper with brothers—however not today. Lance had cast a mushroom cloud over our happy times. Every group unofficially elects their protagonist. Lance was our protagonist—but not today.

As checks were paid, we sauntered to our cars, my eyes focused on Lance. His posture screamed of emotional self-torture. Shoulders slumped, chin buried in his chest and shuffling feet. Normally, Lance stood 6' 3"—erect and proud—not today. Something had taken Lance down. What?

I caught Lance's attention in the parking lot and said, "I know you rode here with Bobby. Ride back with me to the rental house. We'll talk."

Lance's lumbering frame climbed into my Ford as I asked, "What's up, Sherlock?"

He stared at the floorboards, cowering like a man just beaten in a vicious fistfight. No answer.

I shifted the Ford into first gear, popped the clutch and eased out of the parking lot. Lance blotted tears with the sleeve of his flannel shirt. Placing a hand on Lance's shoulder, again I asked, with more compassion, "What's up, Sherlock?"

He finally spoke.

"Yesterday I filed for bankruptcy, lost my car and dropped out of Northeast University, for the second and last time. Not a good day. Today I'm penniless."

"No wonder you spewed doom and gloom over supper. And you only had a grilled cheese sandwich with water. You been eatin' redneck caviar? Short on cash? Ya hungry?"

"Yeah. I'm hungry for somethin' good to happen in my rotten life. Life sucks right now."

"You're the most grounded man in the Carousels," I said. "Do your grieving in private. Climb out of your toilet before it flushes. Resurrect your southern gentleman's persona. Until then, here's $40."

"Rock, you can't afford to carry me."

"Consider it an investment in a good guy temporarily down on his luck."

"Thanks Rock—a bunch," Lance said as another tear crept down his cheek.

"There is one condition," I replied. "Get your head out of your ass."

The following Saturday I made a point to arrive early at the rental house, cornering Big Joe before we went to rehearsal and supper. Our relationship was overtly competitive, although artistically aligned.

In South Louisiana, Big Joe was considered a hard worker, smart, a good musician and a good guy. Woven into the rich Cajun tapestry, Big Joe lived the life of a coonass with gusto and pride. Outside South Louisiana, his coonass ways were strange to most.

"Fortunately, the hearing-impaired drunks at the Carousel Club believe we're great," I told him. "We're packin' 'em in. Conversely, once we get in front of a sober audience, we'll have to raise our game—a lot. Any ideas?"

Big Joe looked me in the eye, considering possible motives behind my question. Like tip-toeing over egg shells, I eased closer—he backed up a step. Not knowing what I'd said to set him off, I extended my palms, up and open. He crossed his arms over his chest and cocked his head to the side, presenting a quizzical look. Perplexed, I searched my brain for a way to reset and start over.

Big Joe had interpreted my comment as a challenge, issued by a North Louisiana redneck to a purebred coonass. Instinctively, I knew a politically safe coonass answer was about to come my way.

"A whistlin' woman and a crowin' hen never come to a good end," he said.

"I'm not talking about whistlin'," I replied. "I'm talking about raising our band to a higher level."

"Wanna walk in high cotton, you gots ta plow da field, Rock."

"Think we've got potential to become a great band?"

"Gots ta plow da field, Rock. Til you bet everythin' on music, every dog will have a few fleas. You gots ta plow da field if ya wanna harvest high cotton."

Outrageously convoluted, Big Joe's puzzling answer seemed to fit our situation: *"The only truth is music,"* as written by Jack Kerouac in *On the Road.*

Chapter 4

1959
METAMORPHOSIS

Enrolling for Tech's spring semester, I stood hopefully before a puffy registrar who held authority over my class schedule for the coming months.

"Weeellllll," she squeaked as she patted her lacquered bouffant hairdo, lest any hair get out of place. "We'll try and schedule you for Monday, Wednesday and Friday classes. Oooooh! You'll have to take Differential Equations at 8 a.m. because that's the only time it's offered. Aaaaaaand, the Advanced Surveying Lab is only available Friday morning. Thermodynamics, Kinematics, and Fluid Mechanics are offered in the afternoons. Sounds hard—I mean those classes sound hard."

"The challenge is that 8 a.m. class Friday morning," I replied. "I work nights."

"Weeeeellllll. You have to have it if you want to graduate with a minor in math. We only offer it at 8 this semester."

"I'll take it."

She licked the lead point of her No. 2 pencil and placed a dampened X next to the math class. Adjusting her pointy, rhinestone-studded glasses, she bounced the pencil eraser on her desk as she gazed upward, apparently seeking Jesus' blessing over my scheduling decision. Her meditation was cut short by what I assumed was a too-tight girdle as she proceeded to squirm her tush in the wooden folding chair. I suppressed the inevitable snicker by biting my tongue until it bled.

When her gyrations apparently succeeded in bringing some relief, she continued to laboriously complete my semester schedule. She licked the pencil every time before carefully placing an X next to the appropriate classes.

Did she have any idea what that act suggests to a 19-year-old full of underutilized testosterone?

I grinned as she had the last lick and last X in place. The born-again evangelical smiled back and handed me the card, pointing toward the cashier.

I felt like a ping-pong ball being slammed between good and evil, straight vs. bent, day vs. night. My Machiavellian life was about to get even more complicated.

During January and February of '59, Rooster pitched the virtues of living life as a three-peckered goat verses remaining a dull engineering student at Louisiana Tech. Needling me became Rooster's favorite pastime. After all, Rooster and the four other Carousels had joined the ranks of college dropouts. Failure loves company.

"You're living days as a goody two-shoes college student and nights promoting sin, dancing, booze and fornication," he would tell me. "The good people of this town would condemn you to Hell if they knew the truth. Your double life is killing you, Rock. Pound your cock inside something warm and beautiful, not inside the pages of another book. Loosen up—enjoy life. Without a doubt, we are."

Rooster was right, although I never admitted my true feelings to him or the Carousels. I grew increasingly wary of the dreaded 3:30

Friday morning drive back to Ruston. The toughest part was staying awake during Friday morning classes.

The lead in my pencil wore down to a nub. A sharpener was nowhere to be found. I never seriously considered taking bennies, although fellow Tech students readily offered them to me.

I'd never been trapped in a perpetual haze until now. I was dumbin' down by the day.

Gray matter was rapidly turning to mush behind slurred words and bloodshot eyes. Sustained concentration was impossible, eroding my analytical abilities like acid on metal. Drifting aimlessly into trite day dreaming, I longed for the rest that comes only at the end of completing a task—not in the middle. Motivation was never a challenge, until now. Exhaustion of body, motor skills and mind extinguishes fire in the belly. Mine was down to glowing embers and thinning gray smoke trails. Chronic blinking appeared, augmented by a nervous tic of the brow.

I am falling apart.

On a freezing Thursday night in February, physically and emotionally spent, I pondered Rooster's words. In my weakened state, I considered sleeping over at the rental house—just one night. Concerned about how sharp or dim-witted I'd be for the 8 o'clock Friday morning Differential Equations test and the 10 a.m. surveying lab, the temptation to sleep over gained momentum by the minute. I knew the risks, but I was exhausted—and it showed.

During our last break Big Joe said, "Ya look like shit! What ya tryin' to prove anyhow? Ain't Superman. *Laissez les bon temps roulez.* In South Louisiana, yo' handle'd be pussy. At Pounder's Bar in Morgan City you'd be tossed for tryin' to be uppity—better dan us. Let me break it to ya Bro: ya ain't better. Everyone sees through ya. Drop the act. Ya need to learn *suave de vive.*

Lance came next. "Normally you're the best kick-ass drummer in North Louisiana, always pushing me to keep up on bass. Here lately, I'm the one carrying you around on my back. I don't know where your grit went, but it's gone. Find a way to get it back. We don't want to look for a new kick-ass drummer and leader anytime soon. You're pushing yourself over the edge."

Smoke let me know that I was welcome to use his crib. "Rocky, I go straight to breakfast and hit the house 'round 10 a.m. I'll crash on the couch."

Easy prey, my defenses sunk to rock bottom. Self-image suffered from too much self-persecution, emerging too weak to resist the easy way out. Muscles ached, head ached and eyeballs ached. My façade, a conjured mask of self-preservation, failed to disguise my pitiful vulnerability against any feeble attack. My grades in Differential Equations and Surveying were okay. Speculating that I could make up the math test later, I caved in. One by one my delusional brain rationalized away my responsibilities. Growing increasingly weary, I gave in to weakness, embracing their invitation to sleep over, finally saying, "Why not?"

A sentence from Jack Kerouac's *On the Road* emerged out of my fog: *"I like too many things and get all confused and hung-up running from one falling star to another til I drop. This is the night, what it does to you. I had nothing to offer anybody except my own confusion."*

The acrid smell of sweaty men and dirty clothes saturated the rental house. Clumsy men moved furniture, slammed doors and drawers and talked loud, obviously never learning how to be quiet at night. Walking around the house, I observed their routine—all new to me. Finally, the guys settled down and hit the sack. I slipped into Smoke's crib around 3:45 Friday morning.

Not too bad.

My eyelids felt like lead, begging to close so I could dream the dreams of angels. Sleep beckoned, but an unfamiliar sound caught my attention. As I looked up, a woman with chestnut brown hair flowing down to her waist stepped into the bedroom doorway. A bathroom light silhouetted her as though she were standing inside a picture frame. She captured my undivided attention with her figure—long and lean. This was no dream.

Without speaking, she slowly slipped the strap of her black dress off one shoulder, then the other, letting it float to the floor like a feather. She repeated the sequence with her black bra, presenting full breasts with large nipples that turned up slightly. Her dark eyes never left me as she moved her thumbs down her side, sliding her panties around her ankles and stepping out with the grace of a ballerina. The sweet aroma of gardenias opening in the morning dew filled the room. She moved with the grace of a dancer.

I said, "You are truly a beautiful creature."

She gently touched my shoulder, sending shivers down my spine. I kissed her fingertips as they passed my lips. Long fingernails made figure eights on my chest, raising a mountain range of goose pimples. I was on fire. As natural as climbing into the saddle of a Tennessee walking horse, she straddled me. Tips of her long chestnut hair danced on my chest like summer raindrops. Silk skin caressed my calluses, creating perfect from imperfect.

She whispered, "Rocky, I waited until I was sure you'd be here tonight before coming over. I have wanted you since the first time I saw you. I want to experience all of you."

I gently placed my hand behind her neck and applied feather-soft pressure until her breast filled my chest. Her body was hot against mine. Her unabashed passion electrified me. I was her prize and she mine—the perfect match.

It was heaven—until a loud police whistle shocked me from my euphoria. Four quick blasts. My head was spinning.

It's a police raid, and my reputation is about to go down the toilet!

While I was about to panic, my chestnut beauty calmly rose and strolled toward the bathroom as if the shrieking whistle had no effect.

What's going on?

As soon as she left my bed, a petite blond appeared. The bathroom light streaming through her open thighs highlighted her terrific figure, and her wicked smile foretold a good time lay ahead.

"Next," she said in a child-like voice. Blondie bounded across the room like a gazelle, jumped in the saddle and seized the initiative. My hands became her tools of pleasure. Full of foolishness, this good-time gal giggled her way to happiness. Finesse was not necessary—athletic is one way to describe her. She bounced, flexed, squirmed, contorted and squealed until the whistle blew again—much too early.

In the blink of an eye Blondie disappeared, replaced by a sultry nymph who surveyed her prey from the doorway. Her gleaming white teeth, high cheekbones, long face and ruddy complexion added to her sensuality.

Pure Indian blood runs deep in this squaw.

Without a word, the nymph devoured me, body and soul. Following pulsating rhythms, a short-lived peace covered us like a soft cloud. Long, lean legs wrapped around me and squeezed—the signal to begin again. Regrettably the incessant whistle blew a third time.

The nymph disappeared, replaced by a brunette sporting double-D melons, begging to be kissed. She titty-slapped my face until my cheeks turned red. I loved it. Her turn, she went doggy, ass shooting skyward, arched back and cheek pressed against the bed sheet.

She kept yelling, "That's my spot," reaching seventh heaven and passing out.

Suddenly I wanted to kill the asshole blowing the whistle.

Incredibly, my short lived anger was exchanged for the night's first prize. Redheads have always turned me on—and the next chickadee to grace my doorway had a topknot that resembled a cardinal, and her voice whistled and chirped a vibrant melody. Red was genuine, freckles and all. Perfect body, bountiful breasts, and sparkling blue eyes. Her unbridled passion led us into positions only mastered by a contortionist. With an exploding crescendo, Red yelled so loud I actually covered her mouth. However, she pulled my hand away and continued to vocalize her orgasm. With a sinister smile little Red devoted every inch of her 105-pound body to satisfying me. With barely enough consciousness remaining, I nestled my head between Red's freckled breasts—safe in heavenly bliss.

That's when the rental house harmonized with a chorus of sopranos and four deep-throated basses, bawdily signaling the free love finale.

The neighbor's rooster crowed, announcing that all is well this day. And, as the day dawned, I realized we had chosen the perfect name for our band.

The Carousels are headed toward pleasures I hadn't imagined. All we have to do is fulfill the rider's fantasies on our Carousel round. No jealousy, no guilt, no moral judgments, no unintended consequences. Laissez les bon temps roulez. Like passing through a translucent membrane, I accept truth—can never return to the other side—morphed from naiveté to enlightenment.

The ack, ack, ack of a Steller's Jay sang me into a nodding dream state. Ack, ack, ack, ack. Sleep transported me inside extraordinary visions, guiding my spirit to walk among the sequoias of Mariposa Grove, giant redwoods of California, pyramids of Giza and the Lighthouse of Alexandria: the wonders of God and man.

The unmistakable aroma of chicory weaved its way through the house, finding my nostrils. Even with the covers pulled over my head, the allure of chicory in the morning was irresistible. I rolled out of bed, drained my lizard, brushed my teeth and put on my tux pants. Smoke was sacked out on the couch. The girls were long gone. It all seemed like a beautiful dream. Bobby sat at the Formica and chrome kitchen table, caressing a steaming cup of French Market Coffee with chicory. It smelled really good.

Bobby was a cocky 5' 8" egomaniac with the physique of a competitive swimmer in top condition—lean and ripped. His jet-black wavy hair and twinkling black eyes highlighted an olive complexion, high cheekbones and a face that every woman loved. There was no denying it; Bobby was a good-looking dude, a natty dresser, with impeccable taste and a peacock strut tinged with arrogance.

Max Starr, Bobby's father, raised Bobby and an older brother following the untimely death of their mother, a full-blooded Kickapoo Indian. Max was the North Louisiana KKK Grand Dragon of the Realm and owner of the largest cotton plantation in the area. With considerable pride, Max enrolled Bobby in the Knights of the

Golden Circle, where he received extensive training and mentoring from an elder Klansman.

Spoiled by Max, who bailed his son out of any unpleasantness that came his way and groomed him to ascend to the Third Klan throne at Max's death, Bobby skillfully leveraged his immense charm, dominating a room with a charismatic aura.

I pointed to the steaming pot on the stove. Bobby acknowledged with his eyes, but didn't speak.

After pouring a mug of black coffee with chicory, I sat quietly with Bobby. The cup of hot java soothed my tired hands and tranquilized my soul. Five minutes passed.

When you've done it all—well—there's no need to talk about it. Rewards lie in savoring the memories in peaceful silence.

I muttered to Bobby in a low tone, "How long has this orgy been going on?"

Bobby frowned, obviously classifying my question as unmanly. However, out of respect for the newbie, he replied, "As long as we've rented the house. It's a nightly ritual around here, at least Thursdays, Fridays and Saturdays."

Big Joe, Lance and Rooster joined us in the kitchen for a mug of joe. Rooster spilled his coffee on the electric burner, creating a mess as the sugar caramelized. Big Joe loaded up his chicory with a large teaspoon of Eagle Brand condensed milk. Lance suggested breakfast. We gathered up Smoke and drove to the Egg Platter.

As we positioned two tables together, an untidy and obviously surly waitress approached, order pad in hand. "Can't come in and move stuff 'round like dat. Der's rules. Who wants' what? Coffee all 'round?"

Orders placed, Lance turned to me and asked, "How's yo hammer hangin'?

"Like a lollypop," I answered. "Wanna lick it?"

Following the obligatory snicker, Lance said, "Isn't this better than falling asleep over a math test?"

"A whole lot better."

"Now ya know what ya been missin'," said Big Joe.

"Gettin' your carrot skinned is the best way I know to clear your head," Rooster added. "Welcome to the club."

The cashier rushed over to set up a tray stand by our table just as our waitress emerged from the kitchen, balancing a huge tray with six dinner plates and six smaller plates of food. She stumbled as she kicked a chair leg, but recovered in time, landing the tray safely on the stand.

Surly as ever, she said, "Dis job sucks. You guys better make dis worthwhile."

We fed our faces with eggs, grits, ham, sausage, biscuits and gravy, washed down with chicory so thick a spoon would stand vertically in the coffee cup. Privately, I welcomed the silence for a final reflection on my guilt—my decision to skip Friday classes.

Bobby read the morning newspaper, lining up fodder for our table discussion.

"What do you guys think about Castro taking over Cuba? New Year's Eve Castro's rag-tag rebel army marched into Havana as Batista got on his private plane and fled with all the money from the Cuban treasury. The New York Times seems to paint Castro as the savior of Cuba. The U.S. and the United Nations are in love with Castro. What do you guys think?"

Everyone contributed an opinion, though none of us had a clue what the future held for Castro, Cuba, Russia, the U.S. or the ramifications of the Mob losing their Cuban gaming monopoly.

Bobby read on, "Alaska and Hawaii admitted as the 49th and 50th states."

Lance said, "While I was in the Army in Alaska, listening in on Russian transmissions, it was easy to tell the good guys from the bad guys. Today it's much tougher to know who or what to believe."

Our babble continued as the food disappeared. Laughter and backslappin' fun became our happy time tonic over brunch.

Following a long Friday afternoon nap, the Carousels kicked off our Friday set at midnight. With eyes wide open, I saw the world through a luminous prism. After the gig, five fresh fillies bought tickets to ride our Carousel.

Waking up much later, with an ear-to-ear smile welcoming my newfound lifestyle, I smelled coffee brewing in the kitchen. Breakfast and brotherhood with the Carousels followed at Pop's Diner. Abundant laughter filled the restaurant with the simple joys of living large. Funny subject matter was easy, highlighted by Lance's spontaneous comedy routine portraying his hatred for working on his father's pig farm in Rayville.

We joked and laughed our way through breakfast and most of the afternoon. Life was great.

Midnight Saturday we were back on stage. My kick-ass drive was back. The Carousels never sounded better. Something had changed—I felt great. Repeating what Bobby called 'a nightly routine,' five eager band-aids showed up for their Carousel ride. With relatively few one-hole scalps hanging from my 19-year-old carnal belt, my initiation continued into the club of unconditional guiltless pleasures and free love.

If things get any better, I'll have to hire someone to help me enjoy it. The metamorphosis from chrysalis to butterfly changes everything. For the first time in months, I'm in a peaceful place.

While I was sippin' coffee with Bobby at the kitchen table Sunday morning, Smoke walked in the back door, sporting bloodshot eyes. I asked, "Wanna go to Shreveport? I'll be back Monday night."

"Yea', sure," he mumbled.

"Pack your poke and let's shag ass," I said.

Throwing my dirty clothes in a paper bag, I jumped in my '40 Ford with Smoke and headed west on Highway 80 to Shreveport and my 20th birthday dinner with Mom. The two-hour drive to spend a weekend with Mom was just the ticket.

She'll probably cook my favorite: cranberry and pecan gelatin salad, pot roast with Irish potatoes, carrots, mushrooms and celery cooked slow in a large black iron pot, English peas and steamed rice with gravy, topped off with

Kayro pecan pie and ice cream. It'll be a great 20th birthday—home and safe with Mom.

Suddenly a line from Jack Kerouac's *On the Road* came to mind, *"Happiness consists in realizing it is all a great strange dream."*

Contrasting Kerouac with Ayn Rand's *Atlas Shrugged* provided balance: *"Who is John Galt? … He was a man who had never accepted the creed that others had the right to stop him."*

I had time in the car to assess my current situation.

Long ago, men of wisdom mapped my destiny. With a high degree of predictability and minimal risks, their road map charted my path through college, career, marriage, children and stature within the Shreveport community. Success is virtually guaranteed, in part due to my adoption of the cultural norms required for a respected southern gentleman.

In stark contrast, the earth's axis shifted on me, revealing a previously unknown world of mystery and grandeur. I'm morphing into a froglet. Exhilarating adventures lie down stream. Fascinating.

Ayn Rand's objectivism surfaced: *"We are fast approaching the stage of the ultimate inversion: the stage where the government is free to do anything it pleases, while the citizens may act only by permission; which is the stage of the darkest periods of human history, the stage of rule by brute force."*

As I navigated the snaky North Louisiana hill country, I conjured up vivid images of a special weekend, pondering its deeper meaning.

Stepping from solid ground into a raging river with currents so powerful that resistance is futile, dark side temptations are sweeping this froglet downstream to an unknown destiny. Neophyte in worldly matters and ignorant of what I need to know to navigate a subterranean culture, I find the lure of the unknown is a powerful magnet, promising colossal adventure. I am standing at a fork in the trail—high road or low road? I have a life-altering decision to make before reaching Mom's. Which path do I choose; stay at Tech or drop out and take a chance on adventure? Who is Rocky Strong?

Chapter 5

1959
20TH BIRTHDAY DINNER

S nuggled in a lump against the passenger door, Smoke snored in rhythm with the car's unbalanced tires rapping against Highway 80's asphalt. Droplets of spittle fell in a steady stream from buckteeth onto his freckled arm. Smoke could eat an apple through a picket fence.

An only child, he was born to a chiropractor father and Seventh Day Adventist mother. Following the death of Hank Williams, the Van Dyke family purchased Hank's house from second wife Billie Jean Williams. Dr. Van Dyke hung out his shingle and performed chiropractic adjustments in the front bedroom, while Mrs. Van Dyke prayed most of the day. By choice, Smoke isolated himself in an upstairs bedroom with his guitar, spending hours on end as a recluse.

Smoke got his handle not so much because he smoked cigarettes and cannabis, which he did, but for his creative ability to blow smoke, spinning tall tales that left the listener challenged to separate truth from fantasy. Smoke's penchant for blowing smoke was widely known within the musician community. Nevertheless, his stories were always entertaining and left us pondering what was truth and what was fantasy.

Dropping Smoke off at his parent's home in Queensborough, I said, "I'll pick you up at 8:30 Monday morning."

Responding with an exaggerated eyebrow tic, Smoke said, "Don't be late."

Motoring five blocks to Mom's, I parked my black Ford at the curb and sat quietly for a moment.

Which path do I choose? Either way, the moment of decision is here.

Mom ran out and greeted me with a big kiss. Excitedly she said, "Happy 20th birthday, Dean. I love you so much."

Only Mom and immediate family called me Dean. It felt really good; almost like returning to the man I used to be.

For the next 18 hours, Rocky is on the shelf. As Dean I'll enjoy Mom, all 90 pounds of her unconditional love and support.

The sound of clanking pots and the mouth-watering aroma of Mom's home cooking emanated from her kitchen. Steam hissed from a covered iron pot. Since childhood, I played games of guessing the ingredients simmering in Mom's pots. Sitting at her hundred-year-old oak kitchen table, I marveled at her home cooking and how she captured the culinary blue ribbon of North Louisiana.

Just for fun, let's see how many ingredients I can name. Rump roast for sure, new potatoes, carrots, celery, mushroom buttons, green peppers and onions sliced thin, four or five pressed garlic cloves, liberal doses of Worcestershire sauce, cyan pepper and salt. I probably nailed it this time because she's prepared this dish many, many times. Her secret ingredient is time, allowing plenty of time for meals to simmer in their own juices. It comes out so tender the roast falls apart. I am truly blessed.

Sure enough, my vision of the perfect birthday dinner was served on a white linen tablecloth, English china and sterling silver flatware. Pulling out her chair, she sat and folded her hands, anticipating the Presbyterian blessing I'd delivered for the past 17 years.

The meal was better than I remembered. The safety, peace and love I found at Mom's exceeded whatever was a distant second.

Following dinner I poured two cups of Maxwell House black coffee. We walked to the cypress swing Dad built, still hanging from a massive limb of a grand oak. As we sipped our coffee, Mom looked at me as only a mother can, smiled and lovingly touched my hand. Many peaceful moments passed before she sighed and said, "Most afternoons at 5:30, your Dad and I sipped coffee and talked about our day here on this swing. Those were very special times for us—just us. I miss him. He's been gone a long time, although, in many ways, he's still here."

A tear rolled down her cheek—and mine.

I can't recall everything about my father's fatal heart attack, being only six years old at the time. Still, I remember the admiration expressed by his Masonic brothers. Dad was a 33rd-degree Mason, Worshipful Master of his lodge and appendant of Scottish Rite. Dad's Blue Lodge purchased his headstone, and his burial ceremony was entirely Masonic. I remember a dozen Masons taking me aside, each saying, "If you or your mother ever need anything, any time throughout your life, come to me. If it be in my power, I will grant your request." But, that was a long time ago.

Mom put her arm around me and squeezed, "I'm so proud of you, Dean. And your father would be proud of you—the apple of his eye and my heart. You are a good man, and the first of our extended family to graduate from college. Can you imagine how much that means to me—and your Dad?"

Mom's love is absolute. But, I have to face reality. My moment of decision is at hand.

Shifting my weight in the cypress swing, I felt the heavy burden of guilt welling up inside. Mom sensed my anxiety, her arm returning to her lap. I spread my arm like the wing of an eagle, pulling her close. She shifted her weight, turning to catch a glimpse of what she already knew. I pulled her closer to restrict probing eyes from peering into my soul.

Too late—My eyes betray me. Mom sees everything. Impossible to hide the truth from Mom.

"Mom," I said, "I've decided to take a break from college."

"What do you mean?"

"I'm exhausted. I don't mind working my way through Tech, but the grind has gotten out of control. I need a break."

The common call of a Blue Jay building a nest was harsh, jeering; jay, jaay-jaay notes, tool-ool, tweedledee, clicking sounds.

Jays are mean, deceitful birds—so am I.

Mom's body visibly shrunk. She looked at the Blue Jay—away from me—obviously to hide her displeasure. Not able to face me, she spoke with a frail voice.

"You know I lost your sister at birth, your brother at three and your father at 40. Now I'm losing you at 20."

Feebly, I replied, "You're not losing me. I'm simply going to take some time off, save some money and return to Tech. That's all."

Regaining her steel constitution, Mom sat up straight, looked me squarely in the eye and spoke with absolute authority.

"I know you better than you know yourself. You've succeeded at everything you tackled: church, Boy Scouts, music, baseball and college. On the other hand once you quit something you never look back. The odds of your returning to Tech are simply ..." she paused. "Please reconsider. Is there anything I can do or say to change your mind?"

"It's just a short break—not the end of the world. I promise, I'll return to Tech one day and get my degree. I swear, Mom."

Standing, Mom turned back toward the Blue Jay, now busily building her nest in the grand oak. An agonizing minute passed.

"Dean, this tears me apart. You know your father only had a fourth grade education. Even though he had a good job on the railroad, he wanted so much more for you. After we lost your father, I've held us together, working downtown at the department store, looking forward to the day when you'd have that diploma in hand and go off to a great career. I'm really struggling with this."

Feeling selfish, I stood and wrapped my arms around her again, saying, "I'm sorry to disappoint you. This will all turn out the way you and Dad wanted. It's only a little side trip."

At that point, all that needed to be said was said. For several hours the subject of Tech never re-emerged. That night I didn't sleep, tossing and turning til dawn. Something was bothering me, and I knew exactly what it was.

Monday morning, the noise of clanging pots bellowed from the kitchen, followed by captivating aromas drifting throughout the house. A big breakfast of black Maxwell House coffee, juice, eggs, ham, grits, and biscuits awaited. As always, she sent me on my way with a full stomach. However, this time I had a huge hole in my gut—gouged out by disappointing the most precious person in my life.

I'll have to make it up to her. As doors close, others open. I can't unsay a cruel word ... have to live with the consequences. I feel like shit!

Her goodbye was like a mother sending her son off to war, perhaps never to see him again. The brown grass of February crackled beneath our feet as we walked to my car. Hugging Mom at the curb one last time, I then climbed in the Ford and drove away from unconditional love. Angry with myself, I said out loud, "This is a major fuckup!"

Smoke was waiting on the sidewalk with satchel in hand. His right eye rapidly squinting, Smoke's stressful time with his Mom and Dad was self-evident.

I said, "Where ya at?"

Twitching eyes and an aggressive itch told me all I needed to know about Smoke's time with his family. Producing a joint from his shirt pocket, he lit up and said, "I can't help it, Rock. I really have to calm down." A sickening sweet perfume filled the Ford, in spite of Smoke's cranking open the passenger window.

"Just this once—never again around me. Got it?"

Smoke nodded, sucked on the marijuana, and held his breath a long time before exhaling in slow satisfaction. There was visible change is his body language, eventually achieving peace in the valley. Tweezers held what was now a quarter-inch roach right up until his final suck.

"I had to get out of that crazy house," he said. "They drive me nuts. If you'd been 20 minutes later you'd be driving up to flashing police cars and a hearse. The coroner would do his job and you'd be looking for a new string man."

Sensing now was not the time to start carrying around Smoke's baggage, I changed focus, asking, "Is this the spot Hank Williams died in the back seat of his Cadillac?"

Smoke snickered before responding with his unique southern lilt. "Actually, his Cadillac was parked in the front yard, right there, straddling the walkway to the front steps. After that long drive back from a gig, Hank and Mr. Jack Daniels died in the back seat from a leaky muffler—carbon monoxide poisoning. At noon the following day Billie Jean came out and found Hank cold as an ice cube in the back seat, along with Jack Daniels neat. That's the real story of how Hank Williams died. I got it directly from Billie Jean—first hand."

Smoke was different. His 6' 2" skeletal thin frame was topped off with curly strawberry-blond hair and a *"What Me Worry?"* smile that never ended. Smoke could stand under a clothesline in a rainstorm and not get wet. In spite of his active tic off stage, on stage Smoke was captivating to the casual observer, dancing as though a puppeteer suspended him from strings, projecting fantastic stage presence and showing no apparent inhibitions. An extravert on stage and recluse off.

Smoke's guitar idols were Tony Mottola, Tal Farlow, Barney Kessel, Joe Pass and Bucky Pizzarelli. He copied licks from each of the famous jazz guitarists with impeccable precision. When I met Smoke, his most prized possession was a brand new, 1957 cherry red, ES-345 Thinline Semi-Hollow Electric Archtop Gibson guitar. He cuddled it like a newborn baby. In spite of his love affair with the Gibson, Smoke never lost his passion to own a custom-made D'Angelica guitar.

Fashioning himself as some sort of secret agent, like Ian Fleming's James Bond, Smoke lived much of his life in fantasy, intrigue, mystery, conspiracy theories and delusional dreams of grandeur, often quoting lines from Fleming's books. If a person wanted to be entertained with the conspiracy theory de jour, or quasi truths behind the Mob, or paranormal messages embodied in mythological Greek characters, or anything related to Agent 007, Smoke was the source.

Most of us were convinced the only reality in Smoke's life was his time on stage. Even then Smoke fabricated a persona to align with some of the great jazz guitarists of the day. Somewhere in his mixed-up mind a creative human soul existed. One could only wonder if Smoke's dream world was more blissful than the daily grind of reality. At some level he lived out more dreams than any of us. Unfortunately, most remained in his head and never became reality.

An hour later I made a left turn off Highway 80 into the Louisiana Tech main entrance.

"Where ya headed?" Smoke asked.

"I've made a decision. Dropping out of Tech this semester—goin' to the registrar's office and make it legal, then to my apartment to clean out my stuff and cancel my lease."

Pleasantly surprised, Smoke said, "Well, all right!"

I still felt guilty—mixed emotions competing on the short ride to my Ruston apartment above the Tick Tock Grill. The familiar grease trap stench welcomed us. Walking into my second-floor apartment, Smoke spotted my feline.

"I've never seen a smilin' cat before. Isn't he a Persian? What's the fluffy white guy's name?"

"Cheshire Cat. This guy's a gal. Deformed at birth or hit by a car—or somethin'. She's always smilin', and she's a great lap cat. Cheshire'll join us on our great adventures in wonderland. I need her approving smiles and lovin'. She's my Marijane."

Smoke surveyed my nondescript student apartment, badly in need of a thorough cleaning. Suddenly, right eye squinting rapidly, Smoke said, "Look at this. Your record collection is fantastic!"

I busied myself packing clothes and books in boxes, barely acknowledging Smoke's comment. While working part-time at a Ruston record store, I amassed hundreds of albums, which qualified my jazz and classical collection as one of the best in North Louisiana.

At least I thought so. Smoke was impressed I had jazz, flamenco and classical guitarists that he didn't.

"You've got Tal Farlow, Bucky Pizzarelli, Andres Segovia, Carlos Montoya and Chet Atkins. Gosh, here's Tony Mottola, Barney Kessel, Herb Ellis, Kenny Burrell and Wes Montgomery. My god, you have the best collection of great guitarists I've ever seen."

I shrugged and continued packing.

Moving stereo equipment and my prized record collection down two flights of stairs proved taxing and time-consuming. Smoke's frail frame was of little help. Stereo equipment went on the back seat and albums in the trunk, beside my collection of favorite books. Goodwill was the beneficiary of old furniture, old clothes, pots, pans and assorted junk.

On the drive from Ruston to Monroe, Smoke slept while I did a mental double take.

Today I abandon the traditional path to becoming a successful, respected southern gentleman. Powerful forces are leading me away from good—into a life of decadence. Dropping out of Tech ... the smart move or a colossal mistake? Only time will tell.

With her motor running in my lap, Cheshire Cat purred, quoting from *Alice's Adventures in Wonderland*. Not surprising, I was the only one capable of hearing the cat's messages: *"Only the insane equate pain with success."*

Chapter 6

1959
RISE OF THE PHOENIX

A distinctive rhythm was self-evident for six hardtails living in the three-bedroom, one-bath rental house. Hardwood floors creaked and boomed as heavy feet made way in and out of community rooms, bathroom and kitchen. I remember everything being inordinately loud. The odor of soiled clothes overpowered the solitary bottle of Air Wick, located on the bathroom floor. The only saving grace was fresh coffee brewing on the stove. As the newbie, I decided to relax and go with the flow.

Tuesday began with breakfast at the Dixie, a restaurant located on the south side of Monroe. An elderly man with a long white beard and wearing a CSA officer's uniform, complete with saber, gold sash and a hat sporting a white ostrich feather, graciously ushered us to a large corner booth that sat six if we added a chair. A huge oil painting of General Robert E. Lee mounted on Traveler, his legendary warhorse, dominated the place. Fifty pictures of Johnny Reb winning battles lined the pecky cypress walls. Sabers, spurs, saddles and Confederate memorabilia filled in blank spaces. A massive Confederate flag covered most of the ceiling, rippling from a breeze pumped through air conditioning vents. The War of Northern Aggression lived on at the Dixie, a gathering spot for those of us holding tight to our southern values and heritage.

Bobby opened with a joke: "What's the difference between a bull moose and a blues band? ... The moose has the horns up front and the asshole behind."

Following a moment to allow everyone to get it, Bobby then turned to me and asked, "So, what's up, Rock?"

"Tech is on hold," I said.

With a smile, Lance asked, "Why do bands have bass players? ... To translate for the drummer. Rocky's IQ just went up 30 points."

Rooster added his endorsement. "You finally figured it out—good nookie trumps everything."

While the others were verbally patting me on the back, Big Joe was attacking his sunny-side-up eggs over corn beef hash, making a gooey mess on the plate. His body language was tense, angry. He hadn't cracked a smile since we sat down. Then he launched his salvo.

"Where ya comin' from n' where ya goin'? Ya leadin' us on a *fais do-do* to nowhere? Lay down ya cards, Bro. I call ya."

Smoke broke in before Big Joe could continue. "Hey, fellows. Rocky just dropped out of college. Back off. Give him room to take a breath."

Banging his fist on the table, Big Joe took Smoke on, mixing Cajun French with English, "*Gar-ici moitier coupon-chum!* I'll ax Rocky anythin'!"

Interrupting Big Joe before he went on a tirade in the middle of the restaurant, I said, "Where I'm coming from and where I'm going? I'm taking this week off to rest up, get in shape and get my head screwed back on. In my absence, each of you have an assignment. Next Monday, right here at this table, cast your vote for one of these options: Door No. 1: *Laissez les bon temps roulez*—simply lay back and enjoy life. Door No. 2: go into training and prepare the Carousels to go on the road. Or, Door No. 3: commit every fiber in your body to becoming big stars in America—whatever it takes to achieve fame and fortune. Each door comes with a price, consequence and rewards. Consider your choices carefully. Remember, with wishes in one hand and spit in the other, guess which one fills up first?"

Watching the facial reactions of everyone at the table, I continued.

"Sitting in the historic Dixie we should remind ourselves that the Confederacy began the War of Northern Aggression with bravado, only to lose in the end because of shortages of capital, natural resources and human attrition. Don't start this war if we can't win. Cast your votes next Monday over breakfast at the Dixie. And, by the way, with the exception of the Thursday, Friday and Saturday gigs, I'm checking out—off the grid."

Bobby asked, "Off the grid—what's that?

Quoting from Jack Kerouac's *On the Road*, I said, "'*There was nowhere to go, but everywhere, so just keep on rolling under the stars.*' Guys, I paid one hell of a price for my ticket on this merry go round. Only space and time will unravel my riddles. I'm disappearing for a few days. Look for me Thursday afternoon at the rental house, where I'll be looking for a bath and a change of clothes. Till then …"

Henry David Thoreau found peace in the woods. So can I.

North Louisiana had plenty of lakes and rivers. Bayou D'Arbonne near Farmerville offered good camping and fishing. I pitched a tent and gave my fly rod a major league workout. Eating what I caught seemed to put life into perspective—'There's no free lunch.' Thursday morning I broke camp and left some of my self-doubt and persecution buried in an earthen latrine.

The following Monday at the Dixie, I waited while our waitress cheerfully wrote six convoluted orders. As she walked away, I put the monkey on the table.

"How do you vote? Who's first?"

Not surprisingly, Big Joe took the lead. "*Trois.* Commitin' to anythin' less is waste. I'm in."

Bobby followed. "Be a star—fame—all the way to the top!"

Rooster's good eye sparkled, registering his vote: "If the second door produces a steady stream of fresh band-aids, count me in. If that works out, then I'll go for the third door."

Lance was next. "Door No. 2. I'm not sure we have the talent to go any further, though I'll give it my all—whatever that's worth."

Somewhere between a wink and a nervous squint, Smoke replied, "Megastar!"

All eyes on me, I said, "It's Door No. 3."

As I sipped my coffee, our meals arrived. Smiles of satisfaction filled faces as good food filled bellies. Then, while downing my last bite of buttermilk biscuit with sausage gravy, I pondered what we had just agreed to do.

The die is cast. Unfortunately none of us have a clue where fame and fortune lie—there's no chart. Adrift in a vast sea without a compass heading or basic seamanship skills, by default, I am their captain. At least Christopher Columbus had funds, experience and leadership skills before casting off. I have none. I'd best get busy captaining the Carousel ship.

Challenge at hand, I surveyed our assets with fresh eyes. Bobby was wiping his mouth with a napkin before blowing his nose into the soiled cotton. Lance took a big swig from his coffee cup, picked up the saucer, tilted and slurped the dregs. Big Joe brushed greasy black hair out of squinting eyes, leaving deposits of scrambled eggs at the peak of his forehead. Rooster played paradiddles on the Formica table with his fork and knife, splattering biscuit remnants on me. Smoke drooled a brown substance from protruding buckteeth into a waiting lap. I picked my teeth with fingernails before clearing wax out of my ear.

Blind leading the blind. We have nowhere else to go, so why not go for entertainment stardom?

"Okay," I said. "Let's get organized."

"I'm for that," Lance replied.

Bobby added, "Yeah. Time for a plan."

"Each of you will be assigned a responsibility," I continued. "Take your job seriously and follow the golden rule. I've tried to match roles with individual strengths."

Chuckling like a child, Rooster interjected, "Is there a role for chief stud?"

Bobby wasn't amused. "Get serious, Rooster. This marks a new direction for the Carousels. Get with the program or get out."

Smoke added, "Yeah. In or out?"

Once more I had to intercede before the situation got out of hand.

"Let's rise above our modest beginnings. Yesterday's missed opportunities will soon disappear in a foggy rear view mirror if we seize control of our tomorrows. Here's my first cut. Big Joe is music director and arranger. Bobby handles stage presence, performance, lighting and sound. Rooster is tune planner and caller. Lance is accountant and administration, and Smoke is in charge of chorography and publicity. I'll handle strategy, bookings, unions and club owners. What do you think?"

"Firs' cut—'bout right," Big Joe said.

Lance added, "Good matchups, Rocky."

"I can fuckup tune calling with the best of 'em," Rooster quipped.

Bobby and Smoke glared at Rooster, but nodded acceptance of their assignments.

Today at the Dixie round table the Carousels bonded in visions of grandeur. Realistically, what choices do we have? Continuing to wallow in North Louisiana mediocrity? That's a dismal alternative when compared to delusional fantasy.

Much like an evangelist minister exhorting his sinful congregation to seek salvation by being born again, I preached my theology to my new disciples seated around the breakfast table.

"Our new schedule begins tomorrow. Monday through Friday, we'll woodshed mornings from 9 to noon. Group rehearsals on Monday, Tuesday and Wednesday from 2 to 4. We'll use the rental house and Carousel Club as rehearsal halls and launching pads. Perfect the Carousel show here, and then we'll take it on the road. Commit to accomplishing something extraordinary, something you'll be proud of—the rest of your lives."

Emboldened, I summarized the master plan.

"Our secret sauce has three ingredients: Superior technique on multiple instruments, eclectic repertory of music genres, and star quality showmanship. Investing equal time and money in each, our goal is to brew our secret sauce into the perfect gumbo. Woodshed five days a week to develop superior technique on multiple instruments. Get busy."

Privately, I reflected on another passage from Ayn Rand's *Atlas Shrugged*: *"If one's actions are honest, one does not need the predated confidence of others, only their rational perception."*

Fortunately, I realized that my self-absorbed imagination can be a one-way street to disaster. They follow because they have nowhere else to go. On the other hand, where else can I go?

Later that afternoon, Big Joe and I had a candid assessment of the strengths and weaknesses of each Carousel member.

"Bobby's *tete dure* is an *esco*; like a *fils-potain*. He's *gate' poput*," Big Joe remarked.

"Tell me about it," I said. "I agree that Bobby is much like a spoiled child. He hates authority almost as much as you."

Big Joe passed up my side jab about him, saying, "Bobby's got da gumbo as a singer, still nothin' as a musician. His pants are too big in the seat. On da other hand, Lance is somethin' else on vocals and okay on bass. Betchya he'll never be good on keyboards. I think I can get him goin' on reeds."

I agreed. "If we get Bobby goin' on drums and Lance on sax, I'll play trombone and vibraphone. We'll have a frontline horn section for R&B and expand our genres to include Latin jazz. That opens up exciting new possibilities."

Big Joe nodded with some skepticism, "Ya wanna play trombone and vibes, then ya gots ta tech Bobby drums."

"I'll teach Bobby drums."

With that, I turned Big Joe loose on the guys. If nothing else, his physical authority would ensure that each Carousel member practiced and practiced until they were performance ready. He loved his newfound authority and laid out a demanding regimen, unique to each player. Woodshedding each morning became our daily routine.

Big Joe's drive created a whirlwind of energy and activity among house residents. Something curious was going on inside his skull, a result of being empowered and respected for the first time in a long time. Leading by example, Big Joe worked harder than any of us. Although his reed work was already superior, he continued his woodshed regime to improve tone, licks and cleanliness on four saxophones, clarinet and flute. When he took out his trumpet and fiddle, it was rough on our ears for weeks. Over time, endless scales produced an acceptable trumpet and fiddle player.

Steeped in rhythm and blues and shit-kickin' Zydeco, Big Joe's style and technique mirrored the great artists of the day, and his musical leadership lorded over our collective progress. Musically, Big Joe was the alpha dog of the Carousels. Regrettably, his interpersonal social skills fell short; a misfit outside his cloistered South Louisiana Cajun culture.

Technically, Bobby was challenged—a self-taught drummer and marginal at best. Highly resistant to authority, he fought my best intentions. Finally I found the key, introducing Bobby to the 13 essential drum rudiments. The routine I drafted for Bobby emphasized the long roll, paradiddle and flamacue. The hard backbeat of the flamacue was particularly effective for R&B and rock. These memory exercises were best perfected in isolation, ideal for woodshedding and Bobby's prima donna personality.

Slowly Bobby grasped the basics of getting around a trap set and, over time, he achieved fundamental competence that became an integral component of our eventual success. Bobby worked hard at perfecting trap drumming and other percussion instruments: conga, timbale, and bongos. I worked hard at avoiding an authority figure persona when coaching him.

When it came to taking classes in music theory, Lance was absent. A year of high school clarinet and basic piano comprised the sum total of his music training. In the summer of '57, the Carousels needed a bass man, so Lance borrowed an electric bass and converted a used jukebox amplifier and woofer. He woodshedded on bass until his fingers bled. In self-defense, he purchased a ukulele felt pick, employing it for the remainder of his Carousel career. The ukulele felt pick created a unique, rich, mellow bottom, similar to double base richness.

Big Joe coached Lance on reed technique, sharing his four saxophones. Mirroring Bobby's success on percussion, Lance eventually achieved competence on reeds, and, like Bobby, helped play a major role in the future success of the Carousels.

Smoke was ideally suited for woodshedding. His guitar work in jazz, ballads, old standards, Brazilian and flamenco music was exemplary. However, he struggled to achieve the rough, aggressive style demanded by R&B and rock. Big Joe and Rooster coached Smoke to introduce a cutting tone to his technique arsenal. Try as he may, Smoke never quite perfected anger and aggression from his Gibson thin line. Otherwise, his bass playing was exceptional—far better patterns than Lance. Intuitively, Smoke knew the styles of the great bassists in big bands, R&B, rock, Zydeco and country.

Additionally, Smoke raised his competence levels on the five-string banjo, mandolin and fiddle, greatly expanding our on-demand repertoire. Within Smoke's areas of expertise, I considered him the finest guitarist in North Louisiana.

The loose cannon in our band was Rooster—crazy like a fox. Piano or organ—it didn't matter. Rooster could dazzle any audience with his accomplished keyboard technique. To show off his talent, he played *Flight of the Bumblebee* at 250 beats per minute while wearing white gloves. He was so impressive, we featured Rooster in our stage show—white gloves under black lights.

When the Carousels needed a traditional Cajun accordion to backup Big Joe's Zydeco repertory, Rooster chose a Mark Savoy, manufactured in Eunice, Louisiana—an authentic Cajun Zydeco squeezebox with buttons and levers, absent a traditional keyboard. Rooster really got into it, playfully squeezing the thing and jumping around the rental house like a one-eyed Cajun. One day, he picked up a chromatic harmonica. His blues bending developed quickly. Then, he surprised us with his skill and sensitivity on ballads.

Rooster was one of the best musicians I'd ever worked with—and the craziest.

In the mid-'50s, I was a big fan of South Louisiana spade bass drum syncopation beats. Lifting my right heel off the bass drum pedal freed my toes to move independently and rapidly, using the axis of my ankle as a fulcrum. A unique independence with dynamic on-call accents evolved. At that time, white drummers didn't recognize the impact or importance of *jig* bass drum patterns. With practice, practice, practice, I mastered the shines' techniques, supplying the foundation freight train drive that supported our unique Carousel sound—particularly effective on R&B and rock.

Throughout grammar school, junior high and high school, my classical training spanned orchestra, band and private lessons. I knew my way around a snare drum, trap set, tympani, marimba, vibraphone, double bass and trombone. While in high school, I acquired a first-generation Leedy & Ludwig vibraphone. Setting it up at the rental house, I woodshedded the circle of fifths every morning over coffee. Cal Tjader and Red Norvo were my idols.

A beat-up student model Pan American trombone got a workout as well. Wanting to play 'bone like J. J. Johnson and Kai Winding, I spent hours on end developing slush-pump embouchure, tone and technique. The transition from double bass to Lance's electric bass was relatively easy. Five days a week I worked mornings on vibes, 'bone, bass and polishing my trap set skills.

Raising our vocal technique and quality required professional coaching. Bobby contracted with a Northeast University professor of voice. Tape recorder in hand for private voice lessons, Bobby shared techniques and exercises with the Carousels. We all embraced voice exercises, learning to open our larynx, singing chromatic scales, forming vowel sounds within the mouth and throat cavity, and recording the exercises for self-critique.

Funny, but effective, we used a stethoscope on our chest to ascertain the origins of tonal quality, striving to drive tone down deep in our chest and gut. A silk handkerchief held over one ear while standing in the bathtub helped achieve a resonance quality.

Bobby mastered the songbooks of Sam Cooke, Jackie Wilson, Ben E. King, Elvis Presley, Chubby Checker, Pat Boone and Ricky Nelson, among others. Lance Love's principal contribution was vocal renditions from the Andy William, Frank Sinatra, Tony Bennett, Brook Benton, Perry Como and Lloyd Price songbooks. Like a sponge, Lance soaked up the tape-recorded voice techniques and exercises, transitioning his voice to a much higher quality.

Big Joe sang the songbooks of Ray Charles, Bobby "Blue" Bland, B.B. King, Fats Domino and most of the Zydeco artists. No one wanted to refine Big Joe's phrasing and tonal quality, fearing any change would destroy his unique ability to mimic the great R&B and Zydeco giants of the day.

Smoke and Rooster could only be trusted with backup doo-wop. Despite my diligent voice exercises, Big Joe pronounced me tone deaf and relegated me to backup doo-wop as well. He was right. Then again I always wanted to sing solo.

We blended into a gumbo of backgrounds, biases, strengths and weaknesses. Comparing record collections of each Carousel, our varied musical taste was self-evident and represented a robust and diverse spectrum. Listening to and duplicating licks laid down on vinyl records is quick, easy and economical. Like loading up a jukebox, we loaded our repertory with favorite tunes, creating an eclectic repertoire designed to satisfy every audience.

Although the Carousels were proficient at reading charts, we preferred head arrangements: listening, reproducing and remembering individual musical parts. We perfected a hundred head arrangements within the first few months. Within a year we mastered about 500, all at performance-ready standards.

Improvements in technique flowed out of daily woodshedding. We became fearless, experimenting with various combinations of instrumentation, harmonies and genres. Not surprising, we developed attitude. During our formative months our standard ensemble expanded exponentially to include four saxes, clarinet, flute, trumpet, trombone, vibraphone, Cajun accordion, frottoir (washboard played with thimbles), fiddle, guitar, electric bass, double bass, organ, piano, harmonica, melodica, mandolin, and various percussion instruments such as conga and timbales.

Within two months we bolstered our repertoire with a Big Band horn section, authentic Zydeco music, country and western, Blue Grass, Delta blues, Latin jazz, Broadway show tunes and classical guitar—a dazzling array of sounds. We traded in our home model Hammond organ for a top-end Wurlitzer with a large Leslie speaker cabinet. I personally guaranteed the loan, cutting a monthly check out of the Carousel bank account. The mighty Wurlitzer produced a big, fat sound, ideal augmentation for our horn section and rendering lifelike Big Band resonance.

Upgrading our personal instruments to professional grade contributed to differentiating ourselves from the average white band, rotating up to eight instruments among six Carousels during each set. As time progressed, we increased the rotation of different instruments played per set to 12. Passing multiple instruments around was unique—a major contributor to building our brand. We were finding our groove.

Chapter 7

1959
THE FOUR FRESHMEN

One of our regulars at the Carousel Club was Roscoe Rossini, the maître d' at the upscale Rendezvous Supper Club. After playing the role of the pompous, tux-attired meet-greet-and-seat host at the Rendezvous, Roscoe headed for the Carousel Club, transforming into his true self, a closet fairy and party animal. Roscoe became a huge Carousel fan, especially of Smoke. One Saturday night Roscoe invited us to be his guest at the Rendezvous for two Four Freshmen shows, Tuesday and Wednesday. We jumped at the invitation.

We arrived at the supper club just before the first show, and Roscoe seated us near the back wall and placed two bottles of champagne on our table. He made a big deal of popping the corks on the pre-chilled champagne bottles and filling our glasses to the proper level. Sheepishly, we noticed that we were the only men in the Rendezvous without jackets and ties. Fortunately, our dark corner table provided protection from incredulous eyes of North Louisiana oil-and-gas men, local politicians, timber moguls and senior management from the paper mill.

Wives and dates were dressed to the nines, with flashy gowns certain to have come from Neiman Marcus in Dallas. Some wore mink coats, draping them over the back of their chairs to ensure the right impression was communicated. Long on money, but short on class, the North Louisiana assemblage barked food and drink orders that could be heard back in the kitchen. Tuxedoed waiters scribbled rapidly, skillfully disguising their contempt for the big tippers. Most men ordered top-shelf bourbon on the rocks. Ladies preferred a Vodka martini with two olives. However, we were not there to impress or be impressed by an audience. Our sole purpose was to see and hear the Four Freshman.

When the four musical giants walked on stage, they were greeted by a good ol' boy standing ovation. Dressed in lavender tuxedo jackets, starched and pleated white tux shirts, lavender studs, black bow ties, black cummerbunds and black tux pants, they looked like male models arriving for an Esquire Magazine photo spread. Electric smiles flashed from glimmering white teeth and sparkling eyes. Instruments in position, they kicked off the show with *Somebody Loves Me*.

Lightning bolts sent shivers up and down my spine. My pulse raced to 110. They were on fire, and so was I. Face flush, my nose kept twitching as nostrils filled with the sweet smell of greatness. All eyes in the Rendezvous were fixated on the Four Freshman as they captured our hearts.

This must be what Baptists experience when they say they were "born again." I became a disciple of the Four Freshman that night. For an hour and a half, I worshiped at the feet of master entertainers.

At the break, Roscoe led us back stage to meet our heroes, where we stammered like country bumpkins when introduced. Despite our awkwardness, the gigantic entertainers were gracious and never talked down to us.

Fortunately, Roscoe facilitated a reprieve, and on the second night we came loaded with carefully prepared questions. Deeply honored to be in the presence of living legends, we embraced their answers as if they were biblical prophecies.

Lance directed the first question to Ross Barbour, drummer and emcee of the group: "What advice can you give us—a local band that wants to go on the road?"

"Trust your instincts," Ross replied. "Listen to your heart. The odds of making it big in the entertainment business are abysmal. In spite of this talent and perseverance will pay off if you commit. Trust your heart and don't quit til you make it."

Bobby fidgeted on the edge of his chair, anxious to ask his question. "How do we make it?" he said. "What's the secret sauce?"

Bob Flanigan and Ross' brother Don Barbour looked at Ken Albers, possibly the Four Freshman's best musician: brass and double bass.

Ken accepted the challenge, replying, "How do you get to Carnegie Hall? Practice, practice, practice. It's a tired old joke, but absolutely true. Master your instruments and pipes. They are the building blocks of a successful career as a professional entertainer. That's your ticket to enter the big show. There's no assigned seating, so be the best at what you do and show up prepared."

Displaying overt hero worship of Don Barbour's guitar and vocal excellence, Smoke was next.

"Your chord selection and singing the 5th or 7th harmony parts are the magic behind the freshman sound. Are you the arranger or is it a collaborative process?"

Don's eyes, now dull from multiple double Vodkas, slurred his answer inside a belch.

"Combination—collaborative in da end. I initiate da chord progressions and vocal parts. Everyone adds somethin'. In da end, we all take ownership of da arrangement."

I looked at Bob Flanagan, trombone and double bass man, asking, "Where are the land mines?"

"Women and drugs," he replied. "Too much of either will blow up your dreams. Manage those and you've got a fighting chance. Good luck."

The meetings with the Four Freshmen inspired us to do whatever it takes to become top entertainers. That night we committed ourselves to step up to the big leagues, eventually competing against the Four Freshmen and other greats. Rehearsals went to four days a week. Our development crept along at turtle speed, yet we persistently moved toward our goal.

Looking for someone to help us with performance techniques, Bobby found a drama professor at Northeast University with a burning desire to get laid. We had the means to satisfy his libido in exchange for his training at the New York Actors Studio, inspired by Stanislavski and defined by Lee Strasberg's Method Acting. He showed us how to draw upon our own emotions during performances. Like sightless men, we clung to Strasberg's Method and blindly walked the walk. Principal training ingredients included living the image of a great entertainer: aloof, mystical, superior and godlike.

Each Carousel articulated his unique mantra over and over in trancelike meditation. I selected a Tibetan Buddhists mantra, *Om Mani Padme Hum*. I quickly shortened it to *Om*. Mantras became our tools as we learned to portray the full spectrum of emotions. Using a mirror we focused on communicating joy, fear, anger, sweetness, sexiness, allure, anxiety, pain and madness. Absurd as these exercises appeared, each Carousel employed his mantra to achieve a high degree of competence as a performer. And it worked.

In the entertainment field a smile is one of the most important performance techniques. Bright white teeth are a must. We brushed ours aggressively with baking soda and a concoction prepared by a whacked-out dentist. Our teeth sparkled, although our gums burned and bled. Each of us spent a great deal of time looking at ourselves in the mirror, developing five smiles: laughter, surprise, happiness, pleasure and seduction. We developed an inventory of smiles, working on them until we consistently displayed them on call.

Bobby helped us wrap our package with new uniforms. We chose off-the-rack tuxedos in three colors from the J. C. Penny mail-order catalogue. Three tux pants and tux shirts, matching bow ties and cummerbunds, one set of studs, a pair of suspenders, and a pair of patent leather shoes for each of us. I wrote checks out of the Carousel checking account—extending our tenuous risks.

Mom crafted a sequined Carousel logo on felt, which looked great on the front of my bass drum. It was classy, until I stuck two Confederate flags in the bass drum keys next to our slogan: *The Pride of Dixie*. Nonetheless, we featured the logo in promotion pictures, letterhead, brochures and business cards, further exhausting our meager bank balance.

Two hairdresser chicks instructed us on hair washing, conditioning, tenting, hair spray and plucked eyebrows. Hair spray had to hold throughout the evening, competing against abundant perspiration. The only hair spray that worked, called Aquanet, contained large amounts of lacquer. Fortunately, it also was the cheapest brand. Unfortunately, it made our hair fall out, causing all kinds of problems. On the positive side our hair remained unmussed in a rainstorm, often resembling a football helmet.

Bobby had a manicurist chickadee teach us to do our own nails, full service. Friday afternoons were devoted to manicures. Most of us could find a band-aid to do it for us. My favorite way to achieve shiny nails was to buff them. Unintended consequences resulted— our pristine manicures attracted women. Some chicks inspected our hands during breaks, obviously a turn-on. It didn't take long to figure out their carnal connections.

A cosmetologist volunteered to instruct us on the selection of theatrical makeup and proper application. Previously, pancake makeup was something I begrudgingly got on my shirt collars and tuxes. Now, I was voluntarily wearing the stuff on my face along with rouge and eye makeup. We commented on feeling queer, but we wore theatrical makeup because it made our facial features appear flawless under bright stage lights.

Dance steps were incorporated into every song. Even the ballads had choreographed action behind the featured singer. Up-tempo tunes demanded action dance steps designed to captivate the audience. Several dance steps were strenuous, mandating athletic ability. Squats and sit-ups became part of our weekly routine in order to perform the physically challenging dance steps in a graceful manner.

We finally began to move in unison. Borrowing steps from the Temptations' dance routines; we took pride in our smoothness and synchronization. Following the musical perfection of a new tune, Smoke choreographed unique dance routines to embellish our performance.

A microphone is both prop and encumbrance. Eating the microphone and obscuring the face are no-nos. Each of us learned correct microphone technique. Bobby studied the sound field ranges and directional sensitivity of each Shure fist microphone and EV microphone. He discovered that positioning a microphone an inch below the chin delivered the best audio results and cleared the face for audience viewing. Gazing at the back row of the audience, over the top of a microphone, was the ideal method for achieving audience connectivity.

The Carousels began to get it. The total package gelled. We drew within sight of professional entertainer status. Achieving greatness had transitioned from a fragile fantasy to a real possibility. Audience accolades inspired our performances at the Carousel Club, while chickadees satisfied our vanities and libidos. And, gate receipts increased. For the first time we had money to invest in ourselves, feeding our dreams of achieving fame and fortune.

The Four Freshman did more for the Carousels than they would ever know. For the remainder of the Carousels journey we held them up as our ideal, routinely comparing our professional persona with theirs. The Four Freshman set a lofty bar.

Then, in the midst of our increasing success, a crisis reared its ugly head with the speed of a king cobra strike. A poisonous puncture wound almost killed the Carousels right then and there.

Chapter 8

1959
DESTINY AND DYNASTY

While at the rental house, our woodshed mornings and ensemble afternoons morphed into a religion. The living room was dedicated to large instruments—vibes, organ, electric piano, practice drum set, large amplifier and record player. Smaller instruments—strings, small amps, reeds and horns—were distributed in the kitchen and bedrooms. Mornings, the house resembled a college music department's rehearsal hall. Isolated in thought, but collective in noise production, we practiced scales, technique, licks, voice exercises and tone development. I'm certain it sounded like bedlam to anyone walking by. Harmony would have to wait til the afternoon group rehearsals, held in the living room or at the Carousel Club.

Our disciplined, yet seemingly chaotic routine continued without fail—until one Monday morning. While I was changing over to four-mallet exercises on the vibraphone, a forceful knock on the front door startled me. Opening the door revealed a disheveled woman about five feet tall with a butt wider than a five-dollar mule. She wasn't alone on the front porch. She had a kid in tow and one cradled in blubbery arms. My first reaction: a homeless person looking for a handout.

I soon found out how wrong I was. The woman addressed me with a heavy Cajun accent. "I'm Marie Robecheaux, Joe's ol' lady. Where's Joe?"

None of us had a clue Big Joe was married or a father. He'd just celebrated his 20th birthday. Then again, the unkempt youngster was at least three or four.

That sly fox.

I yelled out, "Hey Joe! Your ol' lady's here!"

Marie's mouth widened, revealing two black teeth, upper, and one missing tooth below. Smiling back, I motioned for Marie to come in and sit on the couch, removing record albums to make space. She waddled in, but didn't sit.

"Drove up from Morgan City Sunday," she said. "Stayed at da Joe-Dan Motel til now."

From the hallway, Big Joe appeared—stunned, speechless. Still in his drawers and wife-beater undershirt, holding a pair of Levi's in his left hand, he looked like a 230-pound toddler caught with his hand in the cookie jar.

In a voice that dripped honey, Marie turned to him and said, "Hi baby. Came to get ya. Get yo poke and let's go home."

By this time, Smoke, Bobby, Lance and Rooster joined the group, ready to witness whatever was about to happen. We all looked at Big Joe, then at Marie, then back at Big Joe. The weight of the world rested on Big Joe's back—and he ain't Atlas.

Awkward silence thicker than la quete sugarcane syrup froze movement.

Marie finally broke the silence, telling Big Joe, "Papa and yo daddy told me ta come get ya and brung yo home. Let's go home."

Blood vanished from his face as Big Joe visibly deflated, like a pricked balloon headed for the floor. Clumsily, he stumbled a step toward Marie. No words, no kiss, no hugs—no love. He took the infant from Marie, grabbed her hand and dragged her out the front door with the three-year-old trailing behind.

We didn't see Big Joe again until Tuesday afternoon, when he came by to pick up his clothes and instruments. Very little was said as he packed his things and left. Unexpectedly, Big Joe returned Wednesday morning, distraught and showing four days of stubble. Immediately, he sent Rooster to summon me from my morning constitution. Flushing the toilet, I wondered what the next move would be. Without Big Joe, our band was going nowhere.

Big Joe motioned me out to his wife's car, a rusted-out '49 Chevy four-door. For two hours he talked and sobbed—sobbed and talked.

A skid row bum looked better. Big Joe's eyes, incapable of connecting with mine, fixated on rust holes in the Chevy's floorboard. His massive body sagged, suffering under the weight of self-condemnation. Repugnant odors oozed from every orifice. Using the tail of his wife-beater undershirt he wiped away tears streaming from bloodshot eyes, and then used it to blow his nose.

"I'm quittin' da band and goin' home," he said. "Surprised Marie found me, but she did. My life's fucked! Her Papa and daddy sent Marie to get me. Der vice is squeezin' me down. I has to do what de say. I hate being told what to do. Can't stand it. Thought 'bout ways to get out of dis—but short of killing Marie and da kids, I can't escape da vice. I'm fucked! I'm fucked!"

What could I say or do to comfort a broken man who was weeping like a baby badly in need of a diaper change?

My eyes teared up from Big Joe's nauseating body odor. Dirty bare feet and filthy Levis matched his wife-beater perfectly: a collage of coffee, food, blood, mecuricome, and snot. Big Joe began confessing every sin he'd ever committed, seeking redemption. I couldn't give him any of that, although I could provide clear thinking and some better options than going back to Morgan City, taking over his father's machine shop and killing Marie and their kids.

"You're a good guy," I said. "If you lie down with pigs you're guaranteed to get up with shit all over ya. Stop wallowing like a pig in shit. You've made mistakes—you've fucked up. Mistakes notwithstanding, you have choices, and one of them is choosing not to spend the rest of your life in Angola Prison for murder. I've heard that Angola's inmates are 95 percent nigger. You can only sing Ray

Charles to those shines so many times before they stick their big black cocks up your lily-white ass."

"What choice do I have, Rocky?"

"Make a list," I said. "It has to be your list—not mine. However, I'll prime your pump. If you weren't facing this crisis, what would you really like to do with the rest of your life?"

Looking out through the Chevy's dirty windshield, Big Joe paused a moment.

"I'd like to go on da road with da Carousels and make somethin' of my life. So far, I've fucked everything up—lost daddy's respect, knocked up Marie at 15, beat up my LSU math professor fer making' fun of my Cajun accent and runnin' away to North Louisiana."

"Any other options or dreams come to mind?"

"Nope. I jus' want ta run away with da Carousels. The longer we run, the better I'll be. I really need ta find a way ta feel good 'bout somethin'. Da music we make and bangin' chicks are de only dings I care 'bout, but dat's 'bout ta end."

"Big Joe, I can't and won't tell you what to do with your life," I replied. "Even so, be a man. Stand up and take your blows, and remain true to yourself. Do whatever you have to do to find some semblance of happiness. *Suave de vive* is fleeting moments in a human life, so grab it quick, before it disappears. Remember telling me to *laissez les bon temps roulez?* Do what you have to do and do it now. Good luck. Let me know your final decision."

Closing the rusty door of the Chevy, I stood for a moment to watch Big Joe drive away. I shrugged, accepting the possibility that the loss of Big Joe could seal our fate. A mocking bird sang six, no, seven songs of anguish.

Oh well, I can always go back to Tech and get my degree.

Thursday night at nine, Big Joe showed up at the house. He shaved, shit, showered and put on his tux. As though nothing had happened, we played the Carousel Club gig that night. Apparently, Big Joe was back with the band. We never asked and he never spoke of Marie and the kids again. It was like the crisis never happened. And just like that, the calamity passed.

Reflecting on potential ramifications of the crisis episode, I quietly filed articles of incorporation with the State of Louisiana and secured a copyright on the Carousel logo. I wanted legal ownership of the band, bank account, select instruments and brand name—just in case it ever got to the point of mandating "my way or the highway."

That weekend, a group named the Roller Coasters opened at the Southside Club, directly across the street from our gig. The competition was a great six-piece band led by Johnny Ladatta and financially backed by a small-time Mob figure named Smitty Smith. Smitty also fronted a ginmill called the Dynasty Lounge, plus three other Monroe nightclubs. Over the two weekends that followed, we counted cars in both parking lots and determined that the Carousels were out-drawing the Roller Coasters and winning the after-midnight bottle club battle of the bands.

Not surprising, Smitty soon invited me to meet him at his Dynasty Lounge. His reputation for controlling his burgeoning nightclub empire and the Roller Coasters preceded him. I suspected he was setting his sights on controlling the Carousels and me, too. Before leaving for the meeting, I took a long shower, scrubbing away any anxiety that might put me at a disadvantage. Toweling off, I planned my strategy.

Smitty needs me a lot more than I need him. Create a situation where he meets my terms.

Smitty was waiting for me at the Dynasty bar with an open bottle of Jack Daniels Black Label. While pouring me a drink, he offered the Carousels what he termed a business opportunity.

"Here's my number," he said, sliding a napkin in my direction.

I looked at his figure scribbled on the napkin.

"Too low."

I wrote a higher number and slid it back.

"Too high. Let's split the difference."

"I'll talk it over the guys and let you know."

"Give me your answer now. Aren't you the Carousel leader?"

"Look Smitty," I said. "You offer short money and press me for an answer. Did you really believe I'd cave, like Johnny Ladatta? I'm not Johnny, and we're not the Roller Coasters. I'll give you my answer tomorrow."

Leaning back in his seat, his well-known, shit-eatin' grin in full display, Smitty was sizing me up and deciding his next move. I was doing the same with him.

Middle-aged, balding, overweight and impressed with his flashy self-image, Smitty invested lavishly in custom-tailored silk suits, Egyptian cotton shirts, expensive silk ties and Italian shoes. Only a few people knew Smitty packed a .38 snub-nose revolver, tucked in the small of his back at the belt line. One of Smitty's squeezes volunteered his secret to me one night.

Smitty also carried a large roll of cash, bound by a rubber band. I remember the hundred-dollar bills, always on the outside, to impress any observer. One had to admire the dexterity of his performance as he peeled off a payment to the truck driver during the midday beer delivery, performing the peel and pay with flair.

Underneath the gruff facade, the twinkle in his eye gave him away. He was a soft touch for any sob story, particularly if it came equipped with big tits. I didn't have the requisite big tits, or a major sob story. However, I had something he wanted: the Carousels.

Settling with Smitty on a number closer to my original than his, the Carousels soon opened at the Dynasty Lounge for six weeks, six nights a week, cutting back on our after-hours Carousel Club performances to Friday and Saturday only.

With Louisiana's legal drinking age starting at 18, unanticipated consequences emerged at the Dynasty Lounge. Every night young chickadees flew in and perched on show bar stools. Birds on a wire. We named each bird to keep track of 'em: canary, redbird, owl, mocking bird, hawk, black bird, humming bird, cardinal, sparrow, buzzard, and so on.

As we performed on a stage inches above these birds, their adoring eyes and open mouths showed they were hungry for a flight that matched their imaginations. Providing sustenance to a hungry bird for a night seemed appropriate—so we did.

One night a young canary sat at the show bar, right in front of me. On break, I talked to the delicate and shy bird. She told me she was a senior in high school, turning 18 in five months. Apparently a virgin. We met for coffee the following day, after school.

That was the beginning of my eight-year relationship with Barbara Banks, a young, beautiful woman who brightened up my otherwise derelict life. At first, I simply wanted to be with someone normal during the day to keep in touch with my inner good man. Barbara fit the bill perfectly.

Surrounded by workin' girls, bookies, dope dealers and high-stakes gaming shills who worked for Smitty's brother, Marco, mystery and intrigue hung heavy in the Dynasty's underground society. Smoke ingratiated himself with the Dynasty bartenders and pour man. The pour man was Smitty's trusted goon, responsible for cutting the liquor at the Dynasty Lounge and his other nightclubs. According to Smoke, a 30 percent cut by the pour man increased bar profits by 60 percent.

Smoke also unearthed some really shady background on Smitty, his brother Marco and the inner workings of the North Louisiana Mob. With considerable pride and flair, Smoke gave me an eye-opening education of the local underworld. His nervous tic very much in evidence, he began outlining an organizational chart of bosses and crews, naming names. I didn't know how much of this he was making up. All the same, it was interesting.

Perhaps I could use some of Smoke's information to benefit the Carousels. Perhaps not. A fool in his folly can do you more harm than your most ardent enemy.

John L. Nelson

Although Smitty paid the Roller Coasters more than he paid us, we put everything we had into our shows. To Smitty's amazement, the Carousels outdrew the Roller Coasters, markedly increasing the Dynasty's nightly bar receipts. Big Mama, head bartender at the Dynasty and an occasional sleepover for Lance, taught me the golden rule of the bar business: "Keep a running tally of the nightly cash register receipts and set your prices accordingly. Money talks."

Beginning with the Dynasty gig, I delivered an extra spark of motivation just before we kicked off our featured set. The guys came to anticipate my words every night thereafter.

I said, "Create fantasy—sell illusion—project your God Power."

THIRD SET LINEUP—THE DYNASTY				
SONG	ORIG'L ARTIST	GENRE	ENSEMBLE	FEATURE
The Thrill Is Gone	B.B. King	R&B	3 Horns	Big Joe—Vocal, Lance & Rocky
The Night Time Is The Right Time	Ray Charles	R&B	3 Horns	Big Joe—Vocal, Lance & Rocky
Mother-in-Law	Allen Toussaint	R&B	Standard Ensemble	Bobby—Vocal
For The Good Times	Ray Price	Country	Fiddle Solo	Lance—Vocal
Dream Lover	Bobby Daren	R&R	Standard Ensemble	Bobby—Vocal
Bon Ton Roulet	Clifton Chenier	Zydeco	Cajun *Accordion* Frottoir, Washboard, Fiddle + Rhythm	Big Joe—Vocal Rooster, Smoke & Rocky
Hard Times	David "Fathead" Newman	Jazz R&B	3 Horns	Big Joe, Lance & Rocky

Our Day Will Come	Ruby & The Romantics	R&R	Standard Ensemble	Bobby—Vocal
Crying	Roy Orbison	Pop	Standard Ensemble	Lance—Vocal
Stagger Lee	Lloyd Price	R&B	3 Horns	Bobby—Vocal, Big Joe, Lance & Rocky

Bobby took my advice to heart. He lived the role of a megastar: arrogant, aloof, and audacious. Boldly, and almost shamelessly, displaying techniques practiced over previous months, he mesmerized audiences, particularly the chickadees. With no apparent inhibitions, his magnetic personality blended with his music—just the right balance of voice, dress, dance, audience connection and lighting. Every move was so well rehearsed that his performance always appeared fresh and natural. Most of his tunes were up-tempo, captivating audiences with his gyrating dance routines and spins. I beamed with pride when our struttin' peacock fronted our band.

During our often-frenetic days and nights, practicing, performing and polishing our act, brunch was set aside for serious discussions and critical review of current events. With Bobby and Lance volunteering as readers, we received daily updates on happenings around the world. It wasn't long before we recognized a correlation between current events and changing audience tastes in music. Even during our early stages we sensed America's cultural transform. Our challenge was to stay in time with changing times.

One morning, Lance read aloud a news article that proclaimed, *"On the Beach* is the first film to premiere on both sides of Iron Curtain."* Putting down the paper, he editorialized, "We're all going to die from a nuclear blast anyway. It's just a matter of time. This movie simply tells the world...."

"I want ta go down playin' *Waltzing Matilda*," Big Joe blurted out before Lance could finish his sentence. "Bet God wasn't thinkin' 'bout coonass humor when he writ dis drama."

I replied, "I took your advice Joe—I've embraced *laissez les bon temps roulez*. Don't stop me now, just when I've learned *suave de vive*."

Smoke turned serious. "American culture is shifting like quicksand. We have to shift with the sands or be swallowed up. We need to figure out what next year's audiences will be listening to. If we keep doing the same old tunes the same way, we'll be obsolete before we know it. Think about what's coming next fellows. Let's get ahead of the curve—beginning now."

No one responded aloud, but I sensed all heard Smoke's challenge—and took him seriously.

The Carousels began experimenting with audience reaction to the cultural events that played out on the evening TV news programs. We kept a keen eye on nuance, attempting to outwit increasing uncertainty, conflicts and disasters. Challenged, we stayed a step ahead of the psychological tenor of our audiences, most of the time. After all, we were in the escape business.

During our daily brunches, crazy-but-gifted Rooster welcomed input on tune calling and sequencing.

"People are bombarded with bad news every night on TV," he said. "So let's create fantasy and sell illusion, and take our audiences to a happy place."

To my surprise, Rooster began studying the psychological and behavioral sciences, checking out books from the library and consuming the theories of Sigmund Freud like white on rice.

Like teenagers in heat, we never lost sight of the pleasures at hand. For example, there was Big Orange, who sported big pointy tits, a trim body, silky smooth skin and the face of a Molly mule. She often joked about taking afternoon nookie breaks from serving cocktails at the Dynasty Lounge. My curiosity had to be satisfied, so we shared a nookie break one afternoon. I discovered that it was no joke—she was addicted to sex and Orange Crush soda pop, produced by the Nehi Bottling Company. Hence, her handle.

Since I also loved sex and Orange Crush, I purchased two cases of soda and began sharing nookie breaks with regularity, usually following rehearsals at the Dynasty. Big Orange was full of foolishness, a free spirit and a creative lover. Typically we fulfilled our carnal desires, relaxed on stained white sheets, smoked Pall Malls, sucked Orange Crush through straws and giggled away the afternoon.

Lying naked and exhausted one amorous afternoon, Big Orange explained to me the Ten Commandments of an Alcoholic Nursery. Her insight into the world of nightclubs was fascinating, and I listened with interest as she reeled them off:

"Number one, love thy marks. You'll be richer for it. Two, thou shalt not fall in love with every one you sleep with—very juvenile. Three, thou shalt not screw a friend's squeeze—you're guaranteed to lose both. Four, too much seriousness leads to headaches and heartaches. Lighten up."

She smiled at me, sipped her Orange Crush and continued.

"Five, if it feels good, do it—as long as it doesn't harm anyone else. Six, people are who they are—never judge or try to change 'em. Seven, drop the act—everyone sees right through you anyway. Eight, occasionally, do something nice—temporarily restoring faith in mankind. Nine, thou shalt leave generous tips or become known as a loser."

Finally, she asked, "Rocky, can you guess Number 10? Jus'commonsense. It's 'Don't piss off wiseguys—that's stupid and can be deadly.'"

Big Orange was right on all counts. From that day forward, I adopted her Ten Commandments of an Alcoholic Nursery.

Then there was Angelle Devero, a gorgeous Cajun queen from Houma. She embraced her coonass heritage with pride and packaged her attributes just right in all the important places. Her classy, but revealing neckline promised large, luscious melons. As the southern saying goes, Angelle was built like a brick shit house. She leveraged her assets to the max, sitting on her favorite corner barstool at the Dynasty, seeing everything and letting everyone see her. Her seemingly unending wardrobe of expensive clothes complimented her flawless grooming. Angelle was a significant departure from the workin' girls who frequented the Dynasty Lounge. Special and discrete. Whatever Angelle did with men remained a mystery—a mystery most men wanted to solve firsthand.

I asked Lance if he knew anything about her.

"Angelle works for a gaming kingpin and Mob boss by the name of Marco Smith," Lance said, "She is Marco's hostess for high-stakes card and crap games. He pays all her bills. Hotel, food, dresses, hair stylist, drinks, cab fare—everything. In exchange, Angelle is on call night and day, and only to Marco. Between his calls, she frequents the Dynasty Lounge."

Lance added, "I guess you know that Marco backs his brother, Smitty, to front the Dynasty and the other clubs he owns. One call from Marco to the Dynasty Lounge triggers the beginning of Angelle's workday, or workweek. I imagine Angelle excels at her job, providing tantalizing distractions for the marks who show up at Marco's gaming tables."

Most men were either intimidated by Angelle's beauty or feared Marco Smith—probably both. Our Bobby Starr, however, was fearless. One night, following our Dynasty performance, Bobby invited Angelle to breakfast.

The next day at rehearsal, we all were eager to know what happened. Lance was first to ask, "How did it go with Angelle?"

With a sheepish look of embarrassment, Bobby said, "I had too much to drink and passed out—couldn't perform. Nothin' happened." And with that, the Angelle mystery remained unsolved.

A week later Lance asked me, "What's going on between you and Angelle?

At first, I couldn't look him in the eye, pretending to examine the broken tiles on the restaurant floor. Throat dry and tight, I squeaked out a confession.

"A tragedy of missed opportunity," I confessed. "That particular day I was the proverbial three-peckered goat—shooting arrows and scoring bull's eyes. That night with Angelle I reached for a fourth arrow. Angelle was on fire with desire, but my quiver was empty. To add insult to injury the following morning Angelle sent me out to buy manhole covers, and Marco called her in to work—lasting seven straight days and nights. We simply missed our opportunity at *suave de vive*."

Leaning forward, extending his head half way across the table, Lance cocked his head in amazement. "You mean you had the opportunity to devour Angelle's body and didn't?"

The ridges of my nose crinkled as the bitter taste of shame oozed through dry lips. "My spirit was willing, although, at that particular moment, my quiver was empty."

Sitting back in the booth, Lance took a deep breath. "Mind if I take my shot at Angelle?

"Permission granted."

Lance nodded. "If I ever get that beautiful creature in my bed, she'll never leave. That's a promise."

Arrogance fulfilled, Lance delivered. Angelle became Lance's girl. I moved on to pollinate the larger garden, absent Angelle's lush rose.

Freedom to pollinate an entire garden appeals to me, particularly at this point in my mystical adventure. In spite of the dangers, moving from good man to bent man is fun. I'll have to reign in my bent man—but not now—later.

Chapter 9

1959
BIG BROTHER TO THE RESCUE

Lance juggled the relationship with Angelle while enjoying the favors of other women, unbeknownst to Angelle. Laid back and coy, Lance got high marks for discretion and cleverness. His balancing act was working particularly well when Angelle got a call from Marco to go to work. Lance knew the risks, acknowledging that Cajun women had the reputation for blasting a man's cock off if they discovered the guy cheating on them. Angelle certainly had the right friends, the means and the passion to execute a final solution. But Lance loved women, and they loved him.

Meanwhile, I was like a kid in a candy store, falling in love with every warm space between any woman's legs—without discrimination.

Our resident sexologist, Rooster, added to my education: "What doesn't belong in this list, Rocky? Meat, eggs, wife, blowjob? ... A blowjob. You can beat your meat, eggs and wife, but you can't beat a blowjob."

Not done yet, Rooster shot another salvo: "What do you call kids born in whorehouses? ... Brothel sprouts." Crude as he was, Rooster was contributing to my new moral standards—all low.

After sleeping several times with Minnie the midget, I became an embarrassment to the rest of the Carousels, although I didn't know it at the time. Finally, Lance invited me to breakfast one morning at Mama's Table, a blue-plate-special joint known for sugar-cured ham, cheese grits, and Cajun coffee.

Normally laid back, Lance was fidgety, rejecting the first table the waitress showed us, pointing instead to a booth in the back. Nervously flipping through the menu, he slammed it shut, ready to order. As coffee with chicory was served, he ordered a full breakfast. When the waitress left, Lance looked me in the eye.

"Rocky, the guys asked me to talk with you about somethin'. You're our leader. However you can't pull off an air of godlike stature if everyone in the audience knows you're freak fuckin'. Sleeping with dwarfs, midgets, freaks and skanks reflects on the Carousels— and that ain't good. As our leader, you degrade all of us. If you like kinky stuff, at least be discrete. Rocky, stop freak fuckin' Minnie the midget!"

I leaned back against the booth, stunned by Lance's frankness and the truth behind his statement. Stalling for time, I sipped my coffee, finding it bitter. Adding a dash of salt, I sipped it again before responding.

"You're right. I have a responsibility to you guys not to hang out with freaks and skanks. In spite of her special talents, Minnie the midget is history. None of us want to sleep with dogs and wake up with fleas."

Lance nodded. "And I don't like fleas—or crabs. There are plenty of band-aids standing in line to lick your boo-boos. Give 'em a chance to win ya as their prize for a night. One satisfied chick will bring ya ten more. Word travels at light speed among women. Chicks can't keep a secret. Love 'em all with skill and class. I promise, you'll be a lot happier—and so will your Carousel brothers."

Downing his last bite of hominy grits with cheese, Lance continued his sermon.

"They don't have to be drop-dead gorgeous. In fact, the best lay is a grateful lay. In my experience, beautiful women are so self-consumed that they are afraid to muss their hair. God forbid their makeup gets smudged. Clothes have to be carefully hung up before sex. Zero spontaneity. As far as I'm concerned, the worst lays I ever had were with beautiful women. Most were cold fish, more interested in bragging to their girlfriends about sleeping with me than having great sex.

"Moreover, horny guys are constantly staring at your beautiful chick, longing to get in her pants. Much of the time, she's leading them on just in case she needs a warm backup. Beautiful women become practiced at teasing guys into believing they're great in bed. If you ask me, a beautiful woman is a genuine pain in the ass and high maintenance. Nope. Give me an average-looking chick that is grateful, willing to let go of her inhibitions and pass out three or four times during a night of orgasmic pleasure. I'm convinced. A grateful chick is the pathway to heaven. It's gooder'n grits."

A week later, over breakfast at the Last Chance Cafe, Lance and I picked up the same theme.

"Men our age measure happiness by the number of times they get laid," Lance observed. "Most walk around with a perpetual hard-on, desperate to get a babe in the sack. It shows and is a royal turn-off for chicks. On the contrary you and I and the other Carousels are in a heavenly place, with willing chicks all around us. Then again this era of free love isn't going to last forever. So we'd better make the most of our golden opportunity right now.

He obviously was on a roll.

"I'm living completely in the moment. God has given us a free pass, and only God knows when we'll have to turn it in. In the meantime, I'm getting my card punched every day by revolving chickadees. If it feels good, I do it. Millions of men would kill to trade places with us right now. So let's just lay back and enjoy life and free love while it lasts. There'll be plenty of time to worry about the consequences and guilt. For now let's spin the merry-go-round and ride this as far as it'll take us."

I took a sip of joe and replied, "Yep, I fully agree. But I still have a lot to learn about women and should be doing a lot more to expand my carnal confidence and control over women."

"Boy! That's a no brainer, Rock," Lance said in his deep-throated voice of authority. "I thought I was a really great lover until I saw two shines fuckin'. For me, watching them make love was a humbling experience. Those spades made me feel like a pimple-faced teenager, full of naïveté and selfishness. Ebony skin glistened a halo of perspiration from overheated bodies dedicated to satisfying the erotic pleasures of their partners—completely unselfish.

"At the end of the day, I picked a shapely high-yella gal to teach me how to make love the right way—the only way. Everything changed for me. I stumbled on da best way to become an Olympic lover—train with da right coach. Today, we find ourselves in a surreal situation, in the middle of a great free love experiment with an endless supply of coaches, teachers, test subjects and new techniques to explore."

Stunned, I asked, "Do I understand you to mean I should ask a workin' girl to show me how to fuck?"

"Precisely," Lance said. "Didn't you have a music teacher when you learned to play drums and vibes? Then why not do the same here? Just grab a babe with big tits and whisper in her ear, 'I'll do anything you ask. Tell me your wildest fantasies and I'll be your servant. Teach me how to please you tonight.'"

Almost falling over I said, "Holy shit! Have you ever said that before?"

"Last night during our last break, I said those very words to Shirley, that new workin' girl. She asked me to satisfy her six secret fantasies. We did things neither of us had ever done. As a result I got an Olympic lay. I'm always eager to learn more about how to please a woman."

Lance ended his sermon with a promise. "I guarantee—if you do what they ask, every one of them will beg you for more."

Looking at him in amazement, I listened, intent on soaking up carnal wisdom.

"However, a word of caution, and I hope you take this to heart, Rocky. Be selective about who you take into the pleasure zone. You only want Prime Grade A meat knocking on your door at 3 a.m. Treat the band-aids like the skanks they are—focus on satisfying yourself in that situation. It has been my experience that it's all but impossible to dump a skank once you take them into the pleasure zone. So be selective. Concentrate on learning from a pro all you can about becoming a creditable lover. Once you master the techniques, target your carnal knowledge only on Prime Grade A meat. It'll be the sweetest meat you ever tasted—and I mean that literally. Learn the fine art of muff diving."

Four days later, I went to Lance's apartment to borrow toothpaste and brush my teeth. As I squeezed out the white paste and began brushing, Lance came in, sat naked on the toilet and began spraying something all over his balls.

I spit out the toothpaste in amazement and asked, "What is that shit you're spraying on your balls?"

Through clinched teeth, obviously in pain from the burning, Lance groaned. "Black Flag. I have da crabs, and Black Flag twice a day for three days kills crabs. Black Flag beats stabbing the bastards with an ice pick. Want some?"

"Geeze—no thanks. Not today, but thanks for offering," I responded.

This is lunacy—all of it. This could not be happening.

Two days later, I borrowed Lance's Black Flag and began my treatments. Being a little more conservative, I sprayed once a day for two days, recovering just fine. However, Lance had overdone it and was raw from his navel to his knees—miserable. Needless to say, Lance didn't stick his nose or anything else in anyone's business for a week while skin peeled off his midsection. Luckily, Angelle was on a job with Marco during that week. Once again, Lance had dodged a bullet.

What a lesson. All the Carousels washed bed linens, underwear and clothes—twice—and disinfected our apartments with Lysol.

How much lower can I go?

Perched on the windowsill, Cheshire Cat glared in disgust. *"It looks like you ran afoul of something with wicked claws."*

Chapter 10

1960
KINGS OF THE BOSSIER STRIP

B ossier City is little more than a dot on the map along Highway 80, across the Red River from Shreveport. Halfway between Atlanta and Dallas, it's a routine stop for traveling salesmen on an expense account lookin' for a good time. The oil and gas business of North Louisiana and East Texas produced hundreds of blue collar millionaires, all dedicated to enjoying life to its fullest. The Strategic Air Command, based at nearby Barksdale, produced a steady stream of fliers from around the world—also lookin' to party. Traveling salesmen, SAC pilots and ArkLaTex oilmen considered the Bossier Strip, with more than 100 anything-goes nightclubs, as their adult playpen.

Carlos Marcello's Mob money controlled the town. The police and sheriff's departments were well paid to look the other way. However, the Mob made sure marks were safe not only from petty criminals, but also from venereal disease. Every two weeks the health department issued or punched red cards for barmaids, B-girls, workin' girls and waitresses who passed their VD medical exams. Every woman had to have a red card to get and keep one of these jobs. This assured all the johns that they would get a clean twat and a good time.

Money flowed like water on the Bossier Strip. Anything could be had for a price.

Bossier Strip also provided our big opportunity to break out of the small-time. The Carousels were booked to headline at Saks, the crown jewel of the North Louisiana nightclubs.

Saks boasted three full bars, all open 16 hours a day. Two of the bars featured B-girls in skimpy bunny outfits, complete with ears and fuzzy tails. B-girls earned commissions by the drink and got their bonus on couches in the Pit, the world's darkest room.

The fourth section of Saks was the Boom Boom Room—that was all ours.

Saks advertised that it had more neon lights than any place east of Las Vegas and the largest dance floor between Dallas and Atlanta. Although Merrill fronted Saks, everyone knew Carlos Marcello, Mafia Don of New Orleans, was the moneyman. Like most frontmen, Merrill Saks cast an impressive pose, impeccably dressed in custom-tailored suits, starched shirts, alligator shoes and daily visits to his barber. Merrill also special-ordered unique ties from New York: ultra-modern designs with real silver and gold threads that made Merrill stand out, even in the dark interior of Saks. Everything about Merrill was designed to impress, including his practiced savoir-faire.

However, under his Smilin' Jack façade, Merrill Saks possessed plenty of street smarts as he held absolute control over his empire. He discreetly collected an up-front nightly taste from workin' girls, bookies, numbers guys and drug dealers in return for the privilege of allowing them to operate on Saks property.

Merrill's enforcer was Virgil Pusser, Chief Detective of Vice for the Bossier City Police Department. Virgil claimed to be the nephew of the infamous Buford Pusser, Sheriff of McNairy County, Tennessee. Whenever Virgil appeared, you knew that Masher, his right-hand man, was nearby. According to rumor, Masher's unpublished resume included 27 notches on his .38. A visit from Masher guaranteed a bad day.

Insiders knew the rules of the road and stayed out of the ditches. If a naive or stupid workin' girl or drug dealer attempted to ignore Merrill's taste, Masher made them pay—big time.

On the surface the marks never noticed the secret communications occurring at light speed among Merrill, Virgil, Masher, bartenders, waitresses, workin' girls, bookies, and drug dealers. Marks had no chance of walking out of Saks with money in their pockets. The amazing part was that the marks all had a great time and came back for more—again and again.

Saks was the Carousels' first real test. Would our diverse musical lineup attract and hold an audience? We soon found out. The Carousels opened to fanfare and big crowds, packing in 400 a night Monday through Thursday and 600 to 700 every Friday and Saturday. Weekend lines were 20 to 30 yards long, all waiting to get in and see the Carousels. On our first trip to the plate in the big leagues, we hit a grand slam home run.

Before kicking off our featured set, I said, "Create fantasy—sell illusion—project your God Power."

THIRD SET LINEUP—SAKS BOOM BOOM ROOM				
SONG	ORIG'L ARTIST	GENRE	ENSEMBLE	FEATURE
West Side Story (Stage Show—Dance)	Leonard Bernstein	Broadway	Dance, Solo's & Ensemble	All Carousels
String of Pearls	Glenn Miller	Big Band	4 Horns	Big Joe, Lance & Rocky
I Left My Heart in San Francisco	Tony Bennett	Crooner	Standard Ensemble	Lance—Vocal
La Danse de Mardi Gras	Clifton Chenier	Zydeco	Cajun Accordion, Fiddle & Frottoir	Big Joe—Vocal Rooster, Smoke & Rocky
Lonely Teardrops	Jackie Wilson	R&B	Standard Ensemble	Bobby—Vocal

You've Lost That Lovin' Feelin'	Righteous Brothers	R&R	Standard Ensemble	Lance & Big Joe—Vocal
Big Girls Don't Cry	The Four Seasons	R&R	Standard Ensemble	Bobby in Falsetto + 3
Soul Bird (Tin Tin Deo)	Cal Tjader	Latin Jazz	Vibes & Conga's	Rocky & Smoke
Everyday I Have the Blues	B.B. King	R&B	4 Horns	Big Joe—Vocal, Lance & Rocky
Turn on Your Love Light	Bobby "Blue" Bland	R&B	4 Horns	Big Joe—Vocal, Lance & Rocky

We began one set each evening with a modern dance number borrowed from *West Side Story*. The dance routine was intended to bring the audience back into our world. We'd position ourselves in the far corners of the Boom Boom Room, begin snapping fingers and move slowly to the center of the dance floor. The Jets were right here in Bossier City. Five Carousels formed an oblique line on the dance floor, Jet-like crouch and attitude, and danced in unison to snapping fingers. Big Joe's alto sax skated the *Jett Song* from *West Side Story* as he taunted the line of dancers. Sequentially, each Carousel peeled off the line and delivered solo excerpts from *West Side Story* biggest hits: *Maria, Gee Officer Krumpke, Cool, Somewhere,* and *America. Tonight* was our climax—full ensemble finale. The entire performance took less than five minutes, although the impact was extraordinary and long lasting. Our *West Side Story* dance opening became a featured attraction.

Another showstopper included instructors from Arthur Murray Dance Studio. Following their dance party job in downtown Shreveport, they'd make a grand entrance to Saks' Boom Boom Room, go directly to the bandstand and set up chairs in a Big Band formation. This was our cue to play Glenn Miller's *String of Pearls*. We assumed our positions in the chairs: Front line was clarinet, alto and tenor sax, and a back line was trombone and trumpet. I played bone,

Big Joe doubled on tenor sax and trumpet, and Lance doubled on alto sax and clarinet. The mighty Wurlitzer organ augmented by a Leslie speaker cabinet filled in the horn harmony parts, creating a robust Big Band sound. Six to ten Arthur Murray instructors put on a fantastic dance demonstration, covering every inch of the massive dance floor.

Big Joe also could dominate a room, performing R&B and Zydeco hits like *Everyday I Have the Blues* and *La Danse de Mardi Gras* with such panache that a full dance floor and standing ovations were guaranteed. Built like an LSU fullback, he charged into his numbers with such ferocity that the audience had little choice but to succumb to his overwhelming performance.

Hot and spicy like cayenne pepper, too much can ruin an otherwise perfect meal. So we sprinkled Big Joe's hot sauce sparingly into our delicious gumbo. On the other hand, when the time came to spice things up, Big Joe could set a room on fire. Only a few of us knew the difference between Big Joe's mesmerizing talent and stark reality, and we never let his adoring public see his flaws.

In most venues, we featured our best material during the third set, typically playing to our largest audience of the evening. The first, second and fourth sets featured our diverse genres, sprinkled with Top-Ten Hit Parade songs. Always striving to remain unpredictable, we led our audiences through a kaleidoscope of highs and lows within a 50-minute set, creating desire to be part of the Carousel world and remain with us for an entire evening.

Skillfully baiting the hook prior to each break, announcing one or two tunes to be featured in the upcoming set worked its magic. Our break song was *Carousel Waltz*, from Rogers and Hammerstein's *Carousel*. It became another of our featured attractions.

Our success at Saks made the Carousels a hot topic in Bossier and Shreveport. Everyone seemed to know and love us—restaurateurs, waitresses, police, cabbies, flyboys, oilmen, businessmen, truck drivers, and traveling salesmen. Even the ladies at my dry cleaners bragged about being the preferred cleaners of Rocky Strong, leader of the Carousels. We loved being Kings of the Bossier Strip.

During breaks, we worked the room. Unlike most bands, we circulated among the audience, spending a moment at each table and asking the same question: "Enjoying yourself?" Patrons connected with the Carousels, frequently addressing us by our stage names.

Instinctively, we kept an eye on each other during table rounds. That's when I noticed Lance spending time with a serious-looking man in a black suit, tie and white shirt. Once or twice a week Lance huddled with the mystery man for five-minute encounters, usually in a dark corner. Both maintained furrowed brows as they spoke. I wondered why they were speaking in whispers and what was being said, though I didn't pursue it. Straight arrow when it came to drugs, vice and gambling, Lance was reliable and trustworthy.

One night I asked my standard question to a group of Air Force fliers. One answered, "Tonight we party. Next week we drop bombs on *gooks*. I like this a lot better." The other fliers hurriedly shut him down and made light of a highly sensitive topic. They were right—this was neither the time nor place to vent serious commentary on the escalating war in Vietnam. It was time for the pilots to enjoy their R&R. The Carousels were in the escape and illusion business—not the reality business.

On our second Saturday, following our last set, Merrill pulled me aside. "I'm opening the bar up to the Carousels," he told me. "You and the fellows have carte-blanche access to my liquor and B-girls. You just topped our all-time best weekly take. From now on, I'm calling you the Fabulous Carousels."

Getting drunk and laid on Merrill's nickel was fantastic. Then again it also brought an epiphany.

As long as we make Merrill Saks lots of money he'll love the Fabulous Carousels. Conversely, if the money ever stops flowing into Saks, we'll be thrown on the ash pile. Mob-connected frontmen worship money. Within Merrill's Mafia culture, only a fool would believe that money is secondary to anything—anything. It's just business. In the meantime, laissez les bon temps roulez.

Chapter 11

1960
A PROFESSOR'S WISDOM

After breakfast at the Bayou Grill and before our usual rehearsal at Saks, Lance took me to the Show Bar at the Stork Supper Club to meet the professor.

Lance's "professor" was Kenny Livingston, guitar player with the Five Jets.

"I idolize the Five Jets," Lance said as we drove to the Show Bar. "They're where we'd like to be someday. If we catch Kenny before the others show up for rehearsal, perhaps he'll give us tips and advice. He's a true intellectual, their best musician and performer. If Kenny had not chosen to be a musician, he'd be a college professor. I want you to hear pure wisdom direct from the professor's lips."

As we pulled into the parking lot of the oldest high-end nightclub in the ArkLaTex area, old memories resurfaced. As a child, I wondered what kind of deviant acts went on inside. In junior high, I heard they had strippers, comedians and a full band in the main room. Shreveport Baptist ministers referred to the Stork Club as the epicenter of sin and depravity. Perhaps today those teenage mysteries would be unraveled.

Walking under the portico through open doors of the Show Bar, we were hit by a familiar, pungent odor, ever-present in nightclubs the morning after. The process of flushing out stink from the previous night was well under way as giant fans blew yesterday's stench out onto Highway 80. Last night's spilled and spoiled liquor stuck to the soles of my shoes as I tippy-toed across the flypaper carpet. A cloud of nicotine hung heavy, accented by bright neon bulbs lighting up the all-black, 85-seat Show Bar.

There's no mystery in here. If the evening guests could only see and smell the residue of last night's mayhem, this place would lose all its attraction. Miraculously, when the sun sets, gleaming flashing neon signs light the way, spiffy doormen make the unimportant feel important, bunny-clad servers flash cleavage as they polish your table, and an overdose of sickeningly sweet deodorant pumped through air conditioning ducts fully disguise yesterday's sins. Magically, the allure returns.

Lance shouted to Kenny as we navigated through the vacuum cleaner hoses. Lance missed getting tangled in their electrical cords, but stumbled over a mop bucket. Catching his balance, he said, "I hoped we might find you here."

Kenny responded with surprise. "I've been woodshedding, competing with the cleanup crew—they're winning. Tryin' to find a meditation moment."

"Yep. I know that feeling all too well," Lance replied, and then added, "Kenny, I want you to meet Rocky Strong, leader of the Carousels and drummer, among other things."

Kenny extended his hand. It combined the softness of a woman's touch with a powerful grip and was matched by piercing eye contact—all conveying that the professor was a man of substance.

My hand in his, I replied, "Hi, Kenny. Lance expressed the highest regard for you as a professional musician and visionary. He referrers to you as the professor."

Kenny's eyes sparkled. "A visionary. That's an interesting choice of words. I'll see if I can live up to Lance's billing—particularly interesting given my current state of mind."

Lance missed Kenny's cue, barging headlong into a litany of questions: "How did you guys get so good? Who does your arrangements? Where does your comedy and stage presence come from? How did you perfect your act? Any advice for our young band on how to make it big in the entertainment business?"

Without realizing what he had done, Lance's engaging personality and overt hero worship managed to push aside whatever emotional issues Kenny was confronting.

As we arranged bar stools into a triangle, Kenny gathered his thoughts and graciously responded to all of Lance's questions.

"You really are too kind with your compliments. I've seen the Carousels, and you guys are already great. You look terrific, put out a big, fat sound, project professional polish and offer up the widest range of song selection imaginable. And, you guys are drawing huge crowds. The Five Jets are happy to fill an 85-seat show bar on Friday and Saturday. I'm not sure I can add much to what you've already accomplished. You're doing a lot of things right. Don't second guess your success."

Doggedly, Lance continued to press for more. "Kenny, you're always gracious with your praise. Even so, you must have some secret keys to success and lessons learned on how to avoid failure on the road."

Perhaps it was a question Kenny didn't expect, or didn't want to answer. He paused a moment.

"Well guys. You caught me in a particular mood that I normally wouldn't share—or better yet—confess. So here it is, candid and unvarnished. When the Five Jets began we were five close friends who loved hanging together—comfortable in every way. Our music and stage performance reflected our close friendship. Spontaneity and freshness blessed us on stage and off. Thinking as one and performing as one we were completely unselfish—a band of brothers. Like you, we wanted to become great entertainers. So, like the Carousels, we sought the advice of an older group. Their advice to us then is my advice to you now: Women will destroy your dreams of fame and fortune if you allow them inside your brotherhood. Without a doubt, women are your biggest problem."

Lance and I were hanging on every word.

"Professional entertainers invest years in perfecting their talent, bodies and persona in order to present a godlike image on stage. The narcotic of adoration and applause drives us ... never enough praise, approval, special treatment, fan worship. Over time, we begin to believe our own press releases—that we really are special. As a result, we come to demand special treatment, from everyone, all the time. And, we routinely get a free pass for out-of-bounds conduct.

"Elevated to godlike status, it follows that we represent the prize to women. They all want to win us—for a night or a lifetime. Entertainers become their Cinderella story, an escape from reality. Unfortunately over time, our lovers discover that we are not gods and grow weary of catering to exaggerated expectations. Without warning, idolatry enters a really dark dimension. Disillusioned, chicks begin to seek a perverted form of revenge. It's as though we have to repay them for being so starry-eyed stupid. They plot against us to resurrect their self-respect. They scheme to acquire control.

"Once a main squeeze develops influence over an entertainer, they thirst for omnipotent control—including our dreams and brotherhood. However, in time they lose faith that we'll ever achieve their definition of fame or fortune. They simply ride our train 'til it slows, choosing their moment to transfer one night to a faster train, headed in a different direction—toward real fame and fortune. They leave us broken men."

The professor paused and a tear inched down his cheek.

"Goddamn women! If we hadn't allowed women inside our band of brothers, our train would continue on the fast track. Sadly, we argue—all ten of us—all the time. No one wins. Five demonic witches escalate petty jealousies to an art form. Unfortunately, the Five Jets are pussy whipped; impotent to change our downward spiral. Somewhere on our adventure we lost control over our band, our brotherhood, our pride and our dreams. We lost our balls! Sadly, our brotherhood has collapsed ... too late to salvage."

We sat mesmerized by Kenny's outpouring of grief for his dying band of brothers. He looked at me and at Lance as he concluded:

"Hang tough. Don't get serious about a band-aid. Possessive lovers are the kiss of death to a band. Keep your stones rollin'. At some distant point there'll be plenty of time to fall in love, get married, have kids and settle down. Postpone that day until your dreams of entertainment greatness play out—plenty of time to become a straight. Keep women out of your band of brothers and band business. That's the best advice I have. I hope you use it better than the Jets. The Five Jets completely failed the test. Goddamn women!"

A vacuum cleaner began a high-pitched whirrrrr, and the noise shattered the moment.

Lance thanked Kenny, yelling over the vacuum, "You've been generous with your time and advice today. We'll take your advice to heart. The Five Jets are still one of the best groups I've seen. Hopefully, you guys can find the strength to keep your train on track, pointed toward fame and fortune."

We left Kenny sitting there, amid the cleaning crew, staring at the ground-in grime on the floor that no vacuum would ever remove.

As Lance sped his sparkling emerald green Pontiac Bonneville Coupe down Highway 80 to Saks' Boom Boom Room, he said, "The professor is a great man—an oracle. We got more wisdom today from that genius than I bargained for. Goddamn women!"

Naturally I responded, "Goddamn women!"

Chapter 12

1960
BIG FISH IN A SMALL POND

hreveport and Bossier City had more working musicians in 1960 than New Orleans, according to Bob "Pappy" Morgan, secretary of Shreveport/Bossier Chapter of the American Federation of Musicians. The Carousels joined the AFM and began paying dues. Musicians were paid on Saturday nights after their last show. So, on Monday mornings, bandleaders headed down to Pappy's music store to pay union taxes.

I never tested the ritual.

Pappy was a 300-pound bear with a 500-pound voice and a constitution to back it up. He spoke in succinct sentences, barking declarative commands. Once upon a time Pappy played tenor sax with traveling big bands. Just like so many musicians, he grew weary of the road and opened a modest music store in downtown Shreveport.

He held court every Monday as bandleaders from large and small groups filed in with AFM taxes in hand, usually in cash. We would make our deposits, get a receipt and pass pleasure with Pappy over some story that always ended in a big laugh. Just before summarily dismissing the bandleaders, Pappy barked a veiled threat to remain current on our union taxes and dues. We knew Pappy had to have the last word. None of us wanted Pappy's goons shutting down their gigs and livelihoods. We all pacified Pappy.

Monday morning I drove to Shreveport to pay the Carousels' weekly union taxes with an auburn-haired B-girl named Goldie along for the ride. Goldie sported a can't-miss-it solid gold tooth right in the middle of her uppers. Her smile glistened like the grill of a 1952 Buick Roadmaster—big and wide. She also sported a buffed, 116-pound figure, D-cup boobs, sweet-as-sugar face, and hips that wiggled even when she stood still. No guesswork required here.

Goldie and I made our grand entrance into the music store as Pappy was stretching his huge body behind the accessory counter. Sniffing his armpit, Pappy grimaced, and then looked at his watch. I sensed it must be nearing his lunch hour, so I prepared to pay and get out quickly. When his stubby fingers penetrated oversized nostrils and rooted out a yellow substance that immediately went in his mouth, I knew I was right about his lunch time.

Looking up, Pappy did a double take. The scowl on his face said it all as he peered over his reading glasses at Goldie, her sparkling gold tooth and boobs a-gigglin'. In his typical gruff manner, glaring straight at Goldie, Pappy snarled, "You wait here, madam. I have musician business to conduct with this bandleader in my private office." Goldie dutifully turned her attention to the kazoo display.

How appropriate.

Pappy motioned for me to sit down in the chair of inquisition in a cramped office, and barked, "Rocky, do you shit where you eat?"

"Sir?" I said.

"You heard me. Do you shit where you eat?"

Sitting up straight, I responded sheepishly, "No sir. I never have."

Spittle spewing from his mouth, Pappy snarled, "Then why would you parade that whore around in the daylight, especially into my business establishment?"

His question was not intended to be rhetorical, but I really didn't have a good answer. So I dug into my pocket, pulled out the union taxes for last week's wages and placed it on Pappy's desk.

Never looking at the cash, Pappy kept his eyes drilled on mine.

"I hear you have a pretty good band. Is that right? This is a small pond in a big world. Right now you're a big fish in my small pond. If you are any good and have the guts to prove it, you'll get out of my pond and go on the road. That's the only way you'll know if you're worth a damn. Get my drift? Moreover, don't ever show your ass again by parading your whore around in my business or even on the sidewalk in front of my business. There is such a thing as discretion and class. Get some!"

I picked up the receipt, nodded my head twice and got up to leave. At his office door, I turned and said, "If we make it big on the road, will you come out to see my band?"

"I'll come to hear your band if you make it big and your union dues are up to snuff. On the other hand remember this. Some of America's greatest musicians belong to the Shreveport/Bossier Chapter of the American Federation of Musicians, including the late Hank Williams, most of the big name country pickers, studio musicians in Nashville, New York and Los Angeles, Vegas studs, Hollywood cats, and New York Broadway pit monsters. They walk tall in my book. For me to mention you and your band in their company you'll have to get way beyond the city limits of Shreveport and Bossier City. Now get your ass out of here and make something of yourself."

I loved Pappy and I hated Pappy. His wit and manipulation challenged me to the max. On this round, Pappy had the last word. Privately, I swore to lead the Carousels to greatness and never take Goldie into Pappy's again.

After the lecture, I began feeling good again, simply enjoying a beautiful day in ArkLaTex. Hilly sidewalks of Shreveport put us on a downhill slope back to my Ford. As two night people unaccustomed to the brilliance of daylight, we both squinted from unfiltered sun in a cloudless sky. Our pale skin turned pink and our lungs filled with fresh air, replacing the cigarette smoke, rancid alcohol stink, sweaty body odor and cheap cologne of the local bars and lounges.

Touching Goldie's arm, it turned white from light finger pressure, but only momentarily. She smiled before giving me a peck on the cheek. Like two ducks out of water, we waddled down the thoroughfare. Gawking men trudged past, entranced by Goldie's jiggle. I stared at the pavement to avoid eye contact with anyone who might know me or my family. Together, but not together, Goldie and I made way to my hand-waxed '40 Ford, which dutifully took us back to her garage apartment.

That afternoon, I stumbled into the unexpected. Goldie was a burgeoning young artist in the making. I had been hanging my tuxes in her garage apartment closet for a week, not knowing her biggest secret, until today.

"When I was in high school," she admitted, "I began doodling my fantasies in a sketchbook. These renderings are very personal and … well, I've never shown them to anyone—until now. I think you'll find my fantasies interesting."

With immense reverence Goldie slid her beloved sketchbook across the kitchen table, in my direction. I gently opened the leather-bound book to the first page, titled *Inverted Kama Sutra* by Melba "Goldie" Hemingway. What followed were 200 pages of illustrations depicting explicit carnal positions, all designed to please a woman's sexual fantasies. Goldie's illustrations held nothing back—erotic, perverted, and instructive.

Challenged to present just the right reaction, I said, "This is magnificent. I'm deeply honored by your trust and will treat it with the reverence it deserves."

"It's my *Inverted Kama Sutra*, reversing traditional roles of men and woman and fulfilling a higher calling to satisfying sexual desires," she replied. "Honestly, no man has fully satisfied me. I'm rollin' da dice on you, Rocky—are you that man?"

A broad smile exposed Goldie's anticipation of joyous times ahead. Her eyes widened and darted, revealing an inspired mind focused on achieving her life-long objective.

Goldie chose me to reveal her most private and personal secret, extending an unspoken invitation to take her into the pleasure zone of sexual fantasy. I've found my teacher. I'm about to learn the secrets of how to please a woman in a thousand different ways. I'll give it my all and practice, practice, practice … starting on page one.

Lance was right. Whispering a few simple words in the ear of the right chick with experience can earn you a bachelor's degree in pleasing women. Try as I might, after a week of diligent study, we were only seven pages into Goldie's illustrated *Inverted Kama Sutra* book. To be continued …

Chapter 13

1960
FIRST SOUTHERN TOUR

The Carousels' draw at Saks' Boom Boom Room continued to exceed Merrill's and our expectations, but we wanted more.

One day at rehearsal, Big Joe threw down the challenge. "Let's go on da road—see what we can do. Never saw Florida. I'd like to lie on sandy beaches, make love to bikini gals every night. Sound good?"

Rooster cast his vote for Atlanta, Dallas and Houston. "That's where the action is in the South, and that's where the beautiful women are. I'll be glad to oblige all the southern belles who want a taste of me. You can book it."

Lance nominated Nashville. "If we ever intend to cut a hit record, we need to do it in Nashville. There are only three places in America that consistently produce hit records: Nashville, New York and LA. Oh yeah, Memphis and a few other smaller studios produced hits. Although the big three offer the greatest opportunity."

Bobby nominated New Orleans. "At this point I believe scoring big on Bourbon Street is our most important next step. If they love us on Bourbon Street, they'll love us anywhere in America."

Smoke added his vote for New Orleans. "Merrill can get us into the Dream Room. One call to Carlos Marcello and we're in. Kings of Bourbon Street. That has a nice ring to it—don't you think?"

Finally, it was my turn. Everyone looked at me with anticipation. "You guys want to go on the road?" I asked. I'll set up a southern tour. Last Monday, Merrill introduced me to Bianco Alessi, a friend of his who owns a club in Mobile. Mr. Alessi was impressed with the Carousels and asked me to provide dates of availability over the next couple of months. I told him I'd call and set something up."

As promised, a week later I presented the Carousels with a schedule that included Pensacola, Mobile, New Orleans and Atlanta, in that order. The tour spanned three-and-a-half months, ranging from two to four weeks per club. The money was better than Saks. Then again, we needed more cash to handle the increased cost of travel and lodging.

The Carousels anticipated the spread of our magic to a wider audience, capturing hearts, bodies and minds of many southern belles. So before leaving Bossier City, we increased rehearsal time and polished our performance. Professionally prepared, fully loaded and mounted up in four flashy automobiles, six guys began our initial tour.

I arrived in Bossier City driving my old Ford. I drove out of Bossier in a gorgeous, orange and white, 1955 Oldsmobile 98 Starfire convertible. I often referred to it as my pervertible. Smoke purchased a 1950 Cadillac Eldorado and promptly totaled it on a Shreveport telephone pole one night in route to Saks. Without wheels, Smoke asked me for a ride to Pensacola. I agreed.

In route to Pensacola, located in the Florida Panhandle, Smoke talked for hours and hours about Ian Fleming's books, James Bond, the Kennedy family and the Mafia. Smoke had successfully trapped me for 18 hours of driving, taking full advantage of my seemingly undivided attention. I soon found that challenging the authenticity of Smoke's theories only served to increase their incredulity. To be fair, Smoke provided colorful entertainment, and the trip passed without incident.

A fool in his folly can do you more harm than your most ardent enemy. As long as I don't take Smoke seriously, I can enjoy his bizarre theories.

To pacify Smoke, I occasionally responded to his stories with an agreeing smile or nod of the head.

Next stop: Pensacola and the Sahara Club.

Driving all night, rotating drivers, Smoke and I pulled into Pensacola on Sunday ahead of schedule, located the Sahara Club and had lunch at White Sands, a local eatery. We picked up tourist brochures and did what tourists do with them. The gal at the cash register gave me the eye, so I went over and asked her for the name of a good place to stay for a couple of weeks. Two questions and answers later, we settled on the Endless Beach Motel, right on the beach. It was a Mom and Pop motel with low rates—just right.

After we settled in, Smoke wanted to go to the dog track. He smarted up in a white linen suit, blue silk scarf in the jacket pocket, yellow silk shirt, a cocked Panama straw hat and a pipe. I suspected Smoke was acting out his imagined image of Agent 007.

Neither of us had ever been to a dog race. Smoke pranced around, viewed the dogs through field glasses, ordered a shaken, not stirred, martini and generally put on a show. I turned my attention to playing the dogs and lost $20.

Leaving the dog track, I dropped off Smoke at the motel and steered my Olds 98 pervertible toward a Sunday afternoon watering hole. The parking lot at Fantasy was full, somewhat strange for a Sunday afternoon. Entering the dimly lit alcoholic nursery, I spotted a petite angel at the bar and positioned myself on the empty stool next to her. She was primo: short blond hair, flawless complexion, cherubic face, porcelain skin and a well-proportioned 95-pound body.

When my eyes adjusted to the darkened room, I realized I was in a gay bar—and probably the solo straight. I started to walk out, but my Bacardi rum and tonic with a lime twist arrived. Also, the challenge of converting the petite beauty on the next bar stool to a heterosexual lover was too much to resist. Transforming my normal gruff persona into a tender, suave, alluring gentleman presented challenge enough. However, once there, I rolled out my optimum charm to the nymph on my right. She gave me a smile, buoying my confidence.

I can teach this gal what a real man is all about. Before I'm done with her, she'll happily prefer men over …

Gulp!

Before making my next move, a bull dyke claimed the bar stool on the other side of the petite beauty and began competing against me. The dyke was an aggressive gorilla. I countered by morphing into the essence of a southern gentleman. Head-to-head competition ensued—slings and arrows for a full ten minutes. The petite beauty's head was on a swivel, first looking at me, then at the dyke.

Gently touching the nymph's porcelain hand, I quietly whispered in her ear, "I'll do anything you ask. Just tell me your wildest fantasies and I'll be your slave. Will you teach me how to please you tonight?"

Suddenly, the bull dyke went ballistic, grabbed the angel's arm, jerked her off the bar stool and wrestled her out the back door. Experiencing a rude welcome to Pensacola, I learned my lesson and pledged to never compete with a bull dyke again. They always win. What a waste.

Monday afternoon the Carousels moved equipment and instruments into the Sahara Club. Domenico "Dom" Fiorino was a classic Italian frontman, small of frame, good dresser and soft-spoken. I immediately liked him.

"Pensacola's a Navy town," he said, giving me the rundown of our audience. "Most of my patrons are Navy pilots or civilians working at the base. Of course, the dragonflies buzz the fliers every night in hopes of latching on to a husband and a way out of Pensacola. Get the fliers through that door and the dragonflies are certain to be close behind. Your mission is to draw the pilots to our oasis in the Sahara."

With that information in hand, we set up the stage and selected our lineup for the night.

Before kicking off our featured set, I said, "Create fantasy—sell illusion—project your God Power."

THIRD SET LINEUP—SAHARA CLUB				
SONG	ORIG'L ARTIST	GENRE	ENSEMBLE	FEATURE
Sidewinder	Lee Morgan	Jazz	4 Horns	Group
I'm Walkin'	Fats Domino	R&B	4 Horns	Big Joe—Vocal, Lance & Rocky
Cold Cold Heart	Hank Williams	Country	Fiddle	Lance—Vocal
Fortune Teller	Allen Toussaint	R&B	Standard Ensemble	Big Joe—Vocal
La Danse de Mardi Gras	Clifton Chenier	Zydeco	Cajun Accordion, Fiddle & Frottoir	Big Joe—Vocal Rooster, Smoke & Rocky
On Broadway	The Drifters	R&R	Standard Ensemble	Bobby, Lance, Big Joe—Vocal
Poor Butterfly	Cal Tjader	Latin Jazz	Vibes, Guitar & Conga's	Rocky & Smoke
Crying	Roy Orbison	Pop	Standard Ensemble	Lance—Vocal
Watermelon Man	Herbie Hancock w/ Mongo Santamaria Arrangement	Latin Jazz	4 Horns + Conga	Big Joe, Lance & Rocky
I Pity the Fool	Bobby "Blue" Bland	R&B	4 Horns	Big Joe—Vocal, Lance & Rocky

We hit the Navy pilots' bull's eye. Since many were flying off carrier decks the following morning, they came for a boisterous party—and we gave it to 'em. As predicted, dragonflies swarmed the Sahara Club with single-minded dedication. Playing to pilots was three-dimensional: loud R&B, shit-kickin' country and cry-in-your-beer blues. Class and culture would have to wait for Mobile, or New Orleans, or Atlanta.

During our gig in Pensacola, news flashed across the airwaves that a U.S. Airman by the name of Francis Gary Powers was shot down while flying his spy plane over Soviet territory, and amazingly survived, creating the U-2 Incident. Pensacola Naval Air Station went on high alert. Soviet Premier Nikita Khrushchev blasted President Eisenhower, threatening escalation of the Cold War into World War III. Not surprisingly, front-line Navy pilots experienced high anxiety, fearing the worst. In addition to the inherent dangers of flying off carriers, they'd be called on to defend America or attack the Soviet Union. Overnight, Navy pilot attitudes morphed from fun-lovin' clowns into professional warriors.

One of my Louisiana Tech friends had joined the Navy following graduation, applying to become a Navy pilot. I'd lost track of him since leaving Tech. Without notice, he appeared out of the dark on our first break.

After I recovered from my surprise, he told me he was a pilot in training.

"In fact, I make my first solo flight off the deck of a carrier in the morning. I'm here to get drunk and steady my nerves. This engineering student out of a North Louisiana dry Parish is here to raise as much hell as the law allows. I thought I'd say hello before my buddies and I take over the Sahara Club. Our mission tonight is to get drunk and party. I could die in the morning, so I'm living in the moment tonight."

"Let's catch up," I said, pointing to a nearby table. We sat down and he wasted no time filling me in on his Navy service.

"Flying jets is great. It's the most fun I've ever had with my clothes on. Difficult to explain … I feel alive when I'm up there. As long as the Navy lets me fly, I'll make this my career."

"What about the U-2 Incident?"

"Top Guns are sitting on carriers in the Mediterranean and off the coast of Japan. Front liners will get the first call. I'm in line for more training, though realistically, if there is a war, everyone could be vaporized—everywhere. It won't make any difference where we are if the unthinkable happens. Given a choice, I'd prefer to be in my Navy jet."

"Sam, you always were a winner," I told him. "You're getting to fly Navy jets and live the good life. I'm sure you'll be okay. Hope you have a successful career as a Navy pilot. I'm happy for you."

"Great to see you, Rocky. I'd better get back with my gang and accomplish my mission—drunk by midnight. I've got some catching up to do if I'm gonna get even with those wild men. See you around, assuming we make it back alive."

I watched Sam saunter toward his buddies, blissfully happy with his life. Sam did what was expected of him. A bit envious, I had chosen another path.

When we weren't rehearsing or performing, Big Joe lay on the beach by day and laid bikini babes at night, following the gig. At Wednesday's rehearsal, he stepped on stage, looked down at us standing on the dance floor and said, "Guys. Keep yo claws off *mon cher*! On da beach last night, for hours 'n hours, we found *joie de la vie*. Sick of everybody pokin' everybody's *C'est tout*. None of ya can say your *cher's* faithful. Right? Had nuf. *Merci beaucoup*. Now I got Gert!"

Big Joe was really worked up over something or someone named Gert. Even so, Rooster took a risk.

"What's a Gert? The under part of a saddle? A girdle? Did you get sand in her Schlitz while bangin' her on the beach?"

Big Joe erupted. "She's *mon cher*. Keep yo filthy claws off my *cher*. Gert's private stock! Got it?"

Not surprisingly, Rooster was just getting started. "Can we see Gert or do you plan to put a chastity belt on her and lock her away in the tower?"

Spewing spittle, Big Joe yelled, "*Baiser!*"

That evening, during the first break, Big Joe introduced us to Gertrude "Gert" Brown. She cradled a black coffee cup containing a mysterious liquid. Forcing smiles and verbal welcomes, none of us had the guts to touch Gert, not even a handshake. We accepted Gert as Big Joe's private stock. Dispensing with polite decorum, the lovebirds walked away, hand in hand, cuddling at a corner table.

Bobby looked at our faces and said, "Big Joe will get no competition from me. As far as I'm concerned, Gert belongs to Big Joe."

Lance added, "That's one ugly woman—uglier than a lard bucket full of armpits!"

Rooster endorsed the consensus as only Rooster could. "Not only wouldn't I dip my stick in that dry hole; I wouldn't poke that with your schlong."

I nodded in agreement. "She looks like she's been beaten with a bag of nickels and gave back change. Dawg gonnit, y'all. What's in that black coffee cup? Ain't coffee."

Smoke was the kindest. "Well, if it makes Big Joe happy, I'm happy for him."

From that point forward, Gert was a fixture on Big Joe. The upside was Big Joe came to rehearsals with interesting stories about their sexual adventures. In his mind, he was king of the hill when it came to acting out the *Kama Sutra*. His ego artificially inflated, his performance on stage radiated a halo of confidence. Big Joe was living the illusion.

Whatever winds Big Joe's clock, I'm for it. Even so, what happens when Gert takes control of the key? It's not fair—he's such an easy mark. Already, Gert's leading Big Joe around by his johnson. My job just got tougher.

At the end of our gig, we bid Dom Fiorino and the Sahara Club goodbye. Dom and I discussed the Carousels' returning in a few months and agreed to talk about it further on the phone. The Carousels were unanimous: this was fun and a successful gig.

With Smoke riding shotgun and a white ball of fur cuddled in my lap, we headed my convertible west, toward Mobile. Smoke rattled on about Richard Nixon running for president against John F. Kennedy, Khrushchev pounding his shoe on a table at the United Nations, a test launch of a Polaris missile off Key West, the U.S. Supreme Court's ruling that segregation on public transportation is illegal, and another Supreme Court ruling against Louisiana's segregation laws.

On the trip, I did a lot of nodding and uttered an occasional "hummm." With the top down on the Starfire, Smoke's dissertations faded to a whisper, replaced by wind noise at 75 miles per hour. Shirtless, I loved the solitude and warmth of sun and wind caressing my body.

Rarely losing an opportunity to get in the last word, Cheshire Cat meowed, *"To the royal guards of this realm, we are all victims in-waiting."*

Chapter 14

1960
PLAYMATE OF THE YEAR AND SHOTGUNS

Mobile was only three hours west of Pensacola. Bianco Alessi met us at his Variety Club Sunday afternoon, and we moved instruments onto a large, raised show bar stage that overlooked a circular bar and a massive dance floor beyond. After greetings were exchanged, Bianco gave a quick rundown on his audience: "Old southern gentlemen, southern belles with classic charm, bankers, plantation owners, lawyers, owners of distribution companies associated with the port, shipbuilders, welders, and longshoremen. That's why I named it the Variety Club—a delicious cultural concoction."

We carefully planned our sets to feature music that would appeal to Bianco's audience, emphasizing our rich horn section. Sure enough, the Carousels packed the Variety Club. Everyone was happy, particularly Bianco.

Before kicking off our featured set, I said, "Create fantasy—sell illusion—project your God Power."

THIRD SET LINEUP—VARIETY CLUB				
SONG	ORIG'L ARTIST	GENRE	ENSEMBLE	FEATURE
La Dense de Mardi Gras	Clifton Chenier	Zydeco	Cajun Accordion, Fiddle & Frottoir	Big Joe—Vocal Rooster, Smoke & Rocky
String of Pearls	Glenn Miller	Big Band	4 Horns	Big Joe, Lance & Rocky
Cold Sweat	Mongo Santamaria	Latin Jazz	3 Horns + Conga	Big Joe, Lance & Rocky
Soul Bird (Tin Tin Deo)	Cal Tjader	Latin Jazz	Vibes, Guitar & Conga's	Rocky & Smoke
Lonely Teardrops	Jackie Wilson	R&B	Standard Ensemble	Bobby—Vocal
Moon River	Andy Williams	Crooner	Standard Ensemble	Lance—Vocal
Mother-in-Law	Allen Toussaint	New Orleans	Standard Ensemble	Big Joe—Vocal
Behind Closed Doors	Charlie Rich	Country	Fiddle Standard	Lance—Vocal
Watermelon Man	Herbie Hancock w/ Mongo Santamaria Arrangement	Latin Jazz	4 Horns + Conga	Big Joe, Lance & Rocky
Turn on Your Love Light	Bobby "Blue" Bland	R&B	4 Horns	Big Joe—Vocal, Lance & Rocky

Lance filled the role of troubadour; suave, poised and a master crooner. His delivery of *Moon River* caught the attention of every female in the room. His 6' 3" frame moved with the grace of Rudolf Nureyev. However his best feature was connecting with an audience, radiating laser like eye contact with every individual, as though they were the only ones who mattered. His green eyes sparkled at pretty ladies, and theirs sparkled back. Audiences were drawn into his sensitivity as a storyteller. In the style of Sinatra, his phrasing sold the lyrics. In truth, everything Lance did was extremely well rehearsed—and it all worked to precision on stage. Lance got the prize for master balladeer.

During our last break on the second night at the Variety Club, a shipbuilder introduced himself and proceeded to praise the Carousels. Suddenly, pausing mid-sentence, he turned and said, "She's here! She's here! My Playmate of the Year is here!"

As we turned to look, the shipbuilder could hardly contain his enthusiasm, saying, "Honey Dew's here! My all-time favorite exotic dancer! She packs every show at the Desire in downtown Mobile. The owner keeps us guessin' and drinkin' by varying her show times, but I greased the doorman's palm to get her show schedules in advance. She's gorgeous—spectacular body, particularly naked. Too good for Mobile. She's ... wait ... wait ... she's walking straight at me!"

The shipbuilder tucked in his shirt, sucked in his gut and ran his fingers through greasy hair. As his Playmate of the Year approached, the shipbuilder seemed to turn invisible, at least to Honey Dew. Her rebuff caused him to cower and withdraw to the bar for a stiff drink.

Honey Dew made a deep dive into my eyes. "You fascinate me, Rocky Strong. Other than music, what other talents do you possess?"

"Specialize in putting smiles on beautiful women's faces," I replied.

Her eyes tested my bravado. Honey Dew presented movie star beauty, coupled with the innocence of the girl next door. Two hours later, Honey Dew unveiled all her attributes. Dropping to my knees, I worshiped in unholy communion.

Thanks Goldie for teaching me how to please a woman.

The next morning my six tuxedos moved into Honey's closet, and Honey Dew and I did a lot of smiling over the weeks that followed. Pleasing Honey Dew and being pleased by her were among my most rewarding experiences on the southern tour.

An exercise fanatic, Honey worked out six days a week, maintaining an exquisitely sensuous body by sculpturing select muscles. I joined her health club, and we worked out an hour every day, except Sunday.

Two bodybuilders at the gym and regular patrons at the Variety Club were eager to befriend the Carousels, especially me. I thought of them as Mutt and Jeff. Blonds both, Mutt was badly in need of a shower and never spoke. They wore muscle T-shirts only found in *Queer Quarterly* catalogues. The shirts tightly clung to their bodies and helped display impressive definition, massive biceps, broad shoulders and washboard abs.

Jeff did all the talking. "Why don't you meet us Sunday afternoon at Bloody Buckets on Dauphin Island? If you're looking for the real Alabama, Bloody Buckets is the place to be. See you there Sunday?"

"I'll give it some thought. You know, Sunday's are my only day off and I love to relax with Honey Dew." I said with a smile and a wink.

"You can drill Honey Dew anytime, but you can't experience real Alabama except Sundays at Bloody Buckets," he replied. "See you around two?"

Early Saturday morning, Honey sent me out for manhole covers. On a lark, I announced I was meeting a couple of people Sunday afternoon. Honey showed no emotion, simply saying, "Okay. It's best."

Sunday afternoon, I put the top down on my Starfire and casually drove to Dauphin Island and Bloody Buckets. I set the cruise control at 50 mph. My sandy blond hair waived in the wind like the mane of a stallion at full gallop. Shirtless and wearing shorts, I quickly became sunburned from the warm Alabama sun. From a precarious nest perched on a channel marker, an osprey strung together high-pitched whistles and calls, announcing dinner to hungry, begging chicks.

Sundays are great.

Bloody Buckets was a 30-year-old bare wooden shack with expansions made by drunken carpenters. Some 30 Harleys and 40 cars sprawled chaotically in the dirt parking lot while their Alabama owners bent elbows inside. Obviously packed with action, redneck exaggerations and high adventure, Bloody Buckets lured me into the unexplored armpit of a bent Alabama culture.

I spotted Mutt and Jeff sitting at a table adorned with 30 empty Budweiser long necks. I ordered a round, paid and sipped my Bud. Their beers went down in one gulp.

Jeff said, "Rocky, let's go to my car. I have somethin' to show ya."

Making our way to the rear of his 1960 black Lincoln, Jeff looked around to see if anyone was watching us before slowly opening the trunk. There, on the floor of the trunk, were two sawed-off, double-barreled shotguns, two ski masks and two matching denim jackets. Mutt picked up a shotgun, except Jeff put his hand on Mutt's, saying, "Not now—later."

Jeff looked me right in the eye, studied my sober face and posed his question: "Want to make a quick ten grand Thursday afternoon? The dockworkers and ship builders are paid every other Friday. They cash checks at Second National Bank, near the docks. An armored car delivers bags of cash every other Thursday to cover the checks. We need a wheelman Thursday afternoon, about 2 o'clock. Interested?"

These goons believe I'm one of them. Any misstep on my part could get one of those 12 gauges unloaded in my chest.

I answered slowly, shaking my head in a 'no' motion and carefully considered every word. "Jeff. You're talkin' serious money. However, I'm not looking to start a new career right now. I love being a Carousel and want to play this out. Besides, the Carousels rehearse Thursday afternoons. No. I have to pass up your lucrative offer, although you make a wonderful case— but no thanks."

Jeff seemed to accept my answer, saying, "That's okay, Rocky. We have another wheelman, except he's flakey. We just wanted to upgrade that spot. It's okay."

Before closing the trunk of the Lincoln, Mutt reached in, grabbed a denim jacket and a shotgun, wrapping it in the jacket. Mutt and Jeff strolled back into Bloody Buckets mumbling. I quickly climbed in my Olds and cleared out of the dirt parking lot. Turning onto the highway, I heard an unmistakable sound—two 12-gauge shotgun blasts resonating out of Bloody Buckets. I wheeled the Olds into a nearby gas station and pulled around back to hide my orange and white car. In less than a minute, a 1960 black Lincoln sped north in the direction of Mobile, easily exceeding a hundred miles an hour.

Late Sunday afternoon, back at Honey Dew's apartment, I suggested we dress up and go out for a nice dinner.

"I'd love that Rocky," said replied.

We went to Maison de l'Aubrac, playing roles as a southern gentleman and southern belle at a table for two lit by a single beige candle flickering inside a glass pillar hurricane lamp. A French Batard Montrachet filled our glasses, and I offered a toast, quoting from a Cole Porter song. *"Night and day, you are the one. Only you beneath the moon or under the sun. Whether near to me, or far, it's no matter darling where you are. I think of you. Day and night, night and day. Why is it so?"*

Preceded by a charming smile, Honey surprised me by completing the lyrics. *"That this longing for you follows wherever I go. In the roaring traffic's boom. In the silence of my lonely room. I think of you. Day and night, night and day."*

For a fleeting moment, we morphed into straights. The dancing candle highlighted her natural beauty, a radiant femme fatale in supple reflection. Wistfully, we shared intimate affection, tenderness and yes, even a brief hint of love. In contented silence, we held hands. A tuxedoed waiter served succulent courses of escargot, cooked in garlic butter and parsley, Salade César Au Blanc De Poulet Fermier,

Maine lobster, truffle-crusted Dover sole, rhubarb crème brulee, and a hint of heaven poured from a French coffee press.

Returning to Honey's apartment we cuddled like teenagers, watching old black-and-white movies until falling asleep in each other's arms. It was a happy time for me, in spite of not knowing what the future held.

By midweek, Honey wound up and delivered her pitch.

"I want us to go to New Orleans together. I'll get a job and support myself. Never thought I'd be saying this, but we've found happiness together. I don't want this to end. Do you?"

Thankfully, she gave me room to ponder a response.

In a perfect world, Honey and I found happiness together. She's spectacular. We've shut out everything ugly in this world and allowed only happy thoughts inside our relationship. This is fantasy at its best, yet fantasy nonetheless. Her baggage and mine are far too heavy a burden to carry beyond Mobile. The light of day will turn fantasy into an ugly certainty. Sooner or later, we'll wake up to face a nightmare. I must be strong—for both our sakes. I must be strong, with copious compassion.

I stared at the carpet and shrugged like Atlas—implication: "No." Quick on the uptake, she said, "We'll talk about this later, when I have you begging me for more. Fair enough?"

"Fair enough."

Friday morning a Mobile Press-Register headline read, *"Armored Car Robbery Foiled Thursday Afternoon. One Bandit Dead and Two Escape Empty-Handed."*

The last week in Mobile was extraordinary, packing the Variety Club every night with adoring disciples. Friday and Saturday Honey Dew did everything possible to keep me begging for more. However, following a spectacular poke Sunday morning, I got up, washed up and left Mobile alone—limp as a wet noodle—bound for the Big Easy.

Top down on my pervertible, I pointed it in the direction of more adventures in free love.

Who knows—I might hook up with Candy Barr in the Big Easy. I'm transforming from straight man into bent—very bent. Can always return to straight man—however not yet.

Nestled in my lap, fluffy white and smiling, Cheshire meowed, *"Oh, by the way, if you'd really like to know, he went that way."*

Chapter 15

1960
BOURBON STREET

Pulling our instrument trailer onto Bourbon Street Sunday afternoon was exciting. The Carousels loaded gear onto the Dream Room stage and went for coffee and beignets at Cafe Du Monde. Spontaneously, we broke into a white-powdered sugar fight, ending up like badly made-up circus clowns.

Rooster kept up the light-hearted banter for our Big Easy adventure, saying, "On my way to the Dream Room I stopped off at a K&B drugstore and asked the pharmacist to sell me a box of condoms. The pharmacist asked, 'Do you need a paper bag with that, sir?' I said, 'Nah ... She's not that ugly.'"

An old joke, but still funny.

Our budget could not afford sleeping accommodations in the Quarter. Instead, a small mid-city boarding house matched our wallets. The 200-year-old building operated on direct current. Exposed incandescent bulbs lit the room, adding a rustic atmosphere to our adventure.

At sound check on Monday Walter Noto, one of two Dream Room frontmen, called me over to his table. A server immediately presented two cups of black coffee on a table no larger than a dinner plate. Mr. Noto gestured an invitation to take some sugar and cream, then spooned two sugars into what looked like black molasses in his cup and proceeded to extend his warm welcome.

"Merrill Saks expressed high regard for you personally and professionally," he continued. "And Carlos and Vince Marcello saw you at the Boom Boom Room. They loved your band. You couldn't have better recommendations. If there's anything I can do to make your stay more pleasant, let me know."

His manner was gracious, although his steely eyes were intimidating. Walter Noto was an imposing man, impeccably dressed and flawlessly groomed. He displayed class. However, his rutted face resembled a street map of the French Quarter, an obvious clue about his toughness and ability to survive in a brutal world.

I thanked Mr. Noto for his comments and said, "We'll do everything in our power to please you and pack the Dream Room."

Then he got down to business and laid out the ground rules: "Unless you have the equivalent of Keely Smith, do not play ballads on my stage. Even if you have Keely Smith, limit ballads to no more than one per set."

Pointing to his left, he said, "You see that door? It's open to the street about 50 percent of the time, managed by Ralph, our barker. His job is to attract passersby's to the door. Your job is to lure them through the door, inside the Dream Room—and keep them here for the evening. Up-tempo excitement accomplishes the mission. Got it?"

"Got it."

As we talked, I glanced from time to time at the hundred or so pictures adorning the walls of the Dream Room, including icon entertainers on the world stage. Obviously, Keely Smith was Mr. Noto's favorite female singer, and her picture was in a prominent spot. She was the featured singer and wife of Louis Prima, backed up by Sam Butera and the Witnesses. Other stunning pictures on the wall of fame included Al Hirt, Pete Fountain, Phil Harris, Jack Teagarden, Kai Winding, the Dukes of Dixieland, and about 70 other big stars. The Carousels would have to be at our best to make the Dream Room wall of fame.

Before kicking off our featured set, I said, "Create fantasy—sell illusion—project your God Power."

SECOND SET LINEUP—DREAM ROOM				
SONG	ORIG'L ARTIST	GENRE	ENSEMBLE	FEATURE
Watermelon Man	Herbie Hancock w/ Mongo Santamaria Arrangement	Latin Jazz	4 Horns + Conga	Big Joe, Lance & Rocky
What'd I Say	Ray Charles	R&B	3 Horns	Big Joe—Vocal, Lance & Rocky
Fortune Teller	Allen Toussaint	New Orleans	3 Horns	Big Joe—Vocal, Lance & Rocky
Twistin' The Night Away	Sam Cooke	R&R	Standard Ensemble	Bobby—Vocal
Yackaty Yack (Comedy)	The Coasters	R&R	Standard Ensemble	Bobby & Big Joe— Vocal
Old Black Magic	Louis Prima	New Orleans	3 Horns	Big Joe—Vocal, Lance & Rocky
Pretty Woman	Roy Orbison	R&B	3 Horns	Bobby—Vocal, Big Joe, Lance & Rocky
Comin' Home	Booker T & the M.G.'s	Jazz	4 Horns	Rooster—Organ
Sidewinder	Lee Morgan	Jazz	4 Horns	Big Joe, Lance & Rocky
Jolé Blon	Clifton Chenier	Zydeco	Cajun Accordion, Fiddle & Frottoir	Big Joe—Vocal, Rooster, Smoke & Rocky

For the most part, Lance's voice got a rest at the Dream Room, principally because of the strict "no ballad" rule. On the flip side, two thirds of our tunes incorporated three and four horns, augmented by a robust Wurlitzer organ and Leslie speaker cabinet filling in harmony. During our spotlighted set, front line horns were featured in *Watermelon Man, Comin' Home, Sidewinder, What'd I Say, Fortune Teller, Old Black Magic* and *Pretty Woman,* each synchronized with custom dance routines.

A big, fat sound, energy, and action held audiences for our full hour on stage. We packed the house, which translated into a very happy frontman. Our horn section found its groove in the Crescent City.

We reached a spiritual zenith at the Dream Room. A supernatural, nonverbal language flowed at light speed among minds, exposing the bare essence of singular and collective worship. Soul to soul, spiritual connections entered an unworldly dimension that transcended physical limitations. The Carousels held nightly conversations with God. All were invited to worship.

Because loud, up-tempo music helped entice customers through the Dream Room's open-door policy, the entertainment was nonstop. A second band alternated with us on stage, each band delivering a 60-minute set in front of 40 patrons seated at a crescent bar, plus 200 to 300 patrons packed in behind. A transition tune facilitated simultaneous changeover of musicians without missing a beat—no dead air. There was nonstop music for seven hours every night except Sunday.

During breaks, band members occasionally hung out at a narrow bar in a 100-foot-long by 10-foot-wide room behind the stage. Musicians entered and exited the Dream Room stage from this backstage bar, which opened up on Bourbon Street through discretely situated French doors. Only musicians and locals frequented this dimly lit watering hole, some seeking cheap drinks.

On our third night at the Dream Room, Lance was buttonholed at the narrow backstage bar by the mystery man I remembered from Saks. Same black suit, tie and white shirt. Deep in whispered conversation, both had the same furrowed brows, and the bulge at the beltline under mystery man's coat suggested ominous intent. I let that meeting pass without saying anything to Lance. However a few days later, after I saw them together again up Bourbon Street at Felix's Restaurant and Oyster Bar, I confronted Lance.

"Who's the dude?"

"FBI."

"What's he want?"

"Nothin'. Forget it."

"Oooh. Sounds mysterious. Ya part of a grand conspiracy or somethin'?"

"Not now, Rock. Someday—not now."

Once again, I let it drop.

With an hour to burn between sets, most Carousels scattered like a startled covey of quail. All within three blocks of the Dream Room were the showplaces of New Orleans: Al Hirt's, Pete Fountain's, the Famous Door, Preservation Hall, Allen Toussaint's and Clarence 'Frogman' Henry's. Backdoor access got us up close and personal with the greatest musicians in the South. The Carousels were accepted into the bubble-like family of premier musicians—rubbing shoulders with fame.

As we quickly learned, 1 a.m. on Friday and Saturday was the magic moment when the Dream Room transformed into the best party venue in the Big Easy. Two spade bands alternated from 1 a.m. til 8. The party attracted entertainers, musicians, subterraneans, goodfellas, strippers, pimps, workin' gals, bookies, shylocks, barmaids, dope dealers, derelicts of darkness—and the Carousels.

We fell in love with the Quarter and its subterranean subculture. Dark spirits that lurked in us all were set loose. Drinking from communal cups of unbridled pleasure, some of us staggered to Cafe Du Monde for coffee and beignets at dawn. Others surrendered to too much alcohol, drugs and sleep deprivation. Partying every Friday and Saturday, we set free our last remnants of inhibition.

On Tuesday night, a creature right out of Joseph Le Fanu's Gothic novella *Carmilla* approached from the narrow bar hidden behind the Dream Room bandstand. She was what I envisioned a female vampire would look like in real life.

Carmilla was riveting holes in my neck.

"Wanna party, Rocky?" she asked.

I replied, "In this day of free love it must be tough for a workin' gal to make a living."

"I'm not talking about that kind of party," she replied. "I'm inviting you to Jean Val's apartment, above Lafitte's Blacksmith Shop. It's where Quarter dwellers hang out while the tourists snore. Interested?"

Carmilla's straight black hair hung past her waistline, with bangs covering a gaunt face, absent color pigmentation. I had to squint to see eyes, sunk deep inside cliff-like brows. A black robe with a pointed hood draped down her back, disguising her skeletal body.

All she needed was a nearby coffin and the image would be complete.

Her heritage confirmed, I pondered new adventures and nodded acceptance to party at Jean Val's.

"Be here at 1," Carmilla said.

I was and she was. I followed Carmilla six blocks to Lafitte's Blacksmith Shop, a bar located at 941 Bourbon Street. We entered, immediately turned right and climbed a steep flight of stairs to Jean Val's apartment—one massive room over the bar. A peaked thatched roof that soared 20 feet at centerline shrouded the apartment. A heavy gray cloud of smoke masked the peak, allowing only seven feet of oxygen for us to breathe.

Carmilla ushered me through the crowded room of enigmatic faces to an open bar. As I poured myself a Scotch on the rocks with a twist, she scanned the room and nodded to a man playing a piano.

"Our host is co-owner of Vanguard Diving and Salvage, a commercial diver and part-time piano player downstairs at Lafitte's when he's in town," she said as she led me to him.

"Jean Val, this is Rocky Strong, leader of the Carousels—at the Dream Room. His first time to party with us."

Tinkling *St. James Infirmary* on his baby grand, Jean Val looked up and said in a charming southern drawl, "Weeell … indeeeed … from one creative prophet to another … a hearty welcome to you Rocky Strong. Deeeelighted to party with you, Rocky Strong."

A twinkle in his eye said it all. Nothing was out of bounds for Jean Val, obviously swinging from both sides of the plate. His eyes remained glued to mine as he played out *Infirmary.*

Winking, I responded, "It's nice to join your scene, Jean Val. Hopefully, neither of us will check into St. James' Infirmary in the morning."

"Touché Rocky Strong. Weeell done," came back from a smiling Jean Val.

With 50 of her communal friends in full party mode, Carmilla elected to sit on a couch with two strippers from the Show Bar. One offered me a cigarette. It was good. On closer inspection, it had no markings—no label. I sipped my Scotch and had another no-name cigarette.

Carmilla had other tastes—white powder neatly arranged in rows on a sheet of glass that covered the sideboard. Standing next to Carmilla, eyeing the champagne of drugs, was Etta James.

"I love your version of *At Last,*" I told her. "You hit a home run with that old standard. Congratulations."

She snorted a row, shook and slurred, "Yeah, money to party. This line's not buffed … beautiful candy cane."

Carmilla pointed to a bong lying on the table and asked me, "Wanna chase a dragon?"

I don't remember anything else until waking at 4 the following afternoon with Carmilla—naked as a jaybird—lying next to me. Apparently, we were in her apartment. Ugly the night before, she was grotesque in the daylight. I arose, washed up and got out, not knowing where I was or what I'd done. Last look around to make sure I hadn't left any evidence behind, I gently closed the door behind me and slithered down the stairs in bewilderment, exiting onto Bourbon Street.

That night Vince Marcello walked into the Dream Room to say hello and relay a gracious greeting from his brother, Carlos. As the Show Bar frontman, Vince was always operating in promotion mode, this time escorting Blaze Starr on one arm and Candy Barr on the other—parading down Bourbon Street to the Dream Room. Introductions made, I struggled to keep my eyes off Candy.

Niceties exchanged, I leaned forward and whispered in Candy's ear, "Will I see you at Jean Val's tonight?"

She confirmed with a gentle nod and a smile, just before I turned to go on stage. I felt Candy's eyes following me, reminiscent of previous connections, most resulting in a pleasurable outcome.

Chapter 16

1960
SEEDS OF CONSPIRACY

At 1 a.m. I literally ran to Jean Val's. More gorgeous in person than on film, Candy was sippin' Scotch on the rocks with a twist. I poured a Scotch and sat with her on the couch.

I said softly, "Too much anger and hate in this world. Life is the flower for which love is the honey. Love without return is like a question without an answer."

"That's beautiful," Candy replied, obviously unaware that I was quoting Victor Hugo and an old German proverb. "People I meet are hard and mean. You're charming—a cockeyed romantic. Where have you been all my life?"

"Looking for you."

"Look no further, Rocky Strong."

Sometimes, you just know when your time has come. Mind-to-mind connections negate spoken clichés. If you're listening, a tilt of the head, lowering of jaw or parting lips speak volumes. The aromatic scent of almonds foretells ecstasy wrapped within pleasure. The delicate touch of one's hair with longing fingers telegraphs signals of patience, sensitivity and compassion. Truth exposed, you just know—and so does she.

Noon the following day at the Bon Ton Café, I ordered lunch for the both of us: turtle soup, crawfish remoulade and crawfish étouffée. Only natives frequented the Bon Ton. The aroma, taste and ambiance were authentic New Orleans.

Candy's eyes spoke volumes about our spectacular evening together. Her Mona Lisa smile, perfect skin, flawless body and scent of almonds filled my head with joy. Reflecting on the simple pleasure of fully experiencing Candy Barr was a fantasy come true.

Thanks Goldie.

Saturday night I came upon Carmilla talking to Rooster in the hidden bar behind the Dream Room stage. We didn't see Rooster again until Monday at 6 p.m. Bobby and Smoke also fell prey to Carmilla's alluring charms, mesmerized by their discovery of the real subterranean New Orleans' night people. Bobby and Smoke became regulars at Jean Val's; Rooster partied off and on.

Like dogs in heat, Big Joe was stuck inside Gert most of the time, while Lance was busy plugging holes in Blaze Starr and Tempest Storm, strippers extraordinaire. I was having a great time, mostly sober, exploiting Candy Barr and French Quarter culture. Jean Val's party drew me back several times, although I attempted to heed the Presbyterian motto, *'Everything in moderation.'*

Since Lance and I often rode together to the Quarter, we shared our female encounters. Lance and I reveled in living, laughing and loving large—*suave de vive.*

"Rock, we're living the fantasy every man dreams of— uninhibited free love with an unlimited supply of beautiful women. I don't know when I'll have to turn in my free pass card or how many punches I've got left, but I'm gonna fill every inch before … We're having a ball on the road, and I never want this to end. I love gettin' my card punched."

"And we're just beginning this great adventure," I added. "Our punched cards will look like confetti in a year. Till then, we're punchin' away."

"Yeah. This is a win-win situation. Free love provides an opportunity for everyone to be happy. When I was younger, I thought of women only as sex objects. It was all about me. To be fair, many women also see us as sex objects, little more than a means to sexual satisfaction or braggin' rights to their girlfriends. That's not what free love is about. Free love levels the playing field. The objective is to be in the moment, free to give openly of God's greatest gift: ourselves. Our only fidelity is to give unselfishly to our partners. We create joy by delivering pleasure. To use an old showbiz adage, 'We're only as good as our last performance,' just like playing music. I love free love."

The following night on the drive I finally asked Lance about the mystery man.

"What's up with the FBI dude? You involved in something I ought to know about?"

"Sort of."

"Well ... Spit it out."

Pausing for several moments, Lance finally said, "This has to remain confidential. No one can know, especially blabber-mouth Smoke. Agreed?"

"Agreed."

"All this goes back to my top-secret work with the Army in Alaska. Once you're on their list, you never get off. Anyway, the FBI dude is a true southerner, based in Atlanta. He's on a case—actually three."

"Well?"

"One case involves research into the Freedom Riders and Civil Rights Movement. The second deals with J. Edgar Hoover's suspicion that Martin Luther King, Jr. is part of a Communist conspiracy to overthrow the U.S. Government. The third relates to Bobby Kennedy's hard-on for the Mob. All three cases are explosive, although the dude is only the fact finder in the field."

"Fact finder—what's that?"

"He gathers information and passes it on. King's Communist involvement is funneled directly to Hoover. Civil Rights stuff is passed to northern FBI agents. Scuttlebutt involving the Mob is rushed to Bobby Kennedy's organized crime minions. Basically, the way he described it, Kennedy doesn't trust southern FBI agents. Only northern FBI agents are permitted to deal strategically and tactically with Civil Rights, King and Mafia issues.

"Bobby only suspects the truth behind Hoover's hidden agenda, which is gathering evidence for a Communist conspiracy case against King. He said Hoover hates Bobby and Jack Kennedy with a passion, and the Kennedys hate Hoover. On the other hand Hoover's got his private files on both those bastards."

"Since your FBI dude is southern, what's his attitude?"

"He's southern through and through; thinks like you and me. What I'm about to tell you could ruin his career."

"What?"

"My guy's too clever to say it outright, though he hates Bobby Kennedy and his brother—the President. He believes the Kennedys view the Solid South voting bloc as their enemy. Bobby's trying to drive a wedge and break up the southern voting bloc. Divide and conquer. He's using Civil Rights, Freedom Riders and King to divide this nation. It's revolutionary—he's intentionally manufacturing conflict and crisis as a means of achieving self-serving ends. The gullible, stupid Freedom Riders are sheep—Bobby's pawns."

I was trying to absorb this as fast as I could as Lance continued.

"Martin Luther King is a different kettle of fish. King sat in the Oval Office with the President and Bobby. JFK wanted MLK to back off his control over the Civil Rights Movement. Bobby and John wanted to call the shots from the Oval Office. King refused, got up and walked out, snubbing the President and his brother.

"There's a mammoth tension between King and the Kennedys. Jacquelyn Kennedy has Jack's ear, warning that King's despicable character can tarnish the Kennedy image. Her open hatred of King was like pouring gasoline on a roaring fire of distrust. In the end, the Kennedys remain determined to destroy the Solid South and, eventually, Martin Luther King.

"My guy expressed contempt for the self-serving Kennedys and King. My guy gladly reports to Hoover activity pertaining to King's Communist conspiracy involvement to overthrow America, with the ultimate goal of eliminating King."

"What's your role in this?"

"Observer—only observer."

"Lance. We only play wiseguy clubs. As insiders, we know far too much about the rackets. You spillin' your guts on the Mob to the FBI dude?"

"Give me a break, Rocky. I'm not stupid. I'm a patriot. I love America, although I don't believe Bobby and John Kennedy serve America's best interests. To ensure my love of country and southern values, I filter what I tell him, just like he filters what he tells his northern FBI people and Bobby's minions on organized crime. However, I'm reasonably sure he's straight with Hoover, dumping everything he finds on MLK's Communist alliance. I have no problem keeping my mouth shut about wiseguys and Civil Rights issues. Besides, I have no desire to sleep with the fishes."

"Keep it that way—and keep me informed if anything changes. We didn't sign up for mystery, intrigue or gettin' our cock and balls stuffed in our mouths by Mafia hit men."

As if things could not get any weirder, I found that Smoke had begun hanging out with David Ferrie. They would sit at a small table in the dingy narrow bar hidden behind the Dream Room stage, outdoing each other with fantastic stories. Ferrie was one nutty-looking dude—thick black eyebrows, chalky face and a glued-on lid that didn't fit. During our breaks, long discussions between Ferrie and Smoke produced mythological tales, many that Smoke happily repeated with embellishment.

I was soon to hear more than I wanted to know, when Smoke knocked on my door around 11 a.m., saying, "Let's go for oysters and a frosty stein of beer at the Pearl."

"Sounds good. Then we'll head to rehearsal."

Taking our stools at the Pearl on St. Charles Avenue, we fixated on the oyster shucker's dexterity and technique at opening and serving on the half shell in one fluid motion. A dozen more and a second stein down our gullets we mellowed out. Life was good.

With his nervous tic working overtime, Smoke felt compelled to share David Ferrie's stories with me.

"Ferrie's history with Carlos Marcello goes way back," Smoke said. "Marcello began his career in slots and jukes before World War II. Then, when Myer Lansky and Frank Costello needed to hedge their bets against a crackdown by the Kefauver Commission on their New York operations they made Marcello a full partner, opening up New Orleans and the Gulf Coast to gambling and prostitution. Overnight, Marcello became one of the top Mafia Dons, anointed with Black Hand power over New Orleans and the entire Gulf of Mexico operations."

Obviously flattered by Ferrie's trust, Smoke continued to fill me in.

"Ferrie feels the American government is incompetent, suggesting organized crime would do a better job of running America. He hangs around Marcello's ranch outside New Orleans, his clubs in the Quarter and does whatever Carlos asks. Ferrie's ego, storybook and pocketbook get fatter every day."

Smokes eyes widened, right eye squinting several times in quick succession, as he leaned close and whispered, "Ferrie said he actually drove Carlos Marcello to Apalachin when the Mafia Dons got together at the home of Joseph 'Joe the Barber' Barbara. The agenda included grievances between families, settling blood feuds over Anastasia's assassination and putting controls in place over the drug trade. But the number one reason for the meeting was to formalize a para-governmental entity in America, much like the Mafia maintained for centuries in Italy and other European countries.

"Expensive cars with out-of-state license plates aroused the curiosity of local and state law enforcement, who raided the meeting. More than 60 underworld bosses were detained and indicted. The most significant outcome of the meeting was conformation that the Mafia existed, which Hoover had long refused to acknowledge.

"Rocky ... Ferrie was there with Carlos Marcello!"

I asked, "What's the attraction Smoke? You're consumed with goodfella noise. What's the point?"

Smoke frowned at my lack of enthusiasm. "We and you in particular, need to know everything about Marcello. Someday, he'll come to you with a business proposition. We, and you, have to prepare. In my opinion, this information is absolutely crucial if the Carousels are going to come out of this with fame, fortune and our lives. Listen Rock, Ferrie told me that two signs hang over Carlos Marcello's door: *'If you cut off the tail of the dog the head of the dog will turn around and bite you. However, if you cut off the head of the dog the tail of the dog stops wagging on its own.'*"

I asked, "Second sign?"

"*'Three can keep a secret if two are dead.'* You read it over the door on your way out of his office at the Town and Country Motel on Airline Highway."

I grabbed Smoke's skinny arm, squeezed hard and glared into beady eyes. "You're playing with fire. This whole affair is none of our business. We don't mess with the Mob and they won't mess with us. We only make money for the Mob. We're earners. Nothing more and nothing less. If we violate the rules, it'll turn deadly. Stop this conspiracy bullshit. If pressed, that freak David Ferrie will give you up in a heartbeat. You've just become his patsy if he ever needs an out. It's a one-way trip to the bottom of the Mississippi River wearing cement boots. Got it?"

Smoke replied with a sheepish nod and pale face. Even his freckles faded. We finished our oysters and beer and drove to the Dream Room for rehearsal.

Perhaps Smoke took my warnings to heart—perhaps not. I hope he doesn't get himself and me killed. Reflecting on great words of wisdom, a fool in his folly can do you more harm than your most ardent enemy.

Needing compassion from something soft, I had a friend pass a note to Candy Barr at the Show Bar, *"Meet me at Jean Val's tonight."*

Candy and I didn't get out of bed till 5 p.m. the next day, smilin' like clowns in a circus.

What a woman. Dangerous as hell—still worth the risks. Candy's transforming me from a straight man into bent man. I can always return to straight man—but not yet.

The Carousels were Kings of Bourbon Street. Mr. Noto praised our accomplishments, booking us back later in the year for a four-week engagement. Our success at the Dream Room buoyed our confidence. Pointed northeast, we left the Big Easy self-assured that the Carousels could make it big on the national stage. Next stop: Atlanta, Georgia.

Cheshire smiled and purred, *"To the royal guards of this realm, we are all victims in-waiting."*

Chapter 17

1960
SUBTERRANEANS

The Celebrity Key Club mirrored the after-hours' Carousel Club back in Monroe, as well as the Friday and Saturday midnight-til-dawn scene at the Dream Room in New Orleans. Located in downtown Atlanta, its audience comprised musicians, wiseguys, strippers, pimps, workin' gals, barmaids, dope dealers, and derelicts of darkness. In Jack Kerouac's book, *On the Road*, he coined the term *subterraneans* and followed up with a book of the same name. These creatures could be found frequenting the Celebrity Key Club. Opening our act at 11:30 p.m. and closing at 3:30 a.m., we became part of them and they us. Privileged to entertain professional entertainers, we catered to their subterranean taste. They lapped us up like humming birds sippin' sugar water.

Before kicking off our featured set, I said, "Create fantasy—sell illusion—project your God Power."

SECOND SET LINEUP—CELEBRITY KEY CLUB				
SONG	ORIG'L ARTIST	GENRE	ENSEMBLE	FEATURE
A Night in Tunisia	Dizzy Gillespie	Straight Ahead Jazz	3 Horns	Big Joe, Lance & Rocky
The Thrill Is Gone	B.B. King	R&B	3 Horns	Big Joe— Vocal, Lance & Rocky
Walk on the Wild Side	Jimmy Smith	Jazz	Organ Featured	Rooster
Gentle on My Mind	Glen Campbell	Country	Standard + Guitar	Lance—Vocal & Smoke
Spring Is Here	Cal Tjader	Latin Jazz	Vibes, Guitar & Conga's	Rocky & Smoke
Stand By Me	Ben E. King	R&R	Standard Ensemble	Bobby—Vocal
Freddy Freeloader	Miles Davis	Jazz	4 Horns	Big Joe, Lance & Rocky
Watermelon Man	Herbie Hancock w/ Mongo Santamaria Arrangement	Latin Jazz	4 Horns + Conga	Big Joe, Lance & Rocky
Georgia On My Mind	Ray Charles	R&B	3 Horns	Big Joe— Vocal, Lance & Rocky
Work Song	Cannonball Adderley	Jazz	3 Horns	Big Joe, Lance & Rocky

Rooster rocked the rafters with his rendition of Jimmy Smith's *Walk on the Wild Side*. Consistent with his dynamic nature, Rooster launched his acappella 6/8-time signature instrumental—beginning peacefully enough, almost tranquil. Progressively folding in complex fingerings, heightened intensity, rhythm instruments, horns, and volume—lots of volume—Rooster built toward a tidal wave crescendo. Ten minutes in, the audience went wild. Every druggie ran to the head for a fix. Workin' gals confessed to reaching climax. Termites crawled out of hardwood floors to escape the heat. Light bulbs shattered.

Rooster's arms flailed wildly in between arpeggios, his face twisted in bizarre pleasure, the whites of his good eye turned blood red, and his wild, dirty blond hair straightened out like Albert Einstein's. Yep. Rooster found his Valhalla in Atlanta—pervert heaven.

A Night in Tunisia, Freddy Freeloader, and *Work Song* also were instant favorites at the Celebrity Key Club. Big Joe, Lance, and I were challenged to match the masters of progressive and cool jazz. In the world of cool, sophisticates and subterraneans alike accepted us, feeding our egos and libidos. We faked jazz pretty well. Absorbed under cover of darkness, our sins remained hidden from straights as we immersed our souls in bent.

In a place where anything goes, illegal drugs were everywhere. Pretense checked at the door, unbounded energy of the night people blossomed. Bathrooms were gathering places for pissin', shootin' up, and deal makin'.

Draining my lizard one Saturday, a washed-out druggie approached with a deal.

"I needs some bread, Rocky. Gimme a C-note for an untraceable, fingerprint-proof Roscoe."

"Roscoe?" I asked.

"Geeze, Rocky. A piece, rod, heater ... you know, a Smith & Wesson .38 snub-nose revolver, five rounds with a woman's grip—super compact. Acid-removed serial numbers and a rough finish eliminate fingerprints."

"Comes with a holster?" I asked.

"Yeah—sure. I'll even throw in a box of silver tips. Paid four times what I'm askin' 'cause it's clean. I needs juice money now—a C-note and it's yours."

"Here's the deal," I replied. "You hand over Roscoe and I'll give you $20 now plus $80 at closing, after we get paid. Deal?"

"Deal. Where's my Jackson?"

Handing over the twenty, I said, "See you at 4 with the rest of your bread."

Roscoe was compact, and the clip holster fit neatly in the small of my back at the belt line. Instantly, I felt invincible.

The following Wednesday, the FBI dude was back, huddling with Lance on breaks. Since the guy lived in Atlanta, he probably clocked hours with Lance as an excuse to stay home with wife and kids. Anyway, as long as Lance spent time with the spit-and-polished agent, I wouldn't have to get involved. Life was complicated enough.

However, I couldn't resist pulling Lance's chain after the FBI dude left.

"Turning into a snitch?"

"I get more than I give," Lance replied. "I'm not a snitch and never will be."

While in Atlanta, the Carousels rarely gathered for lunch or rehearsal. Spirited by aspirations to learn new jazz cuts by Art Pepper, Herbie Mann, and David "Fathead" Newman, we scheduled a brunch, followed by rehearsal. Bobby selected Aunt Paula's Porch—all-you-can-eat community platter of fried catfish, cold slaw and French fries spun on a lazy susan atop a checkered tablecloth. Rounds of Dixie Beer accompanied the feast. The fried fish was fresh and perfectly prepared. Best yet, the homegrown tartar sauce was exceptional—the best I'd ever had.

Despite the good food, Bobby kept fidgeting in his chair, finally banging the table hard with his fist and drawing attention from others on Aunt Paula's Porch. Lance gently placed his hand on Bobby's, momentarily calming the peacock. Jerking away his hand, Bobby got really lathered up and began speaking the hate speech taught him by Max Starr, his father.

"Any of you been reading 'bout our nigger-lovin' president? He wants to pass a Civil Rights law. Politicians are tryin' to desegregate our schools, turning the FBI and the Attorney General into Nazi storm troopers and putting an Equal Employment Opportunity Commission in place to ensure niggers get paid the same wages as WASPs. It's an attack on our southern values. Politicians sold us out. We're in the middle of a revolution, fellows. Niggers are protesting at Woolworth's lunch counters and launching Civil Right protests all over the South. The worst thing is they don't even get a slap on the wrist for their un-American behavior."

Rooster poured gasoline on Bobby's fire, asking, "What's your final solution for the nigger problem?"

Eyes blazing, Bobby heightened his rant. "What we need are a few cross burnings and a bunch of hung niggers. Martin Luther King, Jr. is probably a Communist—needs a bullet between his eyes. To add insult to injury, Sammy Davis, Jr. married May Britt, a gorgeous white Swedish woman. We should castrate that bastard. The courts are totally against us—can't segregate on public transportation anymore and Louisiana racial laws were declared unconstitutional.

"Goddammit! Our southern heritage is under attack, guys. Kennedy's nigger-lovin' nature is guaranteed to destroy the tattered shreds of what we love about our South. It's bad, guys—I'm ready to kill anyone who threatens our southern values. Where do I sign up for the revolution?

"Calm down," Lance said. "Get your head out of your ass. You wanna be a star on the national stage? Put your KKK bigotry where the sun don't shine—in the nearest trashcan. That hatred will poison an entertainer's career quicker than anythin'. Get beyond your North Louisiana narrow-mindedness. Keep your eye on the prize: fame and fortune. Now's your chance to amount to somethin'. Think positive."

I had to agree.

"Frankly, I've had more fun in Atlanta and New Orleans than the law allows. Even so, we'd better get our heads out of our asses and see what's around the corner—musically speaking. Let's get in time with changing time."

Bobby refused to be pacified. Instead, he bristled, "We're losing the music race, too. Elvis just returned from the Army and released *Are You Lonesome Tonight*. I can feel it—music is changin'. We have to catch a new wave. Let's try something different."

Then again Big Joe groused, *"C'est Magnifique. Tête Dure".* At da top of our game, Bro. Why change what's workin'? Gert thinks we're great—so, we're great. Nuf said."

Big Joe identified the source of his myopic views, telegraphing obstinate closed mindedness to the Carousels' attempting anything new or different. He only knows what he knows. Unfortunately, our limitations are intertwined with Big Joe's limitations.

Five sets of eyes acknowledged the obvious: Big Joe will never embrace what he doesn't understand; still he's our musical alpha dog. So, just like that, cold water doused our zeal for change. Disappointed, I fondled the cards dealt: limited horizons and bucolic thinking. A familiar odor radiated from Big Joe's clothes, their origins impregnated by Gert's pungent elixir. My nostrils twitched and eyes watered.

Not surprising, I remembered a passage from Kerouac's book: *"But why think about that when all the golden lands ahead of you and all kinds of unforeseen events wait lurking to surprise you and make you glad you're alive to see?"*

Our first week back in Monroe, Lance complained of a drip. He passed out from a million unit Penicillin injection. But it stopped the drip. Two days later, I went to the same doctor and received my million units. Atlanta was great fun, although we'd brought back far more than planned to sleepy Monroe and the Dynasty.

The second week, Angelle Devero and Lance Love hooked up—moving in together. Over breakfast at Rebel Yell, I asked Lance,

"You turnin' in your free pass card? Got your ticket punched enough to savor in your golden years?"

"There'll never be enough punches on my ticket, though Angelle's special. For now, I put my ticket in the bureau. Only time will tell."

"A stud cut down in his prime—pussy whipped at 23," I replied. "You said a little over a year ago, and I quote, 'Each of us has fallen into a time warp, without guilt, responsibility, consequences or baggage. For the moment, God has given us a free pass.' Lance, I'm following your sage advice—are you?"

"Busted … hope you have better luck following my advice than I did."

At Thursday's rehearsal Rooster recounted his exploits. "Last night's band-aid kept asking me if I loved her. She said if I told her I loved her she's give me a little nookie. I said, 'Hell baby, I don't love ya', I've simply got a hard-on I'm tryin' to get rid of."

Before kicking off our featured set, I said, "Create fantasy—sell illusion—project your God Power."

THIRD SET LINEUP—DYNASTY LOUNGE				
SONG	ORIG'L ARTIST	GENRE	ENSEMBLE	FEATURE
Lonely Teardrops	Jackie Wilson	R&B	Standard Ensemble	Bobby—Vocal
On Broadway	The Drifters	R&R	Standard Ensemble	Bobby, Lance & Big Joe—Vocal
You've Lost That Lovin' Feelin'	The Righteous Brothers	R&R	Standard Ensemble	Lance & Bobby—Vocal
Lay Your Burden Down	Buckwheat Zydeco	Zydeco	Cajun Accordion, Frottoir, Fiddle + Rhythm	Big Joe—Vocal Rooster, Smoke & Rocky
Yes Indeed	Ray Charles	R&B	3 Horns	Big Joe—Vocals

You Send Me	Sam Cooke	Pop	3 Horns	Bobby—Vocal
El Paso	Marty Robbins	Country	Guitar	Bobby—Vocal & Smoke
Moon River	Andy Williams	Crooner	Standard Ensemble	Lance—Vocal
Tangerine	Herb Alpert & The Tijuana Brass	Pop	3 Horns	Big Joe, Lance & Rocky
Watermelon Man	Lee Morgan	Latin Jazz	4 Horns + Conga	Big Joe, Lance & Rocky

Remembering the time I was a good man, I thought of Barbara Banks, the high school senior I met in Monroe. At that time, Barbara was my only connection to honor and respect—a really nice girl. As soon as the Carousels returned to Monroe, I sought out Barbara to capture sanity, normalcy and my straight man persona. She was still in high school and just about to turn 18. Barbara was on the homecoming court and made beauty in her high school yearbook.

We did simple things—honorable things. Barbara was a starry-eyed virgin, and I was a worn-out slave to decadent living.

For some reason, she loved polishing my Zildjian cymbals. It was an afternoon of activity that involved cleaning cymbals with oxalic acid, followed by Brasso on, then off, repeating several times until they shined like new. I simply loved being with a beautiful woman who was intelligent and innocent. The fact that Barbara was a virgin gave me pause, wondering whether I'd like and respect her as much after … For now, Barbara found shining my cymbals enjoyable, and I loved being with Barbara. She made me feel normal. Who can figure?

But as fate would have it, on the night of Barbara's 18th birthday, I gently guided her passage into womanhood.

Thanks Goldie.

Perhaps because it was new and daring, Barbara began making frequent visits to my apartment. Barbara was falling in love with carnal knowledge and me.

How ironic; I've tarnished the shining symbol of good. What have I done? My bent man is winning the battle for my soul. I've lost my good man.

Chapter 18

1960
BIG MAMA

Later that week, with less than an hour's sleep, a forceful knock on my front door startled me. At 4:30 a.m., my bewildered mind struggled to process the sound.

Was I dreaming or is there a real person knocking?

I tried to analyze who it could be. A jealous boyfriend?

"It's Big Mama! Let me in, Rocky," the voice said.

Dressed only in drawers, I cracked open the steel door, my head spinning, struggling to clear cobwebs from my sleepy brain.

"Big Mama. What's up? Do you need help?"

Big Mama pushed open the door and immediately got to the point.

"Rocky, we need your help with something tonight—right now! Get dressed.... I'll explain on the way."

Big Mama was the head bartender at the Dynasty Lounge. Her handle had nothing to do with her physical size or offspring. She got her nickname by mothering the barflies, barmaids and Smitty Smith, owner of the Dynasty. She was the mother hen, and everyone owed Big Mama something. When there was a problem or someone needed a sympathetic shoulder to cry on, Big Mama was available.

She was great at solving problems and keeping her mouth shut. She gave straightforward, practical advice and was an expert fixer.

Although I had never gone to Big Mama for sympathy or sex, I owed her a lot. She showed me the ropes on how to determine our value to a nightclub owner by monitoring the nightly cash register receipts. Her coaching resulted in Smitty's paying the Carousels a lot more money for our services. We were beholding to Big Mama, and she knew it. Now, here she was, standing in my bedroom, hands on her hips, telling me what to do. I obediently did what she commanded.

Big Mama insisted on driving. She eased her Pontiac out of the Waterfront Oasis Apartments and on to a fog-blanketed downtown street. Straining to see the road through the thick fog, we both squinted and leaned close to the windshield. Within two blocks, she turned left and crossed the bridge leading to West Monroe.

I was finally coming to my senses and my patience was going. "So, what's up?" I asked.

Big Mama did not respond right away. It was obvious there was a lot to say, and she was struggling to organize the information into a coherent, condensed answer.

"Well, Rocky. You know Donna and I share a house together. When I came home tonight, Donna had given herself an abortion. She'd been eating for two for seven or eight months and was extremely depressed. Donna doesn't even know who the father is. Anyway, Donna used knitting needles to puncture her embryonic sack and one of those hand pumps to inject air into her uterus. She aborted the fetus, and when I arrived the baby was lifeless on the bathroom floor, wrapped in Donna's pajama top. Embryonic fluids and blood splattered all over the bathroom, hallway and bedroom.

"Donna was face down on the bed in a pool of blood. I didn't know if she was dead or alive, so I did CPR and she finally began to breathe. Don't know how long her brain went without oxygen, but she is definitely in shock. Glassy eyes and that far-away stare. She's really out there, Rocky. She's in a bad way. Tried to revive the baby, although the little girl never had a chance. The baby would have been a beautiful little girl. Rocky—it was horrible!"

Thank God Big Mama paused. I replayed her story like a newsreel in my mind's eye. The vivid pictures that flashed up were horrific. Emotions stretched to the max, ranging from extreme condemnation to compassionate forgiveness. Befuddled, my spiritual compass was nowhere to be found—cast adrift—emotions racing in a hundred directions, with no bearing. Moreover, I didn't know where Big Mama was taking us.

I finally asked, "So, where are we going?"

With incredible composure, in a soft, but firm tone, Big Mama said, "We are going to the Eternal Rest Cemetery in West Monroe." She said it in a matter-of-fact way, as though it was obvious.

"I cleaned up Donna and the little girl. I called a few of our friends and arranged to meet at the cemetery. You are going to help me bury the little girl, Rocky. You're our preacher. Read a few passages from the Bible and say the right words to properly bury this child. You can do this, Rocky."

Big Mama left no room for argument, nor was I of a mind to object. I simply said, "Okay."

Big Mama handed me a Holy Bible that had been sitting on the seat between us all the time. I hadn't noticed it because we both focused on the fog-shrouded road, which was barely visible.

"Now gather your thoughts and think about what you're going to say and what passages to read from this Bible. I'm counting on you to pull this off."

I was amazed at her calmness after being shocked by the bloody scene at her home. In the midst of utter chaos, she orchestrated everything in this tragic play. I was to be Big Mama's lead character, scripting the appropriate words and feelings befitting this tragic situation.

As we approached the entrance to the cemetery, Big Mama turned off the car's headlights and slowed to a crawl, easing up a gravel road. Squinting, I began to distinguish shapes of cypress trees dripping with Spanish moss like tears into the swampy pools below. I strained to see up ahead and conjured a scene from a horror movie.

A gathering of ghouls standing around an open pit. I expected a malevolent creature to emerge from the adjacent fog-bathed swamps at any moment.

Big Mama stopped the car, took a deep breath, sighed, and touched my hand for reassurance, then slowly opened the door. I sat with the dome light on, frantically searching for the right passages to read at the gravesite, while Big Mama opened the trunk of her car. Illuminated only by the dome light cutting through fog, she cradled a lifeless form in a doll's blanket and walked deliberately toward Donna. Big Mama was so gentle, and we were so illegal. Everything about this was illegitimate.

Stepping out of the car, I recognized the ghouls. Roughly 30 had gathered around a shallow hole in the black North Louisiana earth. Just a few hours earlier, these derelicts of darkness were dancing, drinking and having a gay ol' time at the Dynasty with the Carousels. A mysterious force drew them to this place—a reason only they knew.

Standing on one side of the open grave was Minnie the midget, Jim the out-of-work carpenter, Sebastian the fired vice squad officer, Mike the vacuum cleaner salesman, Sissy the twit, and Ralph the poor little rich boy. At the far end of the pit stood Sarah, a workin' girl; Itchy, a workin' girl with a drug habit that needed scratching; Roberto the pimp; and Manny with a monkey on his back. Flanking the other side of the grave were Jonathan, a sleazebag attorney; Christopher, a bail bondsman; Sam, the town drunk; Robert the bouncer; Paula, a barmaid; Big Orange; and others of equally dubious character. They stood in a semicircle, close together, shoulders slouched, faces down, sheepishly avoiding eye contact with Donna, Big Mama, and me.

This could be a convention of North Louisiana derelicts—all of them present and accounted for, right here, right now. And, I'm about to make a fool of myself as their preacher. What the hell am I going to say to this group that will fit this tragedy?

Big Mama moved to a Ford pickup parked on a slight rise about a hundred feet from the gravesite, its tailgate down. Big Joe and Jimmy the plumber made eye contact with Big Mama. Donna was standing motionless with the empty stare of a mental patient following a lobotomy.

Big Mama tenderly dressed the lifeless baby girl in a doll dress, socks, shoes, ribbons and all. Then she manipulated Donnas' lifeless arms and hands, much like that of a manikin, attempting to involve Donna in the final preparations—clumsily placing the doll bonnet on the dead baby's head, finishing with a bow under the chin.

Big Mama wrapped the fetus in a blanket and placed it in the makeshift casket hastily fashioned out of a pine box that rested in the bed of the plumber's pickup, took two steps back and hugged Donna. Donna didn't raise her arms to share Big Mama's embrace, didn't cry, and exhibited no discernable emotion.

Jimmy nailed the lid on the coffin, each metallic crack of hammer against nail underscoring the irreverence of the moment. The sound echoed off Spanish moss and cypress trees as a painful reminder of the harshness of life—and death.

From where I stood, I could hear Ralph, the poor little rich kid, and Sissy the twit, speaking into their fists in muffled tones. They were judgmental, and Donna was the focus of their wrath.

"Isn't murder a crime?" Sissy mumbled.

"It used to be," replied Ralph with a giggle.

Big Joe approached me, stopping within arm's reach. Big Joe and I were the only Carousels present. He spoke unobtrusively in a whisper, "Rocky, I don kno' if dats my kid or not. Could be, before I met Gert. Ya bout to say words at da grave. Jus' want ya to 'member—Donna isn't blameless here. Still she needs our support more dan anyone here dis mornin'. We've all been where Donna is. Ya words'll mean a lot to us, but Donna is da one that needs your words of forgiveness dis mornin'. To hell with those judgmental assholes standin' 'round a hole. They celebrate someone else's tragedy. Be kind to Donna dis mornin'. What ya say matters."

Stepping back, he moved next to Donna. They didn't touch or speak. Big Joe's tears flooded down his cheeks, exposing raw emotions from the gentle giant. Big Joe did his best to be of some comfort to Donna.

With Big Mama escorting Donna by the arm, they slowly began to move toward the open hole in the cold black earth. Jimmy followed with the casket, a shoebox-sized coffin dwarfed by his burly arms and leather jacket. Big Joe looked at me with hurting eyes as we took our place in the procession, behind the plumber. Big Mama and Donna moved to one side of the open pit. Jimmy placed the casket in the shallow, hastily dug grave. I stood at the foot of the gravesite.

Big Joe hung back just a few steps behind me. When all were in their places, I paused to get my head around this surreal place. Before I could speak, I heard the mournful sounds of Big Joe's clarinet playing agonizingly slow, in the lowest register of the instrument, *Just a Closer Walk with Thee*. Big Joe's liquid emotions flowed down the Selmer and dripped off the bell. Single-handedly, he brought us together, steeped in the tragedy of this moment.

Geeze. You've made this into a jazz funeral—typical of your South Louisiana roots.

I opened the Bible. Big Joe moved to Donna's' side. I stood motionless, saying nothing for a full minute. Not yet dawn; the fog had turned to a grayish white, foretelling the arrival of a new day. There were no animal sounds, no wind, no cars and no evidence of life. Death hung heavy in the air. Tears dried up. There was nothing but the moment and our desperate thoughts. Something died within each of us this morning. Staring at the box lying in the black earth, in our own private way, we dealt with reality: but for the grace of God, any of us could be standing where Donna stands. Or just as likely, we could be where the dead baby girl lay, in a shabby pine box in a shallow grave without a headstone

I waited long enough. My role in this tragic play must begin now.

"Let us pray. Father, help us to understand what is happening here and deal with it in a manner that pleases you."

I read from Ecclesiastes (3:1–15), though I did not announce any scriptural references aloud: *"For everything there is a season, and a time for every matter under heaven, a time to be born, and a time to die, a time to plant, and a time to pluck up what is planted, a time to kill and a time to heal."*

I turned, slowly, deliberately, to the next verse, bookmarked with a decaying damp leaf from the cemetery carpet. I wanted to achieve a tone of reconciliation rather than condemnation. However, I knew that achieving my intent required delivering the next verses with humility and compassion. I took a deep breath, used a low tone, and without reference, read from Peter (4:3 and 4).

"You have had enough in the past of the evil things—godless people enjoy their immorality and lust, their feasting and drunkenness and wild parties, and their terrible worship of Idols. Of course, your former friends are surprised when you no longer join them in the wicked things they do, and they say evil things about you."

Turning to another leaf bookmark, I continued reading from Isaiah (57:3 and 4).

"But you come here, you witches' children, you offspring of adulterers and prostitutes! Whom do you mock, making faces and sticking out your tongue? You children of sinners and liars!"

I was attempting to achieve a particular mindset, thinking to myself, *"is anyone hearing me?"* Undaunted, I read John (8:7) with a little more emotion and volume.

"He lifted up himself, and said unto them, He that is without sin among you; let him first cast a stone at her."

Pausing for a moment, I glared at each ghoul, repeating the same verse, emphasizing the last phrase.

"He lifted up himself, and said unto them, He that is without sin among you; let him first cast a stone at her."

I closed the Bible and stood silent for a moment.

I am the impostor, and these sinners know it. I'm not worthy of preaching to these derelicts. No better than they—simply the one chosen to perform the assignment. My sermon must be brief. Fortunately, my Calvinistic, Presbyterian upbringing fills the void with reassurance that God put me here for a purpose. Now I have to fulfill that purpose, to the best of my abilities, even if I don't fully grasp the meaning behind what is happening.

"All of us here are sinners," I began. "You, you, you, and me. All of us. I am not worthy to stand in this lofty position this morning, except God put me here. And God put you in your places. That is the way it is. Any one of us could be standing in Donna's place this morning. But for the grace of God, we are not—she is. Donna and her unborn baby girl lay broken before us."

A few heads began to nod slightly, and I continued.

"They are the objects of our attention, representing all that is good and evil within each of us. As one of you, I beg you to extend to Donna and this lifeless child whatever compassion, understanding, and love you possess. Perhaps some of you cannot forgive because you're consumed with ridicule and hate. However, if you forgive Donna's sin, you will be blessed with a deeper understanding of life, happiness, and the hereafter. That is not my promise. It's God's promise."

I had done my best. There were no visible signs of agreement or disagreement. Nothing else came to mind so I wrapped it up with a deep sigh.

"And now, for those of you who would like to join me in the 23rd Psalm, you are welcome to do so.

Pausing for a few seconds, I began: *"The Lord is my shepherd, I shall not want ..."*

Initially, hushed whispers were barely audible. Gradually, they transformed into a murmuring chant. Suddenly, I had a revelation.

I'm a foolish impostor, simply passing through this subculture. I'll never be accepted as one of them because my naked soul is exposed. Not that I'm better than they—I'm not. I am utterly transparent, a delusional fool believing that a clever disguise will hide my true self. Yielding to destiny, I submit myself to a higher power that leads me into uncharted waters.

I raised my voice and others followed.

"... Yea, though I walk through the valley of the shadow of death, I will fear no evil, for thou are with me..."

A new dawn was breaking and the fog turned to a white on white curtain. The ghouls were transforming back into humans. The rigidity of anger had softened. Voices spoke clearly in unison as we delivered the final lines.

"*... Surely, goodness and mercy shall follow me all the days of my life: and I will dwell in the house of the Lord forever. Amen.*"

Big Joe moved up the rise behind me, his massive body framed by a saintly halo in the white fog of dawn and black Selmer offering up a spiritual prayer of forgiveness, *Amazing Grace*, in B flat. Big Joe's mournful tones touched our souls, creating a spiritual peace. He became our heavenly connection with God and his forgiveness. Tears flowed down Big Joe's cheeks, onto the ebony clarinet, and finally, rained down to the black earth below. Big Joe's musical prayer ended. Ghoulish eyes bled tears of sorrow and remorse.

I simply and softly said, "Amen."

That morning, at the gravesite of an aborted fetus and a broken woman, God forgave sinners and saints. The horror had ended. Only our memories survived in the privacy of our tormented conscience. None of us ever spoke of this again—ever.

Chapter 19

1960
BLACK SOUL

The Carousels' return to Bossier City brought huge crowds to Saks' Boom Boom Room, in large part because of a mythical image created by Merrill's marketing and public relations efforts. Interviewed on three radio shows and one TV program during our first week, we were full-fledged celebrities in my hometown. Our music was better than ever, and our professional stage presentation had made a quantum leap.

The Carousels were the undisputed kings of the musical intersection of Louisiana, Arkansas, Texas and Oklahoma. Fans drove in to spend a weekend at the Boom Boom Room. Merrill was particularly happy. In exchange for agreeing to appear twice a year, Merrill agreed to promote the Carousels to his friends—club owners and beyond.

During our third and fourth weeks Merrill brought in Jimmy Elledge for two shows a night, Thursday through Saturday. Jimmy's smash hit, *Funny How Time Slips Away*, currently was No. 1on the charts. His personal manager was an RCA advance man, a fellow hired to pay deejays to play RCA records. Jimmy hailed from Meridian, Mississippi, was a closet queer, and a Jerry Lee Lewis fanatic.

The Carousels backed Jimmy's stage show, and I tried to hit on the RCA man for a record deal. However, he was too greedy and his connections were limited to RCA, so I wrote him off.

Jimmy sang *Funny How Time Slips Away* every show, girls swooned and we puked at Jimmy's poor piano playing and marginal imitations of Jerry Lee Lewis. On the other hand he was a showman and a big draw for Merrill Saks, so we smiled and tolerated the pixie dust of the fairy queen.

Big Joe augmented the chord progressions of *Funny How Time Slips Away*, making it much richer and more interesting, reminding me of a Stan Kenton arrangement—Big Band jazz. However, the RCA man insisted we play the music as recorded and not use Big Joe's arrangement. However, we kept the new musical arrangement in our repertoire, with Bobby Starr singing Jimmy's solo and playing tubs, Big Joe on trumpet and tenor sax, Lance on baritone sax. I played bone. The genius of Big Joe's arrangement became a perennial showstopper for the Carousels, making *Funny How Time Slips Away* one of our cornerstone ballads—although never behind Jimmy Elledge.

Before kicking off our featured set, I said, "Create fantasy—sell illusion—project your God Power."

THIRD SET LINEUP—SAKS BOOM BOOM ROOM				
SONG	ORIG'L ARTIST	GENRE	ENSEMBLE	FEATURE
Jolé Blon	Clifton Chenier	Zydeco	Cajun Accordion, Fiddle & Frottoir	Big Joe—Vocal Rooster, Smoke & Rocky
Unchain My Heart	Ray Charles	R&B	4 Horns	Big Joe—Vocal, Lance & Rocky
String Of Pearls	Glenn Miller	Big Band	4 Horns	Big Joe, Lance & Rocky
Unforgettable	Nat "King" Cole	Crooner	Standard + Alto Solo	Lance—Vocal

Whiffenpoof Song	Cal Tjader	Latin Jazz	Vibes, Guitar & Conga's	Rocky & Smoke
I'm Sorry (Comedy)	Brenda Lee (Parody)	Pop Comedy Routine	Standard Ensemble	Bobby in Falsetto
I Did It My Way	Frank Sinatra	Pop	Standard Ensemble	Lance—Vocal
Moanin'	Modern Jazz Quintet	Jazz	4 Horns	Big Joe, Lance & Rocky
A Taste Of Honey	Herb Alpert & The Tijuana Brass	Pop	3 Horns	Big Joe, Lance & Rocky
Work Song	Nat Adderley	Jazz	4 Horns	Big Joe, Lance & Rocky

Another song at the top of the Hit Parade was *A Taste of Honey*. Big Joe put together an arrangement featuring himself on trumpet. Lance and I backed him up and delivered brief solos, although Big Joe's performance was the magic that impressed audiences—and the Carousels. Big Joe came into his own as a trumpeter. His head grew larger as jowls puffed out like Dizzy Gillespie's. His exaggerated body and facial movements diminished the rest of us to little more than buzzin' mosquitoes. Applause was Big Joe's narcotic and he wanted more—and more—and more.

Predictably, the FBI dude from Atlanta appeared once a week, always dressed as Hoover's finest in black on black with a bulge on his right hip at the belt line. Just to show my awareness and interest, I asked Lance, "Are you his only source? Don't let Merrill see you talking with the dude. Go outside in the parking lot."

"Chill, Rocky," Lance said. "I've got this under control."

Gert dominated Big Joe off stage. Angelle moved in with Lance. Betty Booth appeared every weekend, monopolizing Bobby. Keeping track of Rooster and me required a dance card. Rooster was playing his role to the max with nightly one-offs. I split my time between Goldie and band-aids. Smoke kept on spinning conspiracy theories to anyone who'd listen.

Unbelievably, I grew bored with same ol' same ol'.

Something different and wild is what I need. Why not? After all, this is my big adventure.

One night during our break, I spotted one of the high-priced workin' gals sitting at the end of the bar, her regular perch of prominence. A full head of black, Veronica Lake hair partially covered piercing eyes and sunken cheeks. Never taking my eyes off her, I moved down the long row of bar stools, lightly touching disciples seated at the alcoholic nursery.

The tall, trim and expensive brunette winked or blinked in my direction ... wasn't sure which. She knew I wasn't a mark, so I kept moving in her direction out of curiosity, yelling my drink order over the bar, "Scotch on the rocks with a twist."

As I drew closer to her perch, she smiled—an unmistakable invitation. With the coyness of a coquette, she looked away, gaming my desires as easily as strumming a guitar. Cleopatra was a mere understudy to this pro.

Long nails attached to pencil thin fingers lifted the stirring straw from her neat drink and slowly placed it over her long, arched tongue, blatantly hinting at her carnal skills and moral turpitude. Her moist lips closed around the straw as it slowly moved in and out of a luscious mouth. Although the price of admission was rumored to be high, this workin' gal was the best I'd witnessed at revving up a man's libido.

The bartender slid my Scotch over the bar, resting it next to the object of my interest. I brushed by her, reaching for the drink with one hand and grabbing her tight ass with the other. Abruptly, she swiveled her stool around to face me straight on. With the speed of a karate wrestler, she grabbed both my shoulders, aggressively brushing her large breasts against my chest.

Placing her lips close to my ear, she whispered, "If you came here for something wild and erotic, you're in the right place. But if you're Presbyterian, move on—get lost."

Her assertiveness captured my attention and interest, particularly the Presbyterian line. Ready for adventure I said, "I'm not Presbyterian, at least, not tonight."

She moved back a few inches. "If I'm still here in an hour, you're in for the ride of your life."

She was and I was. We drove up to room 666 at the Town and Country Motel, her principal place of business. The room's only illumination: the glow of a 20-watt bulb from a lavender scarf-draped lamp. The sweet allure of incense or hashish saturated drapes and carpet. Twenty candles were scattered about the room. She handed me a box of matches and proceeded to light half while I lit the remaining ten. I wasn't sure who was goin' to ride whom, but our time had come to find out.

Right out of the box, she was different. What I thought was a seductress possessing sensitivity, allure and nuance was not the person undressing before me. She opened a drawer, retrieved an aromatic inhaler and sprayed a misty vapor into her flared nostrils. I declined her offer of the inhaler, wanting to maintain crystal clarity for something "wild and erotic."

She began displaying a nervous itch, her long nails scratching arms and hands, producing abrasions on both her wrists. Right then and there I decided there was only one name to call her: Nervous.

Suddenly, she shook violently, like being hit in the heart with a shot of adrenaline. Just as suddenly, she reached out and grabbed my face, digging those long nails deep into the scalp behind my ears. Her take-charge aggression made it clear that this was her party and she wanted rough sex. Eyes twinkling above sinister lips, Nervous exclaimed, "I love freak fuckin'. You up for this, Rocky?"

"You bet!"

She led me into the abyss of sadomasochism. Her extensive leather collection and cracking whips placed me, then her, into roles of sexual bondage, dominance and submissiveness. Like a child sneaking into a forbidden place, I was excited, terrified, exhilarated. I did what she asked, not knowing if I'd get out of room 666 alive. Nervous was a bottomless pit of creative S&M. I was a fly and she the spider, weaving a web of bondage around what had become a mere caricature of Rocky Strong.

By 5 a.m., my S&M quotient was more than satisfied. Toweling off and dressing, I thanked Nervous and bid her adieu, walking out of her motel room without looking back. On the drive home, I realized that my tuxedo jacket and bow tie were still somewhere in her room. Not up for any more Nervous madness, I decided to keep on driving, hit the sack and pick up my things later. Enough freak fuckin' for one night.

The next day, about 11, I drove back to the motel. As I walked up to Nervous' room, two ambulance attendants and two police officers were at her door.

I turned to one of the officers and said, "I'm Rock Strong, leader of the Carousels. I left my tux jacket and bow tie here last night."

Before the Bossier officer could respond, I walked into the room and saw Nervous lying naked on the bed, a discolored spoon and cigarette lighter idle on the nightstand. A syringe remained in her arm, my bow tie limply hanging around the needle.

Nervous was dead or dying, apparently from a heroin overdose. Inside a ghostlike dimension, her body transformed from life to death. A numinous feeling in my soul invoked fear and trembling, accompanied by a pervasive fascination with the macabre. Involuntarily, I fell into communion with a wholly other, sensing the spiritual ascension of her soul. Nervous's black soul seemed to be reaching up to me in search of a suitable vessel as her next host. Struggling to maintain control over my right mind and senses, I cowered in fear, turning away.

Nervous's black soul seemed to overpower my feeble defenses, swallowing me whole. Emotionally struggling to break free, I reached out to grab my bow tie from her lifeless arm and my tuxedo jacket that was draped over the chair. I stumbled toward the door. The young police officer made a gesture toward me, except the older cop grabbed his arm. I stood at the threshold, turned and said to the cops, "You know where to reach me. Right now, I have to get out of here. That devil is trying to devour my soul."

Celebrity status had saved my ass again. The cops knew who I was—Merrill Saks's favorite. They were probably thinking they dared not mess with Merrill, especially since their chief of police and vice squad were being well compensated by Merrill. If that weren't enough, everyone knew that Carlos Marcello owned the Town and Country Motel.

Standing just outside the threshold, I overheard one cop say to the other, "Why make waves? No one's gonna miss a worthless druggie." The Bossier cops never asked me any questions, ignoring the possibility that heroin could have been stashed in my tux pocket. Still, I was shaken to the core, sensing Nervous' demonic hand reaching out to consume my body, mind and spirit. Terrified, I sprinted to my car—horror-struck by the possibilities.

I'm crossing over to an evil man—devils are consuming me.

My body covered in a clammy sweat, I struggled to gain composure. Recalling Ayn Rand: *"Religion is a psychological weakness … I regard it as evil."*

I questioned everything.

Am I good? Am I evil? Am I the world's biggest hypocrite? Where is my religious strength? Have devils moved into my head?

Bewildered, I drove aimlessly, struggling to figure things out.

I can't show weakness to anyone, particularly Merrill and the Carousels. Only the strong survive. Weak people are summarily crucified in this subterranean world. I have to play this perfectly. First things first. I have to get my head straight—can't show any cracks in my armor. Gotta be strong. How the hell do I do that?'

Don't know why, but I found myself knocking on Goldie's door. When she saw me, I said the first thing that came to mind: "Breakfast?"

"You bet," came from behind a glistening gold tooth. "I'll get dressed."

We selected a remote booth at the Do Drop Inn Restaurant, sat together on the same side, facing a back wall so no one could see us. Goldie sensed my anxiety. Calm, quiet and patient, she provided a tranquil moment for me to recover. Running away from a traumatic event that happened less than an hour earlier required space—lots of space.

I whispered to Goldie, "Order breakfast for us."

She gladly obliged. Cowering in the corner of a rear booth, I was overcome by light-headedness and blurred vision. I placed my head between folded arms on the table, Goldie caressing my hair and neck. Saying nothing, she offered her protection and plenty of space. Blood finally returned to my brain. I sat up and touched Goldie's arm in appreciation.

Food was served and consumed in silence. Finally, I said, "Goldie, I really need a friend. Someone supportive and understanding, without asking questions. It's a lot to ask, but I'm asking you. I'm awfully raw right now."

Goldie gently squeezed my hand and said softly, "Whatever you need, I'm here for you, Rocky. I'm here."

And so, that afternoon I moved six tuxedos and the Cheshire Cat into Goldie's garage apartment. A week of nightmares and cold sweats followed. Goldie became my compassionate angel, lavishing emotional support and compliments that ever so slowly rebuilt self-esteem. Goldie provided space to sort out the madness in my soul, asking no questions.

Without Goldie, my facade would have been stripped away, laying bare my emotional ineptness to lead. Displaying any sign of weakness was certain to be punished. Sixteen hours each day, a dungeon of despair consumed me. For the other eight hours in the day, I forced a painted smiley face for Merrill Saks, the Carousels and an adoring audience.

Has Nervous's black soul taken me over? Nervous was tap dancing on the edge of a straight razor and lost balance. She morphed into the next available host—perhaps me—perhaps the young policeman or the ambulance attendant. Her black soul haunts me every day and every night. Truth remains hidden, yet my nightmares persist. Not even Goldie can know the truth behind my madness.

Cuddled on the edge of Goldie's bed, the Cheshire Cat's motor was running: *Only a few find the way; some don't recognize it when they do; some don't ever want to.*

Chapter 20

1961
FIRST NORTHERN TOUR

braham "Abie" Goldstein was a red-faced, fat, jolly, Jewish booking agent frequenting night clubs on the Bossier Strip, looking for bands and bookings. Abie solicited me on a regular basis. One night at Saks' Boom Boom Room, I responded to his sales pitch, saying, "Sure. Book us a northern tour, to include Nashville and major cities bordering the Great Lakes. Begin with Nashville. Can you do that?"

Abie's head bobbed up and down with excitement.

Within a week, he presented a two-week gig in Nashville's Printers Alley, followed by a four-week gig in Toledo and a promise to book additional gigs around the Great Lakes.

At rehearsal the following day, I laid out the beginnings of the tour to the band.

"Abie got us the Black Poodle in Printers Alley. Two weeks. A last-minute cancellation by Brenda Lee and the Casuals opened up an opportunity for us—with a nice money bump. Just so you know, the agreement names Abie and Dottie LaSalle as co-booking agents. They split 10 percent. Since we net a nice overall increase, I'll sign the contract and return to Abie this afternoon."

Hearing no objections, I continued. "The Kato Club in Toledo is entirely different. We'll play five hours a night, seven nights a week. That's a 35-hour workweek guys; 27 straight nights at slightly more bread than Nashville. Only saving grace is the frontman in Toledo is well connected to Mob clubs around the Great Lakes, and Abie promises follow-on gigs. Flip a coin guys. Ya wanna accept or pass on the Kato Club?"

Following much discussion, Bobby and Smoke's enthusiasm to "test the northern audience acceptance of the Carousels" overpowered dissenting voices. Naïvely, we accepted the terms.

A week later, I distributed six AAA maps and emergency instructions for the road trip. Bossier departure time and ETA in Nashville were set. Big Joe drove his '57 Mercury Marque with Gert and her black cup snuggled close. Lance packed a newly announced pregnant Angelle into his '58 Pontiac Bonneville coupe. Bobby drove an immaculate white '58 Ford flip top with Rooster in the passenger seat. By process of elimination, I ended up with Smoke riding shotgun in my '55 Olds. I was last to leave, packing a roll of cash and Roscoe.

The Black Poodle exceeded all expectations. Mesmerized by the venue and possibilities, we eagerly set up instruments and did a sound check. Designed to feature top entertainment, the 23-foot-wide stage stood a full five feet above the dance floor. The stage was fully carpeted and draped in black; touch switches on the floor controlled professional-grade theatrical lights. A wide variety of lighting fixtures hung on bars in front of the stage and hidden behind a short curtain. With virtually no limits on variety, we could light a solo performer with a sharp focus peanut spot, area light the horn section, or light the full band. Multiple-choice gelatin filters opened up all kinds of possibilities.

Bobby's sound system never came out of the trailer. The house system cost thousands, according to the frontman. Six microphones could be individually customized for reverb, tone and volume. Additionally, up to eight microphone ports were available on the mixing board with individual volume controls.

Every Carousel instrument was set up, consuming the entire stage. Honored to be performing here, my step was quicker and my smile wider. Beaming with anticipation of having reached the threshold of a major turning point in our quest for stardom, I laughed like a child being tickled. Spontaneously, Bobby and Lance laughed, too.

Printers Alley clubs featured Chet Atkins, Boots Randolph, Roy Clark, Brenda Lee, Bill Monroe, Johnny Cash, Glen Campbell, Patsy Cline and Barbara Mandrell, among others, all backed by some of the greatest session musicians in the South. We would be mightily challenged.

This gig is our biggest test yet, eclipsing Saks and the Big Easy. Are we up to this? Can we stand tall with the giant entertainers of the South? Why not stardom, beginning here in Nashville, tonight?

Bubbling over with enthusiasm, Bobby Starr summoned us to the center of the Black Poodle dance floor.

"If we make it big in here, we'll be on our way to hit records, television, Vegas and movies," he said. "This is our big shot at fame. Raise your stage persona. High energy. Mix with the audience on breaks. Make them fall in love with the Carousels. Guys, if we out draw the big stars appearing in Printers Alley, we're ready to cut a hit record and go big time."

Not to be upstaged, Big Joe added, "Expect to beat da best musicians next door, up and down Printers Alley. Out-play 'em."

"I believe tune selection is crucial to our success," Rooster said. "When I call your tune, dazzle 'em. Blow 'em away. By Wednesday, they'll become our disciples."

Lance added his thoughts: "Spend time at customer tables on breaks and be humble."

"Our dance steps have to be crisp and uniform," Smoke said. "I suspect the other clubs have nothing to compete with our choreography and energy. Keep your heads up, make eye contact with the back row and project attitude."

"Great thoughts all," I replied. "Remember. Every moment you're on stage, a top promoter is looking directly at you as his next big star. Turn on your charm and talent. Never relax. It's all about creating and maintaining illusion. Now, let's shave, shit, shower and shag ass back to the Black Poodle and dazzle these disciples."

Before kicking off our featured set, I said, "Create fantasy—sell illusion—project your God Power."

THIRD SET LINEUP—BLACK POODLE				
SONG	ORIG'L ARTIST	GENRE	ENSEMBLE	FEATURE
Sidewinder	Lee Morgan	Jazz	4 Horns	Big Joe, Lance & Rocky
Working Together	Ike & Tina Turner	R&B	4 Horns	Bobby in Falsetto & Lance—Vocal, Big Joe & Rocky
I Pity The Fool	Bobby "Blue" Bland	R&B	4 Horns	Big Joe—Vocal Lance & Rocky
Comin' Home	Lee Morgan	Jazz	4 Horns	Big Joe, Lance & Rocky
Bon Ton Roulet	Clifton Chenier	Zydeco	Cajun Accordion, Fiddle & Frottoir	Big Joe—Vocal Rooster, Smoke & Rocky
Poor Butterfly	Cal Tjader	Latin Jazz	Vibes, Guitar & Conga's	Rocky & Smoke
Country Gentleman	Chet Atkins	Country	Guitar Featured	Smoke
I'm Sorry (Comedy)	Brenda Lee (Parody)	Pop Comedy Routine	Standard Ensemble	Bobby in Falsetto
Since I Fell For You	Lenny Welch	Pop	Standard Ensemble	Lance—Vocal
Mercy, Mercy, Mercy	Cannonball Adderley	Jazz	4 Horns	Big Joe, Lance & Rocky

By Wednesday, the Carousels were outdrawing the big names in Printers Alley. By Friday our uniqueness delivered a packed house and long lines down the Alley. We worked hard, on stage and off, to solidify our position in a town famous for legendary musicians.

When Boots Randolph walked into the Black Poodle, Rooster called for *"Yakety Sax,"* Boots's biggest hit. The first one to stand up and applaud Big Joe's rendition was Boots himself. We gained his respect and, eventually, his friendship.

Three times a week, Chet Atkins made the hundred-step journey from his club to the Black Poodle. Rooster's good eye caught sight of Chet and immediately called for us to perform one of Smoke's featured tunes. Five guys faded to black as Smoke perched center stage on a stool, crossed his legs, positioned the Gibson and consumed the brilliance of a single peanut spot.

Long right-hand fingernails filed to tapered ovals poised near steel strings, now rising to embrace his caress. Smoke employed a Flamenco technique referred to as toque. Polished fingernails flashed on sparkling strings, yielding golden sounds that delighted every ear.

Flawlessly, Smoke delivered *Country Gentleman,* one of Chet's most technically difficult tunes. Chet was the first to rise in applause as Smoke took his bows for a well-deserved standing ovation. Humbled by unbridled adoration, Smoke got higher on applause than anything. In a town of great guitarists, Smoke got what he wanted: self-respect. From that moment forward, Nashville's wannabe guitarists flocked around Smoke during breaks.

Chet was RCA's biggest arranger and recording man and well on his way to executive management. A warm, kind man and a great judge of talent, he connected with Smoke and the Carousels, introducing us to several major contacts in the publishing and record business. Armed with a Chet Atkins's endorsement, we leveraged his praise to the max, opening doors to the dog-eat-dog, cannibalistic jungle of getting a hit record and becoming stars.

Big Joe, Lance, Bobby and I hit the streets, making contact with record producers, publishing companies, studio musicians and A&R men. Our collective efforts produced a backup recording session and a demo for a publisher. Not bad for two weeks in Nashville. The Carousels were learning the publishing and recording business. I inked a four-week contract for a return engagement with Larry LaSalle, Black Poodle manager and brother of Dottie LaSalle. Also not bad.

Just as everything was clicking for us, the lights went out. The Black Poodle and Printers Alley lost their audiences for four straight nights as Americans watched news reports about a ragtag group of Cuban exiles trying to take back their island from Fidel Castro.

The anti-Castro exiles, trained by the CIA, were quickly repelled by Castro's soldiers. Reports claimed 100 freedom fighters killed and more than a thousand captured. Castro proudly claimed victory against U.S. imperialism.

Our country was in shock, and few people felt like partying. Audiences eventually returned to the Black Poodle, except in smaller numbers. A new and powerful competitor emerged, creating a cultural shift from nightclub frivolity to stay-at-home news junkies.

Following our final performance in Nashville, we loaded our instruments into our trailer. AAA maps, ETA and emergency plans distributed to each Carousel, we grabbed a couple of winks and left Nashville Sunday morning at 8:30 in four cars, bound for Toledo, Ohio.

Sunday afternoon, about 50 miles south of Columbus, Ohio, I spotted Rooster on the side of the road, waving arms frantically. I quickly veered to the right and stopped on the grassy shoulder.

"Thank God, it's you," panted Rooster at my window. "Bobby was speeding, got stopped by a nigger sheriff, smarted off, got taken to jail, and his car impounded. Like we discussed in the emergency plan, I stood here and waited for you to come by. Thank God, you came by."

I told Rooster to get in the car and asked if he knew how to find the sheriff's office.

Rooster climbed in the back seat, presenting a map. Smoke sat wide-eyed in the passenger seat. Cheshire's motor was running in my lap.

As we set off for the jail, Rooster detailed the sordid affair.

"We were suckin' on some good shit and Bobby added absinthe to the mix. Neither of us were paying attention to the speedometer, although the nigger sheriff said we were doin' a hundred. Anyway, Bobby's Kickapoo Indian blood boiled over. Bobby bragged about what a big man his father was in Louisiana, but the Ohio nigger sheriff didn't give a shit. All I know is Bobby's father wasn't here to bail him out. I'm afraid that job falls to you, Rocky."

After posting bail and paying cash to get his '58 Ford out of impound, I met a sheepish Bobby Starr outside the jail. I handed Bobby the keys and barked, "This'll come out of your pay. See you in Toledo. Stay ahead of me, just in case."

At the assigned hour Sunday night, four cars pulled up in the alley behind the Kato Club. Six Carousels went inside, only to discover a toilet with a bar, the showbiz term for a low-class club catering to the unwashed. It was located on the north side of the Toledo River in a rundown blue-collar slum. A guy named T-Bone met us with a massive smile and a big, "Welcome!"

His gregarious personality temporarily replaced our initial reaction to his dumpy joint. We unloaded gear and did a quick sound check. The contract called for a Monday opening, so we headed off to secure hotel accommodations and get some well-deserved rest.

As I went to the alley behind the Kato Club, Cheshire Cat's nose pressed against the Starfire's passenger window, staring at something lurking in the shadows. A black, longhair mixed-Himalayan cat arrogantly strutted past on three legs, looking up and smiling at Cheshire with one blue eye and one brown eye. Something interesting was going on between these two felines. Picking up the black alley cat, I placed its nose on the window, opposite Cheshire.

They connected! Opening the passenger door, I sat the Himalayan on the passenger floorboard and assumed my place behind the wheel.

Cheshire curled up in my lap, purring, *"The proper order of things is often a mystery to me. You, too?"*

Not surprising, the Himalayan quoted *Alice: "There is a place, like no place on Earth—a land full of wonder, mystery, and danger! Some say to survive it, you need to be as mad as a hatter … which luckily I am."*

As with Cheshire, my ears were the only ones capable of hearing the black cat's message. Providence confirmed, I named the black Himalayan Mad Hatter, shifted into drive and headed for a place to stay.

Gert and Big Joe selected the Waldorf Hotel—right name, wrong town and zero star rating. Built in 1893, this Waldorf should have been condemned and, even worse, it was situated next to the Toledo River, which stunk like a sewer. On the contrary the weekly rates were right, so we checked in. Disillusioned, Cheshire, Mad Hatter and I fell into a lumpy bed and made zzzzzz's til dawn.

Monday began an arduous, 27-day gig at the Kato Club. After a five-hour opening night, we met Tuesday morning for breakfast at Pattie's Pancake Pantry. Big Joe succinctly summed up our situation, "What da fuck we doin' in dis sewer?"

Rooster added, "You've heard me say many times that if you stand women on their heads they all look alike. Not in Toledo. I'm afraid of falling into one of those bottomless pits and never being seen again."

Bobby continued being the ultimate optimist. "Let's use this as an opportunity to polish our persona. We can reduce rehearsal time to one day a week and focus on tightenin' up onstage theatrics and performance delivery. Certainly have plenty of time to experiment. I see this as a paid rehearsal in preparation for better things to come. What do we have to lose?"

Lance looked directly at me, asking, "Rocky, can you get us out of this disaster and put us into a real opportunity?"

Smoke nodded, endorsing Lance's question and looked at me.

"I agree. This is a cluster fuck," I said. "Beginning today, I'll work on T-Bone, Merrill, Abie and Dottie to get us back on track. In the meantime, Bobby's right. Do this for us, not the Kato Club. Promise yourself when we leave this toilet, the Carousels will be better entertainers."

Heads nodded in agreement. Choking down putrid coffee, undercooked blueberry pancakes and watered-down maple syrup, all six Carousels grumbled our way back to the run-down Waldorf Hotel for a well-deserved nap.

Before kicking off our featured set, I said, "Create fantasy—sell illusion—project your God Power."

THIRD SET LINEUP—KATO CLUB				
SONG	ORIG'L ARTIST	GENRE	ENSEMBLE	FEATURE
Chain Gang	Sam Cooke	R&R	Standard Ensemble	Bobby—Vocal
Dream Lover	Bobby Darin	R&R	Standard Ensemble	Bobby—Vocal
Sherry	The Four Seasons	R&R	Standard Ensemble	Bobby in Falsetto, Big Joe & Lance—Vocal
Your Cheatin' Heart	Hank Williams	Country	Fiddle Solo	Lance—Vocal
Fortune Teller	Allen Toussaint	R&B	Standard Ensemble	Bobby—Vocal
Long Toes	Clifton Chenier	Zydeco	Cajun Accordion, Fiddle & Frottoir	Big Joe—Vocal Rooster, Smoke & Rocky
Moanin'	Modern Jazz Quintet	Jazz	4 Horns	Big Joe, Lance & Rocky

Walkin' To New Orleans	Fats Domino	R&B	4 Horns	Big Joe—Vocal Lance & Rocky
Comin' Home	Lee Morgan	Jazz	4 Horns	Big Joe, Lance & Rocky
The Right Time Is The Right Time	Ray Charles	R&B	4 Horns	Big Joe—Vocal Lance & Rocky

While at the Kato Club, someone Bobby met in Nashville sent him a demo recording of *"Sherry,"* months prior to its release as a single. The demo featured a relatively new group called the Four Seasons, with Frankie Valli singing in falsetto. Bobby perfected his falsetto voice, exposed the Carousels to *"Sherry"* and received standing ovations every time he performed the Four Seasons' future smash hit. Our strutting peacock—arrogant, aloof and untouchable—Bobby became addicted to audience approval. If applause wasn't loud or long enough, he would throw childish temper tantrums during breaks. However, when his gluttonous appetite for applause was satisfied, Bobby was impervious to criticism or authority—and impossible to manage.

On more than one occasion, Bobby stared right through me, like I was invisible. He began to believe his own press releases, fanatically focusing on achieving super stardom. We all knew Bobby's prep began every day around five for an eight o'clock opening. When he hit the stage, his peacock feathers strutted and a blue-collar audience responded with profuse adoration. Bobby Starr was living his dream.

In reality, I'm sure the bikers, dockworkers, auto assembly line workers and skanks thought we looked like clowns on stage, with our polished patent leather shoes and pressed tuxedos. Same for the shylocks, bookies, hookers and dope dealers who preyed on blue-collar marks. With that kind of audience anything could—and did—happen.

On Thursday, Bobby performed one of his featured show tunes, *Mack the Knife*, in the middle of the dance floor. As Bobby strutted through the performance, a biker rode his Harley through the front door, over Bobby's microphone chord and out the back door—with microphone and chord wrapped around the rear wheel of the Harley. We never saw that microphone again, and Bobby refused to do his act on the Kato dance floor anymore.

During the one-day-a-week rehearsal, a bum sprinted through the club and down the stairs to the basement, carrying a bulky black bag. As it turned out, the bum had robbed a bank and was in the process of hiding the loot in T-Bone's basement—but not for long. Snitches turned in the robber for a $10 reward—beer money. The cops judged T-Bone above suspicion, which told me T-Bone was connected. Later that week the amicable bartender, Larry Ladatta, let it slip: "T-Bone's a bagman." Based on his ambition and abilities, Larry was destined to become instrumental in our future.

A semblance of sanity emerged from insanity, supplied by those three notable prophets: Larry, Curly and Moe. Every afternoon at 4, the grainy black and white reruns of *The Three Stooges* flickered on local television. Devotees Lance, Big Joe, Smoke and Rooster replayed the afternoon Stooge routines nightly before going on stage. More than once, Rooster got Lance's finger stuck in his glass eye.

The Stooges' slapstick was exactly what we needed. From that moment forward, one of the first things we did in a new city was search the TV Guide to discover what stations re-ran *The Three Stooges*. We literally scheduled rehearsals around the reruns. Somehow, Larry, Curly and Moe helped us make sense out of nonsense.

To my surprise, T-Bone was a fascinating man, harboring qualities not normally found in a cesspool like the Kato Club. He loved classical music, opera, fine art, history and poetry, demonstrating considerable knowledge of each. He was the only diamond in the rough that shined brightly at the Kato Club.

During one of our many conversations, T-Bone offered to sponsor the Carousels. "I'm going to pay you back, Rocky. You've worked hard for me and I'm makin' money off ya. You're a good earner."

"How do you plan to pay me back?" I asked.

With a sparkle in his eye, T-Bone said, "I'll call my friends and set you up at the Flamingo in St. Paul, the Peppermint Lounge in Peoria and Club Laurel in Chicago."

"Those towns sound right. Are the clubs nice?"

"First class … jus' remember who put ya in the big time."

Within a week, I inked contracts in St. Paul, Peoria and Chicago, just as T-Bone promised. Bustin' our asses for T-Bone paid dividends. He made lots of money off the Carousels and helped us complete our northern tour in style—without paying a 10% booking agent commission. Now, I owed him.

Chapter 21

1961
FINN AND THE BAY OF PIGS

After a couple of weeks in Toledo, my skin was drier than a saguaro cactus and my hemorrhoids ached. I had an overwhelming urge to get out of the Waldorf and far away from the Kato Club. Driving to a nicer part of a stinkin' town, I arbitrarily selected a Red Lobster for lunch. The greeter seated me in a booth by a window. Immediately, a trim, yet muscular figure sat down on the opposite side.

"Finn?" I said, taken by surprise.

"Rocky Strong?" the dude responded.

"God. I haven't seen you since high school," I said. "You were a senior when I was a freshman in orchestra and concert band. I still remember you hitting high C on Sousa's *Stars and Stripes Forever*. You were great."

"And you made all-state band your freshman year," Finn replied.

We asked each other the obvious: what were we doing in a place like Toledo?

"I'm on leave, spending time with my brother," Finn said.

"On leave from what?"

"From the Army—well, a branch of the government actually. I just returned from the Bay of Pigs."

"No shit! How did you get out alive or escape a Cuban jail?"

"I learned a long time ago to never go into something like that without an exit plan. Being a maverick at heart, I've become an old hand at this—and it's saved my ass on several occasions."

I immediately asked for the details.

"I really can't talk about it, due to the super-sensitive nature of that cluster fuck. On the other hand, I'd like to bounce a couple of ideas off you, so I'll share what I can. Okay?"

"Okay," I said.

Finn began by giving me his version of what occurred at the Bay of Pigs.

"Under Eisenhower, Allen Dulles was director of the Central Intelligence Agency, and was instrumental in setting up Operation Pluto, the code name for the planned overthrow of the Castro regime. When Kennedy was elected, his brother Robert assumed control over Operation Pluto. We trained anti-Castro Cuban exiles in Guatemala. Ten of us led 1,200 lightly armed freedom fighters on to the beaches at the Bay of Pigs.

"From the beginning, there were major screw-ups. Air cover arrived early, tipping off Castro an hour before we hit the beaches. We did okay until JFK canceled all future bombing and air cover strikes. Without air cover, Castro's army, artillery and antique planes had time to mount a counter offensive. Their planes wiped out our supply ships. Castro's artillery and soldiers drove us back into the mangrove swamps.

"Left with only my dick in hand, I cursed Robert and John Kennedy for betraying my CIA brothers and the freedom fighters. Those Kennedy bastards abandoned some of America's finest at the Bay of Pigs."

"How did you get out?"

"Like I said, on missions like this one, an independent exit plan is mandatory for survival. For two days we laid in the mangrove swamps, floating in the Caribbean. When it was apparent that the battle was lost, I bailed out, stripping down to my skivvies, this

Rolex watch and a wrist compass. I swam five miles offshore to a predetermined rendezvous point. Fortunately, I hit the unlit small buoy dead on. At midnight, I met up with my buddy piloting a CIA cigarette boat. We waited five minutes but no one else made it to the boat. Today, they're either dead or in a Cuban jail. Following my debriefing at the CIA, I took my leave in Toledo."

"Incredible. And you're alive to tell the story. So, what do ya want to bounce off me?"

"I've been offered two options ... need to pick one by the end of next week."

"They are?"

"I've been offered a slot in Airborne, Ranger, and Officer Candidate schools. If I accept, probably return to Vietnam for my third tour and lead a button-down company into battle as a conventional Army officer."

"The second option?"

Finn struggled a moment to formulate a description suitable for unclassified ears. Finally, he said, "Senior CIA guys I work with are furious about the Kennedys' despicable actions ... cowards ... traitors. They should be shot for treason. To cover up their fuckups, they're looking for scapegoats, and Dulles has become their whipping boy. I suspect they'll dump Dulles, replacing him with a Kennedy minion. Rumor has it the Kennedys plan to bust up the CIA, neuter its effectiveness and minimize future political threats to their legacy, putting their self-interest above America's. They want omnipotent control with all decisions run out of the White House. It'll be a disaster."

He paused again to control his emotions.

"Anyway, reprisals are being discussed at the highest levels. We have the resources, skills, consensus and access necessary to carry off a black ops mission of major consequence—the biggest in history. It'll involve the Mafia, CIA, every sector of the U.S. government, the media, and several world leaders—all of it black ops. Lincoln's assassination will pale in comparison. Although I can't share details, those two slimy bastards could be pushin' up daisies if our guys have their way. That's the essence of my second option. Any thoughts?"

"LSU's Tiger Stadium wouldn't hold your supporters for Option 2," I replied. "If Jack and Bobby were suddenly blown away, southerners will celebrate in the streets. Wow, this is as big as it gets—you'd change the course of history. That said, your decision is way above my pay grade. At least I can appreciate your compelling attraction to the second option. Either way, you have my support—as long as it's right for Finn. In many ways, you're still hitting high 'C's' that give me shivers."

"You know Rocky, when you're really good at something very dangerous, it's difficult to find anything else that turns you on. I'm an expert killer and can dodge bullets with the best of 'em. I love my work. Some say I'm the best. I'd love to be the guy that pulls the trigger on those traitors. Who knows, I just might."

"The perfect metaphor for a life well lived," I said. "You're operating in rarefied air—the big leagues—tap dancing on a razor's edge. I appreciate the narcotic of dodging bullets and being the best at what you do. Giving that up for a traditional button-down job as an Army officer must scare the hell out of you. You'll choose wisely."

Finn finished his lobster, and I mopped up the last of my shrimp scampi. Outside the Red Lobster we hugged and strolled toward our cars. The last thing Finn said was, "If you mention this to anyone I'll have to kill ya." Smiling, he turned the key and drove away.

Finn is a man of substance—am I? My life is frivolous compared to Finn. Today is a wakeup call to accomplish something meaningful with my life. Given the dynamics of cultural change in America and music, I need to get my myopic head out of my tight-wired ass. Compared to Finn, my life is trite."

Monday morning of the fourth week, the phone awakened me from my lumpy bed at the Waldorf.

"It's Goldie—I'm in the lobby. Can I come up?"

Dazed, I said, "Sure … Room 1212."

"Yes, I know. I'm on my way."

Within a minute, Goldie materialized at my door with a worried look on her face, the gold tooth hidden behind tight lips.

"Rocky, on the long drive up I really didn't know if you'd accept me, unannounced and all, or tell me to get lost. Are you mad?"

Still in my drawers, sleepy dirt caked in my eyes, I said, "Goldie, we need a shower."

"You bet," she replied, finally revealing that '52 Buick grill of a smile. We embraced our reunion with vigor. Looking back, Goldie was a breath of fresh air in a rancid town. She went to work at a downtown nightclub, paying her way in every way. I was actually glad to see Goldie.

Six days later, with AAA maps in the hand, the Carousel caravan headed for St. Paul, ETA 2 p.m. Monday. Pushing Smoke off on Lance for the trip, I preferred Goldie next to me as we headed out of Toledo, especially since Smoke just purchased a spider monkey. I didn't relish introducing that monkey to my two cats on the trip to St. Paul. I was surprised that Lance agreed, since he just acquired a German shepherd a few days earlier to keep Angelle company. Not sure he knew what he was in for, traveling with a pregnant wife, Smoke, a dog and a monkey.

Later that afternoon, at a truck stop west of Chicago, Goldie and I ran into Big Joe and Gert. Big Joe pumped gas into his Mercury Marque. I filled up my pervertible.

Big Joe paid for his gas, and then came over to me, saying, "We're done. Wanna split a cabin? Plenty time to make St. Paul by tomorrow. Checked it out—$10 a night—$5 apiece. Ya game?"

Goldie and I also were exhausted. Splitting a cabin seemed okay. After all, we were just going to get some winks and wake up refreshed Monday morning. Goldie overheard Big Joe's question and nodded in agreement.

"Sure, Big Joe," I replied. "I assume they have two double beds— and you don't have a whistle on you, do you?"

"No whistle," he grinned. "Never share Gert. Yep, already checked it out. Two double beds, old-time springs and cotton mattress with strong iron bed frames. Anyway, it's only one night—right?"

Secretly relieved that Big Joe didn't want to play swappin' holes with Gert, Goldie and I accepted. There was no way I could get it on with Gert. Exhausted, Goldie and I were ready for a shower and zzzzz's—I handed over $5.

With Cheshire and Hatter cuddled under my right and left arms, Goldie led us into the dingy truck-stop cabin. Bare wood floors reeked of previous sins. Patches of dried blood left blotchy stains on the walls. A 50-watt bulb hung precariously from the ceiling on twisted wires, hastily tied in a slipknot to rise above our heads. The iron double beds were pre-depression era with mattresses two inches thick and exposed coil springs flattened by 50 years of abuse. The sheets appeared clean, although I suspected the bed bugs were expert at penetrating the thin, hundred-count cotton to dine on our sleeping bodies.

Bummed out, I reflected on a line from Jack Kerouac's *On the Road*: "*My whole wretched life swam before my weary eyes, and I realized no matter what you do it's bound to be a waste of time in the end so you might as well go mad.*"

Gert and Joe showered together. Goldie and I showered separately, principally because we just wanted sleep. Last to exit the shower, I noticed Gert consuming that mysterious elixir from her black coffee cup in one long gulp. Then she opened their Kama Sutra book to one of the hundred dog-eared pages. Instinctively, I knew Goldie's and my anticipated zzzzzz's were about to be usurped.

Big Joe and Gert began with the first page, proceeding sequentially through the book and providing running commentary as they executed various contortions. It was part instructive, part humorous and part grotesque. Whatever they were trying to prove, the implication was that Goldie and I should compete with them for some sort of prize.

At first, Goldie's natural shyness retained the sheet over our activity. However, the bouncing springs and panting from the next bed supplied encouragement. Gert, in between pulsating pokes, asked if we wanted to borrow their book.

Graciously declining, Goldie and I tried to remain hidden under the sheet. Try as we might, passion ultimately prevailed. Our modesty, dignity, moral code and self-respect slowly slipped away as the sheet floated to the floor. The four of us fucked away the afternoon on trampoline beds. In our final hour, joyous laughter, cries of pain, erotic screams, desperate last gasps for air and, finally, a quartet chorus of climatic explosion signaled carnal satisfaction, times four.

Lying on the cotton mattress in a pool of sweat, I covered our exhausted remains with the porous sheet. Goldie and I cuddled in heavenly peace. I whispered sweet tenderness in her ear and gently stroked wet auburn hair off her angelic face. She smiled and fell into unconditional tranquility.

The last thing I did was tend to business. Understanding Big Joe and Gert's insecurities, I rose on one elbow and said, "You guys win the pokin' contest. If I could do what you guys did tonight, I'd charge admission. Good night."

Big Joe sat straight up in bed. "I knew you'd say dat. You guys were close second. Good night."

How much lower can I go? Who is Rocky Strong anyway?

Curled up on the bare floor, Mad Hatter answered my rhetorical question: *"I've been considering words that start with the letter M. Moron. Mutiny. Murder. Mmm-malice."*

Fluffy-white Cheshire Cat purred from a corner of the mattress: *"Every adventure requires a first step. Trite, but true, even here."*

Chapter 22

1961
A TOUCH OF CLASS

Goldie and I arrived at the Flamingo Club in St. Paul on time. Bobby, Rooster, Big Joe and Gert arrived ten minutes earlier. Surprisingly, Lance, Angelle and Smoke were late. Lance was never late. My guilt welled up for dumping Smoke and his newly acquired spider monkey on Lance for the drive to St. Paul.

Laid-back Lance probably lost his cool on the drive as zookeeper, nursemaid to a bitchin' knocked-up girlfriend, and listening to Smoke's endless conspiracy theories. Thank God, I made the trip with Goldie, Cheshire and the Mad Hatter.

An hour later, Lance pulled up alone, his Bonneville filthy from road grime. His obviously spent 6' 3" frame collapsed against the car door.

Bobby, Big Joe, Rooster and I approached.

"What's up Sherlock?" I asked. "Where's Smoke, the monkey, Angelle, and your dog?"

Lance made no attempt to get out of the car. Instead, he lowered the electric window, gritted his teeth, and presented his story to four stooges standing in the alley behind the Flamingo Club.

"I'm exhausted, pissed off, and ready to kill Smoke, Angelle with a kid in the hanger, our German shepherd and that fuckin' spider monkey. The monkey threw sunflower seeds at me from the back seat—all the way from Toledo to St. Paul. Around Chicago, I stopped for gas and offered to give the monkey to a grease monkey. Smoke had a fit and threatened to stay with the monkey in Chicago. Believe me, that was not an easy choice. But, I put Smoke and the spider monkey back in the car and drove on, with a steady stream of sunflower seeds coming from the back seat as my reward. Goddamned monkey!

"If that weren't enough, Angelle had to stop every hour to throw up and piss. To top it off, the shepherd shit on my front seat floorboard carpet—the one I hand-scrubbed in Toledo to make it look new. About 60 miles south of St. Paul, I had to stop or go insane. Wheeling into a motel, we rented one room for the night. As I unloaded the car, Smoke took the monkey cage inside and opened the cage door to let the monkey get some exercise. The fuckin' monkey went straight for the closet. When I tried to hang 12 tuxedos in the closet, the monkey hissed and scratched the shit out of my hand and arm. Look at this! The fucker might be rabid!

"The monkey took over the closet and our lives. I laid the tuxedos on the floor, along with the rest of our shit. Then I looked at the monkey, Smoke, Angelle and the dog, walked out, got in my car, and drove here. Believe me, it's good to see you guys."

By that time, Lance seemed calm enough to help us unload our instruments from the trailer and haul them onto the Flamingo Club show bar stage. We performed a quick sound check without Smoke and went off to find sleeping accommodations.

Goldie volunteered to pay half our rent, all my cleaning bills and buy the food we cooked in the apartment. Searching the newspapers we found an ad from Eiger Brothers Famous Traders offering "Nice one-bedroom apartments with kitchen for rent." It was within a mile of the Flamingo Club. Goldie and I settled in to a clean, 80-year-old brownstone with hardwood floors and a small, yet adequate kitchen. This place was a major step up from the Waldorf in Toledo.

Goldie got a cocktail waitress job at the local bowling alley and made good tips. I-HOP gave Gert a server job.

Preceding opening night, Rooster and I had a long talk about tune selection. We decided to risk everything on introducing *The Pride of Dixie* to these Yankees. Rooster took the edge off the risk by saying, "If this doesn't work, I'll change our set lineups to somethin' else. However, if this works, we'll sell *The Pride of Dixie* to these northern bigots. I suspect they'll love us."

Just prior to our featured set the guys paused in anticipation of my motivation, "Create fantasy—sell illusion—project your God Power."

SONG	ORIG'L ARTIST	GENRE	ENSEMBLE	FEATURE
Jolé Blon	Clifton Chenier	Zydeco	Cajun Accordion, Fiddle & Frottoir	Big Joe—Vocal Rooster, Smoke & Rocky
Moanin'	Modern Jazz Quintet	Jazz	4 Horns	Big Joe, Lance & Rocky
Hit The Road Jack	Ray Charles	R&B	4 Horns	Big Joe—Vocal Lance & Rocky
St James Infirmary	Bobby "Blue" Bland	R&B	4 Horns	Bobby—Vocal, Big Joe, Lance & Rocky
Lonely Teardrops	Jackie Wilson	R&B	3 Horns	Bobby—Vocal, Big Joe, Lance & Rocky
Masquerade	Cal Tjader	Latin Jazz	Vibes, Guitar & Conga's	Rocky & Smoke
Willow Weep for Me	George Benson	Jazz	Guitar & Double Bass	Smoke & Rocky
Sherry	The Four Seasons	R&R	Standard Ensemble	Bobby in Falsetto, Big Joe & Lance—Vocal

THIRD SET LINEUP—FLAMINGO CLUB

Drown In My Own Tears	Ray Charles	R&B	4 Horns	Big Joe—Vocal Lance & Rocky
Proud Mary	Ike & Tina Turner	R&B	4 Horns	Bobby in Falsetto & Big Joe—Vocal
Mercy, Mercy, Mercy	Lee Morgan	Jazz	4 Horns	Big Joe, Lance & Rocky

Bobby Starr was determined to win over Minnesota's Yankees. *St. James Infirmary* and *Sherry* consistently resulted in standing ovations. Even so, Bobby's incredible five-octave vocal range delivered both Ike and Tina's parts in *Proud Mary*. Not yet done, he mesmerized the audience with his rendition of Jackie Wilson's *Lonely Teardrops,* including flawless spins and flashy dance steps, augmented by his crystal clarity on piercing high notes.

Wearing his southern persona with pride, Bobby Starr became irresistible to Minnesota chickadees. He exemplified a strutting peacock better than any man I'd witnessed. On stage, Bobby was on his way to becoming a megastar. Off, he was totally unmanageable. I chose to get out the peacock's way while in St. Paul.

Monday, Tuesday, and Wednesday, we asked Lance the obvious, "Where ya staying?"

The answer was always the same. "I can't get that goddamned spider monkey out of the closet and Smoke won't give it up. We're still at the Miller Motel 60 miles away ... really sucks."

By Thursday's rehearsal, however, Lance arrived smiling. We asked the obvious again.

"I made friends with the young day manager at the motel. I told him about our band, our travels, and the pets we accumulated on the road. He seemed interested in our lifestyle and furry companions. So I asked him, 'Do you like spider monkeys?' He said he always wanted one. So I grabbed his arm and walked him down to our motel room, telling him that spider monkeys were great pets. I offered to trade the monkey for our four-day rent, dead even. The dumb son-of-a-bitch accepted my offer. I opened the door to our motel room, opened the closet door and said, 'There's your monkey.'

"Then I commanded Angelle and Smoke to get their shit into the Bonneville, put a leash on the dog, and we burned rubber out of the Miller Motel parking lot. Yes … I'm happy. Smoke isn't so happy, except he didn't have to pay half of the motel bill. Smoke'll get over it."

A few days later Lance remembered he left the water hose and bucket he used to wash his car. Driving back to the motel, Lance collected both and dropped in on the day manager to ask about the monkey.

The monkey's new owner sheepishly replied, "I couldn't get the monkey out of the closet. Had to move from my room to that room. Still can't get that monkey out. Any ideas?"

Lance said he presented a sympathetic face, shrugged his shoulders, smiled and said, "Actually, I don't know much about the cultural habits of exotic spider monkeys. Good luck."

Upon returning to St. Paul Lance had a serious discussion with Angelle about the German shepherd. She didn't put up much resistance and, in the end, volunteered to find a suitable home for the dog. Lance was regaining some semblance of control over his life—sort of.

The Flamingo Club featured an elevated stage above a 75-foot-long crescent bar. The Carousels were the whole show, except for a Go-Go dancer. The place stayed packed every night with 300 classy patrons, standing six rows deep. All eyes on the Fabulous Carousels, including the Flamingo Club's frontman, Frederico Fabio. I addressed him as Mr. Fabio. He was a suave Sicilian, impeccably groomed and in complete command of his kingdom. Mr. Fabio did a lot of whispering in wiseguys ears as he made his way through his gold mine, smiling and shaking hands with everyone. He was a master at fronting the Flamingo Club.

Our gig coincided with the inaugural season of the Minnesota Vikings. Their first game was against the Chicago Bears, compelling Viking fans to party dressed in purple outfits. The Vikings' starting quarterback was George Shaw. Early on, Shaw was replaced by Fran Tarkenton, who passed for four touchdowns and rushed for one. Tarkenton went on to start 10 of the Vikings' 14 regular season games that year.

The Flamingo Club patrons were fanatical about their new team. Occasionally, Tarkenton showed up at the Flamingo, immediately mobbed by adoring fans. He soaked up adoration like a thirsty sponge. Purple dominated the Friday and Saturday night dress code. We even learned the Vikings' fight song.

One night, displaying an obvious tic, Smoke grabbed me during a break and led me down dark stairs to the Casbah, a subterranean nightclub in the basement. Smoke pointed out the secret rear entrance leading to the alley, requiring a private member passkey. From that moment forward, Smoke spent every break down at the Casbah, spinning yarns and gathering stories from wiseguys and their molls. Smoke had discovered his Valhalla.

As a private club, the Casbah was frequented by Mob figures, politicians, and wealthy married men, each squeezing their moll or girlfriend—all of it incognito. Private booths could easily be closed off with heavy silk curtains. Anything and everything went on behind those curtains. Belly dancers and Middle Eastern musicians provided entertainment, successfully drowning out heavy breathing and an occasional scream emoting from a private booth. The Casbah was classy, exclusive, dark and mysterious. The characters that hung out downstairs were different from the upstairs crowd. One dare not make eye contact with the downstairs crowd for fear anyone of them might be a hit man, which some were.

My focus was upstairs, dazzling the 300-plus Flamingo audiences every night. One night on a break, a well-groomed Negro approached, introducing himself as Charles Rothchild.

"I love your music and showmanship," he said. "I've never heard white boys play R&B that well, until now. But, why are those rebel flags and your slogan *The Pride of Dixie* displayed on your bass drum? Aren't you aware that some of us in the North are offended by your overt exhibition?"

I posted a big southern gentleman's smile. "We're proud of being southern, where Ray Charles, Bobby "Blue" Bland, the Big Bopper, B.B. King, and the greats got their start. Our rich heritage, traditions and culture run deep. Dixie is a beautiful state of mind. Admittedly, my definition of Dixie may differ from yours, but we love the South, and the Carousels really are *The Pride of Dixie*. We're colorblind, and our music reflects our pride and passion."

"Okay, Rocky, we may be from different cultures, although we share the same taste in music," Charles replied. "Let's leave it at that for now."

As we continued to talk, I discovered that Charles was a chemist with Dow Chemical in Minneapolis. He graduated from Northwestern with a master's in Chemical Engineering five years earlier. Charles had class, something this southern boy had never experienced in a Negro.

The following night Charles invited Big Joe, Smoke and me to join him Sunday, our day off, for drinks and partying. We readily accepted his gracious offer to meet at his private club. When Charles walked in, or, I should say, when he strutted in with a gorgeous blond white girl on his arm, my southern roots fell under attack. Perhaps my *Pride of Dixie* speech should have left more wiggle room.

Charles introduced Veronica to the Carousels, and I responded by introducing Gert, Goldie, Smoke, Big Joe and myself to Veronica. One drink down, Charles was ready to move on.

"Let's go to Minneapolis—the Turtle Club," he said. We all agreed and followed Charles and Veronica across the bridge to an unknown, yet highly anticipated destination.

Parking at the curb in a lower middle-class neighborhood, we got out and surveyed the 200 steep steps leading straight up to a two-story house at the top of the hill. Charles pointed up and said, "The Turtle Club."

There was no sign on the house to identify it as a club. Blindly, we trusted Charles, who led the way and dealt with the bouncer at the screen porch door, paying him to let the whiteys inside.

Were we sacrificial lambs?

Crossing the front porch, Charles led us into the vestibule, turned left and descended a steep flight of narrow wooden stairs, into a cavernous converted basement, now a rockin' nightclub. We cautiously followed.

We had time for one drink at the bar before the spade band took a break. Charles whispered something in the bandleader's ear and approached us with a proposition.

"You guys play some Ray Charles, Bobby "Blue" Bland, B.B. King, and James Brown for us. This crowd has never heard blue-eyed white boys play soul music. Show 'em how good you really are."

Stunned by the challenge, we tentatively nodded in agreement. Big Joe slid in behind the Hammond B-3 organ, augmented by two huge Leslie speaker cabinets. Smoke picked up the amplified Gibson hollow body, and I perched behind a Gretsch drum kit. The whites of 300 eyeballs peered out of jet-black faces, daring us to entertain them.

If we don't please this tough crowd, we're certain to never be heard from again … buried deep in the basement of the Turtle Club.

Big Joe paused, tickled the keys with a couple of arpeggios, and then began to wail *Drown in My Own Tears* by Ray Charles. The crowd was amazed. Big Joe dazzled everyone that night.

If you closed your eyes, Big Joe sounded exactly like Ray Charles, a true natural at mimicking great Negro R&B singers. For an hour and a half, Big Joe, Smoke and I entertained one of the toughest audiences we would ever face. Smoke bent his strings like B.B. King, and I provided the freight-train driving foundation with my spade bass drum syncopation beats. Our makeshift trio was a huge hit. Honestly, we loved it, too, and we got out of the Turtle Club with our lives intact. We crossed a couple of thresholds that night, the main one being our self-recognition of how good we really are. The second was to remain humble. Then again our self-esteem and confidence soared.

Chapter 23

1961
A FOOL IN HIS FOLLY

Ivan Eiger owned Eiger Brothers Famous Traders and the apartment Goldie and I rented. We were never sure exactly what Mr. Eiger was trading. Nonetheless, he was proud of his import and export business. He lived most of his days inside a Christian Brothers Brandy bottle. He rivaled Smoke in the telling of tall stories.

One day, he described his resort in upstate Minnesota. According to him, the ten resort cabins rarely rented out, so he closed down the operation. Unexpectedly, he invited Goldie and me to spend a weekend with him at his resort. In part, to challenge the veracity of his tall tales, I accepted his offer with the provision that we would not get there until dawn Sunday morning and would have to leave Monday by noon.

With food, water and kitty litter left in the apartment for my felines, Goldie and I piled into my '98 Olds following the Saturday night Flamingo gig and motored upstate Minnesota to what seemed like a mythical place in Ivan Eiger's imagination.

Arriving at the main building, he greeted us with hot coffee, scrambled eggs, Canadian bacon, and homemade biscuits. After that morning feast, we were directed to a bedroom adjoining the kitchen, where Goldie and I literally fell into the fluffiest, softest, deepest featherbed either of us had ever experienced, disappearing in waves of goose.

Slowly awakening six hours later, we heard lunch being prepared on the other side of French doors. Goldie and I climbed out of the goose down, did our toilette and sat at the kitchen table, watching Mr. Eiger put plates full of food in front of us.

"After lunch, I need your help," he said. "A storm is coming up, and we need to get the boats off the beach and into the boathouse under this building. Adolf will give you a hand."

Following ham steak and German potato salad, I went outside to meet Adolf. He was a 6' 4" German who resembled a linebacker for the Minnesota Vikings. Adolf directed me to grab my side of the 20-foot lapstrake-constructed rowboat and pull it over the logs he had placed on the ground. The boathouse was a hundred feet away, up an incline. I quickly determined that this 70-year-old German was stronger than I was. His side was always ahead of my side, so I gave it extra effort and picked up my side of the assignment.

Six boats in the boathouse, I took a breather and asked Adolf, "Do you live around here?"

"Sure 'nuf. Sixty acres," he responded. "Wonderful property the government gave me after da Indian Wars. Like to see it?"

"Gosh. Well … yes," I babbled. "When can we go?"

Adolf said, "Right after we ask Mr. Eiger if he has anything else for us."

With nothing more to be done, Mr. Eiger said he wanted to tag along and volunteered to drive. Along the way, he pointed out a dance hall built over a lake, where Ina Ray Hutton and the Melodears, an all-girl band, played during the '30s and early '40s. He commented that the movie *Some Like it Hot* was patterned after Ina Ray and her band. Other points of interest pertaining to the good old days made the trip informative and entertaining.

We drove up a dirt road to Adolf's one-room wooden house. No door, no windows, no inside plumbing and one pot-bellied stove. The walls and ceiling were plastered with newspapers, providing meager insulation. Adolf cooked most of his meals over an open pit outside or on top of the pot-bellied stove in the dead of winter.

I had to ask: "Adolf, how did you settle here and how do you spend your days?"

Adolf smiled and began his life story.

"I was hired by the government to chase drunken Indians and people who sold liquor to Indians, mostly out West. In my day, it was a crime to sell alcohol to Indians, and a bigger crime for Indians to get drunk. You probably know—when Indians drink liquor, it poisons their mind. Alcohol makes them crazy. Indians go wild when they drink hard liquor. So my job was to chase and arrest drunk Indians and the suppliers of alcohol to Indians. Wasn't paid for years. The government finally made payment by deeding me these 60 acres. This property has a trout stream, plenty of game, and I plant a garden every spring to grow fresh vegetables. Most nights I sleep 12 hours outside on the ground after reading the Holy Bible until the light goes away. On occasion, I do odd jobs for Mr. Eiger and others to earn a little spending money. I really don't need much. I have everything that is important to me right here. Welcome to my heaven."

Envious of the peace Adolf experienced, I said, "You really have discovered the true meaning of heaven. I envy you, Adolf."

Back in St. Paul on Wednesday, following rehearsal at the Flamingo, Smoke pulled me aside to have a private conversation. Smoke was anxious, blood draining out of his face and his nervous tic working double-time. We drew up a couple of chairs in the back corner of the Flamingo and faced off.

"Rocky, I've been talking to a lot of people up here, but mostly downstairs. What I uncovered over the past three and a half weeks is interesting, but that's not the reason I pulled you aside. The real problem is that the Mob is sending someone in to St. Paul to find out who is asking all these questions."

"Smoke, you can have your fun with conspiracy theories and Mob intrigue. But, one day you'll have to pay for your folly, perhaps even with your life."

Smoke grimaced. "It's not me I'm worried about. It's you."

"What are you talking about?" I snarled.

"The way the game works is I tell them something really juicy and they tell me something juicy. I told them more than I should have."

"What did you tell them Smoke? Don't bullshit a bullshitter. I'll know if you're lying."

Following a lengthy pause, accompanied by rapidly sequenced squinting of his right eye, Smoke sheepishly began, in a southern drawl whisper.

"Over the past three weeks I told Mr. Fabio's girlfriend and two wiseguys that you were Carlos Marcello's fair-haired boy. Mr. Marcello was in the process of signing the Carousels to a personal management agreement and we were destined to become stars. In return, you had an assignment—direct orders from Mr. Marcello— to be his eyes and ears up north. You're to report weekly, only to him, itemizing the action in the northern clubs. You know ... cash register receipts, skimming, drugs, prostitution, shylocks, numbers, and so on. I made you out to be a lot more influential than a simple bandleader. I said that you're a very powerful man."

My blood pressure boiled over. Grabbing Smoke's arm, I squeezed tight, forcing him to look me in my eyes. "Fuck you, Smoke. You might have signed my death warrant. Do you realize what you've done? Fuck you!"

Smoke was a fool, beyond redemption. One cannot reason with a fool.

How do I stop this fool from setting me up for the Big Sleep?

Although I finished the St. Paul gig bearing considerable anxiety, wiseguys never approached me. For the most part, nothing happened. The Carousels finished out the week at the Flamingo Club on a high note. Before going on stage for the last performance, Mr. Fabio pulled me aside, saying, "The Carousels are my highest-grossing band this year. You're welcome back anytime you can work us into your busy schedule."

At 1:15 Sunday morning, we loaded our instruments, grabbed a few winks and pulled out for Peoria. Before leaving St. Paul, I gave serious thought of blowing Smoke's brains out with Roscoe. In spite of the temptation, I decided to head to the epicenter of the Illinois Mafia: Peoria.

Termination may be the best solution for stopping a fool in his folly before we get to Peoria. Nope. I'll wait till Peoria—then I'll snuff Smoke.

On the drive, Goldie did what Goldie does best, and I finally relaxed.

With his motor running, Cheshire replaced Goldie in my lap: *"Well, some go this way, and some go that way. But as for me, myself, personally, I prefer the short-cut."*

The long drive helped me focus.

What probably happened was the wiseguys were pulling Smoke's leg, just having fun with a curious fool. Mr. Fabio never mentioned anything about the incident and he extended a gracious invitation to return to the Flamingo. I hope Smoke's folly ends in St. Paul. Too much to ask?

A hundred miles south of St. Paul, we drove into a major snowstorm—a complete whiteout. Weather reports on the car radio warned drivers to stay off all roads, including major highways and interstates. Slowly navigating two-lane state roads, Goldie and I kept driving south. With an ETA deadline, I elected to persevere.

Otherwise blind on the two-lane road, I tracked taillights of a semi for more than an hour. Growing impatient, I pulled out to pass, only to catch a glimpse of an on-coming truck—air horn blaring—bearing down on Goldie and me.

Trapped, I struggled to wrestle the Olds back in behind the semi, running out of space and time. At the last possible moment, I swung the steering wheel to the left and trusted our lives to fate and the benevolence of a ten-foot snow bank. The car plowed into the snow with an exclamation point, finally settling down. We survived, the pervertible hadn't flipped, although the trailer popped off the ball hitch and lay crippled on its side.

Subtract one. How many of my nine lives do I have left? 'Bout five by my count.

Facing the bitter cold, I climbed out of the '98 and struggled to wrap a chain over the top of the trailer and attach it to the Olds' trailer hitch. I partially deflated the rear tires of the '98, and then instructed Goldie in maneuvering the car, yelling instructions as we slowly flipped the trailer upright. Surveying the damage, I saw that the coupling on the trailer hitch was mangled. In the 55-mile-an-hour blizzard, my hands nearly frozen, I managed to chain the crippled trailer hitch to the Starfire's ball hitch. Then, for half an hour I shoveled snow using my Zildjian cymbal to create a pathway back to the road.

At last, we plowed our way back to the now-desolate road to Peoria. Immediately, I realized the trailer axle had broken loose and the right wheel and tire were suspended six feet outside the right fender, precariously hanging onto the thin axle. Fixing that was beyond my ability and patience. I had no choice, but to drive the Olds and trailer down the centerline of an eerie—and thankfully empty—highway, to allow room for the protruding axle and tire. Fortunately, we didn't meet another car or truck in route as we searched for a welder open on a Sunday.

Eventually, our search was rewarded when we saw Jake's Welding Shop. I begged Jake to fix up my screw-up. Hesitant at first, Jake's resistance began to thaw when Goldie unzipped her jacket and flashed her abundant cleavage. After Goldie displayed her sparkling gold tooth through a massive smile, the welder agreed to weld on a new trailer hitch and fix the axle. I paid Jake for his work. Goldie gave Jake a bonus—a long and very wet kiss.

From the back seat, Mad Hatter jeered, *"Do I need a reason to help a pretty girl in a very wet dress?"*

We proceeded to Peoria and the Peppermint Lounge without further incident. Little did I realize, bigger challenges awaited me.

Chapter 24

1961
SEND ME AN ANGEL

Monday at 1, I entered the Peppermint Lounge. A portly, beady-eyed Italian approached, dressed in a custom silk suit, alligator shoes, and an ostentatious tie that directed eyes straight to his crotch. A raspy voice emerged from thin lips. "I'm Mario Busoni. Welcome to Peoria and the Peppermint Lounge."

Extending my hand, I responded, "I'm Rocky Strong, leader of the Carousels. We are delighted to be with you and hope to draw huge crowds to the Peppermint Lounge during this engagement."

"We're on the same page, Rocky Strong," grunted Mr. Busoni. "Neil Sedaka will be here this weekend for two nights. I booked your group to provide Neil with great backup. Can you deliver?"

"We sure can and will," I confirmed, having heard that Sedaka was owned by the Mob and this engagement was some sort of payoff to Mario. I wasn't curious about the details, so didn't ask questions.

"Good," Mario agreed. "That's exactly what I wanted to hear. Now, set up and I'll see you tonight." Waddling away, he looked like a duck in heat. Balding on top, he stood maybe 5' 7" if he stretched.

The Peppermint Lounge accommodated a thousand patrons on a gymnasium-sized dance floor. Amazingly, the focal point of the room was a Vegas-styled, three-tiered stage. Lighting and sound were first-class, foretelling a great Carousel showcase.

We set up all our instruments to take maximum advantage of the massive stage and venue. Most nightclubs restricted our instrumentation because of their small stages. This stage accommodated everything, including my vibraphone, double bass, and several instruments we normally left in the trailer. The sound check proved the Peppermint Lounge sound system to be among the best we'd experienced. Bobby and Big Joe spent an hour positioning microphones, experimenting with reverb and familiarizing themselves with the robust features offered up by the impressive soundboard.

Meantime, Lance and Smoke explored the lighting system. Five rheostats positioned on the back wall facilitated control over brightness in five sections of the stage. Twelve foot switches neatly located in the hardwood stage distributed on/off lighting control to 12 precise areas. Lance and Smoke aimed theatrical lights and placed tape on the stage to indicate positions for each performer. Spot and peanut lights were set up for featured solo performers, and their positions were marked with tape.

Performing at the Peppermint Lounge could go a long way toward moving us along the entertainment path. Perhaps Neil Sedaka will be our stepping-stone.

Before kicking off our featured set, I said, "Create fantasy—sell illusion—project your God Power."

THIRD SET LINEUP—PEPPERMINT LOUNGE				
SONG	ORIG'L ARTIST	GENRE	ENSEMBLE	FEATURE
Peppermint Twist	Joey Dee	R&R	Standard Ensemble	Bobby—Vocal
Pretty Woman	Roy Orbison	R&R	Standard Ensemble	Lance—Vocal

Chicago	Frank Sinatra	Crooner	Standard Ensemble	Lance—Vocal
Yellow Bird	Arthur Lyman	Latin Jazz	Vibes& Guitar	Rocky & Smoke
Sherry	The Four Seasons	R&R	Standard Ensemble	Bobby in Falsetto + 3
I Can't Stop Lovin' You	Ray Charles	Country	4 Horns	Big Joe—Vocal Lance & Rocky
Sidewinder	Lee Morgan	Jazz	4 Horns	Big Joe, Lance & Rocky
Stormy Monday Blues	Bobby "Blue" Bland	R&B	4 Horns	Big Joe—Vocal Lance & Rocky
Moanin'	Modern Jazz Quintet	Jazz	4 Horns	Big Joe, Lance & Rocky
Jolé Blon	Clifton Chenier	Zydeco	Cajun Accordion, Fiddle & Frottoir	Big Joe—Vocal Rooster, Smoke & Rocky

The first weekend we backed Neil Sedaka's stage show, which brought praise from Neil, the audience, and media critics. Although Neil was generous with accolades, he had no control over which band backed him at different venues. Neil got whatever the clubs provided. He remained cordial, yet ill-equipped to be our steppingstone to Vegas, Hollywood, or a record contract.

The second week Smoke spun a story over breakfast about Albert Busoni, the retarded brother of frontman Mario. During the previous week, I noticed Smoke spending time during breaks with Albert. However, I didn't give it much thought until Smoke told me about their conversations.

"I've been able to get that dimwitted brother to spill his guts, telling everything about his brother's Mafia connections. He'll answer any question I ask. I know that Mario desperately wants to become a made man. He's a powerful man in a town of powerful men. Mario could become made in a couple of years."

All this Mob talk made me furious.

"Smoke, your hobby is out of control, beginning in Toledo as fun, expanding in St. Paul to dangerous, and currently flirting with signing our death warrants in Peoria. In this town, we'll end up inside a can of Spam. You know the Mob owns packinghouses in Peoria and Chicago. Without a body, murder charges can't be brought. Ya really want to end up as Spam?"

Sheepishly, the bucked-toothed, freckled-faced idiot shook his head in denial.

"Smoke! Look me in the eye and tell me exactly what you told the dimwit brother about me!"

Smoke's right eye blinked in double time. "Rocky, it's important they believe you're an important and powerful man. That's the only way they'll respect you and the Carousels."

Fuming, I grabbed his wrist and squeezed as I said, "The only thing they respect is their cash registers ringing—we make them money. We're great earners—that's all. Stop making them money or become a nuisance, and we're history. You've made us a nuisance. Want to die? What exactly did you tell them about me?"

Smoke brightened. "Wait a minute. When I told Albert about you being Carlos Marcello's eyes and ears in the north, Albert realized you are a lot more important than a simple bandleader. Albert believes you have the power to stop his brother from becoming a made man."

"That's the same story you put out in St. Paul. If the Busoni's check us out with Carlos Marcello, we're all dead men. Your frivolous fabrications are pure folly. Because of your stupidity, every Carousel could be sleeping with the fishes or tryin' to cut our way out of a can of Spam."

I considered what to do about Smoke while dipping my rye toast in a runny mass of eggs and sipping cold coffee with salt added to take down the edge of bitterness.

With a day of planning, I could strangle Smoke in the alley with one of his guitar strings. A "G" string will do nicely. Planting a little dope on Smoke's body would be the equivalent of a free pass in this Mob-controlled town.

Breakfast finished, I clinched my fist, pounded the table so loud that everyone in the café stared at me. Glaring into Smoke's startled pupils, I said in triple pianissimo, "Fuck you, Smoke. I'll say this once, so open up your wax-clogged ears. You will stop this conspiracy bullshit now. In spite of your talent, I'm seriously considering kicking you out of the Carousels. You've endangered our lives. If I get wind you're persisting in this folly, I'll personally snuff your ass. Want me to play the big man? I'll wipe you out, hopefully before the Mob gets to me. Do you understand? Am I crystal clear?"

Smoke hung his head, muttering, "I'm sorry, Rocky. It won't happen again."

"There's no free lunch. You buy today," I replied, throwing the check in Smoke's direction.

That night, returning to the apartment around 2 a.m., I was greeted by a sad clown face that showed signs of sobbing for some time.

"I'm pregnant with your baby. Please, Rocky. I need you. I'm desperate. I don't know what to do."

Goldie's eye makeup ran in rivers down puffy cheeks. Shaking violently, she wiped her nose with her wrist, moved toward the window, fondled the curtains and looked aimlessly out, seeing nothing but darkness.

Frozen in guilt, my guts churned as sweat beaded up on my brow. My feet felt like they'd been nailed to the floor. The immense weight of reality consumed me. Stumbling in her general direction, I gently touched her shoulder. She turned, radiating terror from a twisted face. Flinging her arms around my neck, Goldie hung on for dear life—so tight I gasped for breath. Then, like a rag doll, she went limp, 116 pounds of dead weight. One of my arms went under her bent knees, the other behind her back. I carried Goldie to the couch as she hugged harder.

Stroking her dyed auburn hair, I whispered, "You supported me in Bossier City during my most vulnerable time, especially when I'd wake up in cold sweats from horrible nightmares. Goldie, I'm here for you. I'll protect you."

Realizing that I couldn't rationalize with an irrational person, the approach I chose was to repeatedly say, "Everything will be all right." I said it over and over, 20 different ways. We cried together for a while, stopped, and then cried some more. Finally, Goldie's sobbing subsided. Still clinging tightly to my neck, she leaned back and looked me in the eye, asking, "What do we do, Rocky?"

A protracted discussion followed. An hour deep into intense list of options, a rational thread of logical choices evolved. Goldie's grimace slowly relaxed. I wetted a washrag, handing it to her. She wiped her clown face and attempted an all-too-brief smile. Rising, Goldie walked around the room, obviously in deep thought about deciding on the right thing to do. Her eyes came unglued from the floor, looking first at the ceiling then straight at me. The face I'd always thought of as a rosy cherub presented her first real smile of the night, suggesting a decision had been made.

Decisively, Goldie volunteered, "I'll get an abortion. It's the only thing that makes sense."

Awkwardly, we discussed our lack of finances, her fear of doctors and the possibility of my doing it or Goldie performing the abortion herself.

"Do you know anything about doing an abortion?" she asked.

Embarrassed, I relayed my modest involvement with Big Mama and Donna in Monroe when we buried the aborted fetus in a West Monroe graveyard.

Goldie said, "Tell me everything you know—everything about the knitting needles, air pump and outcome."

After telling what little I knew about the actual procedure, she said, "Go get those things. I'll do this myself. I'll need your support—a lot of support."

I drove to the first all-night store I could find, purchasing an air pump designed to blow up inflatable toys. I didn't miss the irony. Checking out, I asked the cashier, "Where can I buy knitting needles?"

"Ya want knitting' needles at 5 in da mornin'? Have ta have 'em now?"

Following the cashier's directions to another all-night store, I found them. Not sure which size to buy, I finally chose the longest ones and returned to the apartment for the dreaded event.

I hope she doesn't end up like Donna—a zombie.

Awkwardly, Goldie took the plastic bags containing the implements of death, held up her hand to stop me from joining her, bravely shuffled into the bathroom and closed the door. I felt lower than a worm, selfishly slithering along the hardwood floor and depositing a slimy trail of excrement for someone else to step in. My worthless, good-for-nothing soul silently screamed in self-contempt.

Everything I do seems to inflict pain and suffering on others. My folly makes waves that break things in my wake. Running from town to town, I'm running away from responsibility, ownership and consequences for my actions. Others are paying a heavy price for my folly and self-centered selfishness. I'm a certified scumbag—a fuckin' shithead.

Head in hands, I sobbed like a baby—and sobbed—and sobbed.

The next thing I remember was a loud thump coming from the bathroom. Opening the door, I saw Goldie lying face down in a pool of blood, next to the toilet. Her breathing was shallow; her pulse barely detectable. I turned her over, performed CPR and placed a folded hand towel between her legs to restrict bleeding. Soaking a full size towel in the bathtub, I rung it out and wiped off detectable horrors. Wrapping her in a fresh bath towel, I picked up a seemingly lifeless mannequin and carried her to our bed. After confirming that Goldie was still breathing, I kissed her cheek and tucked her in for a well-deserved rest.

Returning to the bathroom, my cleanup duty began. Wetting a fresh hand towel, I tied it at the back of my head, covering my nose and mouth to daunt the bitter stench of premeditated murder. Scooping up placenta with bath towels, the toilet received my confession and the bloody mess. Knitting needles and air pump got a quick rinse.

Wrestling with our sins and gargoyles in every corner, I wrapped all visible evidence in a couple of soiled bath towels and stuffed the lot in a large black garbage bag. Like a ghoul, I crept down rickety wooden back stairs to the alley below and hurled the bundle of evil consequences into a community garbage can; the only witness being an owl faintly hooting, *whoo, who-who, whoot, who, whooooooo.*

Predictably, the Mad Hatter issued his warning from the couch: *"Don't take it on an empty stomach and only one tiny little drop at a time; otherwise the experience might burst your shriveled up little heart. Got it?"*

Crisis ended for the moment, our bag of guilt hung heavy, unspoken, still ever-present, challenging our psyches on where we stood on core issues like free love, moral responsibility and right-to-life—all bombarding our souls with gargantuan shame.

Goldie didn't work the rest of that week, and we certainly didn't make love. Goldie toppled headlong into a deep abyss; depression and despair followed.

I supported Goldie throughout. In the end, we agreed: there is no free lunch. Sex was on hold, allowing space for the healing process to reconstruct body, mind and soul. Finally, time and space eased the pain, though not the memories, although we never discussed the horrors of that night again.

Goldie was a prolific poetry reader and writer, ideal background for composing song lyrics. During our moral crisis in Peoria, Goldie channeled her emotions into creating poignant lyrics, and *Send Me An Angel* was the best of more than two dozen she wrote. Reviewing her creative writing efforts provided ample opportunity to praise Goldie for her imaginative artistic beauty. I promised to share *Send Me An Angel* with the Carousels. Perhaps something positive would come from this, given that Big Joe, Bobby and Lance were lousy at lyric composition.

Sure enough, Big Joe and Lance fell in love with Goldie's *Send Me An Angel*, which, unfortunately, created yet another crisis.

Chapter 25

1961
YOUR MOVE—MY MOVE

Big Joe and Lance called a surprise meeting an hour before our last set Saturday night—preview agenda not provided.

Big Joe began, "After dis set, Lance and me leave for Nashville. Cuttin' a record. Be back Monday."

Bobby, Smoke, Rooster and I stared in disbelief.

So much for the brotherhood bullshit.

Rooster was the first to respond. "Cock suckers! You're fuckin' us. Traitors. What about the Carousels? Who's backing you up on this record?"

"The promoters set the rules," Lance said. "The big boys are making all the decisions, controlling the musical arrangements, securing the studio musicians and owning the publishing rights. Everything was set up by the big boys."

Bobby's blood boiled over. "Fuck the big boys! You're betraying us, like Judas betrayed Jesus for 30 pieces of silver."

Big Joe pushed back, "Get real or I'll *je vais te passer une!*"

"The chicken that lays the egg cackles the loudest," Rooster angrily responded. You're tryin' to stuff a *sussette noonie* down our throats and we're gaggin'. You two and a squashed roach make me *fremeers*. Fuck you guys!"

Smoke asked if there was any way to negotiate. "Can we tag along and fill in as side men?"

Big Joe shook his head.

Then it was my turn. "You can't polish this turd," I said. "Your shit's sittin' dead center in our punch bowl. This marks the first time any Carousel put self-interest above our common good.... Out of curiosity, what tune are you cutting?"

Big Joe grunted, "*Send Me An Angel* will be a male duo on side one. We have several others we're looking at for side two."

More treachery.

"Do you have Goldie's permission to cut *Send Me An Angel*?" I asked.

"Not yet," said Lance. "We'll take care of Goldie. She wrote the lyrics and she'll get royalties."

"Like you're taking care of the Carousels?" I replied.

Big Joe and Lance were resolute. Bobby, Rooster, Smoke and I recognized the futility of further discussion, but we never forgave nor forgot their betrayal.

When the last note was played Saturday night, Lance whispered in my ear, "We'll pick up our bread Monday afternoon." With that, he and Big Joe bolted for the door and disappeared on their adventure to Nashville.

Walking toward the glass-enclosed office to get our take for the week, I noticed a serious scowl on Mario Busoni's weathered face.

He can't possibly be angry with me. After all, the Carousels have been his biggest draw and produced the highest take in the history of the Peppermint Lounge. Mario should be kissing my ass for making him money. Anyway, following the Neil Sedaka success last weekend, Mario verbally renewed our contract option by extending us for weeks three and four. I'll get our money and get out of here with minimal conversation.

Offering my hand, I said, "Hi, Mr. Busoni."

Angrily, his right hand slapped my right hand, sending most of our weeks pay floating to the floor of his office. As I bent over to pick up the bills, he availed himself of my subservient position, barking over me like a pit bull.

"You're done here. Get you shit off my stage—right now. Get out of my sight."

Stunned, I rose to a standing position and responded, "What are you talking about? Last weekend you exercised the option for two additional weeks. The Carousels have been your biggest draw and made you a ton of money. We deserve your praise and respect, certainly not a slap in the face."

"Respect! What the fuck do you know about respect?" barked the rotund Italian. "Your disrespect for my brother is a slap of my face. Your guitar player has been terrorizing my brother with crazy stories and threats since you arrived. You don't deserve my respect— you have no honor. Besides, I have a seven-piece band that is out of work and will start Monday night for a lot less money than I'm paying the Carousels. They need me and they respect me. I don't need you anymore. Clear out your instruments and get out of my sight, or you'll regret it."

Oh shit, I thought, *Smoke put me in the cross hairs of the Mob and this Italian wants revenge for offending his immediate family. I need to stall.*

I said the first thing that came to mind. "The Musicians Union secretary will resolve our contract dispute. The union protects my interest and yours. The last thing you want is to be blacklisted by the American Federation of Musicians. Right? A foolish move on your part could shut down the Peppermint Lounge. Now I ask you, would that be the smart thing to do?"

While he glared at me, I grabbed the phone book on his desk, looked up the Musician Union and dialed its after-hours number. The sleepy secretary answered and I stated my case. After clearing his cobwebs, he committed to be at the Peppermint Lounge in ten minutes.

The minutes seemed to crawl by as Mario continued to glare at me until the union secretary arrived.

"Hi Sam," Mario said, grinning ear to ear. "Help me get this asshole out of my club and out of my town."

Mario looked at me as his smile consumed his face. "Sam is my nephew. He grew up in my shadow. Now what, Rocky? Let me put it to you this way: if you don't get your precious instruments off my stage, now, I'll have my boys use them for batting practice. Get your shit out of here."

At that point, I picked up the phone again, dialing the police department number that was displayed on a yellow sticker, pleading my case to the dispatcher. Within five minutes a cop with lots of gold oak leaves on the bill of his cap walked into the glass office, which had suddenly become cramped.

Mario again extended his greeting. "Sorry this shithead bothered you, Alfonso."

With appropriate hand gestures, Mario said, "Alfonso Busoni, meet Rocky Strong. Rocky, this is my oldest brother—the police chief. You already met Alfonso's son, Sam."

Mario then issued his challenge. "I understand from your guitar player that you're Carlos Marcello's private property, his eyes and ears on your northern tour. Mr. Marcello is a great man and has earned my respect, though I don't understand how this gives you any special powers. You probably aren't aware that Carlos has no authority over our turf. You're completely powerless here, a low-life musician, and expendable on my command. I'm calling your bluff. Your move, Rocky."

I did a gut check and decided to raise the stakes, all the way to the Spam factory if necessary. The glass office shrunk as I turned to close the glass door with my left hand. Continuing my turn, my right hand patted Roscoe, neatly nestled in the small of my back at the belt line—just to verify its readiness. Standing less than two feet from the Busoni trio, I manufactured a tough guy persona, assumed a formidable stance, stared each in the eye and began the biggest bluff of my life.

"We'll remove our instruments Sunday morning at 10 o'clock, with the help of your goons standing out there. However, I demand next week's pay, in cash, right now. That's the best option you're gonna get. If you disagree or if any instrument or Carousel is harmed, I promise that Mr. Marcello will personally intervene. Make no mistake, even if you kill me tonight, word will get to Mr. Marcello that he's lost a valuable asset because of three stupid men in Peoria. I can guarantee that you will never become a made man—ever.

Leaning forward, I continued. "Pay me $1,750 now and back off. Your move, Mario."

The cop took off his cap and said, "Step outside, Rocky. We need to talk about this—privately."

I opened the door and walked to the dance floor. Seeing five gorillas in the shadows was unnerving, especially since all of them were lazily swinging baseball bats. But, I had made my play and nothing more needed to be said. As I walked toward Bobby, Smoke and Rooster, I slowly slipped Roscoe out of its holster and into my outside tux pocket. I placed my thumb on the hammer and index finger above the trigger guard and left it there. My sweaty grip was tense, like a tightly wound case hardened spring—up tight.

I struggled to make sense of the situation.

With only five rounds in Roscoe, my first two will be in Mario—heart then head. Brother Alfonso gets exactly the same.... The union guy probably isn't packing, but just to be safe, the fifth round goes in his head. Have to get in close, quick aim, deep breath, and hold, relax and squeeze ... no hesitation. With all three Busoni's down, I'll grab their guns and attack the goons holding the bats. When I cut off the head of the snake, the goons will probably run for their lives. Either way, I'll blaze away until they're all dead—or I'm dead.

Who am I kidding—if I kill Marco and Alfonso, I'm a dead man walkin'. Mob hit men will snuff me before sunrise.

How paradoxical ... Smoke's folly precipitated this predicament, and I'm going to end up as a can of Spam. I should have strangled Smoke with his "G" string—too late now. There's no hole deep enough to crawl into. If Mario emerges without cash in hand, he and his brother plan to kill me. If Mario emerges alone and extends his left hand with the dough, his right hand will be free to draw his cannon, with backup from his brother's .45. If I suspect either option is about to happen, I'll make my move early and keep firing til they're stiff.

On the other hand, if Marco comes out holding greenbacks in his right hand, I may get out of this alive. To pull it off I can't afford the luxury of fear. Stay ready, stay relaxed; hand, arm, body, mind ... relax. A cool head will prevail.

I joined three wide-eyed Carousels on the dance floor, radiating high-anxiety, asking me the obvious question, "What's going on, Rocky?"

"Let me put it this way, if Mario Busoni comes out that door and hands me money, we'll be okay. If Mario emerges without cash in hand, run for your lives. Our answer will walk through that door in less than a minute. Don't ask questions—just react. You'll hear all about it later, assuming we get out of here alive. If one of us survives, call Merrill Saks and Carlos Marcello immediately. Got it?"

Bobby said, "Got it."

Our eyes stayed focused on the glass-enclosed office, observing animated gestures. Finally, heads nodded in agreement. Three Sicilians emerged, two heading for the exit. Marco walked in my direction holding cash in his right hand. With my right hand caressing Roscoe inside my tux pocket, I met Mario in the middle, maintained eye contact, extended my left hand, accepted the dough and said, "Good move. I'll see your goons at 10 later this morning."

Turning to leave, Mario grabbed my tux sleeve, saying, "If my brother and nephew hadn't talked me out of it, you'd be a dead man."

I leaned forward and whispered in Mario's ear, "I think it best we never speak of this again, particularly to our respective bosses. It's as though this never happened, okay?"

"I agree," Mario mumbled.

Motioning to Bobby, Rooster and Smoke to move slowly out the front door, they dutifully obliged. Outside, I encouraged them to go home, promising to meet them for breakfast Sunday morning and explain what just happened.

As I closed the heavy door on my convertible, my steely nerves turned to jello. Overwhelming terror manifested into violent shaking and cold chills. Shallow breathing made me light-headed, forcing me to lie down on the front seat—in hopes of remaining conscious. Tough-guy facade removed, my defenses were stripped naked.

If Mario had knocked on the window of my '98 at that moment, I would not have survived a massive coronary. Fortunately, I regained enough composure to start the engine and motor away from the house of horrors. Twenty minutes later, I reached my apartment and Goldie.

Goldie earned great money as a cocktail waitress, selecting bars that catered to traveling salesmen and businessmen on an expense account. She never worked where the Carousels played; unspoken professional courtesy and all that. Goldie ran her con during the same hours I ran mine. When her shift ended, she preferred to take a cab to our apartment, maintaining the important illusion that some drunk could get lucky and sleep between her beautiful jugs. Goldie was streetwise and played her game to perfection.

That particular night, Goldie patiently waited for two hours. We hadn't made love in ten days, and she was fearful I had latched on to a band-aid to satisfy my manly needs. Opening the apartment door, Goldie immediately sensed my anxiety, telegraphed by my trembling hands and twitching eyes. Four steps inside, Goldie offered to pour a drink.

I said, "A double Scotch on the rocks—and thanks."

Goldie was short on class, but long on compassion. That morning, all I wanted was compassion. She asked no questions, offered no advice and provided lots of space. I wrestled with my demons and refilled my glass.

I admired her capacity to supply blind comfort every time I flirted with madness. Goldie was best at creating a safe haven of security during my darkest moments. Her tender touch was my only connection to reality. On my third double Scotch, I asked myself what might have happened if Mario had chosen another option. An agonizing hour of dreadful thoughts passed over my mind's eye in slow motion.

With perfect timing, Goldie did what Goldie does best. Goldie's gold tooth was the last thing I saw before it disappeared over the object of her affection. Finally, I placed terror on hold, sighed and gave in to the tranquility of Goldie's talents and the anesthetic Scotch.

Fluffy Cheshire replaced Goldie in my lap, purring, *"All this talk of blood and slaying has put me off my tea."*

Sunday morning over breakfast with Bobby, Smoke and Rooster, I spun the events that transpired inside Mr. Busoni's office, leaving out the part about Smoke almost getting us killed, the instruments being reduced to toothpicks and pulling off the biggest bluff of my life. My spin was thin, classifying the extra week's bread as severance pay. Fortunately, placing unanticipated greenbacks in their hands didn't require much explanation.

Conversation quickly drifted to getting word to Lance and Big Joe and locating our next gig. My job was to secure a replacement gig—quick.

I asked Bobby to deal with Lance and Big Joe's betrayal.

"I'm too pissed to deal with those traitors," I told him. "Tell 'em their bread will be waiting for them at my Mom's in Shreveport."

Following breakfast we adjourned to the Peppermint Lounge with trailer in tow. The goons from the previous night were waiting for us, minus their bats. Mr. Busoni was nowhere to be seen. Trailer loaded and travel arrangements to North Louisiana discussed with Bobby, Smoke and Rooster, I picked up Goldie and struck out for Shreveport. The aroma of Mom's pot roast and her unconditional love was my homing beacon.

After lunch on the road, I called Dottie LaSalle at her home in Nashville, potentially risking a dent in my armor. However, she responded with encouragement, offering to work on getting us a gig before our scheduled return to the Black Poodle in four weeks. Our fate and future income was in Dottie's hands, at least for now.

Following a long day of driving south on a beautiful Sunday, I wheeled the '98 Starfire into Saks's Boom Boom Room parking lot. Fortunately, the doors were wide open, with big fans airing out Saturday night's sins. I sat in the car and smoked a Pall Mall while Goldie picked up her bunny outfit and ears, leaving a note for Merrill Saks that she'd be working Monday at 3 p.m. sharp.

I drove Goldie to her garage apartment in Bossier City, carrying her bags up steep stairs. Through travel-weary eyes, we silently acknowledged that our adventure had come to an end. Unspoken, we accepted our fate—it's over.

Terror and guilt devour us for our roles in what happened in Peoria. Best to give this a lot of time and space to heal.

Other than her one-way gift on the couch in Peoria, our lovemaking had been on hold. As if on cue, Goldie flashed her sparkling gold tooth with a twinkle in her eye. I returned a welcoming grin. Volumes were spoken, yet words were absent. Simpatico in the moment, we resurrected her beloved *Inverted Kama Sutra* renderings, consummating in the shower. Exhausted, we stared at the bathtub drain, watching our dirt, grime and contemptuous sins whirlpool down a pipe to the sewer below. I couldn't help but wonder if my life was headed down that drainpipe.

Our chapter has ended, depositing an indelible residue of stained memories for the remainder of our lives.

Early Monday morning, I drove across the Red River to Mom's love and breakfast. Hugs and kisses welcomed me at the door, along with promise of a big home-cooked meal that night.

Thank God I'm home and safe.

Monday afternoon, Dottie called Mom's phone number. I answered. Dottie inquired whether we could open in Louisville the following Monday for a three-week engagement at the Office Lounge. The money was right and the timing was perfect. Our opening day coincided with Derby Week. Dottie said the club was located in an upscale shopping mall near Churchill Downs. I quickly accepted the terms of the contract.

Making calls to Bobby, Rooster and Smoke was easy. Since Big Joe and Lance had not called to pick up their bread, I anticipated a confrontation. Still furious with their treachery and betrayal, I decided to keep my powder dry until the right moment presented itself.

They finally called Tuesday afternoon. Neither they nor I mentioned the Nashville recording session, but they were elated with opening Monday in Louisville. The idea of playing near Churchill Downs during Derby Week struck a positive chord. Conversations quickly transitioned to picking up juice money. In the end, each preferred I hold their cash til Louisville. There'd be a right time to collect suitable retribution for Lance and Big Joe's disloyalty.

Said my three-legged Mad Hatter: *"You're not the same as you were before. You were much more … muchier. You've lost your muchness."*

The Cheshire Cat responded, *"Most unpleasant metaphor. Please avoid it in the future."*

Chapter 26

1962
DERBY TOWN

Reggio Greco, manager of the Office Lounge, met us Monday at 1 for orientation and set up. Black on black with sparse accents of red, the Office Lounge décor was perfectly suited for customers who wished to be incognito with their lovers. The shopping center developer and owner of the Office Lounge spent a lot of money turning this place into a class act, boasting an excellent stage layout, sound system, lighting, and professional management in the name of Reggio Greco.

Dottie LaSalle drove her new, white 1962 Cadillac convertible to Louisville, welcoming us on opening night. The Carousels achieved rave reviews, and Dottie took most of the credit for her brilliance and trust she maintained with high-end club owners. She needed my praise to bathe her fragile ego, in addition to the ten percent commission I was paying her. I spun her up with lavish compliments, overusing the word brilliant several times when describing her booking agent talents. It worked.

She believed everything I said, largely because she wanted to. With her bleached platinum blond hair, toothpick skinny frame, tits the size of fried eggs, and an expensive white dress to cover it all up,

Dottie beamed with pride and self-importance. She was queen for a night, taking full credit for discovering the Fabulous Carousels and permitting Reggio Greco to benefit from our magic spell.

On our first weekend, Smoke, Rooster, Bobby, and I went to America's premier horse race—the Kentucky Derby—to soak in the grandeur of the Sport of Kings. With mint julep in hand, Dunhill lighter flashin', and a fashionable cigarette holder supporting a black coffin nail, Smoke led our way into ostentatious self-delusion. A Panama hat added a rakish look to his wardrobe.

We bought programs and studied statistics like seasoned gamblers. In the end, Rooster bet on his favorite color: brown. Bobby went for the highest odds. Smoke bet the trainer. My $10 bet went on jockey Bill Hartack, ultimately returning about $90 to my poke. Smoke's bet on Roman Line, with Tennessee Wright as trainer, paid just under $40 on a $4 bet to show. Bobby's and Rooster's pockets were lighter by $10 each. Overall, the adventure added to our education and savoir-faire.

Perhaps because thoroughbred racing was in full swing at Churchill Downs, we broke the Office Lounge record for highest cash register take. To everyone's amazement, the following week started off even better.

We had fallen in a bucket of shit in Peoria and come out smelling like roses in Louisville. Were the Carousels this good or just lucky?

Before kicking off our featured set, I said, "Create fantasy—sell illusion—project your God Power."

THIRD SET LINEUP—THE OFFICE LOUNGE				
SONG	ORIG'L ARTIST	GENRE	ENSEMBLE	FEATURE
Yakety Yak (Comedy)	The Coasters	Pop	Standard Ensemble	Bobby, Big Joe & Lance—Vocal
Cathy's Clown	The Everly Brothers	Pop	Standard Ensemble	Big Joe & Lance—Vocal

Soul Bird (Tin Tin Deo) Whiffenpoof	Cal Tjader	Latin Jazz	Vibes & Conga's	Rocky—Vibes
Funny How Time Slips Away	Jimmy Elledge w/ Big Joe Jazz Arrangement	Pop—Big Band Jazz	4 Horns	Bobby—Vocal, Big Joe, Lance & Rocky
Sidewinder	Lee Morgan	Jazz	4 Horns	Big Joe, Rocky & Lance
Stormy Monday Blues	Bobby "Blue" Bland	R&B	3 Horns	Big Joe—Vocal, Lance & Rocky
Just a Gigolo	Louis Prima	New Orleans	3 Horns	Bobby—Vocal, Big Joe, Lance & Rocky
For Your Love	Ed Townsend	Pop	Standard Ensemble	Lance—Vocal
Stand By Me	Ben E. King	Pop	Standard Ensemble	Bobby—Vocal
Watermelon Man	Herbie Hancock w/ Mongo Santamaria Arrangement	Latin Jazz	4 Horns + Conga	Big Joe, Lance & Rocky

The diversity of our audiences spanned the globe, with racing enthusiasts flying into Louisville for Derby Week and remaining for much of the racing season. The Office Lounge was a magnet, drawing sophisticates and the money crowd. Although I'd played *Whiffenpoof* many times in many clubs, my velvet tone, four-octave Deagan vibraphone yielded the longest and loudest applause at the Office Lounge. *Whiffenpoof,* from Cal Tjader's *Soul Bird* album, required four- and five-mallet chords combined with long, intricate two-mallet runs.

Normally, good technique was enough, but I took it to another level with the addition of dramatics. Yarn-covered mallets on thin bamboo shafts waived wildly on technically easy parts—lots of show. Elbows waiving like chicken wings, hands jumping over the tops of one other, exaggerated body, and face gestures—the whole dramatic scene played out during easy passages. On the other hand, to get through technically difficult passages, I abandoned dramatics and emphasized good technique. Candidly, when compared to the great vibe men, my dramatics were the only differentiator—rehearsed showmanship during live performance.

On break, a well-tanned man dressed in a Palm Beach white linen suit, blue pocket scarf, blue shirt, and yellow-and-blue polka dot tie approached.

"Great vibe work, Rocky," he said. "Have you ever considered moving to New York?"

"Why do you ask?"

"I produce Broadway shows and jazz records. Actually, my money comes from Broadway, although I spend far too much on my fetish—great jazz. Ever hear of Blue Note records? I'm a silent partner.

"Impressive," I replied.

"Louisville is the thoroughbred racing capital of the world. New York is the Broadway show and jazz capital of the world. If you want to be recognized as a great musician, you're simply in the wrong town. Your mallet work is exceptional. Cal Tjader, Milt Jackson, Red Norvo, and newcomer Gary Burton could use some competition. Are you up to that? Want to move to New York?"

"Tell me more."

"You'll gig in the pit orchestra of *Hello Dolly* while you put together an album for Blue Note. I'll be your sponsor."

"That's a very generous offer," I said. "Deeply appreciated. However, I'm on the road with the Carousels, with steady bookings for six months. What about moving the band to New York?"

"Nope. I'm only interested in you and perhaps your guitar man. What about it?"

"Perhaps someday—but I can't commit right now. Perhaps in a few months. Give me your card and I'll call when the time is right. Okay?"

"Ya know—very few people turn me down. Here's my card. When you call, tell my secretary you are the vibe man from Louisville.

That'll get your call through to me. In the meantime, you hammer good mallets, Rocky. Will you play Tjader's *Spring Is Here?*"

"You bet—upcoming set."

As a result of that brief conversation, I told Rooster to increase the number of vibe tunes in our Louisville sets. Admittedly, my ego lapped up praise like an alley cat on cream.

Another surprise surfaced during our Louisville gig. Joseph "Big Joe" Robecheaux and Gertrude "Gert" Brown co-signed a note to purchase a new, 28-foot travel trailer and a brand new Jeep truck with four-wheel drive and towing package. They were exceedingly proud of their new home and Jeep, well past the bragging point. Their insecurities were showing, so I spun them up to believe we all loved their trailer and truck.

Not to be outdone, Lance Love, Angelle Devero and Norman "Smoke" Van Dyke co-signed a bank note for a custom, two-bedroom 42-foot house trailer designed and built at a Louisville factory. Actually, since Lance had declared bankruptcy two years earlier, Smoke and Angelle's credit probably made the difference. Just glad Lance hadn't asked me to co-sign.

Smoke designed his front bedroom and private bath. Several of us considered Smoke's blueprint layout peculiar. Even before it was built, we called Smoke's 8 by 10-foot domicile the bat cave. Lance and Angelle designed the remaining 32 feet, which included a full kitchen, dishwasher, upscale appliances, washer and dryer, and several premium furnishings. Lance traded in his Bonneville on a new Chevrolet 2500 truck with towing package, manual stick shift on the floor and four-wheel drive, financing the truck at the same bank he used to fund the trailer purchase. The customized 42-footer would be ready in nine weeks, coinciding with the end of our Atlanta gig.

Observing from the windowsill of my Louisville apartment, Mad Hatter purred, *"Yes, yes—but you would have to be half-mad to dream me up."*

CHAPTER 27

1962
THE SHOW MUST GO ON

On our return trip to Saks's Boom Boom Room, Merrill Saks secured a special rate for us to room at the Town and Country Motel, the pretentious, quasi-classy, one-story sprawling motel on the Bossier Strip owned by Carlos Marcello. In addition to the Carousels, the Town and Country residents included strippers, hookers, B-girls, other musicians, assorted subterraneans, weekend partiers from Arkansas, Oklahoma and Texas, and traveling salesmen looking for a memorable time. The Town and Country also harbored horrific memories for me—nightmares of Nervous' madness.

Merrill continued to be the perfect frontman: suave, super dresser, good businessman, all-knowing about which cops to pay off and demanding his B-girls get their red cards punched every two weeks. A different custom-made tie with solid gold and silver threads glistened on his chest every night as he ruled over his empire. Merrill sported a gargantuan ego that dimmed the neon lights out front. He could charm the hood off an executioner.

He catered to the Carousels and me because we were great earners, his biggest draw. I monitored the Boom Boom Room cash register receipts by bedding Caroline, the head bartender. A running tally of nightly receipts came in handy if I ever wanted anything from Merrill. Although he went out of his way to make us happy by opening up the bar and his B-girls to the Carousels on Saturday nights, I knew he was all business when it came to money and contract commitments—tough and tight. Fortunately, I also knew where Merrill's line in the sand lay and I never crossed it, although I pressed it hard.

Before kicking off our featured set, I said, "Create fantasy—sell illusion—project your God Power."

THIRD SET LINEUP—SAKS BOOM BOOM ROOM				
SONG	ORIG'L ARTIST	GENRE	ENSEMBLE	FEATURE
Cold Sweat	Mongo Santamaria	Latin Jazz	4 Horns + Conga	Big Joe, Lance & Rocky
I Pity The Fool	Bobby "Blue" Bland	R&B	3 Horns	Big Joe—Vocal, Lance & Rocky
String of Pearls	Glenn Miller	Big Band	4 Horns	Big Joe, Lance & Rocky
Bring It On Home To Me	Sam Cooke	R&B	Standard Ensemble	Bobby—Vocal
Big Girls Don't Cry	The Four Seasons	R&R	Standard Ensemble	Bobby in Falsetto, Big Joe & Lance—Vocal
Ramblin' Rose	Nat King Cole	Crooner	Standard Ensemble	Lance—Vocal
Alligator Purse Avec	Michael Doucet	Zydeco	Cajun Accordion, Fiddle & Frottoir	Big Joe—Vocal Rooster, Smoke & Rocky
Spring Is Here	Cal Tjader	Latin Jazz	Vibes, Guitar & Conga's	Rocky & Smoke
Stand By Me	Ben E. King	R&B	Standard Ensemble	Bobby—Vocal
Working in the Coal Mine	Allen Toussaint	R&B	Standard Ensemble	Big Joe—Vocal

Lance's velvet voice was ideally suited for Nat King Cole's hit, *Ramblin' Rose*. His purity of resonance, tonal quality and phrasing were impeccable. Lance piggybacked effectively on Bobby's voice, guaranteeing applause every time from an adoring audience. We generally positioned Lance's ballad in the middle of our sets, bookended with up-tempo tunes. Band-aids gawked stage side, audibly sighing with desire.

On more than one occasion, Lance discreetly accepted band-aid overtures, taking maximum advantage of the Pit, the world's darkest room, located in the rear of Saks behind the massive main bar.

His explanation: "Might as well harvest boo coo honey from the big garden while the queen bee's a buzzin' in the hive."

Rooster preceded the start of our rehearsal with his wisdom of the day. "Did you know that in the human body there is a nerve that connects the eyeball to the anus? It's called the anal optic nerve, and it's responsible for giving people a shitty outlook on life. If you don't believe me, pull a hair out of your ass and see if it doesn't bring tears to your eyes."

Before kicking off the Friday's first set, Merrill buttonholed me to announce his latest attraction.

"Rocky, on Monday I'm bringing in a blond bombshell that captivated the Biloxi Gulf Coast and New Orleans. Her name's Venus Cruz, and she's breathtakingly beautiful—but also private property—and requires special handling. Venus will be here Monday afternoon for rehearsal, and I want you to make her happy. She's been working for friends of ours on the Gulf Coast and New Orleans."

I knew exactly what Merrill meant by "friends." That evening, I shared the news with the Carousels. Big Joe was the first to respond, growling, "She's yours to manage. We'll back her, but I won't kiss her ass."

Smoke was much more enthusiastic. "If we do this right, Merrill will set up a personal management contract with Carlos Marcello. This is a real opportunity to move up."

Monday afternoon we arrived on time for rehearsal. Venus Cruz was late. Rooster and Bobby complained about playing second fiddle to a chick. Big Joe and Lance added their frustrations to the mix. Twenty minutes inched by. Impatiently, we waited for the tardy bombshell to show.

Twenty-five minutes after the established start time, Venus finally walked through the Boom Boom Room door. Six jaws dropped and 12 eyeballs popped out like pipe organ stops. She astounded all with her beauty, gracefully strutting down the massive dance floor like a high-fashion model on a Paris runway. We all took pleasure in watching her jiggle. Venus was a Barbie Doll, complete with big hooters. Her lips glistened as if she just licked them. Her silky blond hair, baby smooth skin and makeup by Merle Norman framed piercing blue eyes. Yep—she had alluring charms that tantalized the imagination.

Venus spoke in a soft, sensuous voice, "Is Rocky Strong here?"

I closed my gaping mouth, gulped, took two steps forward, extended my hand in welcome, peered into her baby blues and said, "I'm Rocky. Welcome to Saks's Boom Boom Room and the Carousels. Nice to meet you, Venus."

Her delicate porcelain hand slipped easily into my clammy, callused paw. I loved touching her, even in a simple handshake. With my left hand I motioned to the guys behind me and said, "Let me introduce you to the Carousels." Ushering her down a makeshift receiving line, I said, "Meet Joseph 'Big Joe' Robecheaux—lead vocals and music arranger; Lance Love—bass, sax and lead vocals; Bobby Starr—emcee, lead vocals and drums; Marion 'Rooster' Badcock—keyboards and tune caller; and Norman 'Smoke' Van Dyke—all strings and choreography."

Venus gracefully took their right hands in turn, placing theirs in hers and covering both with her left hand in a gentle caress. Venus's beauty broke down all barriers, sweeping away all remaining resistance as she said to each, "I'm delighted to meet you," repeating their names, progressing the routine down the receiving line.

Big Joe broke the ice. "What's ya show, tunes, keys, tempo and routine?"

From her opera clutch, Venus handed Big Joe a paper, laying out two complete shows. The paper contained the names of each tune, key, tempo and director notes. Big Joe studied it and said, "Let's start at da top and shorthand dis. Da firs' is *Just a Gigolo* in the key of G. Tempo is 120 beats per minute. Rooster, give us da melody line and tempo."

Each of us went to our respective instruments and began filling in around Rooster's lead. Big Joe walked over to Venus and said something we could not hear. She nodded an agreeable smile, picking up a portable microphone and began singing *Just a Gigolo*.

Venus didn't have a strong voice. In fact, Bobby had to turn up the volume on the PA system to achieve adequate amplification and projection. And we had to turn down our instrument volume—a lot. Venus's voice was more sensual than strong—in the style of Peggy Lee. The first run-through she sang it straight. The second time she moved to the middle of the dance floor and went into character, delivering a professional entertainer's presentation that made you forget her thin voice. Venus had all the moves and tools. She was captivating, even in rehearsal.

We rapidly went through her list of tunes, one by one, using musician shorthand to compress and accelerate the rehearsal process. Big Joe and Venus directed nuances, dynamics, entrance and exits. Venus appeared satisfied with the Carousels and said so through her gestures and approving smile—sufficient reward coming from a goddess.

As we approached the end of the rehearsal, Venus asked us to join her on the dance floor. We obediently assembled. She led us through the way she wanted introductions and how to handle encores and exit speeches. Big Joe appointed Bobby to handle emcee work. Then Bobby and Venus sat together at the nearest table and worked out the script.

As we were about to wrap things up, a strange man entered the room and walked toward Venus. He appeared to be Hispanic—a rarity for North Louisiana. The spic was not particularly attractive or special in any way. Unexpectedly, Venus announced without fanfare or discernable emotion, "This is Luis, my husband. He led our Latin show band in Biloxi and New Orleans. Luis is a reed man."

Curiosity satisfied, that ended that.

Following rehearsal, as Rooster and I walked out the front door Rooster said, "That spic must have a joystick the size of a telephone pole to keep that gorgeous creature hanging around."

I nodded in agreement, wondering how much truth there was in Rooster's penetrating philosophical statement.

Before kicking off our featured set, I said, "Create fantasy—sell illusion—project your God Power."

VENUS CRUZ'S FIRST STAGE SHOW				
SONG	ORIG'L ARTIST	GENRE	ENSEMBLE	FEATURE
Just a Gigolo	Louis Prima	New Orleans	Standard Ensemble	Venus
Bill Bailey	Bobby Darin	R&R	Standard Ensemble	Venus
Fever	Peggy Lee	Jazz	Standard Ensemble	Venus
Jock-a-Mo	Sugar Boy	New Orleans	Standard Ensemble	Venus
Peel Me a Grape	Peggy Lee	Jazz	Standard Ensemble	Venus
Our Day Will Come	Ruby & The Romantics	Light Jazz	Standard Ensemble	Venus
Do You Know What It Means To Miss New Orleans	Pete Fountain Style	New Orleans	Standard + Clarinet	Venus & Big Joe
Hit The Road Jack	Ray Charles	R&B	3 Horns	Venus

That first evening, Venus's performance delivery was flawlessly professional. The Carousels backed her show without a hitch. Obviously, she had received dramatic training, delivering compelling gestures of a seasoned stage performer. Dancing and moving with grace, class, and jiggle in all the right places, she was incredibly sexy. My impressions were that Venus was destined for much bigger things than North Louisiana. She possessed special talents and knew how to leverage these attributes to best advantage.

Surprisingly, the Bossier crowd never warmed up to Venus. The consensus of some of our regulars: "Venus Cruz is a bit too sophisticated for us rednecks. She needs to be in Vegas or on TV."

I was sure rednecks of North Louisiana had never seen a woman as perfect as Venus Cruz. Every night Merrill, the Carousels, bartenders and the B-girls complimented Venus on her terrific performance and beauty. We all liked her, in spite of the redneck audiences remaining lukewarm.

Between shows, Venus sat in a small room just off stage and to the right of my drum kit. I felt her eyes on me—all the time. I lapped up her adoration like a suckling infant, loving every moment. My performance on stage commanded most of my focus, but I always felt the penetrating warmth of her baby blues. She only came out of the back room for her two shows a night; otherwise, she remained back stage and stared at me. We rarely spoke more than a couple of passing words.

The week rolled on, and we changed a few numbers in her show to reel in the rednecks. Unfortunately, Venus's act never caught fire in Bossier. Polite applause was the best she got.

On Saturday, during the break prior to her final show, Venus came out of the back room and grabbed my arm, leading me to an isolated corner. With great tenderness she placed my hands in hers, looked into my eyes, saying nothing for a full minute. Then she spoke directly from her soul to my soul.

"Rocky, I couldn't take my eyes off you all week. I love watching you move. I dream about how it would be with us."

Dumbstruck, I struggled to find the appropriate response. I knew I didn't have those feelings for Venus—lust yes; love no.

Venus is one of the most beautiful women I've ever seen. Of course I want her, but at what price? She's married. Perhaps my lack of interest turned her on. On the other hand, her possible ties to the Mob, her marriage thing, leaving tomorrow for Las Vegas with her husband, and gettin' my horn waxed most nights are legitimate reasons to take pause. I have to get a grip on my emotions and not cave in. If I'm to err it must be on the side of caution. Besides, this really is too much to digest in one gulp.

Two long deep breaths later, I looked Venus Cruz in her baby blues with all the compassion I could muster and said, "Venus, I had no idea you felt this way. However, this is more than I can handle. An impossible situation. You're leaving with your husband for Vegas in the morning. There's no time to deal with this, at least right now. What can we do?"

Squeezing my hands in hers she said, "I don't know what to do, Rocky. You figure something out, and I'll come to you. All I know is I want to be with you."

Venus had to begin her final stage show in less than two minutes. I took out my Carousel business card, handed it to Venus and said, "My mother's home address and phone number are on this card. When you get set up in Vegas, drop me a line with your new address and phone number. I'll contact you."

Venus took the card, smiled and said, "Anything you say, Rocky. I think I love you."

Letting go of Venus was like letting go of a high trapeze without a safety net. I slowly turned and strolled the length of the dance floor.

"I must be dreaming. Did I just hear what I think I heard? Oh well, I may never see her again. Anyway, she's probably a femme fatale.

I forced a smile as I entered the bright stage lights, stepping up and on.

Before we kicked off the set, Lance grabbed my sleeve, shielded the microphone with his hand and said, "I'm going to miss Miss Goodbody. She's really something else. If I ever get the opportunity to crawl in the sack with that, I promise you: she'll never leave my bed. I'll put a permanent smile on her kisser."

Lance had no clue that Venus had a thing for me—not him. I saw no point in pissin' on Lance's fantasies, so I let it slide, manufactured a grin, climbed into my Slingerland drum kit and said, "Kick it off, Bobby!"

Arriving at my motel room, three-legged Hatter groused, *"The Jabberwock, with eyes aflame, Jaws that bait and claws that catch. Beware the Jabberwock, my son, the frumious Bandersnatch! —He took his vorpal sword in hand. The vorpal blade went snicker-snack. He left it dead, and with its head he went galumphing back…. Rocky, it's not all about you, you know."*

Chapter 28

1962
EARNING NASHVILLE'S RESPECT

The Black Poodle Club in Printers Alley was the top show place for any band and particularly well suited for the Carousels. Two weeks prior to our second gig there, Dottie LaSalle convinced her brother Larry, manager of the Black Poodle, to insert display advertisements in the entertainment section of the newspaper: *"Fabulous Carousels Return to Printers Alley December 2."* We opened to standing-room-only crowds and lines of hopeful patrons 20 yards down the Alley. Dottie also lined up two radio interviews and a television interview on a noon program.

During their breaks, Boots Randolph and Chet Atkins became regulars at the Black Poodle. We frequently reciprocated with visits to their club, ironically called the Carousel Club.

A mutual admiration society among professional musicians developed, shared openly through the house sound system upon entry by the stars to our club and the Carousels to their club. We couldn't pay for better endorsements. Although Printers Alley offered seven great clubs within a two-block range, audiences tended to oscillate between the Black Poodle and the Carousel Club. Our mutual admiration society boosted audiences, increasingly made up of the Who's Who from Music Row: session musicians, record promoters, arrangers and recording engineers and legitimate big-name stars who called Music City their home.

Before kicking off our featured set, I said, "Create fantasy—sell illusion—project your God Power."

THIRD SET LINEUP—BLACK POODLE				
SONG	ORIG'L ARTIST	GENRE	ENSEMBLE	FEATURE
La Danse de Mardi Gras	Clifton Chenier	Zydeco	Cajun Accordion, Fiddle & Frottoir	Big Joe—Vocal Rooster, Smoke & Rocky
All Blue	Miles Davis	Jazz	3 Horns	Big Joe, Lance & Rocky
The Thrill Is Gone	B.B. King	R&B	3 Horns	Big Joe—Vocal, Lance & Rocky
Crying	Roy Orbison	R&R	3 Horns	Lance—Vocal, Big Joe & Rocky
Masquerade	Cal Tjader	Latin Jazz	Vibes, Guitar & Conga's	Rocky & Smoke
Crazy (Comedy Routine)	Patsy Cline (Parody)	Country	Comedy Parody	Bobby in Falsetto
Willow Weep for Me	George Benson	Jazz	Guitar & Double Bass	Smoke & Rocky
Sherry	The Four Seasons	R&R	Standard Ensemble	Bobby in Falsetto, Big Joe & Lance—Vocal
A Taste Of Honey	Herb Alpert & The Tijuana Brass	Pop	4 Horns	Big Joe, Lance & Rocky
Drown In My Own Tears	Ray Charles	R&B	3 Horns	Big Joe—Vocal, Lance & Rocky
Working Together	Ike & Tina Turner	R&B	3 Horns	Bobby in Falsetto Big Joe—Vocal, Lance & Rocky

Cold Sweat	Mongo Santamaria	Latin Jazz	4 Horns + Conga	Big Joe, Lance & Rocky

Bobby's falsetto voice found new disciples for his brilliant parody of Patsy Cline's *Crazy*. Using only a bobbed black wig as prop, Bobby underwent a metamorphosis, becoming Patsy Cline in the flesh. Machismo abandoned, Bobby licked his little finger, daintily brushed back his eyebrows, and went feminine. Having studied Patsy's gestures from television clips, Bobby delivered all her moves with perfect precision.

Every eye in the audience was glued to our performing peacock. When Bobby's tongue licked the microphone while singing the lyric, *Crazy—for thinking that my love could hold you* ... (lick, lick, lick), the audience went wild in laughter, then stood in prolonged applause. In a town of country and western megastars, Bobby's parody became the talk of Nashville. Our peacock strutted above mere mortals.

Not surprisingly, Big Joe became jealous of Bobby for stealing his spotlight. Big Joe's natural charisma began to tarnish as he tried too hard to regain his role as alpha dog. Though Big Joe was enormously talented, the rest of us knew he was forcing himself on the audience, sacrificing allure, fantasy, and likeability in search of emotional acceptance. His insecurities were showing. Overall, the Carousels gained ground as Big Joe struggled to recapture his moment in the spotlight.

I created a strategic plan for attacking Music Row and its record producers, publishing companies, studio musicians, A&R men, and recording studios. My focus was to secure a record deal, a hit record, and album. To maximize potential effectiveness, I assigned Bobby, Big Joe, Lance, and Rooster to cultivate specific targets. Their objective was to open doors. They eagerly began their assignments. Big Joe saw this as his opportunity to regain our respect, which he'd never really lost in spite of suspecting he had. Off he went to prove his self-worth.

Assigning Smoke the task of gathering intelligence was right up his alley. His job was to discover names, titles, decision-makers, the going rate for studio musicians, rates for recording sessions, royalty percentages paid for lyricists, melodies, and original recordings. Smoke threw himself into his assignment.

Dottie welcomed my invitation to participate in securing a record deal. Of course, the potential of a ten percent commission brightened her baby blues. Dottie and I made rounds, gaining access to some of the giants in the record business. Based on the audience Dottie identified, I sensed our actions offered the best potential for producing a record contract. The seeds were planted, and each Carousel diligently watered and fertilized their assigned rows.

Our collective efforts produced two recording sessions backing wannabe artists, four new-tune demo sessions for publishers and two self-demo tapes of Carousel original material. We were learning the record business, becoming regulars at Owen Bradley, Mercury, Capitol, RCA Victor, Studio B, Columbia, and Decca studios.

Individually, most of us achieved some success. Chet Atkins offered me sideman session gigs on two occasions. However, my focus was on recording the Carousels as a unit. In my mind the road to stardom ran through Nashville, and the Carousel bus was our best vehicle. Even Big Joe and Lance bought into the concept of riding the Carousel bus to stardom. Admittedly, their attitudes were influenced by their failed attempt to go it on their own a few months earlier.

Our contract called for a six-week engagement at the Black Poodle to include a weeklong break for Christmas, re-opening New Year's Eve, and playing out the first week of January. This provided an opportunity to spend Christmas with our families in North Louisiana. I called Abie Goldstein and secured two dance gigs Christmas week, at good money, fully funding our payroll and trip to Louisiana. Before leaving for Shreveport, I mailed a letter to Venus's secret post office box in Vegas, reporting our progress, wishing her Merry Christmas, and inviting a rendezvous.

Back in Nashville for New Year's Eve, we played out our contract with immense satisfaction. Dottie booked us back for a midsummer opening at the Black Poodle. Saturday night, we packed up and left with smiles on our faces and maps in hand, headed for Atlanta.

On the 250-mile drive, Smoke sat shotgun, pontificating on the same tired yarns. I knew Smoke's story inside and out, tuning his volume down to triple pianissimo for the duration of the trip.

As Smoke droned on and on, Mad Hatter looked at me through his blue and brown eyes. I was never sure which eye to focus on—certain the answer lay in my subconscious predisposition as to whether I was looking for sunny or shitty commentary. I focused on the brown eye.

Hatter's motor ran: *"I thought all you guys were wiped out years ago.... Why do I always have to be the Mad Hatter? Why can't you be the Mad Hatter for once? Oh, all right, I'll be the Mad Hatter again! You like hats? I'm mad about hats! Well, then, I rest my case!"*

Between Smoke's rambling and the Mad Hatter's philosophical observations, I began daydreaming.

I'm pretentious, fallaciously operating under Kerouac's influence. Be that as it may Jack used drugs to minister to his madness. I'm on my own, much too sober to exploit this magnificent opportunity; an oddity among subterraneans. Time to let go—laissez les bon temps roulez—before it's too late. Live more, laugh more, and love more ... that's the ticket.

Entering Kerouac's mind revealed insights fraught with risks. In *On the Road,* a brief dialogue between Dean and Sal came to mind: *"Sal, we gotta go and never stop going til we get there." "Where we going, man?" "I don't know, but we gotta go."*

Chapter 29

1962
36 TAILORED TUXEDOS

Two months earlier, Abie Goldstein had mailed us a contract outlining a four-week booking at the Casbah in Atlanta, in part to make up for what we called the Toledo toilet treatment. The money was right, particularly given that it was for a five-night-a-week gig. Favorable hours consisted of three-and-a-half hours Tuesday through Thursday, and four-and-a-half hours on Friday and Saturday. The Casbah was located in an upscale shopping center in Buckhead. Expensive Middle-Eastern décor was augmented by a gourmet menu—lots of shish kabobs flaming on skewers—and superior service.

Our first hour-and-a-half featured dinner music; mostly old standards and special requests from the audience. The second set gradually transitioned from dining to dance music, and final sets were all dance. The Casbah clientele consisted mainly of southern aristocracy and businessmen on an expense account. The average table generated $75 per seating, with two turns a night. We began at 7, ending at 10:30 Tuesday through Thursday, and 7:30 to midnight Friday and Saturday.

Circulating patron tables on breaks, we struggled to elevate our vocabulary and manners. On one such occasion, a well-dressed man sporting a southern colonel's goatee and lion's head cane asked me to join his party for a drink. Following introductions, he commented, "Your slogan, *The Pride of Dixie,* caught our attention, and the Confederate flags mounted on your drum clearly indicate where your loyalties lie. Are you familiar with the United Daughters of the Confederacy or the White Citizens Counsel?"

"Yes sir—and ma'am," I added, looking at the matriarch seated at the table.

Dressed in a masculine-cut dark suit jacket and tailored skirt, with two mink skins and three long strands of cultured pearls caressing her shoulders and neck, the matriarch radiated wealth and power. A large diamond and ruby-studded Stars and Bars pin focused attention above large breasts, and a pillbox hat topped off a perfectly coiffed hairdo. Expensive perfume with a hint of gardenia fought against too much rouge and blood-red lipstick. A faint smile cracked through a serious expression—revealing the face of an aging Confederate patriot. Leaning forward, the matriarch held up her hand, indicating to the colonel to yield the floor.

Her green eyes focused on me, peeling away lingering pretenses hidden under my facade. With a raspy voice degraded by too many Picayune cigarettes, the matriarch said, "I presume your southern history is complete regarding the War of Northern Aggression."

"Yes ma'am."

"Are you familiar with Andersonville?"

"Of course. The Confederate's prison camp used to incarcerate bluebellies."

"That's right, Rocky—those despicable bluebellies. I am inviting you to join us for a gathering this Sunday to honor the man who commanded Andersonville prison, Henry Wirz. Commander Wirz was the only Confederate officer executed for committing war crimes. Unjust ending for a truly great man. His descendants are flying into Atlanta this Saturday for a Sunday ceremony in Andersonville. The United Daughters of the Confederacy and the White Citizens Counsel are honoring Commander Wirz for making the ultimate sacrifice. Can you and select members of your band join us Sunday in Andersonville for lunch and the memorial ceremony? Of course, you'll be our guests."

"Thank you for the gracious invitation," I replied. "I'll talk with Bobby Starr and Rooster Badcock about their plans this Sunday. Can I call you with our RSVP?"

Batting long, false eyelashes four times in quick succession, she pulled out a card engraved with her name and address: Helen Walpole Brewer, 610 Fifth Avenue, Penthouse, New York City, New York. On the back, she penciled in: Westin Buckhead 404-796-8735.

As I read her card, she answered my unspoken question.

"Actually, I live in New York; I'm an actress—Broadway. I also write radio scripts, and I'm a literary and theater critic. Yet rest assured, I was born in Birmingham, Alabama, and my veins bleed CSA."

My shiny white teeth broke through previously parsed lips.

"I'll let you know if we can join you Sunday. Either way, I'll call your number with our RSVP."

"I look forward to your call. In the meantime, continue to proudly display our colors throughout you travels. Spread *The Pride of Dixie* to all those northern bigots, just as I do from my perch in New York City. Always be the southern gentleman you appear to be. Rest assured, we are very proud of you for displaying where your loyalties truly lie. The South will rise again! Also, be sure to invite Bobby Starr and Rooster Badcock over to our table for a drink."

Before kicking off our featured set, I said, "Create fantasy—sell illusion—project your God Power."

THIRD SET LINEUP—CASBAH				
SONG	ORIG'L ARTIST	GENRE	ENSEMBLE	FEATURE
Freddie Freeloader	Miles Davis	Jazz	3 Horns	Big Joe
Funny How Time Slips Away	Jimmy Elledge w/ Big Joe Jazz Arrangement	Pop—Big Band Jazz	4 Horns	Bobby—Vocal, Lance & Rocky

Spring Is Here	Cal Tjader	Latin Jazz	Vibes & Conga's	Rocky—Vibes
Bye Bye Love	The Everly Brothers	Pop	Standard Ensemble	Big Joe & Booby—Vocal
Do You Know What It Means to Miss New Orleans	Pete Fountain	New Orleans	Clarinet Featured	Big Joe—Vocal
Have You Met Miss Jones?	Joe Pass	Jazz Guitar	Guitar & Double Bass	Smoke & Rocky
All The Way	Frank Sinatra	Pop	Standard Ensemble	Lance—Vocal
Tangerine	Herb Alpert & The Tijuana Brass	Pop	3 Horns	Big Joe, Lance & Rocky
String of Pearls	Glenn Miller	Big Band	4 Horns	Big Joe, Lance & Rocky
Dis Here	Cannonball Adderley	Jazz	3 Horns	Big Joe, Lance & Rocky

Lance delivered a beautiful rendition of Sinatra's *All the Way*. Big spenders and their ladies loved Lance's voice, frequently requesting ballads covered by his extensive repertoire. His vocal exercises in Monroe were paying big dividends. Projecting excellent tonal quality and phrasing, he consistently impressed our sophisticated audience. This country boy, son of a Louisiana hog farmer, had risen from sloppin' da hogs to a stage of distinction, lording over southern aristocracy audiences with an air of belonging. Lance was living his dream.

Herb Alpert's version of *Tangerine* also struck a positive note at the Casbah. On first playing through the tune, Big Joe's arrangement mimicked Herb Alpert's recording. On the second playing, Big Joe's chord progressions expanded exponentially as his trumpet lead hit screech notes like Maynard Ferguson in a Stan Kenton arrangement. I loved both versions, commenting to Big Joe at the break, "You really are a diamond in the rough—an incredible musical arranger—a real talent."

"Danks, Rock," he said, chest expanding and chin rising with pride. A wide smile split a ruddy complexion, exposing a mouth full of pearly white teeth brushed daily with baking soda.

With the assistance of his CPA brother, who was handling the books for a mobile home manufacturer in Monroe, Bobby designed a new 30-foot trailer. The price was near manufacturer's cost, and delivery was scheduled the week we reached Monroe, our next booking. Bobby also purchased mobster Marco Smith's black on black 1961 Cadillac Sedan D'Elegance, title transfer to take place when he reached Monroe—perfect timing for Bobby's self-image and new towing requirements.

During the first week in Atlanta, the Carousels were in desperate need of new threads, in large part from sweating for nine months in our previously attractive, but currently rotting tuxedos. Bobby researched Atlanta clothiers and settled on Zimmerman's. With Bobby's impeccable taste guiding our selection, we voted on colors, styles, and accessories. Black, red, wine, gray, royal blue and robin-egg blue tuxes were selected.

Zimmerman's priced out our final selection, which included six custom-tailored tuxedos, six pleated tuxedo shirts, six sets of matching studs, six matching bow ties, four color coordinated cummerbunds, two matching tux vests, three sets of suspenders, and two pairs of patent leather shoes. Extending the numbers out, the total amounted to 36 complete outfits; everything except drawers and socks.

I took a long look at Zimmerman's estimate, our corporate checking account balance, and the business risk. With abundant encouragement from five Carousels, I committed to spend everything we had in the corporate account on the first-class outfits, handing over a deposit with a guarantee to pay the balance upon delivery. Zimmerman's promised final fittings and delivery within three weeks, just prior to our scheduled pullout of Atlanta. At a minimum, the Carousels would look fabulous. Moreover, we had contracts for seven continuous months: Monroe, Bossier City, Nashville, New Orleans, Muscle Shoals, Nashville, Chicago, and Louisville.

Creating awesome desirability on stage, Lance and Big Joe put on their chastity belts the minute they stepped off stage. What a paradox! Riding to and from the gig together, Big Joe and Lance missed all the fun of being on the road and gettin' their tickets punched.

As the Casbah clock struck 10:30 and midnight, respectively, Cinderella's carriage turned into a pumpkin. Bobby, Rooster, Smoke, and I morphed from four beautiful stallions into lowly gutter rats, leaving professional persona behind as we raced into downtown Atlanta's subculture. Atlanta jazz clubs and bottle clubs were magnetic, sucking us down the rabbit hole, stepping through the looking glass. We had a great time experimenting with forbidden fruits of Atlanta, nothing was out of bounds. Smoke busied himself spinning yarns that lunatics found bizarre. Bobby, Rooster, and I perfected our rodent instincts, searching for cheese in every nookie and crackie.

The fourth week in Atlanta, I got my million-unit penicillin shot to stop the drip and pissin' pain. Needing an emotional lift, the Great Bolo came to mind. He was a guy who loved the Carousels, going all the way back to our first Atlanta appearance at the Celebrity Key Club. The Great Bolo hung with the Carousels during our current gutter rat period and his disciple like devotion could prove fortuitous.

The Great Bolo had been a professional wrestler operating under that moniker in nationally televised wrestling matches. His ring uniform consisted of a full-face ski mask. The kicker was that he glued a hard metal disk to his forehead before covering it with the mask.

A couple of well-placed and well-staged head butts to an opponent's noggin and the Great Bolo's right hand consistently went up as the winner. Lots of blood gushing from opponents' foreheads paid extra, and the show provided a means to move up earnings. Without warning, his wrestling gig ended when, as the Great Bolo tells it, "A rookie just breaking into the big show blew out both of my knees one night." After his ring injury, the Great Bolo sold the rights to his professional name, using the money to purchase a used car lot in Atlanta.

Perhaps it was Johnny Walker talking, but he offered to sell me, at his cost, a 1959 Cadillac Coupe de Ville he just took in trade. The Great Bolo showed me the actual invoice to prove the price he paid for the Caddy. The next day I washed and drove my Olds pervertible into his used car lot. The Great Bolo made a generous offer for the '55 Olds, and we struck a deal.

A quick call to my Shreveport banker arranged financing, and I drove the gorgeous pearlescent white Caddy coupe with black interior and silver threads off the lot. My Cheshire Cat grin was matched by the car's glittering grill. The sleek fins prominently displayed four horizontal bullet taillights, admittedly the most ostentatious automobile ever made.

It had long been my habit to read the daily newspaper during brunch. This was the only true contact I had with the real world. However, I read the paper with a skeptic's eye. I rarely read the Classifieds, although today I scanned the columns and found, *"Eighteen-Foot Travel Trailer—Must Sell Today—Great Price."* Although brief, the description provided the location and lot number. On a whim and wanting to sport around Atlanta in my almost-new '59 Caddy, I drove into the mobile home park and searched out the lot number and trailer.

A handsome, 6-foot guy bounded out the trailer door, stuck his head through the passenger window of my Caddy and asked, "Looking to buy a travel trailer?"

I nodded.

His partner also emerged from the trailer, a real knockout sporting a gymnast's figure and soft smile. She never spoke a word, although her dancing eyes spoke volumes. She wanted out of Atlanta, and fast.

The guy immediately began a verbal tour of the trailer.

"It's very spacious, great kitchen, large bath and shower, comfortable double bed, and plenty of closet room and storage."

How he stuffed all those adjectives into an 18-foot travel trailer amazed me, but didn't fool me. Once inside, it looked okay for my modest requirements.

Five minutes into his rapid-fire sales pitch, I finally got my first question asked, "Why are you selling it?"

Ten minutes later I knew his and her life story. The highlights included the two of them going on the road as magicians and adagio dancers. According to his telling, the entertainment business changed dramatically when the Beatles invaded the scene. Club owners and television variety shows stopped booking traditional magic acts. As an alternative, the duo worked up an adagio dance routine, but with marginal success. Bookings were scarce and money was short. They were headed out of Atlanta and back to Wisconsin.

I nodded in sympathetic agreement, posing my second question, "What is your absolute lowest price?"

The man shuffled the dirt with his bedroom slippers, glanced at his gorgeous partner, saying, "If you buy it right now, $300. We want to drive to Wisconsin tomorrow afternoon. The trailer and title are yours if you have the cash. The trailer is worth triple that amount—we have to go home. We really have to go."

Nodding, I said, "I'll be here at 9:30 tomorrow morning. Locate a Notary, sign over the title, and I'll hand you the bread. Do you want a check, cashier check, or greenbacks?"

"Greenbacks and nothing larger than a twenty. I'll locate a Notary today and look for you tomorrow at 9:30. We have a deal."

That particular day I was thinking clearly enough to stop by the trailer park office and ask the manager where I could get a commercial travel trailer hitch installed on my car. He provided the names of three places, then recommended "Iron Benders." I arranged for Iron Benders to install a heavy-duty trailer hitch on the Cadillac following the title transfer.

The following morning the ex-magician/ex-adagio dancer and I concluded the title transfer and changed palms with $300 in cash. I spent the remainder of the day with Iron Benders and the following day inside the trailer, installing my stereo system and building racks for my prized record collection. At last, I could spend quality time listing to music I loved: jazz, classical, Big Band, Broadway, Latin, and love-makin' music.

As a house warming to myself, I entertained Salome, *"The Best of Atlanta."*

At my recommendation, Smoke purchased a 1958 Lincoln Continental from the Great Bolo. He put new tires on the beast, had the motor tuned up, and washed the monster every day. I embarrassed Smoke into installing a trailer hitch on his Lincoln to pull the Carousels' instrument trailer. He'd sponged off us long enough.

Not done yet, the Great Bolo sold Rooster a 1960 Chevrolet Impala coupe, in excellent condition. Until this purchase, Rooster never owned a decent set of wheels. He actually cleaned himself up a bit and demonstrated a modicum of self-pride.

The Carousels left our mark on the Atlanta entertainment scene and left much of our money in the hands of various Atlanta vendors. Final fittings of our custom tuxedos completed, we accepted delivery and I paid Zimmerman's.

Accolades and praise emanated from Casbah management. They wanted to ink a contract for a return engagement. However, I chose to leave the date open for a number of reasons. My hope was the Carousels could secure bigger money by cutting a hit record and capture a Vegas gig. A return option to the Casbah was best left open, at this time.

Sunday morning, my brothers pulled out of Atlanta and headed west to Monroe. At 8:30, Salome, *The Best of Atlanta,* appeared, offering a goodbye poke. It lasted three hours, expanding my adventure, in spite of delaying my departure. Once again, good nookie trumped responsibility.

With his blue eye sparkling, Mad Hatter purred, *"No wonder you're late. Why, this watch is exactly two days slow."*

Chapter 30

1962
BLOOD DONORS

We traveled Interstate 20, east to west, from Atlanta to Monroe. My 18-foot trailer pulled beautifully behind the Caddy. Leaving Atlanta five hours behind schedule, I saw no Carousels waving on the side of I-20. Given that Lance drove to Louisville to pick up his new, 42-foot trailer before driving to Monroe, he and Angelle were on their own. Big Joe pulled his 28-foot trailer from Atlanta to Monroe with his new Jeep truck. Rooster and Smoke were driving newly acquired used cars. I was relieved to make the trip without incident.

Three trailers set up at Whispering Pines, with Bobby's joining us midweek. Everything about travel trailers was new to us greenhorns. Leveling jacks, hooking up water, sewage, and electricity all sounded easy when the salesmen delivered their pitch. A week later we were still adjusting to our new digs, but overall we loved the idea of never having to move six tuxedo outfits from motel room to motel room, hopefully ever again. In addition, Cheshire Cat and Mad Hatter loved my new crib.

Cheshire Cat rapped, *"After all this time, coming all this way, you're getting far too close to stop. Get a grip on this rock and get a grip on yourself if you're gonna make it to the top."*

Before kicking off our featured set, I said, "Create fantasy—sell illusion—project your God Power."

THIRD SET LINEUP—DYNASTY LOUNGE				
SONG	ORIG'L ARTIST	GENRE	ENSEMBLE	FEATURE
Boy, What a Night	Lee Morgan	Jazz Version	4 Horns	Big Joe, Lance & Rocky
Harlem Shuffle	Boogie Kings	R&B	4 Horns	Bobby—Vocal, Big Joe, Lance & Rocky
Hello Rosa Lee	Clifton Chenier	Zydeco	Cajun Accordion, Fiddle & Frottoir	Big Joe—Vocal Rooster, Smoke & Rocky
Eleanor Rigby	Stanley Jordan	Jazz Version	Acoustic Guitar	Smoke—Acoustic Guitar
Walk on the Wild Side	Jimmy Smith	Jazz	Organ	Rooster—Organ
Behind Closed Doors	Charlie Rich	Country	Fiddle	Lance—Vocal, Big Joe & Smoke on Fiddle
Whiffenpoof Song	Cal Tjader	Latin Jazz	Vibes, Guitar & Conga's	Rocky & Smoke
Moon River	Andy Williams	Ballad	Standard Ensemble	Lance—Vocal
Everyday I Have the Blues	B.B. King	R&B	3 Horns	Big Joe—Vocal, Lance & Rocky
Watermelon Man	Herbie Hancock w/ Mongo Santamaria Arrangement	Latin Jazz	4 Horns + Conga	Big Joe, Lance & Rocky

Following Monday's opening at the Dynasty, I called Barbara Banks' mother at home. She was delighted to hear my voice and told me Barbara was working at an insurance agency, though she planned to enter college the following semester. Never falling victim to shyness, I drove to the insurance agency, arrived at 11:15, walked right in and stood staring at Barbara's long blond hair. She was on the phone, facing the rear wall, and focused solely on assisting a client. So as not to disturb Barbara, I placed a finger over my lips, signaling to the other insurance clerks. They snickered, but complied.

Gazing at her, a beautiful angel, I felt honored just to be in her presence. Missing her purity, I felt noble.

Barbara finished the call and wheeled around in her chair to make notes in the client file. Then she saw me standing 20 feet away. A big smile dominated her face, and she screamed, "Rocky!" Barbara ran into my arms and planted the juiciest kiss I'd had since leaving Monroe. She really felt good. By this time, four insurance clerks cheered and applauded.

I simply said, "Lunch?"

At the nearest sit-down restaurant, we ordered lunch and held hands like teenagers. I felt clean again. Tales of happenings and travels passed pleasure for an hour. Our magical relationship confirmed we picked up where we'd left off. Once again, Barbara and I bonded. This canary represented hope that true happiness was possible. Barbara was special.

The following day over lunch, our small talk included the recent death of Marilyn Monroe from an overdose of sleeping pills to John Glenn orbiting the Earth in Friendship 7. Then she asked if I plan to one day return to Tech and get my engineering degree.

"I think about it every day," I replied. "Right now, I've got a bad case of wanderlust. I'm having a ball, trying to catch the brass ring. If I miss it, I'll go back to Tech and graduate. But wanderlust draws me deeper into adventure and living life large."

"How long?"

"Hard to say. This is the first time I've allowed myself to let go and run with the wind. One day, responsibility will replace frivolity. All I know is I've got more running to do before settling down as a straight."

"I also share wanderlust," Barbara confessed. "Don't have your talents or the opportunity to see the world, but I need to live, laugh and love more before settling down. Maybe we'll meet on the other side of wanderlust."

I loved feeling normal.

Barbara Banks is beautiful, pure, and smart. I could do a lot worse. Our time will come one day. Hopefully, there'll be enough good man left in me to make her happy.

Adorned with new threads, new tunes, and a polished stage show, we impressed the alcoholic nursery crowd at the Dynasty. Maturing as performers, we presented a gracious and humble aura to a packed house. Being home recharged drained batteries.

Smitty cashed in. Big Mama remained in charge, keeping me informed of the nightly take. Life was good.

Then, time stopped for 13 agonizing days during October 1962. The Cuban Missile Crisis dominated everyone's attention, thrusting the world into panic. The average American citizen wondered how President Kennedy would react after discovering that the Soviets were surreptitiously building bases in Cuba for a number of medium-range nuclear missiles with the ability to strike most of the continental United States.

A year before, the U.S. had installed its Thor and Jupiter missiles in Britain, Italy, and Turkey—more than a hundred missiles having the capability to strike Moscow with nuclear warheads. The Soviets, badly behind the U.S. in the arms race, wanted their smaller missiles to be close enough to attack the U.S. mainland.

During the Cuban Missile Crisis, the country lived under a dark cloud of uncertainty. Audiences at the Dynasty Lounge changed from party-going players to fatalistic drunks, living out what they believed to be their last days on earth—hooch in hand. Selling dreams and fantasies to fatalists every night presented an incredible challenge, although an army of drunks arrived determined to die dead broke.

For several heart-stopping days, we watched as the world came close to nuclear war. Kennedy ordered U.S. armed forces at their highest state of readiness ever, and Soviet field commanders in Cuba were prepared to use battlefield nuclear weapons to defend the island if it was invaded. Luckily, Kennedy and Soviet Premier Nikita Khrushchev maintained diplomatic relations and thermal nuclear war was averted.

Tensions eased on October 28 when Khrushchev announced that he would dismantle the installations and return the missiles to the Soviet Union, expressing his trust that the United States would not invade Cuba. Further negotiations were held to implement the October 28 agreement, including a U.S. demand that Soviet light bombers be removed from Cuba and specifying the exact form and conditions of U.S. assurances not to invade Cuba. As part of the deal, although unknown by most Americans, the following year the U.S. would quietly remove its missiles from Turkey.

Twenty-four hours after the crisis ended, our fun-and-folly players were back, celebrating the wonderment of being alive. Smitty was happy. The world had returned to near normal, and so had the Carousels.

Our fourth Thursday in Monroe, Lance frantically banged on my trailer door, "Angelle delivered a boy, except she's bleeding badly, and we have to provide eight pints of blood right away!"

"Sure Lance," I said. "Have you contacted Big Joe, Bobby, Rooster, and Smoke yet?"

Nodding, Lance jumped in his truck and sped out of Whispering Pines, headed for the hospital.

Six Carousels and two barflies each contributed a pint of blood. In the waiting room, we discussed Angelle's medical condition. Big Joe said that Gert had gone with Angelle for her first and only prenatal doctor visit in Atlanta. Everything seemed okay at the time, but Angelle had gained a lot of weight and might be in danger of being toxic.

Bobby asked, "What's toxic?"

Lance responded, "I really don't know, but it ain't good."

Smoke was optimistic. "Everything will be okay. Don't worry. We have done everything we can for now. It's up to Angelle and her doctors."

Two days later, Angelle Devero and Lance Love carried a healthy boy out of the hospital. The Carousels and two barflies formed a silly honor guard at the hospital exit, taking the edge off of what had been a serious situation. Angelle and Lance smiled ear to ear. They really appreciated our concern and support. Indeed, their smiles were a welcome sight, happiness having disappeared from both their faces for the past ten months on the road. Mother and baby were fine, although Angelle remained in bed the following week because of blood loss and exhaustion. Gert tried to play friend and care giver, with marginal results.

Back at my trailer, Mad Hatter's black whit played out, *"If you knew time as well as I, you wouldn't dream of wasting it!"*

Chapter 31

1963
TRANSITIONS

Sunday morning, we towed four travel trailers and one instrument trailer from Monroe to Bossier City—an hour-and-a-half trip. We set up at the Red River Rendezvous Trailer Park. Like conquering heroes returning from war, carrying bounty as proof of our victories, we paraded into Bossier as champions—displaying new threads, digs and shiny autos as evidence.

Betty Booth spent the first week with Bobby in his brand new mobile pad. Angelle and Gert dominated Lance and Big Joe inside their respective tin cans. Smoke hung out in his bat cave. My 18-foot trailer was an oasis of joy, freeing me from musty motel rooms and allowing me to blast away with my favorite records.

Rooster secured a hotel room and became disturbingly quiet … until Monday.

While going through a sound check at the Boom Boom Room, Rooster announced, with a straight face and serious tone, "You guys are whoremongers! I've lost all respect for ya and the lives you lead. Yesterday, I gave up my sinful ways. A really good person came into my life. Sunday, we went to her Pentecostal church and I accepted Jesus Christ as my Lord and savior. I became a born-again Christian, baptized into the Holy Spirit. Nothing will ever be the same for me. I'm quitin' the Carousels. You have my two weeks' notice ... last day is a week from this comin' Saturday. Good luck and goodbye!"

We were stunned for a moment. Then, Bobby doubled over in laughter. When he could speak, Bobby asked, "Surely you're jokin'—aren't you? Playin' a practical joke on us? April fool's?"

Lance laughed along with Bobby, waiting for Rooster to break into a smile. When that didn't happen, Lance turned serious.

"What are you talking about, Rooster?" Lance asked. "You're the biggest pussy hound in the band—cock always on the hunt for a hen in heat. You're breakin' your own golden rule—'Never fall in love with just one snatch.' And ya have the balls to call us whoremongers because you've fallen in love with a born-again Holy Roller who speaks in tongues? What can her tongue do that other chicks can't? Holy Roller takes on a whole new meaning. Rooster, you've lost your mind and your balls."

Big Joe barked, "Ya judge us? Snakes'r higher dan ya. Got religion, too?"

I said nothing, trying to make sense of Rooster's pronouncements.

Can he make the leap and forgive himself? Does he have any clue as to what this means? Should I try to change his mind or just let it ride? What's best for the Carousels?

Smoke mumbled, "Are you serious or is this a big put on? You really in love?"

"I told you," Rooster replied, "I'm a born-again Christian now. I'm quittin' the Carousels and quittin' sinful life. That's it. You can't talk me out of this. Get another keyboardist. You have two weeks."

I nodded, leaned in close and whispered in Rooster's ear, "Does this mean you're not going to kill your ol' man the day he gets out of prison? Read the Sixth Commandment and Exodus 20:13, *'Thou shalt not kill.'* Good luck and goodbye."

Rooster sneered, wheeled and stormed out of Saks, headed for his born-again, holy-roller life and newfound fidelity to a single honey hole obviously capable of speaking in tongues.

Monday night during our first break, I drove down the Bossier Strip to talk with Mathew "Dallas" Fingers, a sideman keyboardist and lead singer carrying a four-piece band at the Side Car, part of the Stork Club and Show Bar complex. Next afternoon Dallas auditioned with the Carousels at Saks. We all agreed: Dallas was a good fit.

He sang lead on tunes other Carousels couldn't handle, expanding our eclectic repertoire by 20 percent. Dallas also played a style of organ and piano fingering that produced a raw sound, ideal for blues and R&B. Within two weeks, Rooster left and Dallas stepped in as our keyboardist, one of four lead vocalists and the Carousels' tune caller. By Friday the Carousels were a better band, although our culture was changing.

Before kicking off our featured set, I said, "Create fantasy—sell illusion—project your God Power."

THIRD SET LINEUP—SAKS BOOM BOOM ROOM				
SONG	ORIG'L ARTIST	GENRE	ENSEMBLE	FEATURE
West Side Story (Stage Show—Dance)	Leonard Bernstein	Broadway	Dance, Solo's & Ensemble	All Carousels
String of Pearls	Glenn Miller	Big Band	4 Horns	Big Joe, Lance & Rocky
Bring it on Home to Me	Sam Cooke	Pop	4 Horns	Bobby—Vocal, Big Joe, Lance & Rocky
Cold Sweat	Mongo Santamaria	Latin Jazz	4 Horns + Conga	Big Joe, Lance & Rocky
My Way	Frank Sinatra	Crooner	Standard Ensemble	Lance—Vocal

You've Lost That Lovin' Feelin'	Righteous Brothers	R&R	Standard Ensemble	Lance & Big Joe—Vocal
Johnny B. Goode	Chuck Berry	R&R	Standard Ensemble	Dallas—Vocal
Sherry	The Four Seasons	R&R	Standard Ensemble	Bobby in Falsetto, Big Joe & Lance—Vocal
Poor Butterfly	Cal Tjader	Latin Jazz	Vibes, Guitar & Conga's	Rocky & Smoke
Turn on Your Love Light	Bobby "Blue" Bland	R&B	3 Horns	Big Joe—Vocal, Lance & Rocky
Georgia On My Mind	Ray Charles	Country	3 Horns	Big Joe—Vocal, Lance & Rocky
Moanin'	Modern Jazz Quintet	Jazz	4 Horns	Big Joe, Lance & Rocky

Dallas was the youngest among us, idolized the Carousels, and frequently expressed his appreciation for being chosen to be part of the band. He was born in Shreveport to born-again Christian Southern Baptist Convention parents. Literalists when interpreting the Holy Bible, his parents condemned anything and everything fun, including dancing, drinking, and fornicating.

We honestly didn't know how Dallas would deal with the free-wheelin' life of the Carousels. A massive gulf between myth and reality existed. Can Dallas handle this?

When we officially hired Dallas, he insisted on offering up a prayer to Jesus, which lasted a full five minutes, covering just about everything and ending with, "God grant the Carousels international stardom and abundant riches."

Fortunately, we old-timers had the good sense to leave reconciliation of fantasy and reality up to Dallas.

God's will be done. We're changing during changing times.

Soon after he joined the Carousels, Dallas introduced us to Mary Bishop, his main squeeze. Since high school, Mary was in love with

Dallas and Dallas with Mary. Young and naïve, they cuddled like doves and rose above the cesspool of Carousel life.

Dallas was a truly good person. On the other hand, it was painfully obvious that he was struggling to create a balance between right and wrong. His other emotional burdens were inherited from his father's fervent hatred of niggers, integration, Jews, and the Kennedys. The complexities of good, evil, and racial prejudice wrestled inside Dallas' brain.

Feeling leader-like one day at rehearsal, I shared my thoughts with the Carousels on changing during changing times, saying, "We are the best we've ever been, guys; booked for the next five months into Nashville, New Orleans, Muscle Shoals, back to Nashville, and into the Windy City. However, times are a changin' in American culture and musical taste. The days of happy tunes and carefree, fun-lovin' audiences are in decline. Daily newspapers and nightly television play and replay divisive conflicts within civil rights, Vietnam, and southern hatred of the Kennedys. This destructive narcotic is sucking audiences out of nightclubs—most glued to their televisions.

"Change or perish. Buy a super-sized bottle of Pepto Bismol and begin listening to lyrics by Bob Dylan, Joan Baez, Belafonte, and Peter, Paul & Mary. Dylan's *The Times They Are A-Changin'* previews what's comin', guys. Baez and Dylan promoted their music during Martin Luther King's March on Washington. Now that's scary. *Blowin' in the Wind* by Peter, Paul & Mary turns cynicism into an art form. You don't have to like these artists, but you'd better understand where music is headed in America—they do. They have tapped into a generational revolution and so should we. Our future depends on it."

Finally, I issued a warning.

"If we don't act now, the Carousels won't make the footnotes of American music history. The Beatles, Four Seasons, and Elvis picked up on the freedom movement and societal discontent. Their latest lyrics chronicle new directions. They're changin' with the times.

Today we're at the top of our game, but we can't rest on laurels. Be creative—catch the next musical wave. Have new lyrics and material ready for Nashville, guys. Over the next five months we've got two shots at securing a major record label in Nashville. Carpe diem!"

Playing Saks's Boom Boom Room reminded me of Venus and, as luck would have it, another letter arrived from Vegas to Mom's address. Venus's letter left no doubt that she wanted us to get together. Remembering her beauty and passion, I composed a return letter, suggesting a rendezvous in New Orleans, seven weeks away.

About the same time Barbara Banks phoned from Monroe and left a message with the Saks bartender, saying, "I need to see you this weekend. A friend will drop me off at Saks Friday night and pick me up Sunday afternoon. Okay?"

"Absolutely," I said when I returned her call. "We'll have a ball in Bossier."

"I'll see you Friday night at Saks," she replied in an uncharacteristically weak voice.

Barbara arrived during our last break. Following the Carousels' final set for the night, she and I went to breakfast and held hands— just like old times. Clearly, Barbara was preoccupied. Respecting her space, I backed off and waited 'til she was ready to lay down her cards. Our night together was wonderful, although different—heightened passion with flashes of desperation. Something had changed. Wonder what?

Saturday morning I offered to fix breakfast in my trailer. Barbara asked for oatmeal.

I said, "Sure. I have oatmeal. Want some raisins, cinnamon, and cream?"

"No. Just oatmeal—perhaps a sliced banana."

Busying myself in the tiny kitchenette of the trailer, I served black chicory coffee while the oatmeal cooked on the small burner. Within twenty minutes I handed Barbara a steaming bowl of oatmeal with sliced bananas. She spooned a bite, cooled it with a gentle blow and slowly ate.

"It's good, Rocky. Thanks."

Then, looking at me, she quietly said, "I'm pregnant with our child."

Stunned, I staggered back.

Barbara reached out for my hand. "You don't have to say anything right now. Just listen and be supportive."

"You are …?"

Barbara interrupted my clumsy response. "Be quiet and listen, Rocky."

I nodded and placed both of her delicate hands in mine.

"I've given this a lot of thought and prayer. All I want from you is understanding and support. We are so young—just beginning our lives. Neither of us is ready to settle into marriage and raise kids—not right now. I love you Rocky. But, I know in my heart we can't make it—not with this pressure hanging over us. When this is behind us …"

I tried to interrupt and say something, but Barbara placed a finger over my lips.

"I don't know if you remember Marge and Major Hickok and their side-kick, Mack McManus. Major and Mack fly two crop dusters, and Marge handles ground crew and accounting chores for their company—Dusty Wings. Their Monroe contract is up; next stop Austin, Texas. I'm going with them. Marge knows I'm in a family way and offered me a job doing their books, ordering chemicals, fuel, and setting up new clients. We leave next week. Marge and I will drive the truck while Major and Mack fly the biplanes to Austin."

Barbara touched my lips again, continuing. "Part of my decision is based on the Baptists around here. I refuse to wear the Scarlet 'A' on my breast the rest of my life. They're so narrow minded and hypocritical—quick to judge and slow to forgive. Getting out of town will get me away from their condemnation and give me a chance to find some semblance of happiness.

"Putting our child up for adoption is best for everyone. I'll pick an adoption agency and deliver our baby, probably in a town where Dusty Wings has a contract. Neither of us should know the name of the adopting parents. In nine months I'll contact you. That's the time and place I'll need your love. Okay, Rocky?"

Overwhelmed, I pondered the gravity of Barbara's practical mind. Finally I said, "I don't deserve your love. You're the best thing that ever happened to me. I'm so sorry...."

She interrupted me again, softly saying, "When there's nothing to say—shut up. Until tomorrow afternoon, simply be understanding, compassionate, and gentle. As for the rest of our time together, what have we got to lose?"

At the foot of our bed Cheshire purred, "*Only a few find the way, some don't recognize it when they do—some ... don't ever want to.*"

Perched high on the bureau, Hatter winked his brown eye, offering, "*You don't slay? Do you have any idea what the Red Queen has done? You don't slay.*"

With five days to go at the Boom Boom Room, Merrill Saks cornered me following rehearsal.

"I talked to a number of club owners on your behalf," he said. "I also had a long talk with Carlos Marcello about a personal management contract. Carlos saw you here and at the Dream Room. He's interested and wants to move forward with an agreement."

A personal management contract with Carlos Marcello guarantees fame, fortune, and success, but at what price? I'd take orders from Merrill and Carlos—whatever they command—just like Sinatra, Tony Bennett, Neil Sedaka, Neil Diamond, Fabian, the Four Seasons, and a hundred other top-flight entertainers. Freedom and control will become a thing of the past. The Mob will own us—dictate every move—control our lives.

"I'll think about it," I said. "Like to know details before committing. I assume each Carousel will have to sign a personal management contract with you and Carlos."

"That's right. It's all or nothing. In about six weeks you'll be in New Orleans. I'll arrange a one-on-one session with Carlos at the Town and Country Motel. Think about making it big with our backing. This is an opportunity of a lifetime: fame, fortune beyond your wildest dreams."

Chapter 32

1963
HAVE TRAILER, WILL TRAVEL

Setting up four travel trailers in an upscale Nashville trailer park eclipsed our setups in the red clay of Bossier City. Access to a swimming pool, rolling hills, bike paths, and hiking trails beckoned at our front door. Dallas moved in with Bobby, although he spent most of his day in my 18-footer. Dallas was a trip. Long discussions ensued, spanning a wide range of subjects, philosophies, and theology.

Carousel trailers were located in one section of the sprawling mobile home park. Given our erratic hours and wild parties, musicians were corralled far away from the family section. George Jones and Tammy Wynette frequently came and went to the trailer parked across the street. Although both were married to other people at the time, their trailer was a love nest, rocking off the leveling blocks on two occasions. One sunny afternoon, I helped George re-level and stabilize his trailer, yet could do little for his crumbling marriage and self-destructive life style.

Who am I to be judging George and Tammy? I am no better.

Cooking became a new passion for several Carousels. Funny how food replaced nookie as our principal topic of conversation. Lance and Smoke bragged on Angelle's Creole and Cajun cabbage rolls, rue-based crawfish étouffée, jambalaya, chicken and andouille sausage gumbo, and red beans and rice with andouille sausage.

Not surprising, Big Joe was the cook in his family, relying on his rich Cajun heritage. Seafood gumbo, white beans and rice, pork chops, Creole-baked fish, sautéed shrimp, and grillades were his favorites. Bobby and I were redneck, North Louisiana cooks, growing up on eggs, ham, grits, steak, meatloaf, potatoes, poke salad, greens, peas, squash, eggplant, beans, and iced tea to wash it all down. Bobby and I limited our menus because of time constraints and small kitchens, even though we all loved to cook and eat in our trailers.

Once again Dottie and Larry LaSalle did a great job with advance newspaper and radio advertising. Headlines read: *"Triumphant Return of the Fabulous Carousels to the Black Poodle."* Dottie and Larry deserved my admiration for superior promotion. Of course, Dottie was earning her ten percent, and Larry received a lucrative bonus from the Mob bosses.

Excited about our return to Printers Alley, we customized our *West Side Story* routine for the Black Poodle dance floor and stage.

A terrific duo played behind the Black Poodle bar two hours before the Carousels mounted the stage. The duo returned to fill in our first break. I typically arrived early to relax and catch their act. They were classy entertainers.

Before kicking off our featured set, I said, "Create fantasy—sell illusion—project your God Power."

THIRD SET LINEUP—BLACK POODLE				
SONG	ORIG'L ARTIST	GENRE	ENSEMBLE	FEATURE
West Side Story (Stage Show—Dance)	Leonard Bernstein	Broadway	Dance, Solo's & Ensemble	All Carousels

Orange Blossom Special	Ervin and Gordon Rouse	Country	Fiddle, Banjo & Guitar	Big Joe & Smoke
Sherry	The Four Seasons	R&R	Standard Ensemble	Bobby in Falsetto, Dallas, Big Joe & Lance—Vocal
Soul Bird (Tin Tin Deo)	Cal Tjader	Latin Jazz	Vibes, Guitar & Conga's	Rocky & Smoke
Jolé Blon	Clifton Chenier	Zydeco	Cajun Accordion, Fiddle & Frottoir	Big Joe—Vocal Dallas, Smoke & Rocky
Stand By Your Man (Comedy)	Tammy Wynette	Comedy Parody	Fiddle & Guitar	Bobby in Falsetto
All I Have To Do Is Dream	The Everly Brothers	Country Crossover	Standard Ensemble	Bobby & Dallas
Eleanor Rigby	Stanley Jordan	Jazz Version	Acoustic Guitar & Double Bass	Smoke & Rocky
Hit The Road Jack	Ray Charles	R&B	3 Horns	Big Joe—Vocal, Lance & Rocky
Watermelon Man	Herbie Hancock w/ Mongo Santamaria Arrangement	Latin Jazz	4 Horns + Conga	Big Joe, Lance & Rocky

Dallas attended church our first Sunday in Nashville, then met me for breakfast at Pop's Place. We read *The Tennessean* newspaper over ham, scrambled eggs with cheese, grits, and biscuits covered in sausage gravy. The paper's Sunday magazine's front-page feature article was titled, *Have Trailer, Will Travel*. The article title was a take-off of the popular TV show, *Have Gun, Will Travel*, featuring Richard Boone as a gunslinger-for-hire named Paladin. The article spotlighted the Fabulous Carousels and our gypsy journey in four travel trailers. Our promotion picture filled the cover page of the magazine.

The article certainly seemed to encourage readers to go on the road and see America. And I hoped it beckoned readers to know more about the wonderful life as a Fabulous Carousel.

Excited to share the good news, we paid up and rushed to Lance's trailer to congratulate Smoke on his public relations accomplishment. Neither Lance, Angelle, nor Smoke had read the story, making it all the more enjoyable. I ran to Bobby's and Big Joe's trailers, inviting them to Lance's place for the great news. Reading the article over and over again, Smoke got more pats on the back that Sunday than any day in the history of the Carousels.

The three weeks that followed brought in many recording stars, promoters, public relations executives, and record company executives, all asking the same question, "How did you get *The Tennessean* to publish this article?" Big shots of Music City confessed how hard they had to work to get just a line or two about their artist in *The Tennessean*, with minimal success.

The music community was abuzz with the article and the Fabulous Carousels. I lost count of the band-aids who begged to go on the road with the Carousels. The Black Poodle was packed every night with long lines of patrons running down the Alley and around the corner. We were becoming well known in Music City.

Similar to our second trip into Nashville, we resumed our strategic plan and attacked the Music Row market with vengeance. The *Have Trailer, Will Travel* article provided exceptional leverage for getting in to see the decision-makers. Dottie lined up a couple of big-time record producers. Negotiations began with several major labels and our hopes soared. However, as before, no major recording contracts were offered. The net result of our solicitations produced three studio back-up recording sessions, two demos for publishers, and one studio session featuring our original material.

"Our big break will come when a money man steps forward and shares dreams with the performing talent," Smoke said. "Predicting the timing of our big break is impossible."

Persistence appeared to be the only part of the equation we could control. A couple of pep talks to keep trying were delivered, the right elixir to bolster Carousel attitudes. We all kept trying.

On the last Thursday at the Black Poodle, Big Joe announced he was marrying Gert at the courthouse at 10 a.m. Saturday, in Judge Morris's chambers. We all managed to be there on time, standing stunned at the one-minute legal proceedings and sterile nature of signing the marriage certificate. Fortunately, Angelle took pictures of Big Joe, Gert, and the judge, saving the day and memorializing the event.

Adjourning to the Black Poodle for a celebratory drink, the joy of it all was missing, in large part because of the lack of planning. Finally, handing Lance their boy, Angelle orchestrated what turned out to be the saving grace of an otherwise clumsy morning. As best man, Lance offered a toast and congratulatory speech to Big Joe and Gert. The rest of us said nice things and wished the newlyweds a happy life.

For the first time in memory, Gert's mysterious elixir swirling in her black coffee cup was absent. Their marriage day marked the first time in 14 months Gert was not in the bag before lunch. Later that afternoon, however, the black coffee cup reappeared, remaining ever-present thereafter. Even on her wedding day, Gert looked like she'd been beaten with a bag of nickels.

The next day, a letter arrived from Venus, addressed to me at the Black Poodle. She outlined her driving plans from Vegas to our next gig in New Orleans.

Anticipating the joy of finally hooking up and returning as Kings of Bourbon Street, my reply to Venus was a little over the top. However, given the sacrifices she was making to be with me in the Big Easy, it seemed important to reassure her of a receptive welcome waiting in the Crescent City.

The last line in my letter promised a telegram the day I arrived in New Orleans, to include the name of the trailer park, address, lot number, and directions. I sealed, kissed, stamped, and mailed the letter. The next step was to get my ass to the Quarter and Venus.

Chapter 33

1963
THE BIG EASY

I was the last Carousel to pull into Bayou Gentilly Trailer Park. Following Lance's, Big Joe's, and Bobby's rigs, my trip from Nashville to New Orleans passed without incident. I was as limp as a worn-out condom, so I went to bed after setting up my trailer. Monday morning came early. We set up instruments on the Dream Room stage, grabbed beignets and coffee at Café Du Monde, cleaned up, dressed, and shagged ass back to the Dream Room for opening night.

Walter Noto was even more welcoming than on our first trip to Bourbon Street, respectfully mentioning Merrill Saks and Carlos Marcello. However, he reminded me that the Dream Room was an up-tempo club—no ballads. It felt really good to be playing again in this historic place. Paying homage to the hundred pictures on the performer wall of fame provided the right spark to jack me up for the four weeks ahead, especially when I discovered a photo of the Carousels displayed prominently.

I looked forward to reconnecting with Candy Barr. Regrettably, she was traveling a circuit, currently dancing at the Carousel Club in Dallas. Missing Candy saddened me, but Venus would soon fill the void.

I issued encouragement before beginning our featured set: "Create fantasy—sell illusion—project your God Power."

SECOND SET LINEUP—DREAM ROOM				
SONG	ORIG'L ARTIST	GENRE	ENSEMBLE	FEATURE
Watermelon Man	Herbie Hancock w/ Mongo Santamaria Arrangement	Latin Jazz	4 Horns + Conga	Big Joe, Lance & Rocky
I'm Walkin'	Fats Domino	R&B	4 Horns	Big Joe—Vocal, Lance & Rocky
Sherry	The Four Seasons	R&R	Standard Ensemble	Bobby in Falsetto, Dallas, Big Joe & Lance—Vocal
Lonely Teardrops	Jackie Wilson	R&B	Standard Ensemble	Bobby—Vocal
Orange Blossom Special	Ervin and Gordon Rouse	Country	Fiddle, Banjo & Guitar	Big Joe & Smoke
La Danse de Mardi Gras	Clifton Chenier	Zydeco	Cajun Accordion, Fiddle & Frottoir	Big Joe—Vocal Dallas, Smoke & Rocky
Soul Bird (Tin Tin Deo)	Cal Tjader	Latin Jazz	Vibes, Guitar & Conga's	Rocky & Smoke
Comin' Home	Lee Morgan	Jazz	4 Horns	Big Joe, Lance & Rocky
Turn on Your Love Light	Bobby "Blue" Bland	R&B	4 Horns	Dallas—Vocal, Big Joe, Lance & Rocky
Sidewinder	Lee Morgan	Jazz	4 Horns	Big Joe, Lance & Rocky

Tuesday morning, as promised, I sent Venus a telegram disclosing the trailer park, address, and site location. Excited about seeing her after all these months, I anticipated her ETA, a week from Friday—only ten days away. Assuming she would be driving all the way from Vegas, arriving exhausted, I wondered if our written words would match our body chemistry.

With two alternating bands every night at the Dream Room, each of our sets lasted an hour, with an hour off between. During breaks I made the rounds. Fats Domino was at Al Hirt's Club. Erma Thomas played next door to Pete Fountain's place, and the Dukes of Dixieland were at the Famous Door.

Every night, like stink on shit, Smoke and Bobby headed for Jean Val's party over Lafitte's. I joined them once or twice a week. Life was good.

Also, the FBI dude was back. Lance's body language confirmed his cool head. No need to pester him with paranoid questions—not this time.

Smoke and David Ferrie also reconnected in the narrow bar back stage, huddling and whispering during every break. Smoke's involuntary right eye tic became more pronounced, as his twang sang the lilt of a true Southerner. One Wednesday, before going back on stage, Smoke said he wanted to talk privately about something really big coming down. We agreed to meet the next morning.

Smoke knocked on my trailer door early Thursday morning and suggested we go to lunch before our scheduled rehearsal at the Dream Room. Smoke chose Mosca's, an innocuous wooden building on the West Bank, Highway 90, near Westwego. Mosca's was noted to be Carlos Marcello's and his Mafia family's favorite dining spot and hangout. Inside, the walls were clapboard white with floors scrubbed bare from nightly brushing with bleach—immaculate. White starched tablecloths and wooden ladder-back chairs rounded out the modest decor. Obviously, great food and service were Mosca's draw.

As first timers in the quasi-private Mob club, Smoke and I attracted suspicious glances. Still yet, Mama Mosca graciously greeted us, reciting the menu of overwhelming choices. Her homemade pasta was complimented by succulent menu specialties such as Oyster's Mosca, Shrimp Mosca, crawfish étouffée, Redfish Coubion, and eggplant stuffed with river shrimp, among other mouth-watering entrees. Two frosty steins of draft Dixie Beer were served and we settled in for a leisurely lunch. On several occasions Mama Mosca refilled our steins to ensure complete satisfaction with her cuisine and service. Smoke's dining fantasies paid delicious dividends—at least on this day.

After we ordered, Smoke pulled out a pocket-sized, spiral-bound note pad, referring to his haphazard scribbles before he began speaking. There were many moving parts to Smoke's convoluted puzzle, accompanied by a rapid, repetitive, non-rhythmic facial muscle tic associated with his right eye.

He began with the punch line: "Carlos Marcello, along with Santo Trafficante, Jr. of Tampa and Johnny Roselli of Chicago, approved a plan to assassinate President Kennedy."

Patting the small of my back to make sure I had Roscoe, I leaned forward and whispered, "You crazy? We'll be tonight's veal marsala if you don't shut up. Why did you pick this place, of all places, to lay out a Mafia assassination conspiracy? You nuts?"

"Atmosphere. They'd never suspect us because we're insiders."

"Perhaps inside a coffin. We're earners. No more, no less. You're living in fantasy land—completely delusional."

"Rocky, you're dead wrong." Pointing to his scribbles, Smoke twanged on, "My notes document everything David Ferrie knows about a potential JFK assassination—right down to the smallest detail. This is not fantasy—it's very real."

"You're about to spoil my lunch and afternoon."

Referring to his scribbles, Smoke said, "Lauren Hall was a cellmate of Trafficante while in a Cuban jail. Hall's the go-between for Lee Harvey Oswald, one of three patsies in the secret plan. The Cuban Democratic Revolutionary Front, the Committee to Free Cuba, Clay Shaw, Guy Banister, and Victor Marchetti are accomplices. Three cities have been proposed as assassination targets, requiring different patsies in each: Thomas Valley is the patsy in Chicago, Eladio Lopez for Tampa, and Lee Harvey Oswald in Dallas."

A fool in his folly can do you more harm than your most ardent enemy. Smoke continued to decipher messy scribbles.

"There was a secret CIA plot, with Bobby Kennedy's blessing and code-named Amworld, to assassinate Castro. The CIA approached Trafficante and paid him big bucks to carry out the plan. Amused, he shared the Kennedy and CIA naiveté with his Mafia friends, pocketed the payoff and forgot about the assassination plot. Trafficante simply took the money and laughed all the way to the bank."

"Where is this leading us, Smoke?"

"As far as the Mafia bosses are concerned, the opportunity to turn this unholy alliance with Bobby Kennedy on its head is simply too good to be true: assassinate JFK instead of Castro. After JFK's assassination, Bobby will become politically impotent. Then the Mob will be free to deal with Castro in their own way."

Smoke droned on with great excitement about David Ferrie's conspiracy theory. Temporarily distracted by his rapid eye blinking, I lost track of the complicated connections and date sequences, responding to Smoke with a lot of head nodding and "uh-huhs."

The arrival of our food put an end to Smoke's rambling—at least for a few minutes. Consuming my Italian crab salad, Redfish Coubion, homemade square pasta, and Dixie Beer—fantastic food—I passed pleasure. Smoke slurped his turtle soup and devoured crawfish étouffée, squeezing assassination conspiracy details in between bites.

Finally I posed, "What do you want me to do about it, Smoke?"

Smoke sat back in his chair, showing disgust that I had missed the essence of his story.

"If the assassination of President Kennedy takes place, the Carousels' future with Carlos Marcello and the Mob ends—we're history. Mr. Marcello won't have the interest or time to mess with us. Secondly, the killing of JFK could rapidly escalate into a global war. That's what I'm talking about. We've got to be prepared. Now is your golden hour to come up with a way out of a really fucked-up situation."

"OK, Smoke. I'll give it some serious thought, but don't get in any deeper. You already know too much. I've pulled your ass out of a few messy situations, yet I'm powerless if you get fitted for cement shoes. Besides, the rest of us will be sleeping with the fishes if Marcello gets wind that you are the canary singing about this. For God's sake, cool it, Smoke."

When we paid up, I thanked Mama Mosca for a delicious meal and sauntered to the parking lot and my car. Mama Mosca yelled from her doorway, "You boys are always welcome here. Come back anytime." I inhaled a lungful of fresh air, belched and got my second taste of Red Fish Mosca—better the first time, I thought.

On Thursday of our first week at the Dream Room, Vince Marcello made his nightly journey from the Show Bar to the Dream Room, adorned with strippers who just arrived from the Carousel Club in Dallas. Vince grabbed my arm during a break. "Rocky, I have a message from Carlos. Can we talk privately?"

"Sure Vince. Let's go in the kitchen," I said, gesturing toward the rear café doors.

Vince was the little brother with a big message to deliver.

"Carlos is occupied with a major project and simply cannot meet with you during the next few weeks. He wanted me to convey his personal apologies and say he's interested in revisiting the item in question during your next trip to the Dream Room. He assured me that this delay is unavoidable, but sends his warmest regards to you and the Carousels."

I shook Vince's thin, clammy hand and looked straight into his black, beady eyes.

"Message received. Extend my regards to your brother. Looking forward to picking up the item in question during our next gig in New Orleans. By the way, I hope your brother's major project works out to his liking. Be sure and convey my respects."

One evening, Carolyn Jones, my favorite teller at Pioneer Bank in Shreveport, showed up unannounced and obviously seeking some fun during her New Orleans vacation. After my gig, we strolled through the French Quarter, stopped at Cafe Du Monde, and then walked to the parking garage where my '59 Caddy was presented with fanfare by an attendant, who was tipped handsomely.

We got in and I asked, "Where to?"

Carolyn slid over to my side and said, "I want to see where you live, Rocky. Can we go there?"

Twenty minutes later, the windows of my 18-foot trailer began to steam up with passion—but not for long.

Carolyn confessed, "I'm a virgin. I'm not sure. Not sure if … if this is the right time to …"

I can afford to be cool with this one. After all, Venus Cruz arrives at my trailer door Friday morning. Got to rest up for Venus.

Carolyn and I smooched for an hour, taking me back to my teenage years. Moving at a snail's pace, her runaway emotions battled it out—good versus evil. My patience was rewarded when she placed my hand on her luscious bosoms.

I'm about to hit a home run. I'll rest up tomorrow.…

Unexpectedly, Carolyn rebuffed my advances.

"I want you—terribly—but I'm scared. Don't know … It's all so new … I'm not sure, Rocky."

"I'm not sure." The kiss of death for an otherwise blissful roll in the sack.

Experience taught me that women who hold back on their passions are terrible lays. Besides, Carolyn's good-versus-evil battle going on in my bed became a royal turnoff. Cuddling in each other's arms, fully clothed, yet thoroughly disheveled, Carolyn and I drifted off to sleep on top of the bedspread.

Anyway, I need my rest. Venus will be in my bed in less than 28 hours.

Cheshire purred, *"He wants to set the princess free. He's got lots of hats, but he's lots of bats. You know, it just ain't meant to be."*

Chapter 34

1963
ONE DAY EARLY

Aknock on the door of my tin can startled me. Glancing at the clock, I said aloud, "Who the fuck is this at 6 a.m.?"

Carolyn wriggled next to me, but didn't awaken. Not giving a shit about my disheveled appearance or trying to be cordial, I opened the trailer door and glared down at the stranger standing on my patio. The creature wore Indian moccasins, faded and frayed blue jeans, a dingy gray sweatshirt with worn neckline and holes in the sleeves, pointy old lady glasses, no makeup, and an ugly scarf with a floral pattern covering dirty blond hair that hadn't been combed in days.

Surely, this creature is a street person looking for a handout.

"You don't recognize me?" the creature asked, raising her chin and peering at me through those pointy glasses.

I studied her face, searching desperately for an answer. I rubbed sleepy dirt out of my eyes and stepped out of the trailer to the patio below for a closer look.

"Nope. What can I do for you," I said with a tinge of anger in my voice.

"Rocky, it's me ... Venus."

"Holy shit!"

"I drove all night to get here a day early. Robert helped me drive in exchange for getting him to New Orleans."

Awkwardly, I looked back inside the trailer to see if Carolyn was visible, then down at my rumpled tuxedo pants, limp suspenders and the lipstick-stained tux shirt with shirttail flappin' in the breeze. I could feel Carolyn's makeup on my chapped face from last night's smooching. I looked back to Venus, but didn't step toward her, and she made no move toward me. We stood on the patio, embarrassed and speechless.

This is a cluster fuck.

"You have someone with you," she finally said. "I'll leave you alone."

Venus spun around and returned to her car at a rapid pace. I followed at a trot. Standing outside her car window, I asked, "When will I see you, Venus?"

She answered my question while pushing the button to raise the electric window.

"Later," she said.

Her next word was directed at the guy behind the wheel: "Go."

Obviously the driver was Robert, a skinny, bearded and balding dirty man with a glazed look radiating from dilated eyes, suggesting heavy drugs at work.

The white Oldsmobile station wagon moved down the street, too fast to run after, but much slower than normal. I watched intently until it turned the corner and disappeared. I couldn't discern if Venus was crying, angry, or anything. She sat motionless in the passenger seat, looking straight ahead. I asked myself a hundred questions, most coming back to, *what does "later" mean?* I didn't have a clue where Venus went—no way of getting in touch.

Will I ever see Venus again?

Off balance and angry with myself, I tried to clean up my mess. I awakened Carolyn and hurriedly drove her back to her hotel, skipping breakfast on the lame excuse that she wasn't used to staying up all night and needed her rest. I mounted a forced facade of gracious concern as I dropped Carolyn's ass off at the front door of the Monteleone Hotel in the Quarter.

My Caddy sped back to the trailer—no Venus. Agonizing over not knowing the results of my fuck-up, I waited for Venus Cruz to reappear.

Friday morning, exactly 26 hours after seeing Venus drive out of my life, I was again awakened by a knock on my trailer door. The sound was different, softer. I put on my newly acquired black silk robe and opened the door. Venus stood before me, beautifully quaffed, Merle Norman makeup expertly applied, and dressed in a baby blue velour jump suit, all the while radiating a sweet scent of jasmine. She looked fabulous. Venus was the perfect Barbie Doll. Bounding to the patio, I wrapped my arms around her, gave a mighty hug and began spinning her around, airplane style.

Venus had no choice but to put her arms around my neck, if for no other reason than to avoid being slung off to Thibodaux.

When I finally put her down, we both were dizzy from spinning. Still wobbling, I gently kissed Venus on her moist lips, slow and tender. God, she felt good. The electricity and body chemistry were fantastic. Still, there was more to explore. I led her inside my aluminum cocoon, offering to brew us a pot of Café Du Monde coffee and scare up some scrambled eggs and biscuits for breakfast.

Her baby blues pierced my soul as she answered, "Anything you want, Rocky. I'm all yours."

Friday evening I emerged from my tin can at the last possible moment, sped to the parking garage in the French Quarter and ran to the Dream Room stage, barely making it as the transfer tune began to play. When the last note of our last set sounded off the Dream Room stage, I sped back to my trailer and Venus. I repeated the frantic dash Saturday night, and we didn't leave the love nest til Monday afternoon, stepping out to cooing Ring Neck Doves, blue skies, and a clean fresh breeze.

Our relationship blossomed like a rose—ever mindful of sharp thorns. Fairytale days followed. Tenderly, we took turns at peeling away layers of emotion, fondling each other's essence. Like drug addicts craving a fix, our combined thirst was unquenchable.

Radically different heritage and backgrounds were laid bare. Venus had minimal exposure to classical music or formal education. I flipped on the stereo and played Ravel's *Boléro*. The stereo's woofer vibrated our libidos. Venus's amorous tendencies stimulated, she instinctively knew what to do—and we did it. Beginning that day, Venus made regular requests for *Boléro*.

Rachmaninoff's *Second Piano Concerto*, one of my favorites, elicited a different reaction from Venus—a somber and serious honesty.

"I've never heard anything this beautiful. Thank you for bringing me into your world."

Mood set, we began exploring our respective childhoods, family, religion, philosophy, goals, likes and dislikes, fears, passions, the meaning of life, and a hundred other subjects, all drawing us closer by the day. The more Venus talked, the more she cried. Tenderly, I kissed tears away as they rolled down her flawless face, binding our trust.

On Tuesday morning of the last week in the Big Easy, I listed Venus's attributes and extraordinary qualities. It took me 20 minutes to say everything. Sweet jasmine dominated the humble abode as she leaned forward and whispered, "I hope you continue to see me in this light. However, I'm not that person. But, I'll try to live up to your image of me."

That afternoon, Venus turned the tables on me.

"Grant me as much time as I need to say something really important. Don't interrupt or question me until I've finished. Okay?"

I nodded in agreement and sat quietly.

"Rocky, you are good to the core, trustworthy. You're blessed with vision, creativity, leadership, boundless energy, and loyalty. In spite of all that, you are not streetwise—far too trusting—totally naïve. In a way, your goodness is your biggest weakness. Your strong character will be your downfall, particularly in the entertainment business. In spite of trying to appear tough, people see right through you. You see no evil, even when it stares you in the face ... blind to the ugliness of this world."

Pausing only for a breath, Venus continued, "On the other hand, I wish I were that person you described this morning. I'm not. You are blinded by love for something or someone who does not exist. I'm carrying lots of baggage: raised in the Ninth Ward, growing up in the sewers of New Orleans. What I am today, I learned from the school of hard knocks. I'm streetwise and hard as steel, disguising my true self in a beautifully wrapped package with a big bow and smile. I'm a long way from the person you described this morning. Open your eyes before taking your next step. I'm ... We're ... Just open your eyes, Rocky."

"Venus," I replied, "We are who we are, and, if we're lucky, our strengths and weaknesses will balance out."

"Yes, Rocky," Venus agreed. "We are who we are."

Friday, November 8, 1963, marked our last weekend in New Orleans. Transporting the Carousels, our travel trailers, and several automobiles from the Big Easy to Muscle Shoals on Sunday required attention. With our trusty AAA maps and emergency plans drafted and distributed to the Carousels, Venus and I crafted our own plan. Sunday morning she'd drive her station wagon and I'd pull the travel trailer with my Cadillac. Plans set, we looked forward to the trip.

Saturday night the Carousels finished the Dream Room gig and loaded the instrument trailer. For some reason we didn't have room for my Deagan vibraphone, a clumsy instrument even when packed up. I decided to drive home, get Venus's station wagon, drive back to the Dream Room, and load the vibraphone in the back of her vehicle. She readily agreed. Parking her big Olds on Bourbon Street, in front of the Dream Room, I opened the rear door and began loading the vibraphone.

That's when I spotted an anxious-looking man running towards me from the doorway of Whisky Joe's. Whisky Joe's sat directly across the street from the Dream Room, catering to alcoholics and lost souls with nowhere else to go at 2:30 Sunday morning. The man stared at the Olds station wagon, at me, then inside the front seat.

He took a step back, looked at me again, and said with confusion in his voice, "Dat's my car. You're drivin' my car. Got da title to dis car and you're driving it. Why?"

I shrugged my shoulders and raised an eyebrow—implying ignorance.

The man collected his thoughts.

"Ya don't remember me, do ya? I'm Luis Cruz—Venus's husband. You're Rocky Strong, aren't you?"

I nodded in agreement.

With a voice that left no room for negotiations, Luis said, "Give me da keys to my car or I'll call da police and have ya arrested for grand theft auto!"

He only had to say it once. I tossed Luis his keys. Satisfied with my response, he softened his rigid appearance and tone, studying me with considerable curiosity. I began to move to the back of the station wagon to get my vibraphone, but his hand motion stopped me.

Luis moved in close, apparently to avoid the gathering drunks who were becoming curious about our confrontation.

"Rocky, I had no idea it was you," he said. "Venus left Vegas in da middle of da night, while I was sleepin'. No warning. I didn't know where she went. For da first time in three weeks, I now know where Venus is. She's with you."

Obviously struggling in indecision, to say more or simply drive away, Luis heaved a warning shot my way.

"I promise ya one thing. Venus will break ya heart, just like she broke mine—many times. Suddenly, Venus goes crazy—totally nuts. No warnin'—jus' flip's out. She's like a caged bird, willin' to do anythin' to get away. Suddenly, she's gone. No one knows why or where. Three weeks ago she flew away from me and Vegas. She's done dis before—lots of times."

As we faced each other at 3 in the morning, a busboy from the Famous Door carried out a load of spent beer cans, dumping them into a 55-gallon barrel at the curb. Two drunks wrestled like orangutans a hundred feet down Bourbon Street. The stench of vomit snaked its way up from the gutter, bringing tears to my eyes. However, Luis Cruz wasn't done yet.

"I'll bet you don't know anything about our daughter and son. For da past two years, Alicia and Ricky lived wit Venus's sister in New Orleans. Venus can't handle day-to-day livin', being a mother or wife. I still don't know what's going on in her head or how to make her happy. Venus dumped terrible pain on me, da chillen, sister, mother, and lots of good people."

Luis seemed to grow three inches by straightening his back and raising his chin to look me in the eye. With three deep breaths, he struggled to clear the cobwebs from a brain numbed by too much Bacardi. Finally, he cleared his throat and stepped in close.

"Venus dumped enough garbage on me to last a lifetime. I've had it. No love left—just pain. Da nightmare ends right here—now. She's all yours. Wish you luck, but she'll break your heart, too."

As if on cue, the ten-piece spade band inside the Dream Room boomed out Bobby "Blue" Bland's version of *I Pity the Fool*. Luis and I looked at each other—captured by the moment—questioning—pondering—accepting.

Sensing my naiveté, Luis smiled, silently reveling in his hard-won wisdom, as poignant lyrics wafted onto Bourbon Street, delivering a haunting prophecy. Like a prize fighter, the spade singer wailed his punch lines as Luis bobbed and weaved sobriety away from another all-night drunken stupor.

> *I pity the fool, I said I pity the fool*
> *I pity the fool, I said I pity the fool*
> *That falls in love with you*
> *And expects you to be true*

Oh, I pity the fool

Look at the people
I know you're wondering what they're
doing
They're just standing there
Watching you make a fool of me

...

Oh, I pity the fool, I pity the fool
That falls in love with you
I pity the fool, I pity the fool

...

She'll break your heart one day
And then she'll laugh and walk away
Oh, I pity the fool ...

Bobby "Blue" Bland's provocative lyrics captured everything Luis wanted to say.

Luis helped me unload the vibes and secure them inside the Dream Room storage closet. Then he treated himself to a self-rewarding laugh, climbed into the Olds and drove away. I hailed a taxi, instructing the cabbie to drive to Bayou Gentilly Trailer Park. Welcoming the drive time to think this through, I considered Luis's position.

He lost Venus and is understandably upset, getting revenge by saying those ugly things to poison Venus's and my relationship. On the other hand, checking out the two kids is easy. Checking out Venus's craziness will take a little longer. She could even turn out to be the femme fatale Luis described. C'est la vie. Venus is a delectable passing fancy—simply playing a transitory role in my big adventure. Got to keep this in perspective. Laissez les bon temps roulez.

As I got out of the cab, Venus anxiously asked the obvious. I decided to keep most of Luis' comments to myself. It would do no good to confront Venus with more baggage. The loss of the Olds was enough trauma for one night. I presented a story minimizing the loss of the station wagon. I kept repeating three themes: "I'm not going to jail for grand theft auto; Luis will never bother you again and everything will be all right—you're safe with me."

Venus didn't sleep that night. I slept four hours, waking at 8 a.m. After hooking my trailer to the Cadillac, I drove by the Dream Room and picked up my Deagan vibraphone. Leisurely, I drove to Muscle Shoals, with Venus snuggled next to me like a scared rabbit. Putting miles under our asses, we left the Big Easy and Luis Cruz behind—distancing ourselves by the hour. As we pulled into the trailer park in Muscle Shoals, Venus began to relax—finally.

No one said this would be easy.

Cheshire Cat: *"Those who say there's nothing like a nice cup of tea for calming the nerves never had real tea. It's like a syringe of adrenaline straight to the heart!"*

The Mad Hatter: *"Of course. Anyone can go by horse or rail, but the absolute best way to travel is by hat. Have I made a rhyme?"*

Chapter 35

1963
A LIVING LEGEND AND A DEAD PRESIDENT

The Lamplighter in Muscle Shoals was an upscale country club, complete with its own air strip, 36-hole golf course, and a clubhouse that catered to fine dining and dancing six nights a week. Entering through large double doors, I began my standard routine, soaking up ambiance like a sponge. I asked myself, as I always did upon entering a new club, *Will the ghost speak to me today? Be quiet and listen. Listen.*

A welcoming lobby led to a rich mahogany walled barroom, adorned with lighted pictures of famous golfers and a massive oil painting of Robert E. Lee, spotlighted behind the 20-foot-long bar. There was an easy transition to the main room, with 28 tables dressed in white linen, and adorned with silver and china settings and fresh yellow roses. Separating the tables was a highly polished, virgin pine dance floor, 20 feet wide by 60 feet long, leading up to a raised stage, complete with red velvet curtains.

Moving slowly around the 80-by-80-foot dining room, I listened for the whispers of ghosts past. As hardwood floors creaked, I thought I heard something—twice. At last, I ascended five steps to a backstage packed with lighting and amplification panels. Stage left, a small sign above a toggle switch read, "Curtain—Up to Open, Down to Close." I flipped it up, took a deep breath, and walked to center stage—surveying new territory to be conquered. Thinking to myself, *We'll create magic here. Our God Power will reign on high.*

The Carousels provided much of the entertainment, beginning with an early cocktail hour, transitioning to fine dining, and then dancing. Our experience at the Casbah in Atlanta supplied a great template. During our breaks a terrific, six-piece Mariachi band made the rounds at tables. They hailed from Mexico City. Wearing traditional Mariachi outfits, the group consisted of three guitars, one bass guitar, and two violins. Each musician had an excellent singing voice. The group lived out back in a trailer provided by the Lamplighter.

Old-moneyed patrons arrived with friends halfway through the cocktail hour, drank moderately, inquired into the chef's recommendations, ordered the appropriate wines with dinner, and engaged in the fine art of small talk. They requested tunes by Glenn Miller, Tony Bennett, the Four Freshmen, Pete Fountain and Cal Tjader.

The nouveau riche arrived before the cocktail hour, drank fast, boasted about their net worth, ordered the largest steaks on the menu, and requested the latest rock and roll tunes on the Hit Parade. The Carousels made a point of catering to both old-money and new-money patrons.

The principal Lamplighter owner was Mrs. Charlotte Lee, widow of the recently deceased Jefferson Lee, whose proud bloodlines traced back to the South's most famous Confederate general. As rumor had it, Jefferson Lee had a fatal heart attack one night while visiting Melba Moore, his concubine who was known to all, except Mrs. Lee.

At 35, Charlotte Lee was a knockout, with a shapely figure, China-doll face, and a hair style only achievable with daily visits to the beauty parlor.

The widow Lee assumed an active role in managing the family business. She brought in a man by the name of Judd Phillips as minority partner and general manager of the Lamplighter's restaurant, bars, and entertainment. Judd was the brother of Sam Phillips, owner of Sun Records.

Judd had been Sam's advance man and road manager for most of Sun Records' megastars. The more Judd drank his beloved Wild Turkey, the wilder his stories about international tours with Elvis Presley, Jerry Lee Lewis, Johnny Cash, Roy Orbison, Roger Miller, Howlin' Wolf, Carl Perkins, Charlie Rich, Junior Parker, and Rufus Thomas, among others.

In the late '50's and early '60's, Sam Phillips exploited the best black blues melodies, lyrics, and artists, commercializing them into white versions of what is called rock and roll today. Sam preferred the studio and negotiating artist contracts. Judd did whatever Sam told him to do, mostly coddling big-name artists and arranging road shows in various countries, states and cities.

The Carousels had a fantastic opening week. All Lamplighter patrons were members of the country club, owned businesses or were independently wealthy, cloistered in the North Alabama culture. From points of origin throughout the South, fly-ins ventured to the Lamplighter for golf, fine dining, and the Carousels. We made a point of visiting guest tables during breaks, making small talk, receiving requests, and creating a bond with customers. Our pressed tuxedos and manufactured charm lasted about one minute at each table, moving on before we embarrassed ourselves.

We quickly developed a cadre of regulars, whether old-money families or nouveau riche business owners looking for a stiff drink and a juicy steak after work. Old-money preferred mid-week dining at the one-seating-a-night elegant venue.

Venus joined me at the Lamplighter for a couple of hours once or twice a week, all decked out in her Barbie Doll finest. She looked classy. The regulars asked us, but mostly Venus, to join them at their table. Venus made wonderful small talk and reeled in both the old- and new-money gentlemen with equal ease.

When she spoke fluent Spanish to the Mariachi musicians and sang *Sabor a Mi,* and *Tu Solo Tu*, the nouveau riche North Alabama rednecks were visibly impressed, commenting too loud and too long. Of course, old-money was equally impressed, but restrained their emotions in typical subdued fashion.

Venus limited her Lamplighter appearances, although she was always welcomed. My stock went up markedly with Charlotte Lee and Judd Phillips, and Venus became an asset to furthering the Carousels' true objective: securing a record contract with Sam Phillips.

Mary Bishop, Dallas Fingers' main squeeze since they were freshmen in high school and also a fervent, born-again Southern Baptist, joined us in Muscle Shoals. Mary was cute as a bug, sweet, shy, and living in sin with Dallas at the Muscle Shoals Motel, adjoining our trailer park. This marked their first venture into round-the-clock sex, satisfying pent-up premarital carnal pleasure.

Just proves that good sex trumps hypocrisy.

Dallas was in the process of reconciling his fundamentalist biblical beliefs with reality and life on the road as a Carousel. Since Dallas joined the Carousels, he preferred to hang out with me, although he shared Bobby's trailer. I prudently chose to hide the many ugly chinks in my armor.

When Mary arrived, she and Dallas began hanging out with Venus and me. We were perceived to be older and wiser. Truth be known, Venus and I didn't want to burst their bubbles, so we kept our bent lives and rancid secrets to ourselves. Fortunately, our façade was all Dallas and Mary saw.

Once or twice a week, Gert, with her ever-mysterious coffee cup in hand and Angelle arrived at the Lamplighter, always sitting at a table near the stage. However, when Venus and Mary came to the Lamplighter, they sat in the middle, typically joined by Lamplighter guests, exchanging conversation and laughter. It quickly became apparent that tension was brewing among Gert, Angelle, Mary, and Venus. Privately pleased that Gert and Angelle voluntarily isolated themselves from the Lamplighter regulars, I spent extra time with Big Joe and Lance during rehearsals, breaks, and at the trailer park. All I cared about was the Carousels' working as a cohesive team.

The Carousels worked hard to increase the frequency of guests. Judd and Mrs. Lee were pleased with the results. Of course, Judd took all the credit. In truth, I wanted something from Judd, and Judd needed the Carousels or a promising new artist to redeem himself with his brother, Sam Phillips, owner of Sun Records.

Picking what I believed to be just the right moment, I posed the question: "You think Sun is looking for fresh new talent? Why don't you introduce us to Sam? You can be our sponsor."

"Great idea, Rocky," he replied. "Wild Turkey got between two brothers, but it's time we get back together."

According to the grapevine, Judd repeatedly screwed up dates, travel schedules, venues, and contracts, alienating many of Sun Records premier artists. Two artists left the label, blaming Judd's incompetence for their decision. Some say Sam Phillips booted Judd before losing other artist. Falling from grace and dead broke, Judd convinced Mrs. Charlotte Lee to let him manage the food, beverage, and entertainment division of the Lamplighter Country Club. His first big management decision was to book the Carousels. Judd longed to get back to the good life with his brother.

Judd rented sophisticated recording equipment, mixing board, and high-end Telefunken microphones. He played sound engineer while the Carousels cut demos of original material. The sound engineering quality was terrible, but the band sounded good. I hoped Sam's good ear would hear through his brother's lack of sound engineering skills.

I was paying a price for the promise of Judd's sponsorship. He grabbed on to me every break and bent my ear on how the Carousels were going to get him back in with his brother. The more Wild Turkey he consumed the louder he talked, the wilder his road stories became, and the bolder his promises to turn the Carousels into megastars. Mrs. Lee had to ask Judd to quiet down and step into the kitchen for conversation. Judd became belligerent, spewing venom at her—the person who signed his paycheck.

Fortunately, my time with Judd lasted no more than a 15 minute break. I issued encouragement before beginning our featured set, "Create fantasy—sell illusion—project your God Power."

THIRD SET LINEUP—THE LAMPLIGHTER				
SONG	ORIG'L ARTIST	GENRE	ENSEMBLE	FEATURE
West Side Story (Stage Show—Dance)	Leonard Bernstein	Broadway	Dance, Solo's & Ensemble	All Carousels
String of Pearls	Glenn Miller	Big Band	4 Horns	Big Joe, Lance & Rocky
I Left My Heart in San Francisco	Tony Bennett	Crooner	Standard Ensemble	Lance—Vocal
Jolé Blon	Clifton Chenier	Zydeco	Cajun Accordion, Fiddle & Frottoir	Big Joe—Vocal Dallas, Smoke & Rocky
You've Lost That Lovin' Feelin'	Righteous Brothers	R&R	Standard Ensemble	Lance & Big Joe—Vocal
Big Girls Don't Cry	The Four Seasons	R&R	Standard Ensemble	Bobby in Falsetto + 3
Soul Bird (Tin Tin Deo)	Cal Tjader	Latin Jazz	Vibes, Guitar & Conga's	Rocky & Smoke
In This Whole Wide World	The Four Freshman	4 Part Harmony	Standard Ensemble	Bobby, Dallas, Lance & Big Joe
All I Have To Do Is Dream	The Everly Brothers	Country	Standard Ensemble	Bobby & Dallas—Vocal
Come Fly With Me	Frank Sinatra	Big Band Standard	3 Horns	Lance—Vocal, Big Joe & Rocky

On Friday, November 22, at 12:50 p.m., Central Time, Dallas Fingers banged on my trailer door.

Terror radiated from his wide blue eyes. Voice trembling, Dallas said, "President Kennedy has been shot in Dallas! He may even be dead! Turn on your television!" With that, Dallas spun around and disappeared back to Mary Bishop and the motel.

Venus turned on the small black-and-white TV as we joined 200 million Americans for a CBS News Bulletin, delivered by a teary-eyed Walter Cronkite: "… President Kennedy died at 1 p.m. Central Time, some 38 minutes ago."

We shuttered in disbelief at words spoken by the most trusted newsman in America.

Stunned, my jaw dropped to my chest and my eyes widened to catch sight of some perspective. Hot flashes began in my chest, rushing to the top of my head, rattling hair follicles. An imaginary vacuum sucked my breath away, leaving only light-headed bewilderment. My knees weakened and I sat down on the bed, next to a trembling Venus. She gasped for air and reality. Ruby cheeks disappeared, replaced by an ashen face desperate for blood and oxygen.

Her head shook left to right in disbelief murmuring, "No—no—no—no—this can't be happening!"

Cold sweat beads bathed her brow like droplets of acid eating into a naked brain. Aggressively scratching her arms, first redness then blood appeared on porcelain-smooth skin. Placing my hands over hers, I stopped her scratching. Instantly, she threw her arms around my neck, hugging tight as she sobbed, "Never let me go. Hold me tight, Rocky. Never let me go!"

Another CBS Bulletin came at 1:50 p.m. when Walter Cronkite announced that Kennedy's suspected assassin, Lee Harvey Oswald was arrested at a Texas movie theater in Dallas."

Like all Americans, Venus and I stayed glued to the TV during Oswald's booking into the Dallas jail. Live TV cameras captured Oswald's first public comments, linked to his alleged role in the assassination of John F. Kennedy.

"I didn't shoot anybody.... They've taken me in because of the fact that I lived in the Soviet Union. I'm just a patsy!"

Immediately I thought of Finn.

"We have the resources, skills, consensus, and access necessary to pull off a black ops mission of major consequence—the biggest in history." Makes sense—the validity to Finn's and Smoke's stories have just been confirmed. My conversation with Smoke at Mosca's simply laid out one piece of a much larger puzzle. Don't know which option Finn accepted, but his second outlined what just happened in Dallas. If that's the case, the public will never know the truth behind Kennedy's assassination. The bottom line is, I trust Finn's version.

On the other hand, Smoke thinks he knows everything that happened—from David Ferrie in New Orleans. Although the Mafia role is important, it's only one component of the black ops conspiracy. Even with an incomplete chessboard, if Smoke blabbers, he and the Carousels could be in grave danger.

Every TV channel covered every minute detail of the transfer of JFK's body from Parkland Hospital to Love Field, the casket loading on to Air Force One, and the reported swearing in of Lyndon Baines Johnson as President of the United States. Live pictures of the plane taking off from Dallas and landing in D.C. preceded removal of the casket from the rear of Air Force One and a belated statement by America's newest president.

I called a 6 o'clock meeting at Lance's trailer. At my invitation, Mary, Angelle, Gert, and Venus also attended.

Beginning the meeting in a somber, yet firm tone, I said, "Friends, the show must go on. We're in the illusion, fantasy, and dream creation business. This is our job. In spite of this we can't ignore today's events. I'll go in early and talk with Mrs. Lee and Judd. It's their club and they'll determine what happens next.

"Assuming we play tonight, my only request is to begin with a 50-beat-per-minute, 32-bar choke cadence, transitioning into *America the Beautiful*. Big Joe, you handle the musical arrangement. Dallas, your job is calling the right tunes the rest of the evening, a job none of us want tonight. Bobby, minimize emcee work tonight.

I'd be happy if we don't announce any tunes, just play. Otherwise, demonstrate class and dignity."

"I know several of you are dealing with rampant emotions. Some are upset over the assassination of Kennedy. Some are celebrating JFK's death. Keep your opinions away from the Lamplighter. Never offer a response to a customer who hated President Kennedy. Do not express your honest opinions in public—not at the Lamplighter, the cleaners, restaurants or gas stations. We can talk openly among ourselves and say anything we want—venting among ourselves is a good thing—but never in public. America and the Carousels will get through this. We'll be okay."

Dressing in my black tuxedo, I went to the Lamplighter an hour early. Mrs. Lee was nursing a double Scotch at the bar, alone. I approached slowly and sat two stools down. The bartender came over, nodded but said nothing.

I said, "Glenlivet—double—on the rocks."

Mrs. Lee looked my way, smiled, and said, "I've had too much death in my life over these past few months. Sometimes I want to hide and cry for a week. Ever feel like that?"

"On occasion, everyone feels that way. Good Scotch helps relieve the pain," I replied, lifting my glass in a toasting motion.

She responded by lifting her glass and made eye contact for the first time. The whites of her eyes were gone, replaced with blurry purples and reds. This classy southern belle was losing it. Her steel magnolia persona had wilted.

I decided to back off and simply disappear from her pity party, saying, "We will do our best to deal with the patrons this evening. Neither of us know what to expect tonight, although we'll handle this situation with respect and dignity."

Judd Phillips picked that moment to come through the front door of the Lamplighter in a rage. I elected to head him off before he screwed up Mrs. Lee's head even more.

"Judd," I said as I stopped his beeline for Mrs. Lee, "Tonight presents a challenge, but the Carousels will do our best to adjust to the situation. Do you have instructions regarding this evening and our presentation?"

Judd was staring at Mrs. Lee, but finally looked at me and said, "What? Oh yeah, this evening. Just keep it medium and we'll see how the audience responds. Just do whatever you think is best. Okay?"

I felt like a rodeo clown whose job it was to distract pissed-off bulls from trampling tossed riders. Dance as I might, this bull was determined to trample the wilted steel magnolia sitting at the bar.

Nodding in agreement, I stepped out of Judd's way and walked into the dining room. There sat one regular, Charlie Mack. No one else was in the room, not even a waiter. Charlie owned the NAPA franchise for the Muscle Shoals area. He was a nice person who dined with us every evening and stayed until 10 p.m. He always invited Venus to sit at his table. Although Charlie was not married, he was gracious to Venus, the consummate southern gentleman. Charlie had a master's degree in engineering from MIT, made his money at General Motors, and returned to a quieter life in North Alabama. He loved hunting, fishing, and the friendly atmosphere. Charlie was a happy man, even this evening, sitting there as our only customer.

Like pallbearers, black-tuxedoed Carousels mounted the stage. I began a pianissimo, choked 32-bar drum cadence on the floor tom, at an agonizingly slow tempo. Big Joe had done his job well, beginning the first verse of *America the Beautiful* as an instrumental— very somber. The second time through, Lance sang the first verse. We witnessed Charlotte Lee, Judd Phillips, three waiters, two busboys, the dishwasher, and two cooks crying like babies.

Next, with no introduction, Dallas sang *God Bless America*. We all wept. Dallas called a third tune, an old standard, raising the mood, but only slightly. The fourth tune was somewhat brighter.

At that point Judd came to the edge of the stage, called me over and said, "That's it, Rocky. I'm shutting this down. Tell your people to go home. I'll contact you when we decide to reopen the Lamplighter. By the way, you did a great job tonight."

Chapter 36

1963
THINGS NEVER ARE WHAT THEY SEEM

Early Saturday morning, Smoke and I walked to the river and sat on a grassy knoll. Smoke's tic accelerated as he expounded, "Two weeks ago, according to David Ferrie, a four-man team of shooters were to be flown from Italy into Winnipeg, Canada. Chicago, Tampa, and Dallas were the targeted hit cities. Once the go-ahead was issued, Ferrie would fly the hit team from Canada into the selected city. Following the hit, two goodfellas driving two cars would lead the escape. If Dallas was selected as the target city, they'd escape to Mexico on isolated back roads through the Texas desert.

"However, I got the distinct impression that none of the shooters would make it to the Rio Grande—at least alive. The southern Texas desert is the perfect place to bury secrets, evidence and bodies. That leads me to the high-value of a patsy like Oswald. Remember the sign hanging over Marcello's door, *'Three can keep a secret if two are dead?'* What's next? Rocky, this thing is just beginning."

We talked for half an hour. As Smoke exhausted all he knew or thought he knew, I reflected on Finn, adding plausibility and dimension to a grand conspiracy. Satisfied with my understanding of what really happened in Dallas and what will happen in the days ahead, I wound up my conversation with Smoke and returned to my trailer and Venus.

Following a light lunch, I shared my plans to meet daily with the Carousels, explaining our band of brothers to Venus. She didn't understand the brotherhood part, but welcomed the free time "for me to deal with my devils and the assassination."

Out of the blue Venus volunteered, "I hated the man and his family. I believe the Kennedys were destroying the South. Evil people. Be that as it may, for some reason, I feel guilty about the assassination. I have to work through this in my own way."

Saturday, about 2 p.m., I took a walk to give space to Venus and me. On a lark I located a pay phone and tracked down Candy Barr at the Carousel Club in Dallas. A man answered, "Carousel Club—Jack Ruby."

"This is Rocky Strong with the Carousels. I want to speak with Candy Barr."

"Just a minute—who are you, anyway?"

"Rocky Strong—friend of Carlos and Vince Marcello, Walter Noto and Merrill Saks. Let me speak with Candy."

Following a brief pause I heard a lovely sound: "Hello Rocky. I miss you."

"How you holding up?"

"Not good. Dallas is crazy. Have to get out of here. When can I see you?"

"That's not a good idea right now. What's the scuttlebutt on the ground in Dallas?"

"Jack's gone schizoid, cryin' like a baby. Yesterday, following a long phone call with Carlos Marcello, Jack lost it. They talked again today. Jack says he's going to kill Oswald. Still the way he says it is strange, like something or someone … All I can say is Jack's being squeezed."

"What are the Dallas cops saying? What's their take on this?"

"That's really weird. Dallas cops said federal agents took control of everything; the Texas Book Depository, Parkland Hospital, and the Texas Theater. Federal agents took over Oswald's interrogation, Kennedy's hospital records, the car Kennedy rode in ... everything. Most of Dallas is shut down. The feds are hiding somethin'—somethin' big. Everything's upside down—smoke and mirrors, if you know what I mean. The world has gone schizoid. When will I see you?"

"Like you, I'm on a circuit and can't pack up and leave. I needed to check up on you to see if you're okay."

"I'm caught up in something bad—really bad—and I'm not okay. This is the beginning—not the end. I'm scared, Rocky."

I promised that we'd hook up as soon as possible.

Walking back to the trailer park, I knocked on the door of Bobby's trailer. Black twinkling eyes appeared.

"What's up, Rocky?" Bobby said, motioning me inside.

He handed me a cup of CDM chicory, and we sat quietly together, watching a somber epic event play out on his television.

In muted intonation, the commentator said, "... a horse drawn caisson carries the casket of our dead leader in front of thousands of morning citizens flanking the route from the White House to the Capital." The TV commentator's voice was solemn, detailing every nuance' in whispered tones. "... following the caisson is a single horse without a rider, boots reversed in the stirrups to signify a fallen leader looking back at his troops...."

Bobby turned down the sound before speaking.

"You know my Dad's the Grand Dragon in North Louisiana with the Third Klan and a member of the White Citizens Counsel. He raised us to hate niggers, Jews, and the Kennedys. I literally cheered when JFK's brains splattered all over the Lincoln. Everyone I know hated Kennedy's anti-segregationist agenda. Strangely I feel guilty, as if I personally pulled the trigger on him in Dallas. It's confusing; glad he's gone, but feeling strange...."

"I know," nodding, "your feelings are natural and human."

Bobby took a sip of chicory and continued, "Rock, I'm concerned about something else. What's the future of the band? Will this disrupt our road to fame? Are we fucked?"

"Too early to tell, although I have the same questions. However, I have a suggestion for turning tragedy into triumph. We need fresh material for the recording studio. Go to the Muscle Shoals library. Read Joseph's Campbell's, *The Hero with a Thousand Faces,* then read *The Giving Tree* by Shel Silverstein. There's several hit records imbedded in those books and they intersect with the JFK assassination. If that's not enough, pick out songs from a hymnal at church and get inspiration for our Nashville recordings."

Bobby brightened and responded, "Good advice. I'll clear my mind, go to the library, read, and compose. I guess a brand new verse of 'Dixie' would be out of the question—or would it?"

We sipped CDM and chewed on lighter subject matter. Following ten minutes of relaxed trivia, I sensed our time was right to say goodbye.

Lance Love was outside his trailer working on an electrical hookup. Approaching, I asked, "How's the future pig farmer doing today?"

Lance laughed and responded, "My cow died last night, so I don't need your bull." We both laughed at the old southern greeting.

"Just getting this plug changed out. Has a short. Actually, I had to find some excuse to get out of the trailer. Going nuts in there. The television reporters are depressing—the dramatization of the casket transported on the caisson and its placement in the Capitol rotunda was melodramatic. The steady line of mourners passing by the casket to pay their respects—it'll go on till the funeral on Monday. Angelle is sobbing her eyes out, the baby has a terrible cold, and Smoke is hanging from the ceiling in his bat cave, glued to the television and smokin' loco in his hookah. I can't take being around all that negativity. Outside is fresh air and sanity. What's up with you?"

"I'm making the rounds. Checking out Carousel heads."

Motioning for us to sit in Lance's folding chairs, I asked, "What are your thoughts—the Kennedy assassination?"

Lance responded, "I can't tell the good guys from the bad guys anymore. Everything's turned upside down. The politicians and news media spin everythin', covering up the truth. Can't trust …"

Pausing for a long time, Lance continued, "Actually, President Kennedy screwed up—a lot. The Bay of Pigs, Cuban Missile Crisis, civil rights, and Vietnam, just to name a few. I wouldn't give him the sweat off my balls. This country is better off without the bastard. Maybe Johnson can get this country back on track. As for the future of America, that's the huge question mark."

I responded, "Tell the truth and shame the devil."

Lance then said, "This will jar your preserves. The FBI dude drove over from Atlanta this morning."

"Well?"

"Actually, he asked some interesting questions."

"Such as?"

"He asked if I'd heard anything about a CIA-Mafia plot to kill Kennedy. He also asked if I knew anything about a CIA black ops plan or cover-up. Anything that sheds light on the Kennedy assassination?"

"Do you?"

"Not really, but I'm not stupid. I didn't share my speculations with the FBI dude. He's looking for something to report to his bosses. Any off-the-cuff remarks I make might get me hauled in for questioning by those northern FBI gorillas. Even if I knew something, mum's the word."

"Speaking of patsies," I said. "It's best you know something explosive. Smoke's our Achilles' heel—two bricks short of a load. While we were in New Orleans Smoke spent time with David Ferrie, who laid out the entire Kennedy assassination plot and named all the patsies, including Oswald. This conversation took place in the narrow bar behind the Dream Room stage. Smoke's a loose cannon. That's probably why he's so spaced out on Tijuana tea today. One slip of the tongue in the wrong circles and Smoke sleeps with the fishes—and you know we'll be next in line."

"Mother fucker! He fell out of a tree and hit every branch on the way down. I'll kill that son-of-a-bitch."

"The line forms behind me. I snatched his balls out of the fire in Toledo, St. Paul, and Peoria. Sooner or later we'll have to face up to a final solution."

Following a long pause, Lance said, "Sometimes I feel like an ox yoked to a Conestoga wagon. My load gets heavier every day. I spend every cent I make on car notes, trailer payments, food, and baby supplies. Financially, I'm strapped.

"Another thing—I planned to go on the road and plug holes in chickadees. I'm jealous every time I look at you and Bobby. I try not to think about it, although I fantasize over your relationship with Miss Goodbody. You're doing exactly what I intended, but I've turned into an ol' man at 24. This picture isn't right. I really need to lighten my load and get this picture right."

I replied, "Take your free pass card out of hiding and get it punched. We're living in times of guiltless free love. You set my standard and issued my free pass card. Come on—rejoin the party."

Lance raised an eyebrow before saying, "Interesting idea—shitty timing."

We finally laughed together, reveling in the joys of swapping-hole parties and the magic whistle at the rental house in Monroe. We belly-laughed ourselves into exhaustion. Finally, sensing Lance had a good grip on reality and his emotions, I rose, waived my hand across my waistline like James Dean, and strolled off toward my next stop.

Big Joe and Gert were washing their Jeep, sobbing like babies. I asked, "Is this a good time or should I come back later?"

Big Joe said, "Get funk off us."

"Get fuck off you?" I asked.

"No. Funk. Funk. Ya know—depression."

Gert spoke, "Don't you hate what happened? Crazy Oswald put our country into a tailspin. Kennedy wasn't perfect, but he was our president—my president. He's gone. Been crying ever since."

Big Joe added, "The last time I cried like dis was when mama passed. Never got to say 'I love ya.'"

I said, "Replace despair with creativity. Compose new tunes in tune with our times. Treat this as opportunity in masquerade. Our recording session with Judd last week will take on a life of its own— with introductions to his brother. That's done. On Monday I'll buy a Roberts tape recorder and we'll cut new demos at the Lamplighter, circulating our new material around Nashville. Focus on Nashville and securing a record deal. Dump the funk. Get back on the road to victory."

"That's good, Rock," Big Joe responded. "Replace down with up. Good thinkin'."

Gert took a sip of elixir from her cup and said, "I'm in a funk, too. What should I do?"

I said, "Stand by your man. Open up your *Kama Sutra* book and give him plenty of lovin'. That'll raise you both out of the funk."

Incredibly, Big Joe displayed a boner, visible through wet, stained pants.

Thank you God for sending me Venus instead of Gert.

For Saturday night supper, Venus cooked a big pot of chicken and andouille sausage gumbo. Her rue was among the best I ever tasted. On the table was potato salad on lettuce leaves and a pitcher of ice tea. I sprinkled filé on my gumbo, took a sip, smiled, and said, "Very tasty."

When the last morsels disappeared from our soup bowls, Venus moved to my side of the table and said, "Hold me, Rocky. I feel safe in your arms. Tell me everything will be okay. Hold me tight."

Tenderly, I whispered, "Everything's okay. We'll be okay."

Her jasmine cologne overpowered the stench of a nation in mourning.

A red-tailed hawk soared gracefully over the river in search of prey. Cumulus clouds moved between sun and earth, offering solace to weary eyes. Lying swaddled in tenderness we found peace together, eventually drifting into shameless sleep that lasted til dawn.

Chapter 37

1963
REQUIEM

Early Sunday morning, I walked up to Room 8 of the Muscle Shoals Motel. Through the open curtains I could see Dallas and Mary, eyes glued to the TV set. Dallas and Marry looked up and opened the door before I could knock.

"Hi, Rock," Mary said. "Come in."

"I see you're staring at the television," disapproval in my voice.

Dallas said, "We are, but I'll turn it off."

Motioning to the outside I said, "Let's take a walk and enjoy a beautiful morning in North Alabama."

Dallas turned off the TV and the three of us walked fifty yards to the Tennessee River, made small talk, and enjoyed each other's company. The bright sun warmed our bodies and spirits. At what seemed the appropriate time I asked, "How are you guys holding up?"

Dallas began, "I tell ya. Mary, me, and our parents are glad President Kennedy's dead. Kennedys are nigger lovers. They were destroying the South. He got exactly what he deserved—bullets pumped into his brain. Mary and I prayed for an hour this morning, thanking God he's finished. We feel much better now, knowing that God's will has been fulfilled in Dallas. God protects us. Praise God!

God's prophecies are coming to pass. Maybe Johnson can turn this around."

As Dallas spoke, Mary's head nodded in agreement.

Dallas continued, "People in the North don't understand where southerners are comin' from. When the Civil War ended and the Emancipation Proclamation came in, freeing the slaves destroyed our southern economy."

"Where did you hear that?" I asked.

"My Dad teaches American History and Mom's a librarian," Dallas said. "Also, they learned a lot from their parents and grandparents about what really happened back then."

"What really happened?" I asked.

"The wealth of the South was invested in slaves to work the fields and perform jobs necessary in an agrarian society. The total investment in the South's labor force was larger than the North's total investment in all their industries. With the stroke of a pen, the South's major asset became worthless. Without labor to work the fields and no money to repay bank loans, greedy northern carpetbaggers gobbled up plantations for pennies on the dollar. To this day, we hate the North for raping our culture and economy."

I asked, "What else did your parents teach you?"

"The slaves lost, too—nowhere to go to support themselves or their families. Southern plantations that survived the carpetbaggers gave the ex-slaves and their families' jobs, housing, food, medical care, and education. Most successful plantations worked on the task system, opposite the gang system. Actually, that's where sharecropping originated. Since then, southerners have taken care of niggers out of the goodness of our Christian hearts. And for the next hundred years the South's black and white interdependence remained in balance— until Dr. Martin Luther King, Jr. and the Kennedys came along."

"You hate both King and the Kennedys?" I interjected.

"King is the typical nigger preacher, ignorant of Holy Scripture, using them as tools to fornicate with members of his congregation. On many occasions King said he wanted to fornicate with white women, and did. Adultery is one of the Ten Commandments, and he committed it all the time. King is probably a Communist. He's doing all this marching and stuff for money, fame, and power. Only the young, ignorant northern students and stupid niggers support King. He's a terrible human being, along with Stokely Carmichael, Rap Brown, and Malcolm X—despicable scum."

Dallas was on a roll, and I watched in fascination while he continued his white supremacist rant, exposing the bigotry in every pore of his body.

"Anyway, the Civil Rights Movement is a Communist plot. The Kennedys are in cahoots, using King to break up the South, destroy our southern heritage, our spirit, and the Southern Baptist Convention. Kennedys are Catholic and hate Baptists. King and the Freedom Riders are Kennedy's frontline soldiers.

"It's a conspiracy to overthrow the South and integrate the races. Over time, race becomes blurred by intermarriage and dummin' down, making America ripe for the pickin'. If this continues, we could have a nigger president, leading to socialism, and a Communist takeover. The Kennedys, King, and Freedom Riders are dividing the South and the America we love. They must be stopped. Oswald's bullet was only the first. Mark my words, there'll be more blood spilled."

"Who will get the other bullets?" I asked.

"That's easy," Dallas replied. "MLK and Robert Kennedy, top my list."

Mary asked, "Where do you stand, Rocky?"

"America lost her innocence November 22. We'll never be the same. Throughout history, when subjects assassinate their king, the empire falls into chaos, disorder, and ultimately, collapse. Everything changed Friday. Innocence is no more. All of us are victims and to blame."

"Are you saying Kennedy was a king?" Mary asked.

"A metaphor, Mary. Metaphor, as in symbolic. Our king was killed by one of his subjects. We are all to blame. A cancerous hatred is sweeping over American culture. Hatred destroys. Love nourishes and builds. I prefer love over hate."

"So where do you stand, Rocky?

"I'm a political centrist, neither left nor right of center. I see both sides objectively and prefer the high ground—staying out of the ditches. I try to be a good Presbyterian and Calvinist. The bottom line is I'm just Rocky. Good enough?"

"No. That's not good enough," Mary answered. "We've been open with you. Where do you stand?"

"Presbyterians believe that God is in charge; not man. Granted, it's often inconvenient to understand or accept God's plan for us, particularly when faced with justifying slavery, the Civil War, destruction of southern culture, world wars, JFK's assassination, or the MLK's Civil Rights Movement."

"So, you believe God pulled the trigger, not Lee Harvey Oswald?" Mary said.

"I didn't say explaining God's plan is easy. Actually, I don't know the answer to your question. Also, I don't know why I'm out here on the road instead of graduating from Louisiana Tech. I only know that I'm here for a reason and trust a higher power to chart my course. That's why I call myself a centrist—it's much easier than explaining Calvinism and predestination."

I've just exposed the tip of my iceberg. Facing facts, I'm way off course—at least the one set by the Mason's and perhaps God. Today, the bad within me has pushed out good. Dear God, have your will with my life. Give me the wisdom to understand my mission and the courage to carry it out.

Mary's demure nature and soft-spoken voice turned militant, her tightening facial muscles readied for shouting slogans only the Daughters of the Confederacy could appreciate.

"I've always believed the South will rise again, break away from those corrupt politicians in the North. This is a sign from Heaven. The wrath of God descended on John Kennedy! 'Thy will be done.' This is our time to reconstruct the Confederacy. We'll take back what is rightfully ours. Praise Jesus! The South will rise again! Praise Jesus!"

She only heard what she wanted to hear. There's a boiling cauldron of hate in Mary's belly. Her public façade of the straight-laced Pollyanna disguises a bigot. *Charming and cunning as she can be, its best I never let my guard down with Mary. She'll never see my iceberg below the water line.*

"I welcome your candor in private—others may not," I told her. "Many will be offended by crediting God for Kennedy's assassination. We should bite our tongues in public, particularly given our celebrity status. As an entertainer, taking political positions is the kiss of death. Please take this to heart as we get back on our road to fame and fortune."

Both nodded in agreement. Walking from the river back to the motel Mary made an unexpected announcement: "Dallas and I are talking about getting married. What do you think, Rocky?"

I said, "Wonderful. You two have my blessing, support, and congratulations. You'll be blissfully happy. A long, rich life together. Congratulations. You two found happiness hidden in the midst of despair. Hang on to your handle and go for it."

Upon returning to their motel room Marry turned on the TV, immediately fixating on JFK's casket lying in state in the U.S. Capitol rotunda. As I was leaving, I overheard a snippet of the commentator, "... over 90 world leaders are here to pay their respects to our fallen president. They are joined by a seemingly endless line of mourners, expected to last all day and all night—right up until they transfer the casket to St Matthews Cathedral for the funeral service on Monday ..."

I knocked on Lance's trailer door. Angelle appeared in a shapeless moo moo and stringy hair that hadn't seen shampoo for at least a week. She opened the sliding glass door and invited me in. Remaining outside I said, "Let Smoke know I'd like to talk with him—outside."

Angelle nodded and disappeared to knock on Smoke's bat cave.

Smoke appeared unshaven, mussed hair, still in pajamas, and reeking of pungent reefers. I insisted that he come outside and sit with me, and he reluctantly nodded.

Stumbling to the patio, Smoke was so stoned, his tic temporarily disappeared. He carried black French smokes and a Dunhill lighter, lighting up as we sat. Smoke never passed up an opportunity to foster his James Bond self-image, stoned or not. Unfortunately, he consistently failed to hit the mark.

Ignoring his poor theatrics, I said, "Smoke, you got most of this assassination conspiracy thing right. How do you feel about being privileged to insider knowledge weeks before the assassination took place?"

"Not sure how I feel," Smoke slurred. "I'm afraid your predictions hit da nail on da head. Ferrie could give me up in a heartbeat. I'm livin' in da moment and flyin' high. Right now, I'm untouchable."

"Other than me, who knows the full story?"

"Uh … Uh … No one."

"Keep it that way. Our lives could depend on you keeping your mouth shut."

Smoke said, "I keep thinkin' 'bout David Ferrie tellin' me all dat stuff. Why would he do dat if he weren't settin' me up?"

Smoke's inherent limitations are focused on the narrow picture that the Mafia assassinated Kennedy. In Toledo, my buddy Finn laid out the full scope of the assassination plot and black ops cover-up. Smoke's only got one piece of a much larger puzzle. He must never know what I know. I'll leave Smoke twistin' in the wind to deal with his vulnerability as Ferrie's patsy.

I asked, "So, what's next, Smoke?"

"Remember? I answered dat question at Mosca's. Da Carousels future wit' Marcello is dead. Merrill Saks is dead. Da music business—dead. Dis assassination ding will throw America into World War III. Who needs da Carousels in da middle of a war?"

"Touché, Smoke. We both know this is only the first act in a three-act tragedy. Sober up and keep your mouth shut."

On a beautiful sunny Sunday in Muscle Sholes, I strolled back to Venus and my tin can around one. Upon entering, Venus had just turned on the television to get an update. An anxious announcer fumbled with words to describe what had just taken place. Reruns of someone shooting Oswald were playing on TV, over and over, recorded on a loop tape. An excited reporter said, "This morning, Sunday, November 24, Lee Harvey Oswald was being led through the basement of Dallas Police Headquarters toward an armored car that was to take him to the nearby county jail. At 11:21 a.m. Central Standard Time, Dallas nightclub operator Jack Ruby stepped from the crowd and shot Oswald in the chest, the bullet striking several organs, penetrating his stomach, and tearing his vena cava and aorta. Oswald was taken unconscious by ambulance to Parkland Memorial Hospital—the same hospital where doctors tried to save President Kennedy's life two days earlier. Lee Harvey Oswald was pronounced dead at 1:07 p.m. Central Standard Time, Dallas, Texas."

Instantly, I understood the consequences of what just happened. *Everything Finn said was true. Smoke's information from David Ferry was true. Bet, we'll never learn who pulled the trigger on Kennedy. It certainly wasn't Oswald. If Smoke goes down, we'll all go down. This isn't what I signed up for.*

Sunday afternoon, I began a three-mile run by the river. The solitude was the perfect tonic for clearing clutter that had rattled around in my brain. Afterward, I rested in the shade of a large water oak. As I strolled back, Venus was sun bathing on a quilt, scantily dressed in a halter-top and short shorts. I gazed at my beautiful Barbie Doll—gorgeous; one of the most beautiful women I'd known.

A full minute passed before she sensed my presence.

"Welcome home, my love."

Inside our magic cocoon we found peace, locking out a chaotic world.

Monday morning, Smoke and I took a walk. Still stoned, he stumbled to the river as I held his arm in support.

Smoke said, "Ruby's Carousel Club rotates strippers with Vince Marcello at da Show Bar. Dis connection points straight to Carlos Marcello. Ferrie can give me up any day now."

For the first time, Smoke was scared.

I said, "Could James Bond be trusted with a secret?"

Brow furrowed, Smoke replied, "Always."

"Become 007. Lock your secrets away from the bad guys. A tight lip will save your life. As far as Ferrie ratting you out, we'll monitor the pressure coming down on Carlos Marcello. That'll tell us if Ferrie is going to serve you up as his fall guy. Think James Bond—think cool."

Smoke staggered back to his bat cave, pluggin' back into his beloved hookah.

The only way to crawl out of depression was to unplug the television. Venus and I limited TV time to 20 minutes a day, just to keep in touch. Monday afternoon we saw rerun clips of JFK's funeral mass at St. Mathews Cathedral and the temporary grave site and eternal flame ceremony at Arlington National Cemetery.

Devotees to 24 hour television coverage of the JFK assassination saga became zombie-like, approaching catatonic. Those of us choosing to restrict TV to a few minutes a day emerged mostly sane. Venus and I searched for happiness elsewhere. I believe it saved our sanity.

My extensive record collection provided the great escape. Miles, Dizzy, Chet Baker, Tjader, Coltrane, Brubeck, Four Freshmen, Lee Morgan, Ramsey Lewis, and 50 other jazz greats became our security blanket.

Given that Monday was a National Day of Mourning, I contacted Judd Phillips by phone to get instructions. Judd told me to bring the Carousels back to the Lamplighter stage Wednesday night. Until then, my record collection kept Venus and me smiling. Emotionally, we ran away.

That afternoon, we began a daily routine that included working out, long walks among the hardwoods, and picnics on the banks of the Tennessee River. Venus caught two trout and prepared Trout Veronique for dinner, served by candlelight. We escaped to a place removed from reality.

Five-day stubble removed from glum faces, body and hair washed for the first time in days and mind slippage adjusted, the Carousels prepared to officially end the mourning period for ourselves and our audience. Carousel attitudes were spot-on as we reopened the Lamplighter Wednesday evening, radiating a positive aura with our wine-colored tuxedos.

Our audience was exhausted, ready to put the horror behind them. Clearly, defrosting frozen emotions was our mission. A large crowd, particularly for a Wednesday, was ready to party, and we led them back to some semblance of normalcy.

The Carousels successfully ended our third week by premiering a new stage show on Friday and Saturday. The show was a grand success. Judd was impressed and said so, many times. Mrs. Lee was equally pleased, expressing her desire to contract us for a return engagement. During our fourth and final week, we delivered the new stage show on alternating nights, fine-tuning as needed.

I purchased a Roberts 1770D reel-to-reel tape recorder to cut demo tapes. Tuesday, Wednesday, and Thursday rehearsals focused on recording Bobby, Dallas, Lance, and Big Joe's original material. With ten hours invested, we emerged with ten original cuts. Bobby, Big Joe, Lance, and I dialed for dollars to set appointments with record producers, publishers, and studios in Nashville. Most granted us an audience to preview our new material.

Venus and I settled into normalcy, enjoying life in the North Alabama hill country. Over breakfast Friday, our last week at the Lamplighter, Venus delivered an announcement.

"I have pressing bills and have to go back to work to earn money. I called my old boss in Biloxi, put a small band together, and I open Monday."

Finally, I responded. "Reluctantly, I'll support your decision. Missing you is a gross understatement, but I'll not stand in your way."

"Thanks, Rocky. Sometimes I feel like a caged bird—have to fly away, just to make sure I'm still free. Letting me go to Biloxi tells me everything about our future together. I need the money and time to think about us."

Inadvertently, something I said or did Saturday triggered Venus' desire to cancel her Biloxi trip. In the end, Venus went south to Biloxi Sunday morning, and the Carousel caravan motored north to Nashville.

My tin can in tow, I felt odd, alone for the first time in two months. The big Caddy engine purred easily through the three-hour journey while I assessed the universe and my place in it. The more I pondered, the larger my migraine. About an hour into the drive, I abandoned trying to make sense out of nonsense. *I really need to let go and enjoy life as it comes. Suave de vive.*

From the Cadillac floorboard Mad Hatter again recited his favorite quote: *"The Jabberwock, with eyes aflame, Jaws that bait and claws that catch, Beware the Jabberwock, my son. The frumious Bandersnatch. He took his vorpal sword in hand. The vorpal blade went snicker-snack. He left it dead, and with its head He went galumphing back. It's all about you, you know."*

Cheshire Cat meowed contempt for Hatter, *"That was rude, you are! Rabbit knows a thing or two and I myself, don't need a weather vane to tell which way the wind blows."*

Chapter 38

1963
CELEBRITY HERO

Following the JFK assassination, Americans stumbled around like zombies in a fog, not knowing if their country was going to war against Castro, Khrushchev, Mao Tse-tung, or all three. Fundamental truths fell under scrutiny. Conspiracy theories, Vietnam protests, rioting in the streets, and rejection of everything authoritarian sparked mass migrations toward social anarchy. Alcohol and drug consumption exploded. Young Americans were dropping out—escaping into hooch, acid, blow, bongs, angel dust, amp, apple jacks, aunt mary, and auntiemma. From that moment on, America changed.

In spite of the doom and gloom, the Carousels attacked Nashville with renewed enthusiasm, on stage and off. Our new stage show was a hit. Spontaneous applause was expected and received. Both Dotty and Larry LaSalle were ecstatic with the results. Larry's Mob boss was pleased.

Before kicking off our featured set, I said, "Create fantasy—sell illusion—project your God Power."

THIRD SET STAGE SHOW LINEUP—THE BLACK POODLE				
SONG	ORIG'L ARTIST	GENRE	ENSEMBLE	FEATURE
West Side Story (Stage Show—Dance)	Leonard Bernstein	Broadway	Dance, Solo's & Ensemble	All Carousels
Orange Blossom Special	Ervin and Gordon Rouse	Country	Fiddle, Banjo & Guitar	Big Joe & Smoke
Stand By Your Man (Comedy)	Tammy Wynette (Parody)	Country Comedy Routine	Standard Ensemble	Bobby in Falsetto
Twistin' The Night Away	Sam Cooke	Pop	Standard Ensemble	Bobby—Vocal
Soul Bird (Tin Tin Deo)	Cal Tjader	Latin Jazz	Vibes, Guitar & Conga's	Rocky & Smoke
Who's On First (Comedy Excerpts)	Abbott and Costello	Comedy Routine	None	Big Joe & Dallas
Slow Motion Baseball (Comedy) Excerpts from *Casey at the Bat*—Author Ernest Thayer	Strobe Light—Slow Motion Comedy of Baseball Game	Comedy Routine	Dallas—Baseball Stadium Organ	Bobby, Rocky, Smoke & Big Joe
Malagueña	Smoke	Classical	Acoustic Guitar	Smoke—solo
A Taste Of Honey	Herb Alpert& The Tijuana Brass	Pop	3 Horns	Big Joe, Lance & Rocky
Charlie Brown (Comedy)	The Coasters	Comedy Routine	Standard Ensemble	Dallas & Smoke
Jolé Blon	Clifton Chenier	Zydeco	Cajun Accordion, Fiddle & Frottoir	Big Joe Vocal Dallas, Smoke & Rocky

Dallas carried the spotlight with his comedy versions of *Who's On First* and *Charlie Brown*. Although Big Joe and Smoke participated in the routines with some funny lines and gestures, the audience couldn't look away from Dallas' rubbery facial expressions and hilarious body language. Genuine talent was on display, and Nashville showed its appreciation with standing ovations every time he performed what ultimately became classics.

That success pulled Dallas to a featured spot on at least one tune during each set. Good looking, a captivating stage presence, and a good musician, Dallas spread his wings in Nashville. He was no longer the newbie. We made room for his growing talents.

At Wednesday's rehearsal Bobby boasted, "The Carousels are the magic sauce for the Black Poodle—we're gods. What puzzles me is what we're doin' to create the illusion of greatness and, better yet, how do we repeat the process?"

Sensing my time was right to paint visions of grandeur, I took a risk, knowing I could potentially be laughed off my precarious perch.

"Musicians, entertainers, actors, and sports figures are anointed with extraordinary powers as seen through the eyes of an adoring public," I began. "Celebrity heroes only exist in the minds of our audiences. Audiences fantasize about tapping into celebrity heroes' spiritual energy. In truth, fans are searching for a means to overcome their ineptness, unhappiness, despair, and bankrupt souls. We are their heroes, leading them into fantasy, releasing them from mundane lives. We become their pathway to redemption … resurrection. Any reactions?"

Lance said, "Ain't dat some shit? Pretty good yarn, Rock."

"The way you laid it out kinda makes sense," Bobby added.

Big Joe grunted, "Dare ya go again … bein' da pompous ass smart aleck."

Smoke said, "Go on, Rocky."

Continuing, I said, "Celebrity is all about self. Hero is about the welfare of others over self. A paradox. A celebrity is someone famous. A hero can be many things, although in general he's someone who contributes positively to other people, but he's not necessarily famous. When we strike the right balance between the celebrity in us and the hero in us, we achieve a magical state—the secret sauce. Fans thirst to believe in something larger than themselves, eagerly signing up as disciples.

"Yeah. That's it." Bobby said.

Elaborating, I said, "However, entertainers who symbolize god-like powers are seen to suffer one prime weakness: hubris. Ironically, entertainers are naturally arrogant. It is difficult to balance celebrity with humility. The message here is avoid hubris."

Bobby said, "You're nuttier than a squirrel turd, but it smells good."

I said, "To make this simple I call it God Power—a spiritual conversation between fans and us. Consciously or unconsciously we compel audiences to worship the Carousels. They happily respond because they need us. If you choose to embrace God Power, you'll capture the secret sauce recipe. Channel celebrity into creating and feeding your disciples. But remember, avoid hubris."

Lance eloquently summed up, "That's gooder 'n grits."

Two weeks prior to Christmas, Venus flew to Nashville for five days. The grace and tenderness she exhibited in Louisiana and Alabama was replaced by a femme fatale. With one exception, Venus avoided any mention of Biloxi or her past. The exception: "I got a Mississippi divorce from Luis. I'm free of him and that life. I'm yours, if you'll have me."

Her third night in Nashville, Venus joined me at the Black Poodle, sitting at the piano bar. A husband-and-wife duo began playing two hours before the Carousels' first set and during our first break. From her prime vantage point, Venus watched the Bobbie and

Billy duo perform, and later struck up a conversation when they took a break. It proved fortuitous.

They asked if Venus was alone or with someone.

"Yes," Venus replied. "I'm with Rocky Strong, leader of the Carousels."

"Great band," Bobbie said. "One of the best we've played opposite in a long time."

Billy added, "I wish they could meet Stan Zuckerman. He'd fall in love with the Carousels."

"I've heard of Stan Zuckerman," Venus replied. "Isn't he a big-time personal manager? Is he your personal manager?"

"We wouldn't have it any other way," Bobbie said. "We simply let Mr. Z know an area of the country we want to see, and he lines up a tour. He's always placed us in class clubs at good money. We love Mr. Z."

"Who else does he manage?" Venus asked.

"His current stable of artists is large and impressive," Bobbie said. "Andy Williams, Perry Como, the Beach Boys, Pat Boone, Bobby Darin, Danny Thomas, Tony Bennett, Ricky Nelson, and more. We are one of only two small acts he handles. Mr. Z watches over us like a father. Want his business card?"

Venus extended her hand and Mr. Z's business card graced her palm.

On our ride to the trailer park after the gig, Venus told me about her conversation with Bobbie and Billy and excitedly promoted possibilities for the Carousels.

"Get Mr. Z to come to Nashville—your best venue for showcasing the Carousels. Once he sees your act, I know he'll offer you a personal management contract. This could be big—really big."

"We've been approached by Merrill Saks and Carlos Marcello on that, although ..."

Venus interrupted me, exclaiming, "You do realize that Carlos Marcello is no longer your passport to fame and fortune. He's busy distancing himself from the JFK assassination. Find a replacement. Now!"

"And you believe Stan Zuckerman could be our passport?"

"Rocky, a personal management contract with Mr. Z opens doors to the big show. Bobbie and Billy agreed to provide their recommendations, but you have to make this happen."

The following morning, the sound of loud clacking exploded from my dusty manual Underwood typewriter. After composing a letter to Stan Zuckerman on Carousel letterhead, I included a brochure, business card, and 8x10 glossy in an oversized envelope.

Venus beamed with pride that I'd taken her advice to heart. We posted the package to Mr. Z that afternoon.

I waited until I was driving Venus to the airport before giving her a Christmas present. She loved the pearl earrings in spite of being embarrassed—no Christmas gift for me.

Hugging for a long time at the gate, I realized that letting Venus go was not getting easier. As I leaned in to consume my last whiff of jasmine, brainwaves synchronized between us, raising the hairs on my neck. Beginning at her head and ending at her toes, Venus trembled with electric passion. Her hand rose to brush away hairs covering my forehead, her touch as soft as a velvet glove.

Why did Venus come to Nashville? Did she have an agenda, and was it satisfied? Did I miss something? Venus presented a new facet of her fractured personality, a different woman—wonderfully sensual, although very nervous, consumed with anxiety and a hint of desperation.

Women. Who can figure 'em? There are a lot of mysteries and dangers surrounding that woman. Venus is grand, as long as I don't look too deep into her history and ulterior motives … just enjoy our blissful time together and avoid complications. Just lay back and let the good times roll.

Dallas and Mary planned their wedding in Nashville the week before Christmas. Bride in Cinderella white and Carousels in black tuxes, we all arrived at the Baptist Church for the marriage ceremony promptly at 11 a.m. on a Wednesday. Big Joe gave Mary away. Bobby was best man, and I was asked to be Mary's maid of honor. I grinned, but accepted my new role, knowing that Venus would have been Mary's first choice. So I played Venus's understudy, recognizing the implications of Mary not asking Angelle or Gert—an unmistakable affront.

The newlyweds celebrated their reception in a private dining room at Denny's Restaurant. Each of us paid for our meals. Dallas and Mary were beaming with joy—particularly now that their born-again Southern Baptist Convention asses were legal. Congratulatory speeches from each Carousel and female companion, beginning with Bobby and ending with Gert, reinforced our bonding. Our band of brothers and sisters rejoiced in Dallas's and Mary's blessed event.

I'm privileged to be invited inside their circle of trust. Deep-seeded prejudices, strong devotion to the Southern Baptist Convention and uninhibited passions bind them—perhaps ensuring a blissful marriage that'll last a lifetime. Have they discovered what I'm still seeking?

As was the case a year earlier, our contract with the Black Poodle included a four-week stretch, off Christmas week, return to reopen New Year's Eve and play out the first week of January. Leaving the big trailers in Nashville, we towed the instrument trailer to North Louisiana for Christmas, our families and a couple of gigs.

Being home with family for Christmas and a week of relaxation was wonderful. In six years on the road, I never missed being home for Christmas with Mom.

Following Nashville, our next stop was the windy city—Chicago!

Grousing from the floorboard, Hatter meowed, *"Do you know why they call me Hatter? Because I'm always there when they pass the hat, so to speak."*

Cheshire's motor ran, once again citing her favorite quote, *"To the royal guards of this realm, we are all victims in-waiting.*

Chapter 39

1964
NORTH BROADWAY AND ABSINTHE

Searching the *Mobile Home Park Bible* for a Chicago park near the club proved futile. Chicago and the surrounding area had an ordinance prohibiting trailers of any kind. The closest park was 60 miles from Club Laurel, which was located on North Broadway, too far for Bobby and me.

Sunday afternoon Big Joe, Lance, and Smoke set up their trailers at the Wuthering Heights Mobile Park, resolving to drive an hour and a half each way to Club Laurel. Bobby and I got permission from Club Laurel management to park our trailers in the alley behind the building. We slept in them Sunday night without heat or electricity. Early Monday morning, we rented a furnished apartment with a small kitchen near our gig. The newlyweds rented an apartment in the same building.

That afternoon, I knocked on the club's stage door, ready to check out the venue. An aging spade porter with a gimp leg opened the door.

"Ya da Carousels? I's been waitin' fer ya. Brung yo stuff thru here and set up."

He motioned in the direction of the massive stage with his worn-out broom, sweeping occasionally just to stir the air. Six Johnny Rebs stepped inside.

Very old, still very impressive, I thought. Turning to the white-haired porter, I asked, "You been working here long?"

"'Bout 30 years now. Used to work for Big Al. But da feds put him in da Big House. He was good ta me, but he's passed now. Da Marconi's gave me dis job because I keeps my's mouth shut. Don't many people do dat now-a-days, but I does."

"Not telling any secrets today?"

"No way. If I does, that'd be my last."

On time at 2 p.m., Guido Marconi met us with a gracious welcome. He looked and sounded like Santa Claus. Guido mentioned Carlos Marcello and Merrill Saks, then quickly volunteered that he never personally met the gentlemen.

"One of my associates filled me in about your connection with these fine gentlemen."

Once again, Marcello and Saks were opening doors for the Carousels, even though I suspected Marcello's interest had waned. Guido and his brother, Gino, were frontmen and well connected. Successfully running Club Laurel for many years, Gino worked two weeks and Guido worked the following two weeks, rotating management responsibility and their vacations with family.

Guido provided the cook's tour, pointing out famous entertainers and bands on his wall of fame. It stretched a hundred feet with 300 glossy-framed photos in 8x10 format. Pictures of Count Basie, Stan Kenton, Woody Herman, Glenn Miller, Tex Beneke, Frank Sinatra, Andy Williams, Tony Bennett, Louis Armstrong, and Ella Fitzgerald were prominently displayed, along with photos of 290 other entertainers on the Club Laurel wall of fame.

"Count Basie and Joe Williams will be here Sunday night," Guido told me, "and Stan Kenton will be in the following Sunday. After your last set Saturday, make room for the Big Bands. Store your instruments here," pointing to a storage room with a padlocked door.

We couldn't ignore it. Chicago rhythms were different. I'm talking about the rhythm of body language, speech patterns, eye contact, mysterious conversations with hands cupped over mouths, under-the-breath whispers in ears, and Damon Runyon characters right out of *Guys and Dolls*. Didn't take us long to realize the wider the pinstripes, the longer the collars of their custom-made shirt collars and the cup size of their molls indicated family ranking.

For two hours that night, men in pinstriped suits and Mob flappers scrutinized our band with discriminating eyes. Pretty sure they viewed us as southern hicks. Mightily challenged, we set out to do what southerners had done to Yankees many times—out-fox the fox with southern charm.

During our third set, we defrosted their icy challenge with our stage show. Loud applause was matched by genuine compliments during breaks. By the end of the first evening, we'd moved from hicks to charming southern gentlemen. They were easy prey. We out-foxed the fox.

On breaks, we made a point to visit tables with the men wearing the widest pinstripes, slathering on good ol' boy southern charm like molasses. By mid-week, the Chicago Mob, their molls, subterraneans, derelicts of darkness, and marks turned from their table discussions to the action on stage.

We studied our subjects as if they were aliens from a distant planet, discerning their entertainment tastes, political and religious views, and the unspoken, yet distinctive rhythms of the Chicago Mob. By week's end, we had galvanized our connection.

Friday, during a break, I approached the waitress' serving station, putting up one finger, my routine signal to the bartender: Scotch on the rocks with a twist. With a smile and a wink, he passed over my drink.

On a perch next to me sat a high-priced workin' gal—same perch every night. For the first time that week she acknowledged my presence, posing her question wrapped in surly tone, "What are you Confederates doin' in Yankee country? Lost your compass? Lost the Civil War, hung blacks, did everything you could to stop civil rights, and you killed America's greatest president. You are not welcome here."

"We were invited here. So far, everyone except you loves us."

"I don't love you—unless you're willing to hand over greenbacks. Far as I'm concerned, all southerners are redneck bigots. Take yourselves back across the Mason Dixon line and don't come back until you get some education, class, and musical taste."

"The North might have won the War of Northern Aggression, but we're winning the entertainment war for class and musical taste," I replied. "If you stop hating yourself long enough to listen, you'll begin to appreciate *The Pride of Dixie*. To prove my point, ever hear of Van Clyburn, Ray Charles, Bobby "Blue" Bland, B.B. King, Fats Domino, Elvis Presley, Al Hirt, Pete Fountain, Allen Toussaint, Ray Price, Hank Williams, Roy Orbison, Lloyd Price, Brenda Lee, Nat Adderley, or Miles Davis?

"Want more? I can name hundreds of southerners who dominate records, national radio and television. We've already won the war of musical taste in America. We stopped fighting the Civil War a hundred years ago. Today, we're lovers of great music and entertainment. Unless you're tone deaf or blind to everything beautiful, just lay back … *laissez les bon temps roulez*. You might also want to learn *suave de vive*. Speaking as a poorly educated redneck bigot, I suggest you also might pick up a book on French to English translations. As for now, *baszd meg magad*."

Before kicking off our featured set, I said, "Create fantasy—sell illusion—project your God Power."

THIRD SET LINEUP—CLUB LAUREL				
SONG	ORIG'L ARTIST	GENRE	ENSEMBLE	FEATURE
West Side Story (Stage Show—Dance)	Leonard Bernstein	Broadway	Dance, Solo's & Ensemble	All Carousels

Southern Nights	Allen Toussaint	R&B	Standard Ensemble	Bobby—Vocal
Big Girls Don't Cry	The Four Seasons	R&R	Standard Ensemble	Bobby in Falsetto + 3
Soul Bird (Tin Tin Deo)	Cal Tjader	Latin Jazz	Vibes, Guitar & Conga's	Rocky & Smoke
Pretty Woman	Roy Orbison	Pop	Standard Ensemble	Lance—Vocal
Moanin'	Modern Jazz Quintet	Jazz	4 Horns	Big Joe, Lance & Rocky
The Thrill Is Gone	B.B. King	R&B	4 Horns	Big Joe—Vocal, Lance & Rocky
Cold Sweat	Mongo Santamaria	Latin Jazz	3 Horns & Conga	Big Joe, Lance & Rocky
Turn on Your Love Light	Bobby "Blue" Bland	R&B	4 Horns	Bobby—Vocal, Big Joe, Lance & Rocky
Sidewinder	Lee Morgan	Jazz	4 Horns	Big Joe, Lance & Rocky

While we were traveling from city to city, civil rights agitators were traveling through the South, causing a ruckus. Reconciling our southern values with our love of spade R&B rose to the surface. Bobby loved the Sam Cooke songbook. At that time, Cooke was at the top of his career. Most of his new releases reached No. 1 on the charts within a week. *You Send Me* and *Twistin' the Night Away* were among our most requested tunes.

Talk was that when Sam Cooke heard Bob Dylan's *Blowin' in the Wind*, he couldn't believe a white man wrote the song. Sam was determined to write an equally powerful lyric, resulting in *A Change is Gonna Come,* composed on his tour bus in May 1963. He had long felt the need to address the situation of discrimination and racism in America. However, his fear of losing a largely white fan base held him back.

Two major incidents in his life changed his mind. The first was the accidental drowning death of his 18-month-old son, Vincent. The second came October 8, 1963, when Sam and his band tried to register at a white-only motel in Shreveport and were arrested for disturbing the peace. Both are represented in the weary tone and lyrics of the piece, especially the final verse:

There have been times that I thought I couldn't last for long

But now I think I'm able to carry on.

It's been a long time coming, but I know a change is gonna come.

Cooke died in December, 1964, fatally shot by the manager of the Hacienda Motel in Los Angeles. At the time, the courts ruled Cooke was drunk and disorderly, and the manager killed the 33-year-old singer in self-defense. Since then, the circumstances of his death are widely debated. Some accounts accuse the motel manager, Bertha Franklin, and a prostitute of robbing and murdering Cooke. The fact that he was a known womanizer helped spread a rumor that he was fatally shot by a crazed husband who caught Sam in bed with his white wife. We'll never know what really happened that night.

A Change Is Gonna Come became Sam Cooke's farewell address and final hit.

Given that Bobby Starr was being groomed to ascend to the North Louisiana KKK Grand Dragon of the Realm and lead the Knights of the Golden Circle when his father died, Bobby was confronted with an extraordinary crisis of conscience—one destined to change the direction of Bobby's life.

Prior to Thursday's rehearsal, Bobby and I shared a meal at Lao Sze Chuan. Bobby was all lathered up over Sam Cooke's death and inner conflicts over his core southern values.

I told him, "Bobby, this Sam Cooke thing is eating you alive. Back off and relax. We're simple entertainers—not judge and jury on racial issues. *Laissez les bon temps roulez.*"

"I'm ripped apart," he replied. "Don't know if I'm capable of compromising my southern values by performing *A Change is Gonna Come,* a protest song of extraordinary power. We show disciple-like worship of R&B spade music, while two Confederate flags stick out of your bass drum and are prominent in the Carousel logo. Shit, our slogan is *The Pride of Dixie.* I'm torn between my love of spade music and my commitment to the KKK."

"Like I say every night before kicking off our featured set, 'Create fantasy—sell illusion— project your God Power.' And, if you need more words of wisdom, here's Big Orange's fourth commandment from her Ten Commandments of an Alcoholic Nursery: 'Too much seriousness leads to headaches and heartaches. Lighten up.' Number 7 also fits your situation: 'Drop the act—everyone sees right through you anyway.' *Suave de vive.*"

"Once in a while you actually make some sense," Bobby replied.

In the end Bobby performed *A Change Is Gonna Com,* as a tribute to the late great Sam Cooke. Love triumphs over hate.

While in Chi Town, Bobby and I wrestled the scheduling challenge: who gets the apartment and who sleeps at the band-aids pad? However, we worked it out fairly well, resolving that communal copulation and free love made good bedfellows. The foldout couch was a blessing. Chicago, my kind of town.

Sharing an apartment with Bobby was revealing. His drive to achieve stardom was all consuming. Bobby invested copious energy into achieving his dream. Every day, he performed voice exercises using a stethoscope to pinpoint the origins of tonal quality, a silk scarf over one ear to maximize resonance, and vocal exercises to open his larynx and throat cavity.

I routinely finished my toilette, including hair spray and tux, in about 20 minutes. Conversely, Bobby maintained a disciplined, 90-minute regimen so as to appear absolutely perfect on stage. He always looked terrific, putting my thrown-together package to shame.

With one bathroom in a small apartment, nothing was private— at least not for long. One day, searching for Carousel promotion materials, I opened a drawer that contained Bobby's stash, which included a fifth of absinthe labeled *la féeverte.* I recalled reading somewhere that absinthe was an addictive psychoactive drug and had been banned in the U.S. It was used to achieve creative inspiration by artists, writers and thespians during the 19th and early 20th centuries.

Bobby's supply of *la féeverte,* a bag of grass, roll-your-own paper, baggie of white powder, and a bottle of bennies diminished daily. However, when he climbed on stage, Bobby's charisma captivated audiences, produced by his chemical concoctions.

Chapter 40

1964
I'M NOT YOUR DADDY

Waking up exhausted on Friday, I offered to buy Bobby lunch at a Hungarian restaurant in the neighborhood. He and I loved their food and unique culture. I could taste Beef Noodle Paprikash three blocks away. Bobby loved their crepes and strudel dish.

Our Hungarian waiter approached, asking, "Etlap?" Not knowing what he said, I nodded and menus were presented.

The waiter pointed to specials of the day, pronouncing them in Hungarian. Feeling adventurous, Bobby pointed at one of the mystery lunches and I pointed at another. Our departure from southern soul food expanded our culinary and cultural palettes. The aroma of musty wood furniture, moldy carpets, and Budapest body odor fought with the delectable aroma wafting its way out of a kitchen filled with yelling cooks. The authentic atmosphere competed with authentic Hungarian food. Fortunately, the food won.

Musicians dressed in gypsy garb played the cimbalom, gypsy violin, and cobza. Welling up with joy from uncluttered contentment, I soon had tears creeping down my cheeks, transforming to full-blown weeping at the beauty bursting forth from the Hungarian trio. Out of the corner of my eye, I caught Bobby wiping his tears away with his sleeve. Hungarian kávé was served without interruption by our waiter as we dried our eyes.

For the next half-hour, Bobby and I simply relaxed in the cradle of the gypsies. Life was good.

When the trio took a break, I turned to Bobby.

"This is your life and I'm not your judge, nor your daddy. However, if I were your daddy or brother, I'd have you committed to a drug rehab to dry out. My question is, how hooked are you on the shit you keep in the drawer under the sink?"

Bobby's black eyes twinkled, as he responded, "My shit's my business. It's my body and I can handle shit just fine. I can quit any time I choose—and do from time to time. I find the boost I need to climb on stage at Club Laurel and dazzle audiences. Applause is my addiction, Rocky—not absinthe, weed, coke, or bennies."

I tried one more time.

"Bobby, we're having the time of our lives, evidenced by last night's orgy. Reaching for the brass ring is exciting. My only concern is when we catch it, will we have the strength to hold on? Remaining clear-headed and in control of my faculties is my way of fully experiencing life. Dulling my senses down or up with drugs only dilutes the joy of living the dream. I want to remember everything that happens, clear-headed and alert. Bobby, that shit will eventually do you in. It's your life, but think twice about choosing another path to achieving fame. You can make it big without a monkey hanging on your back."

Bobby blew me off. "Just let it go, Rock. Let it go."

It's obvious. I'm talking to a committed drug addict. Nothing short of drug rehab will save Bobby Starr from self-destruction. A year, two at best, before he starts pumping H into his veins. In the short term, Bobby Starr is captivating on stage—though at what price?

Do I save Bobby Starr from drug oblivion or step aside? The bottom line is I'm not Bobby's daddy.

Club Laurel introduced us to our most diverse clientele. Colorful main characters dressed to the nines paraded in processional packs from street to tables, always positioning themselves at the edge of the dance floor in prime position for viewing and being viewed. Bosses and underbosses, accompanied by their mistresses, sat inside a protective ring of soldiers, seated nearby and always with one hand inside their suit jackets.

Chicago Mafia made up 20 percent of the Club Laurel audience: bosses, underbosses, consiglieres, capos, soldatos, associates, hit men, and career thieves. Of course, the Chicago Mob's cadre of drug dealers, shylocks, bookies, hookers, pimps, extortionists, and strong-arm collection goons were there as well.

Marks frequenting Club Laurel included businessmen, executives, traveling salesmen, bankers, politicians, habitual gamblers, and drug addicts. Abundant subterraneans rounded out the guest list.

For Smoke, hit men held a special fascination after a recent Mob hit on a *canary* made front-page news. However, the best story could be heard at the bar, detailing how the canary's cock and balls were stuffed in his mouth before he received a bullet in the brain. Other tantalizing stories passed freely at Club Laurel, adding to our streetwise education and adventure.

Adding to the Chicago ambiance, the city boasted the largest Catholic diocese in America and I soon learned about the inner turmoil roiling the Catholic Church in America after the death of Pope John XXIII in 1963 and the emergence of Pope Paul VI. Pope John established the Second Vatican Council, which made far-reaching changes in the way Catholics celebrated Mass. Many parishioners eagerly embraced the changes, such as priests facing the congregation and speaking in English. Conversely, they rebelled against rumors of a possible reversal of Vatican II by Pope Paul VI.

In direct contrast with southern Catholics, many of whom were fervent devotees of the traditional Latin Mass, Chicago Catholics angrily voiced their discontent with anyone wanting to turn back the clock.

The potential split between northern and southern Catholic factions fired up emotions. And when the Southern Baptist Convention was folded into the mix, the religious brew boiled briskly.

Recognizing that the Carousels were southerners entertaining northerners, I created our party-line response to the nightly debate raging at Club Laurel. Explaining the cultural differences to Dallas and Mary—our Southern Baptists—and Big Joe and Angelle—our South Louisiana Catholics—required diplomacy. I gave it my best shot and squelched all discussions at Club Laurel that dealt with any religious or civil rights subject matter.

It worked. We focused on entertaining a sophisticated Chi town audience and avoided all talk of religion.

Every Tuesday, Wednesday, and Thursday, we rehearsed at 4:30 p.m., much later than normal. This permitted Big Joe, Lance, and Smoke to drive in on rehearsal days and drive back following the gig. Dinner near the club was part of their standard routine on those days. About half the time, Bobby, Dallas, and I joined them.

At one of our get-togethers, Bobby wiped ketchup from his mouth, sipped iced tea, and complained about the changing musical tastes in our country.

"The Beatles are taking over music in America," he began. "*I Want to Hold Your Hand* is Number One. *Can't Buy Me Love; Twist and Shout; She Loves You; Please, Please Me;* and *A Hard Day's Night* are also at the top of the charts. Shit! Some 73 million people watched the Beatles on 'The Ed Sullivan Show.' It's a British invasion of American popular music, guys. What's the message here?"

Big Joe replied, "*Rocachah.* Dat's all. *Pesque Moustique, maringouin.* 'Sides, Gert says we're great da way we are. 'Nuf for me. Don't change nothin'."

Professor Kenny Livingston's warnings are coming to fruition. Gert's leading Big Joe around by his one-eyed-jack, controlling everything that comes out his mouth.

Lance immediately challenged Joe's statement that the Beatles are a passing fancy.

"I don't think so. The first time I heard *I Want to Hold Your Hand,* I knew this could be the death of the Carousels. Our dreams of fame and fortune are fading, now that Marcello is out of the picture and the Beatles are dominating the charts and television."

Dallas asked, "What's next, Rocky? How we going to compete with the Beatles?"

"I may have a surprise for you guys in a few weeks," I said. "However, it's premature to talk about it now. When I know, you'll know."

Storm clouds have moved in, covering the stars in heaven and the future of the Carousels. They all see what's happening. In spite of being the best we've ever been, it may be too late to change direction. We're mired down—lured into believing our own press releases. What's our next step? What should I do?

During Wednesday's rehearsal, I watched as Guido Marconi counted out five stacks of greenbacks, and then carefully placed each stack under five coffee cups and saucers on the bar. At 5 p.m. sharp, two cars pulled up in front of Club Laurel. One was an unmarked police car, the second car painted bright red, *Chicago Fire Chief* emblazoned on the door.

Three police officers with lots of oak leaves, one fire chief with matching oak leaves and one suit walked in and mounted bar stools in front of their stack of greenbacks, each sealed with a coffee cup and saucer. Greetings exchanged, Guido told a joke and everyone laughed. Five immaculately groomed occupants on bar stools relaxed in casual conversation, passing pleasurable time with their host. Guido graciously poured fresh coffee, supplied sugar, cream, and polite conversation. Coffee finished, the parade reversed, and five dudes returned to their respective cars—elapsed time one minute. Of course, five stacks of cash disappeared—magic.

Welcome to Chicago.

Big Band sounds blew the roof off Club Laurel every Sunday. We saw Count Basie, Stan Kenton, Woody Herman, and Harry James. The Marconi brothers let us in, gratis. During a break, I talked with Stan Levey, legendary drummer with Stan Kenton. I idolized Stan since I was a freshman in high school. Although not the flashiest drummer, Stan's drive and pristine technique were the best of the Big Band drummers. I knew everything about him: Born in Philadelphia, he was considered one of the earliest bebop drummers and played with Dizzy Gillespie's group in 1942 at age of 16. Soon after he went to New York, where he and Dizzy worked with Charlie Parker and Oscar Pettiford.

A left-handed drummer, Levey played on more than a thousand recordings with Dizzy Gillespie, Charlie Parker, Miles Davis, Stan Getz, Ella Fitzgerald, Peggy Lee, Frank Sinatra, Nat King Cole, and with bands such as Quincy Jones, Skitch Henderson, and The Tonight Show Band. Levey also was said to be an accomplished photographer, snapping pictures throughout his drumming career.

"Life on the road is grueling," Stan told me. "Different venues every night. No time to get my carrot gnawed. It's always, 'Back on the bus, boys.' Fuckin' Beatles, Elvis, and English bands—they're assassins. America's finest musicians are leaving the profession in droves, unable to support their families. Cultural changes are destroying great music and America. Admittedly, I'm a diehard. The narcotic of playing with Stan Kenton is like sitting at the right hand of God. My dream is to go out playing Pete Rugolo's arrangement of *Peanut Vendor* with Maynard Ferguson's screech horn leading me through the pearly gates."

Our last week in Chicago, Gino Marconi approached, extending many compliments and requesting our open dates. Thanking him for his confidence, I promised to provide available dates and write a contract before leaving Chicago. We signed contracts that Friday.

The Marconi brothers were a class act. Our last night, Gino said, "I'm confident Carlos Marcello will position the Carousels to achieve great things. Just don't forget us when you move up to super stardom."

Next stop, Louisville, absent the Derby.

My companions to Louisville were Hatter and Cheshire. Predictably, Hatter snickered, *"You have a regrettably large head! I would very much like to hat it!"*

Cheshire Cat shed white hair and her advice, *"The uninformed must improve their deficit, or die."*

CHAPTER 41

1964
BOBBY'S CRISIS

We set up four trailers at the Derby Mobile Home Park in Louisville. Then, Monday morning, we drove to the Office Lounge and set up our instruments on stage. Reggio Greco met us with a big welcome, admitting that crowds were down since we left. To boost sagging attendance, he had placed newspaper and radio spots announcing the return of the Fabulous Carousels.

"We'll draw an audience," I told him. "Once they catch our new stage show, you'll have a packed house."

Opening night, Reggio handed me a letter from Stan Zuckerman in Los Angeles.

"At this moment I manage a robust stable of top entertainers and am not seeking to expand," the letter began. "However, Bobbie and Billy had some nice things to say about the Fabulous Carousels. I will consider reviewing your band when it becomes mutually convenient, in part because my brother lives in Nashville. When do you anticipate the Fabulous Carousels will play the Black Poodle again? Regards—Stan Zuckerman."

I shared the Zuckerman letter with the guys, providing my explanation of how this came to pass and Stan's background. Sensing no discernable reaction to the Zuckerman letter or my comments, I stuffed the letter in my red tux pocket as we kicked off the first set.

Like Chicago, we presented our stage show during the third set. The audience was blown away, evidenced by seven standing ovations during the hour-long show. Quickly, the crowds grew. Weekends brought SROs and a waiting line down the mall concourse. The Fabulous Carousels returned to Louisville and our disciples were packing in shoulder-to-shoulder in the alcoholic nursery.

Before kicking off our featured set, I said, "Create fantasy—sell illusion—project your God Power."

SECOND SET LINEUP—THE OFFICE LOUNGE				
SONG	ORIG'L ARTIST	GENRE	ENSEMBLE	FEATURE
Watermelon Man	Herbie Hancock w/ Mongo Santamaria Arrangement	Latin Jazz	4 Horns + Conga	Big Joe, Lance & Rocky
I'm Walkin'	Fats Domino	R&B	3 Horns	Big Joe—Vocal, Lance & Rocky
Sherry	The Four Seasons	R&R	Standard Ensemble	Bobby in Falsetto + 3
Booginin'	Clifton Chenier	Zydeco	Cajun Accordion, Fiddle & Frottoir	Big Joe Vocal Dallas, Smoke & Rocky
Orange Blossom Special	Ervin & Gordon Rouse	Country	Fiddle, Banjo & Guitar	Big Joe & Smoke
Just a Gigolo	Louis Prima	New Orleans	Standard Ensemble	Big Joe—Vocal
Masquerade	Cal Tjader	Latin Jazz	Vibes, Guitar & Conga's	Rocky & Smoke
All Blues	Miles Davis	Jazz	4 Horns	Big Joe, Lance & Rocky

| Everyday I Have the Blues | B.B. King | R&B | 4 Horns | Big Joe—Vocal, Lance & Rocky |
| Sidewinder | Lee Morgan | Jazz | 4 Horns | Big Joe, Lance & Rocky |

Apparently Bobby's stash of absinthe, pot, angel dust, and bennies had been augmented with sexual enhancement drugs. In Louisville, Bobby set new records for three-peckered goat encounters. By the end of our first week, Bobby's face and body resembled Count Dracula. Worried about his health, I went to his trailer for a cup of joe and conversation.

Bobby greeted me with bloodshot eyes under heavy eyelids and a befuddled expression on his pallid face. An odor of almonds gushed from his heavy breathing. He functioned just enough to motion me inside before turning to retrieve a bra hanging from the chandelier, panties from the stove, and a red dress from the couch—evidence of last night's triumph. As he tossed garments through a bedroom door, I overheard unintelligible mumbling, then watched a thin band-aid emerge and quickly exit.

Bobby, much like a robot, scooped out coffee grounds from a French Market coffee can, filled the percolator with water, assembled the stem and basket, and plugged in our morning joe.

Bobby Starr was a physical and emotional wreck, mumbling half sentences while aggressively scratching his balls through an open house coat. As the coffee began to perk, images of Pinocchio's growing nose resembled Bobby's johnson, now standing at attention, uncontrollably pulsating up and down like a conductor's baton, synchronized with the rhythms of his percolating coffee pot.

Bobby's normally pristine trailer was in total disarray, reeking of sickening sweet marijuana, an empty muscatel bottle, and two half-filled glasses containing six drowned roaches. Having shared every indignation six guys could possibly experience together, personal modesty disappeared long ago. What remained was raw, the residue of a communal, decadent lifestyle.

I smiled at the bizarre tableau, but caught myself before laughing out loud.

Hot black joe in hand, I said, "We've been good buddies on the road; a once-in-a-lifetime adventure we'll remember forever. Although I'm not your daddy or blood kin, I am your brother of sorts. So far, I've been able to bail you out of some pretty messy scrapes. That's what friends do for friends. However, you've taken a radical left turn, revealing a self-destructive side that gives me pause. Just so I'm prepared when the time comes, I brought this measuring tape to get specifications for your casket. While I'm at it, do you have any final request before I ship you back to North Louisiana in a pine box?"

Bobby managed a half-hearted chuckle.

"You have been a good brother and friend," he replied. "And you haven't hovered over me, told me what to do with my life, or judged me. Thanks for that. All the same, before you measure me for that casket, but only if you keep your mouth shut, I'll let you inside my head."

"Keep my mouth shut? Do you have to ask?"

"Nope—but this is really embarrassing."

"Have I ever ratted on ya? Now, what's going on inside Bobby Starr's skull and body?"

He struggled for words.

"What you tried to say in Chicago was ... I cut you off too soon at the Hungarian restaurant. It kills me to say this—you were right. The cock has come home to roost. Rocky, I've got a bad case of limp dick. My cock won't crow without a daily dash of shark fin or rhinoceros horn. I either walk around with a perpetual hard-on or live with the shame of a limp dick. This ain't good for a guy trying to become a megastar. Limp dicks don't become megastars—they turn into jokes for comedians. I don't want to turn into a joke. I guess I've let things get a little out of balance."

Biting my tongue til it bled, struggling to suppress an irrepressible cackle at the ridiculousness of Bobby's dilemma: limp dick versus perpetual boner.

In the midst of Bobby's perverted egocentricities, he was more afraid of not being known as a stud stallion than simply curing his limp-dick problem by cutting back on drug consumption. Just goes to prove that ego is a powerful force.

"Out of balance!" I shouted. "You've jumped into the Grand Canyon without a parachute and no quick way to sprout wings. You're so far out of balance you're flying upside down. Bobby Starr is dancing on the edge of a razor blade. Even sober, it's challenging to maintain balance on a sharp straight edge, but near impossible when you add a pharmacy of mind-altering drugs. Continue the path you're on and you're certain to slip one day and slice off your precious cock. One missed step and all that shit will kill you. Before I give you a way out of this limp-dick dilemma, stand up so I can measure your height and width. A mortician is waiting for these measurements."

"Enough with the jokes," Bobby replied. "This is serious. What's my way out?"

"Back off absinthe, pot, angel dust, bennies, rhino, and shark. This too simple for ya? The alternative is being buried in a casket for eternity. Back off enough and you'll find that shark and rhino are little more than a passing bad dream. Your limp-dick problems will go away."

"How long will it take before my dick gets hard on its own?"

"Word on the street is it'll take two or three weeks if you go cold turkey—a month to six weeks if you simply taper off. That's up to you."

Not sure I could keep a straight face any longer, I excused myself under the guise of drainin' my lizard. The bathroom mirror reflected a laughing clown, emitting perverted humor at audience expense while caustic yellow urine splashed in the toilet. The clown in the mirror finally laughed out loud.

After all, I am the ringmaster of this circus.

Five minutes later I left, satisfied that Bobby would survive his excesses, at least for the next few months.

Based on loose talk from braggin' chicks, incapable of keeping secrets about their sexual conquests, I gathered that Bobby returned to near normal within six weeks. Our peacock survived, though his body and brain had paid a price. I laugh every time I think of Bobby's limp-dick saga.

Mostly, Big Joe and Lance could be found hanging out at their trailers, often outside reading the newspaper or performing maintenance on their vehicles. Dallas and Mary rented a hotel room. Three of my brothers turned into old married men, except Lance and Angelle weren't married. Lance complained about Angelle's bitchin', while Big Joe bragged about his erotic adventures with Gert. Dallas—a newlywed in love—was enthralled with legally—and religiously—screwing Mary. Smoke cloistered himself in his bat cave. Heavy gray clouds from la-la-land gushed under the door.

Every morning, I habitually read the newspapers on my patio. The nylon straps on my folding chair had begun to fray and sag from overuse. However, the deeper my butt sank in the nylon, the more comfortable my attitude. Everything and everyone was at peace, as every morning began with a clean slate.

Two small nuthatches sang their big songs of happy times as they fed worms and insects to their chicks in a meticulously woven nest. Cottonwoods burst in explosive blooms, blowing wispy seed pods my way in a whimsically orchestrated ballet.

The prize of my morning was sipping Riley Coffee Company's freshly brewed CDM joe with chicory. The aroma of rich Columbian beans weaved their way to my nostrils, eager for the morning seduction into a pleasurable peace.

Chapter 42

1964
THE SCORPION AND THE FROG

aturday night, during our second break, Venus called the Office Lounge, asking for me. When I answered the phone, her message was brief: "Would you mind if I fly up to Louisville?"

"Sure—come on," I said. "When will you be here?"

"In the morning—Sunday. Is that okay?" she asked with a quivering voice.

"Sure thing. What time?"

"Sunday ... Delta Airlines ... 9:30 a.m. arrival."

Early Sunday morning, I cleaned and flash-scalded four green peppers while browning ground sirloin in a black skillet. Chopped-up onions, parsley, shredded carrots, squeezed fresh garlic, heavy helpings of Worcestershire, and seasonings got mixed in with rye bread soaked in red wine. Mixing the ingredients together, I stuffed the concoction into four pepper shells and placed the result in a covered dish, refrigerating for later. Two foil-wrapped, medium-sized sweet potatoes went in the oven at 325 degrees. Electing to put a fresh salad together later, I cleaned the kitchen, showered, dressed, and drove to the airport.

Predictably, Venus jiggled her way off the plane. Before I could say hello, she completed the French kiss she began at the airport in Nashville. Needless to say, I was glad to see her.

With the silliness of two teenagers, we giggled and squirmed during the short drive to my trailer, in nervous anticipation of what lay ahead. Her scent of jasmine flashed back the Cinderella times of two lovers committed to fulfilling destiny.

This slipper fits nicely.

Following a spectacular morning in the sack, we broke for intermission. Attention turned from the bedroom to the tiny kitchenette, as I placed a half-inch of water in a Pyrex dish containing four stuffed peppers and baked it in a pre-heated oven at 325 degrees for 30 minutes. Sweet potatoes were on the counter, fully cooked, and ready for popping in the last ten minutes. I tossed a garden salad and placed it in the refrigerator to chill.

As Dvorak's *New World Symphony* warmed our souls, Venus watched my every move, reminding me of her stares at Saks' Boom Boom Room. I loved her eyes on me and she loved my attention to pleasing her.

I added blue cheese dressing to the salad, divided it into two small plates, and then placed the steaming stuffed peppers, and sweet potatoes on two dinner plates.

Turning to Venus, I said, "Dinner is served. Where would you like to eat?"

Barbie Doll and I ate dinner in the middle of my bed, naked as jaybirds in a newborn nest.

On Monday, Venus showed yet another side of her complex personality. Twisting a Kleenex between fidgety fingers, her anxieties were apparent. As she shredded the tissue, she mumbled unintelligible fragments that sounded something like, "Shameful, despicable." She shook her bobbing head left to right in a "no" motion. Another mumble under her breath, "Wretched witch." Her long face lost its Barbie Doll charm as bulging eyes pleading for someone to love her.

What's going on?

As I passed the couch, she reached out and tugged on the tail of my wife-beater undershirt, twisting it one way and then another. Sensitive to her emotional frailty, I saw Venus as a China doll; fragile, delicate, vulnerable. Somewhat unexpectedly, I felt compelled to extend tenderness to this frail canary. Extending my hand, I raised her to a soft kiss of safety.

Whatever the source of her pain, I was determined not to ask questions, particularly ones dealing with her past. Instead, I tried to spin positives.

"We make our own happiness. Venus, how would you describe happiness?"

"I want to remake myself into the person you described during our first week together in New Orleans," she replied. "So far, I've made a mess of my life. I want to start over. Starting over is scary, but with your help, I can become whatever you want me to be. I love you, Rocky."

Venus scares the bee-jesus out of me. It never occurred to me that I'd be asked to assume responsibility for Venus or her happiness. Til now, our relationship was wonderful, although transitory. Living in the moment was perfect. Tasting the nectar of many flowers in an unlimited garden of great beauty was the natural thing to do for a musician on the road—at least at my age.

Apparently, Venus had a different plan. Not yet ready to sacrifice freedom, I sensed the restraints of her carefully laid snare. Obviously, Venus had arrived in Louisville with an agenda. I need time to think this through and escape her snares.

I made light of her heavy comment, saying, "Venus, you'll find happiness inside yourself. No one person can make you happy. Happiness is solely your responsibility. However, I can promise you no pressure, lots of laughs, and a really good time. What better gift can I give you? Let's live in the moment."

It wasn't what she wanted to hear.

"I need more," Venus replied, tears rolling down ivory cheeks. "I need you to love me."

She placed her face on my chest, tilted baby blues up at me and asked, "What can I do to get you to love me?"

Finally revealed, Venus's trip to Louisville was designed to throw a net over my young ass and put me in her cage. She was either emotionally bankrupt or desperately in love with me. Either way, her desire to own me as her ideal soul mate was driving her actions.

Trying again to defuse the mood, I said, "Let's give our relationship space and time. Like they say: live, laugh, and love more. Everything good comes to those who are patient. Let's be patient."

Ravel saved me. At that moment, *Boléro* dropped down on the turntable and woofers boomed, vibrating our libidos. Venus's indecisions and frailties vanished, replaced by a take-charge guide into our special place. I had to admit that her carnal knowledge was extraordinarily well developed; a spectacular lay. Emotionally and physically satisfied, I congratulated myself on escaping her snares, at least this round.

Gotta be mentally quick to out-fox this fox.

The next few days, I danced around her cleverly designed traps. Saturday night, Mary Fingers and Venus came to the Office Lounge. Venus was pursued by every horny toad in the club and she put on a seductive yet classy show. The better the actress, the more natural the performance. Only I could recognize her mastery of seductive sorcery, having fallen victim myself on occasion. Amazed at how easily she dominated a room, I watched in fascination as she mesmerized onlookers. Amused by her attempts to make me jealous, I sat back and enjoyed her performance.

Early Monday morning I went out to buy cigarettes. On my return, I found Venus curled in a fetal position, sobbing uncontrollably, a bundle of pain headed toward deep depression. I had no idea what triggered her radical mood swing. But, the beautiful person I left sleeping peacefully had transformed into a tormented caricature of Venus—displaying symptoms certain to puzzle any psychiatrists. Wanting to demonstrate tenderness, I took her to a park for a picnic. She loved it, commenting, "You're a cockeyed romantic."

Light conversations on trite subjects steered us away from Venus' darker moods and her not-so-hidden agenda. She began to relax as I massaged her back and neck. We lay in the sun and drifted off in a long snooze.

I awoke around 5, awakened Venus, gathered up our picnic leftovers, and drove back to the trailer. Quickly changing into my gray mohair tux, I sped to the Office Lounge for Monday night's performance.

Venus, still under the mysterious force Tuesday morning, was an emotional wreck, coiling in pain, crying like a baby. I felt like a bad court jester, attempting to make a distraught queen laugh—perhaps even be happy. No laughs so far. I selected a record, Stravinsky's *Rite of Spring,* dropping it on the turntable. The 33-minute masterpiece resulted in the exact opposite reaction I'd intended.

Cuddling Venus also did little to improve things, so I squeezed fresh orange juice, percolated Community Coffee with chicory, scrambled eggs with cheese, Canadian bacon, and Pioneer biscuits with honey. I forced her to eat something. Venus continued to cry, to the point of exhaustion.

Washing dishes, I stayed out of her way—a big challenge inside an 18-foot trailer. Venus was a basket case, wrestling with dark emotions. The harder I tried to appease, the more I failed. Feeling the fool, I thought of ways out of the abyss. Deep depression was not far behind, so I asked Venus a question to get her talking, encouraging her to vent.

"Perhaps I can help you dump your heavy load," I said. "Why are you so sad?"

Venus sat up straight. She asked for a wet washcloth, which I readily provided. Still sobbing, she began regurgitating pent-up anguish, hurling horrific images onto the walls of my little trailer.

"I did some horrible things as a teenager on the back streets of New Orleans. Think the worst and I did 'em. At 17, I married Luis because I was pregnant with Alicia and Luis was sort of nice to me. Neither of us had a high school diploma. Our economic prospects were bleak; a Latin man in South Louisiana and a new mother with an infant in her arms. Luis did his best to support us, playing sax around New Orleans. He was an okay musician, but would never be a great sax man. Following the birth of Alicia, my boobs blossomed. Luis taught me to jiggle and sing a little. We put together a Latin band that was different, adding a percussionist and keyboardist. Things got better, though work was spotty."

I had the good sense to shut up while she revealed her personal Greek tragedy. I wasn't sure if I had lines in her tragedy or was simply her audience. At this moment, I chose to be the audience.

"One weekend, we drove to Biloxi, to Club Capri, right on the beach. The owner was interested in my big boobs and our stage show. He believed both would attract the airmen from Keesler Air Force Base as well as traveling salesmen motoring through the Gulf Coast. I jiggled, danced and sang. The airmen and salesmen only came to see my body—not for my singing or brains. To make ends meet, I occasionally made extra money ... The club owner made all the arrangements, handled the financial transaction with the marks, giving me my share the following day."

After a pause, she said, "Rocky, during this period, heavy guilt consumed me, pushing me into a deep depression. At first, drugs provided an escape. Then I really crashed hard from the drug scene, more than a couple of times. See these scars on my left wrist? Those two are from the first time I tried to kill myself. Luis found me in the bathtub, unconscious, the water red with my blood. He got me to the hospital just in time.

"Later I gave birth to Ricky, and my craziness got worse—much worse. I felt trapped in a loveless marriage; a reluctant mother and rapidly turning into a workin' girl. I hated myself. Once again, drugs eased the pain, but not for long. Again, suicide appeared to be the only way out. See these scars on my right wrist? My daughter found me on the bathroom floor. She was smart enough to dial '0' pleading with the operator to send the police. The hospital staff saved me, though I wish they hadn't."

Sobbing again, Venus kept moving her story forward, despite the tears.

"Luis and I worked, off and on, at Club Capri in Biloxi. My body was bringing in marks and I paid our bills on my back, detesting every minute of it. Luis tried to make the best of things, but had few options—so we continued to repeat our death spiral, over and over and over. I signed a personal management contract with the club owner based on his big promises. Nothing really changed except he dominated our lives and became our jailer. He enrolled me in a health club and modeling school, sent me to Merle Norman for makeup training, bought me theatrical gowns and controlled what I did and who I did it with. He owned me.

"I hate shackles. One night I ran away from Biloxi, Luis, my kids, everyone—ran to my sister in New Orleans and hooked up with another wiseguy who booked me into hotel rooms with wealthy businessmen. Three to five times a week, anonymous johns paid big money for my body. The wiseguy supplied me with plenty of drugs, and I took more than my fair share—sky-high all the time. In a moment of clarity, suicide seemed the only way out of my failed life. Before I pulled the trigger, Luis found me and brought me back to Biloxi.

"We left Alicia and Ricky with my sister in New Orleans. I dried out in Biloxi—went cold turkey, which was the hardest thing I ever did in my life. Running on the sandy beaches of Biloxi got me clean and human again. As soon as I was able, Luis and I returned to Club Capri. Predictably, I fell off the wagon and went into my deepest depression so far."

Venus paused, wiped her face with the wet washcloth, and then continued.

"That's when I demanded we get out of Biloxi. I really couldn't handle the pressures of living. Fortunately, Merrill Saks was vacationing in Biloxi and booked me into Saks's Boom Boom Room. We passed by New Orleans to visit my sister, Alicia and Ricky. Luis and I drove to Bossier City and the rest you know, except for Vegas.

"Following Saks, Luis and I drove to Vegas without a gig or prospects of work. The musicians union required a full year of permanent residency before issuing a union card. Luis was banned from playing music, so I became a cocktail waitress and finally landed a job downtown at the Mint in *Artists and Models,* their big room gala review. With only feathers attached to my twat and headgear—that's it—I pranced around with boobs giggling and arms stretched out like an airplane propeller. I drank vodka like a fish to build up courage before walking out there naked.

"My body brought the marks into the Mint and marks paid me good money for private parties after the show. Hated myself in Vegas. Then again, that's how I supported Luis and me. The only thing stopping me from blowing my brains out was Rocky Strong. Your letters gave me hope. You saved my life, Rocky."

Now sobbing like a baby, Venus came to the end of her monologue.

"When I ran away from Vegas and Luis, I ran to you. Rocky Strong is the best thing that ever happened to me and my best chance to find happiness. Since we've been together, I realize I can't live without you. Rocky Strong is my knight in shining armor—my redeemer—my salvation."

At that point, Venus fell under the dark wings of desperation. Uncontrollably, she sobbed herself into an exhaustive state, collapsing in a ball on the bed, like a deflated balloon in repose. Emotionally drawn in by her tragic tale, sensitive to her pain, I instinctively knew I was being played. I comforted her anyway, saying only, "You're safe with me. Everything will be okay."

Venus had changed the rules of this game. My frivolous folly as a three-peckered road musician was under attack by an accomplished seductress. This fox is on the verge of being out-foxed.... She's zeroed in on my goodness—counting on my good man to step forward and be her shield against the ugliness of her past, become her white knight protector and slay the dragons. She wants' me to remake her into the happy queen. Shit! She's playing me like a fiddle.

Sure enough, on the Friday of our last week in Louisville, Venus wound up and pitched the perfect curve ball.

"Rocky, take me with you to Toledo. I'll make you the happiest man on earth. Sending me back to Biloxi is a death sentence. I swear ... I'll kill myself if you send me away!"

As her baby blues searched my face for a reaction. Her right hand unhurriedly reached in her clutch, pulled out a double-barreled .45 Derringer and placed it on the bed between us—inserting an exclamation point on her threat. Blood drained from my face and my asshole puckered from the possibilities of what could happen next. The ground was falling out from under me, leaving me suspended in midair without wings. Stunned, I wrestled with sanity.

Depending on my answer to her Toledo question, Venus is crazy enough to put the first slug in my brain before killing herself. Do I have the guts to call her bluff and say "no"? I'm trapped inside life's game of chess, played on a giant field of squares. I'm a pawn to the Queen of Hearts. I've stepped through the looking glass. The Red Queen's in my bed and has a gun with my name on one of those bullets. She's my antagonist; cordial, seductive, ruthless, and utterly mad. The Red Queen sets the rules and controls the outcome. This game just turned deadly....

Ready as I'd ever be, I reached down inside my brain and recalled one of Aesop's fables and proceeded to tell it as calmly as I could, considering the gun lying between us.

"Venus, let me tell you a story. A scorpion and a frog meet on the bank of a stream, and the scorpion asks the frog to carry him across on its back. The frog asks, 'How do I know you won't sting me?' The scorpion says, 'Because if I do, I will die, too.' The frog is satisfied, and they set out. But in midstream, the scorpion stings the frog. The dying frog has just enough time to gasp, 'Why?' Replied the scorpion: 'It's my nature.'"

Taken aback, Venus said, "I could never hurt you, Rocky. I'm happier with you than I've ever been in my life. Yes, I've done terrible things and stung a lot of good people with my poison—it was in my nature—no more. You saved me. I've changed. I want to be with you the rest of my life. I love you Rocky and want you to love me."

I looked at the Derringer, weighed my options and the risks. Venus' body was tense with anticipation. Her tight ass squirmed on the bed sheet, eager for me to make up my mind. Venus stared at me, but inched her hand closer to the Derringer.

God knows what's next. It's futile to negotiate in a rational manner with an irrational person. I can't take the chance of calling her bluff. This is Russian roulette, and I'm not even holding the gun. My choices are death by Barbie or live to fight another day.

In an instant, I decided to take the path of practicality and hopefully diffuse the crisis. Irrationally rationalizing away reality, I convinced myself I could control this game once we get to Toledo. Playing the fool of fools, my gut screamed the only answer that made sense.

As casually as I could appear, I said, "Okay. Don't make a big deal of it. You and I will go to Toledo together."

Exuberant, she threw her arms around my neck, jumped up and wrapped her legs around my waist, squeezing hard, like a giant python in a death grip, crying out, "Hold me, Rocky! Hold me! Hold me tight! I can't live without your love. I am totally yours—forever!"

Flattered by her hero worship, in truth, I was terrified by the possibility of Venus' committing suicide on my watch—and taking me down with her.

This moment marked the first time I faced a life-or-death ultimatum: "I'll kill myself if you send me away." Venus' clever trap was sprung. Has the sorcerer snared her prey? Do I have the guts to escape? I'll have to make my move in Toledo. Who is Rocky Strong?

Witnessing everything atop the chest of drawers, three-legged Hatter meowed, *"I wouldn't let you do it if I didn't think you'd be okay."*

Cheshire Cat purred: *"Well, some go this way, and some go that way. But as for me, myself, personally, I prefer the short-cut."*

Chapter 43

1964
OPPORTUNITY KNOCKS

S aturday night, following the last note at the Office Lounge, we loaded the instrument trailer and hooked it up to Smoke's car. All I had to do Sunday morning was hook my trailer to the Caddy and pull it to the Toledo Mobile Home Park. Ranking the four Carousel trailers, my tin can was the easiest to set up, hook up and pull on the road. Venus and I secured the trailer and were on the road within 20 minutes—intentionally last in the caravan, AAA maps distributed to the guys, and a roll of dough in my pocket.

Monday morning, Venus cooked whole-grain pancakes with pecans and honey. Washing it down with orange juice and Community Pure Blend Coffee, we felt great. As Venus washed dishes, I was separating my dirty clothes from clean when I found the letter from Stan Zuckerman I had stuffed in my red tuxedo inside pocket. Dishes washed, dried, and placed in the cabinet, Venus turned to me and wanted to know what I was reading. I handed her Zuckerman's letter.

As she read, Venus got excited.

"You did it, Rocky—fantastic! I'm so proud of you. Stan Zuckerman is as big as they come in the entertainment industry. If you get him into the Black Poodle, it's almost guaranteed he'll sign a contract with the Carousels."

With that encouragement, I dusted off my manual Underwood and typed a second letter to Zuckerman. Succinctly, I provided Black Poodle dates and financial arrangements, which included paying his round-trip plane ticket from Los Angeles to Nashville on the Carousels' nickel. In closing, I reminded him of his desire to visit his brother while in town.

Venus was ecstatic, insisting we post my letter right away. Happy that Venus was happy, I also promised to call Zuckerman within four days.

Monday afternoon, I shook hands with Larry Ladatta, club manager and frontman at the Peppermint Lounge. Larry had been the head bartender at the Kato Club during our first Toledo trip. Larry made good and currently worked for club owner Luca Esposito, a well-connected Mob figure and owner of a grocery chain in Northern Ohio. Three months earlier, Larry had contacted me to alternate with the Four Seasons.

Best of all, Larry and I were buddies. A shrug of the shoulder, a half grin, a wink of the eye, or touching one's nose with a flick were equally effective means of communicating without words. Larry and I had found our groove.

It was entertaining to see Larry's expression when he met Venus for the first time. Emerging from the ladies room, Venus approached like a superstar model. Larry appeared awestruck, pausing a moment before tentatively extending his hand. He could barely speak, paralyzed by Venus's beauty, mumbling, "You're … I'm … It's … Welcome …"

I was embarrassed for Larry, but Venus turned on her charm and graciously accepted his bumbling introduction. When Venus took his hand, Larry seemed to melt before our eyes.

I saved him from further embarrassment by saying, "Larry, let's have a drink and talk about the music profile of your marks and what you want us to do over the next four weeks."

Venus took my lead, excusing herself. Watching her saunter away, Larry asked me, "Where did you come up with that gorgeous Barbie Doll?" Italian male that he was he had completely lost his cool in Venus's presence.

"Just one of the fringe benefits of being a good musician on the road," I said with a smile and a wink. "Now, lay out your plan for the month."

As we each sipped our single malt Scotch on the rocks, Larry adjusted his boner and tried to compose himself and get down to business.

"Okay," he said. "The next four weeks—right? The Four Seasons will be here for two shows a night, this Friday and Saturday. The Carousels will lead off the first set and play the third set. The Four Seasons will play the second and fourth sets. Ideally, there should be absolute minimum downtime between their sets and yours. Dead air … the kiss of death. The Four Seasons will do a sound check Friday afternoon. They requested the use of your tubs, organ, electric piano and amplifiers. They plan to plug their bass into your amp. The club sound system will remain in place, though they may provide a sound engineer, twisting the dials.

"Between now and then, just do what you guys did at the Kato Club. Our audience is much more sophisticated. Oh yeah … pack the house every night. We need a big gate for the Four Seasons and standing room only for the Carousels. Give me all you've got and I'll take care of you and the Carousels. Mr. Esposito is well connected and can make things happen for you and the Carousels—assuming you make him money. Money is all he cares about, Rocky."

"Larry, the Carousels will deliver. You'll be pleased with how far we've come since the Kato Club. We'll make a lot of money for you."

Larry grinned. "It's my ass if you don't."

Opening night was a smashing success. Big Joe owned the audience with his melodramatic renditions of *"Turn on Your Love*

Light" and *"Hit the Road Jack."* Every eye in the joint was glued to his coonass movements, sound and nuance. All those days practicing in front of a mirror were paying big dividends as Big Joe's ego swelled two sizes larger than his hatband. If he hadn't weighed 230 pounds, I'm sure he would've levitated over the crowd.

During Tuesday's rehearsal, I challenged the Carousels to put on their God Power. The guys adopted an air of arrogance, producing the illusion of superstardom. Table topics with the patrons on breaks cemented our personal connections with marks.

Exceeding Larry's expectations, we took the Toledo audience on a nightly entertainment ride of their lives. Money flooded Larry's till. By Thursday of the first week, there was standing room only and lines outside, all waiting to see the Fabulous Carousels.

Before kicking off our featured set, I said, "Create fantasy—sell illusion—project your God Power."

THIRD SET LINEUP—PEPPERMINT LOUNGE—TOLEDO, OHIO				
SONG	ORIG'L ARTIST	GENRE	ENSEMBLE	FEATURE
Bon Ton Roulet	Clifton Chenier	Zydeco	Cajun Accordion, Fiddle & Frottoir	Big Joe—Vocal Dallas, Smoke & Rocky
Turn on Your Love Light	Bobby "Blue" Bland	R&B	4 Horns	Big Joe—Vocal, Lance & Rocky
Sidewinder	Lee Morgan	Jazz	4 Horns	Big Joe, Lance & Rocky
I Wish You Love	Nat King Cole	Old Standard	Standard Ensemble	Lance—Vocal
Twistin' the Night Away	Sam Cooke	R&R	Standard Ensemble	Bobby—Vocal
Malagueña	Andalucía by Ernesto Lecuona	Classical Acoustic Guitar	Guitar Solo	Smoke— Acoustic Guitar
Crazy (Comedy)	Patsy Cline	Country Comedy	Fiddle	Bobby in Falsetto

Tangerine	Herb Alpert & The Tijuana Brass	Pop	4 Horns	Big Joe, Lance & Rocky
Hit The Road Jack	Ray Charles	R&B	3 Horns	Big Joe—Vocal, Lance & Rocky
Moanin'	Modern Jazz Quintet	Jazz	4 Horns	Big Joe, Lance & Rocky

Perhaps naïvely, I began discussing the Carousel's strategic plans with Venus. Venus knew a lot about the ins and outs of the entertainment business and the inner workings of the Mob. Intuitively, she grasped the potential of the Carousels. Like a sponge, she soaked in every detail, classifying, categorizing and storing information, preparing her strategy and dissertation.

Her street smarts turned my vision on its head, repositioning money and fame ahead of the shallowness of cabaret adoration. Venus's focus provided the germination of a new plan—a quantum leap to fame and fortune.

The Red Queen sets the chess game rules and controls the outcome. I'm the high-trapeze flier pondering the triple summersault without a safety net. Missing the catcher is certain death, splattering brains all over the floor of the Big Top. If she fails to catch me, my epitaph will read, "Rocky was crazy for getting involved with Venus." Ultimately, I'm struggling to balance self-preservation with trusting Venus as my catcher. I stand at the crossroads.

The Four Seasons were great on stage, but at war off. Dysfunctional except during performances, the Seasons were held together by money and fame. The bass player and Frankie Valli regularly hurled verbal salvos at each other in the alley behind the Peppermint Lounge during breaks. Aloof off stage, they never mingled with the audience. However, the Four Seasons' sound and show were fantastic—setting the Peppermint Lounge on fire.

On two occasions, I talked with the bassist, Nick Massi, and keyboardist Bob Gaudio. Each was preoccupied with internal band wars, offering little opportunity for the Carousels to piggyback on their success. However, they complimented the Carousels, encouraging me to go for the brass ring by cutting a hit record.

Focused on recordings as their preferred pathway to fame and fortune, they didn't provide any introductions or opportunities for me to leverage. More disturbingly, they echoed my fears that Beatlemania was taking over American music, potentially marginalizing the Four Seasons along with the Carousels.

I thought we held our own with the Four Seasons, one of the hottest groups in America. Regrettably, they were making the big bucks, and we were just another cabaret band on the road.

Monday at 12:20 p.m., I called Stan Zuckerman's office in Los Angeles (9:20 a.m. Pacific Time). His voice was strong, positive, articulate, and decisive. So was mine, thanks to a drink of honey, lemon, and hot water an hour earlier.

Following niceties, Mr. Zuckerman said, "I know I'm repeating, but I'm not seeking to add to my stable of artists. However, your reputation intrigues me. As you know, my brother lives in Nashville. Although I don't want to create false expectations, I would be interested in accepting your kind offer to fly me in to review your group at the Black Poodle. It's your nickel."

"I agree," I said. "Nonetheless, I want us to meet prior to the performance and the morning following your review, since it's our nickel and risk."

Satisfied with our understanding, Mr. Zuckerman replied, "I'll have my secretary contact you at the Peppermint Lounge in Toledo. You two can work out flight schedules and my ETA."

After that conversation, I wheeled the '59 Cadillac into Good Ol' Home Cookin', Venus at my side. We joked and giggled as the waitress served up western omelets with all the fixin's. Buttering biscuits, doling ketchup on my hash browns and splashing hot sauce on my omelet, I relayed the essence of my phone conversation with Zuckerman.

Three sentences into my delivery, Venus erupted, raising arms like a prizefighter who just won the championship. Her pearly whites glistened through a smile broader than the grill of a 1956 Lincoln Continental—well close.

In the high voice of a little child she said, "You did it, Rocky. Yeah! I'm so proud of you. Tell me everything!"

Venus stood up, threw her shoulders back and moved her tight ass and plate to my side of the booth, planting a sloppy kiss on my puss. Her porcelain hand caressed my arm as she whispered in my ear, "You're fantastic, Rocky! I can trust you do exactly what you say. Never known anyone who kept their word like you. How did I ever live without you?"

Following breakfast, I drove to the country, parked at a rest stop and led Venus on a walk in the woods. For half a mile we followed a lightly traveled hiking trail through cottonwood trees on the shoreline of a babbling brook—well out of sight and sound of Toledo's ugliness. The cottonwoods were bursting with blooms, blanketing the sky with ten thousand puffy little clouds floating on a cool breeze.

This place was paradise to eye and ear. Birds sang their songs of joy. A cottontail rabbit hopped across our path, stopping to inspect us before moving on. Chipmunks chased each other over grass and leaves. As we got to the edge of the cottonwood tree line, three shrews briefly raised their heads in curiosity, interrupting their feast on grubs in an old log. The air was accented with a faint hint of jasmine.

I led Venus to the center of a winter wheat field, and we spread our arms and twirled like whirling dervishes. The soft stalks of wheat smelled clean and fresh, particularly to my nicotine-stained lungs. Like playful children engaged in a mock wrestling match, we rolled around and giggled away the afternoon, au natural. Returning to my trailer, we were red as beets; full-body sunburns, complimented by massive smiles. Blissfully happy.

Tuesday afternoon Venus delivered her "pump up Rocky's ego" speech, listing all my attributes, plus several I didn't have. For balance, she did deduct points for my terrible singing voice. Not knowing where she was headed, I remained quiet and let her talk.

My patience paid off.

Venus concluded her dissertation with, "I want to spend the rest of my life with you, Rocky. In spite of my history of messin' up, you are the love of my life. I'll try to keep my demons out of our loving relationship, but I'm scared—really scared. Need your understanding and love to survive. Will you reach out to me—save me—love me?"

She's leading me through a dance—step forward, step back, slide sideways. It's Salomé's dance of seduction. Creating allure and desire—Venus's strong suit. Tease me with a little peek at her sexuality, step back, twitch a little more, pause, wiggle again, and WHAM, I'm helplessly under her spell. She's mastered the tango. If I dance her dance, I could be out-foxed by this fox—or is it fox-trotted?

Fortunately, it was time to go to the Peppermint Lounge.

Chapter 44

1964
UNCLE REMUS

When I arrived at the club, Larry handed me an envelope. His curiosity matched mine. Venus Cruz's name was written in large printed letters. No address, stamp or return address.

I said, "Where did this come from?"

"Luca Esposito handed it to me this afternoon with instructions to make sure Venus gets it and responds by Friday—whatever that means."

"Have any idea what's inside?"

"No, although Mr. Esposito was serious, and that's never a good sign. Want me to steam it open?"

"Nope. It's none of my business."

"It could become your business real quick if the Mob is after Venus. Stubby double barrels have a peculiar way of not caring who's out front."

"Yeah. You're right about that. I'll keep you posted," I replied, stuffing the envelope in the inside pocket of my tux and mounting the stage.

Following the gig, I searched for perspective—and a friend. Once again, Lance's rapier wit and desert-dry humor became my elixir. Country as they come, his brilliant insights and wisdom were loosely wrapped in absurdities, sometimes crass, but always astute. Lance accepted my breakfast invitation to Sloppy Joes.

A black cloud of cigarette smoke hung so low we had to duck to make out the hostess—obviously a retired hooker, grossly overweight with leathery skin—who pointed us toward a table in the back. The wooden floors creaked as we passed tables of boisterous arguments or drunks with their heads buried in their hands. At 2 in the morning, the place was jammed with elbow-bending barflies, subterraneans and musicians badly in need of sobering up before hittin' the sack. Lance and I sat down at the designated table. Leather Skin recommended the house special: biscuits and red-eye sausage gravy.

Lance said, "Great. Make it two, plus coffee."

As Leather Skin waddled away, I said, "I've never had red-eye sausage gravy before—you?"

"Oh yeah. My grandma's cookbook had seven meat and gravy recipes. Her book gave us choices of pork, venison, chicken, chitins or goat. We could mix and match several, including white flower, brown roux, red eye or jalapeño green. I've had 'em all; still I loves da red-eye gravy with swine sausage best. Of course, our pigs were always fresh slaughtered."

"Other than your grandma's cook book, what other books were around?"

"We used a Gideon Bible as a door stop, but *Uncle Remus* got a serious workout."

"Really? *Uncle Remus?*"

"I was the second of 13 kids. When I learned to read, my job was to put the younger ones to bed. *Uncle Remus* was the only children's book we had, so I read every story—over and over. In time, I had memorized most of the stories—in full dialect. Actually, I credit *Uncle Remus* for getting me interested in acting and entertainment. Guess I'm a ham at heart. One story in particular—da *Tar-Baby*—was not only my favorite, it was my brothers' and sisters' favorite, too. When I went away to the army, *Uncle Remus* sort of became my bible—the foundation of my religious beliefs."

"That's nuts. Never heard of *Uncle Remus* stories used in a religious context. You're pullin' my leg—aren't you?"

"Why not *Uncle Remus*? All religions are based on stories and myths. There's always a central character dat ya pulls fer and wants to be like. I simply chose *Uncle Remus* for my myth and Br'er Rabbit as my hero. Everything you need is in there: morals, right, wrong, mystical spirits, humor, Heaven, Hell—everythin'. So far, it's worked out okay for me—better dan most screwed-up Christians and Jews I've known."

"How did *Uncle Remus* work for you in Alaska?"

"Up there, the Christians and Jews were worried sick about the Russians' setting off a nuclear missile strike and killing all of us. I simply saw it as another *Uncle Remus* story—just another myth that'll end with Br'er Rabbit comin' out okay. In the middle, there were many twist and turns, yet somehow he'd find a way to win the day. I simply trusted … Well, you know … Anyway, who'd want to kill Br'er Rabbit?"

Giving Lance an opening to show off his Uncle Remus dialect, I asked, "So, what would Br'er Rabbit say about our adventures on the road and our women?"

His eyes beginning to sparkle, Lance sat back and easily slipped into the plantation Negro dialect used by Joel Chandler Harris.

"Br'er Rabbit pacin' down de road—lippity-clippity, clippity-lippity—dezez sassy ez a jaybird. He'd say lots 'bout da times we's livin' in. He'd gwine to jump head firz' into free love, devil-may-care, fun-lovin' happy, breaking all da rules, out-smartin' Br'er Fox and gettin' high on life. He'd scorn hard drugs, da draft, da Vietnam war, taxes and de out-of-control government. Even so, overall, Br'er Rabbit would say America's livin' in da best of times. He'd say we's needs to smile more, laugh more, and love more while dis last."

"And women … what's Br'er Rabbit's take on women?" I asked.

"Know anythin' 'bout rabbits? Br'er Rabbit'd never gets 'nough nookie. Br'er Rabbit really loves da ladies. Settlin' down with just one jill is out of da question. Dat's simply not in his nature."

"Why?"

"'Cause he knows dat women'll always beez a mystery. No rabbit or man alive can figure what goes on inside da female skull. Think they'll do one thing and de dooz da opposite. Worse yet, nookie becomes der anvil to hammer da shackles on ya—den dey tries to change ya into what's dey thinks dey wants—a pussy-whipped tin man. Nope, settling down with just one jill is not fer Br'er Rabbit— and it wasn't for me, til I met Angelle. Frankly, I finds myself with the right jill in da wrong place and times. Not sure how dis will turn out... terrible timin'."

"What happened?"

"*Uncle Remus* didn't have stories 'bout serious stuff, like love and responsibility. So I's don't have *Uncle Remus* to save me from dose dings. I wuz mostly happy tryin' to beez like Br'er Rabbit ... never getting' 'nough nookie. Guess I'll have to rethink dis a bit."

Finally, I posed the question I wanted to ask all along: "What would Br'er Rabbit say about Venus?"

Ready with an answer, Lance replied, "Firz, Br'er Rabbit lusts fer Br'er Fox. She's gorgeous, cunning, and lethal. Still yet Br'er Rabbit sez, 'Watch out! Br'er Fox'll gots ya stuck hard to da Tar-Baby. Tu'n me loose, fo' I kick de stuffin' outen you,' sez Br'er Rabbit, but de Tar-Baby, she ain't sayin' nuthin'. She des holt on, en de Br'er Rabbit lose de use er his feet in de same way. Br'er Fox lay low. Den Br'er Rabbit squall out dat ef de Tar Baby don't tu'n 'im loose he butt 'er crank sided. En den he butted, en his head got stuck. Den Br'er Fox sa'ntered fort', lookin' dezez innercent ez wunner yo' mammy's mockin'-birds."

"Refresh my memory," I said. "Did Br'er Rabbit break loose from da Tar-Baby?"

Through a mischievous grin, Lance, now the muse, had his opening.

"Now, dat's da big question, isn't it? Some say he got's loosed 'im—some say he didn't."

"Well?" I posed.

"You'll finds out pretty soon," Lance said. "As I sees dis, Br'er Fox's got's ya stuck hard to da Tar-Baby. Co'se Br'er Fox wnater hurt Br'er Rabbit bad ez she kin. Will Br'er Fox snatch out ya eyeballs, t'ar out yer as by de roots, en cut off ya legs, skin ya dis time? What's ya gonna do Rock? Dat's da real question? Ya smart 'nough to break loose? Wills ya skip out des ez lively as a cricket in de embers, or be roastin' over Br'er Fox's dinner fire? Dat's da question only you can answer Rock."

"Okay, now translate for me," I said.

Before answering, Lance dipped a paper napkin into his water glass, washed his mouth and hands, then dried them with a clean paper napkin. Moving painfully slow, Lance lit a Picayune cigarette and took a long drag. For a brief moment, the caustic stink from his match overpowered the stench of nearby vomit radiating from a drunk who hadn't made it to the head in time.

Blowing the Picayune smoke skyward, Lance tested my patience while crafting his answer. Finally, he let fly a gargantuan fart as prologue to his wisdom.

"Rock, you're livin' out my grand plan—free pass card gettin' punched into confetti. Honestly, I'm envious of what you've done with my advice, especially your current squeeze, Br'er Fox. There's a big world out there. Keep reminding yourself, you're living in free-love times—the best of times. Don't fuck up a good thing—like I have. Keep on being Br'er Rabbit and out-foxin' Br'er Fox."

I said, "You can always get your free pass card out and get it punched into confetti."

"Yep—I could, though my plan didn't take into account love and responsibility. I'm too young fer dis, but its da way it is. Since I'm saddled with dis, I see ya goin' down the same path. Take my advice: do as I say—not as I do."

Nailed by my buddy, he sees things as they are, not as I'd like them to be.

"Am I that transparent?" I asked.

Raising his chin to the high posture of authority, my friend declared, "Rock, you're with the wrong woman at the wrong time. Your mind has gone to mush, taken over by an awfully shrewd Br'er Fox dats gots ya stuck hard to her Tar-Baby. I've watched her lead you around by your dick, but figured you're smarter dan dat. If ya 'member, Br'er Rabbit figured a way to get unstuck from Tar-Baby, and so can you. It's okay to love 'em and leave 'em. Dat's what Br'er Rabbit'd do. Dat's free love. Take my advice: Fuck Br'er Fox's brains out, den move on down da road with a big smile on da face. *Laissez les bon temps roulez.*

"Remember what Professor Kenny Livingston told us in Bossier City? Unfortunately, we're making all the wrong moves and our women are taking over our band. Say it with me Rocky: Goddamn women! Say it, Rocky: Goddamn women!"

I said it with Lance: "Goddamn women!"

Standing on my trailer's patio at 3:30 Wednesday morning, I removed the mysterious envelope from my tux pocket, holding it like a hand grenade. Collapsing into sagging webbing of my lawn chair I pondered its contents.

What's in the envelope? Am I getting in too deep? Is there more to her story than she's telling? Am I in the line of fire?

Perhaps Lance is right. Whether it's lust or love, spending the rest of my life with Venus is too idealistic, though I can't help but wonder. Besides, I'm at least a thousand punches shy of my free love quota. Why stop now? On the other hand, if Venus and I could only bottle today's happiness.... Admittedly, she's offering up a triple summersault without a net. Risk taker that I am, this one's a whopper. She's screwed up everyone she's touched. Luis Cruz said it straight out in New Orleans. Venus's confessions confirmed everything. And now this envelope thing. Is the Mob after her—me? Am I guilty by association?

Quietly entering the trailer, I placed the envelope in plain sight on the counter. A half empty Dewar's Scotch bottle sat next to a tall empty glass. Undressing, I climbed into bed, lying next to an unresponsive Barbie Doll. A million questions consumed my gray matter. Sleep remained elusive until sunrise.

Just outside my door, Mad Hatter and Cheshire Cat made their toilette in a nearby sand pile, returning to the patio to comment on what just happened.

Looking straight at Hatter, Cheshire pointed her paw at Venus sleeping inside the trailer, purring, *"Oh, by the way, if you'd really like to know, he went that way."*

Hatter snickered, *"Warning. Don't take it on an empty stomach and only one tiny little drop at a time; otherwise the experience might burst your shriveled up little heart. Got it."*

Chapter 45

1964
BOBBY WEARS ORANGE

"Bobby's in jail and is being transferred to the state penitentiary!" Dallas was yelling and banging on my trailer door at 8 a.m., Wednesday morning. Literally jumping up and down, Dallas' eyes twitched and his hands waved like a brakeman on the railroad.

As I stumbled to the door, I noticed that Venus and the envelope were nowhere to be found. For now, that would have to wait. I managed to get Dallas inside so he could tell me the full story. His eyes popped and spittle spewed as Dallas reached both high and low 'C's' within a single sentence. The bottom line was Bobby had too much to drink, smoke or sniff, and, as a result, took several swings at a couple of nigger cops in a Toledo restaurant about four hours ago.

"Bobby is charged with drunk and disorderly conduct, drug possession, and resisting arrest. He's in the city jail, scheduled to be moved to the state penitentiary later this morning. What do we do, Rocky?"

"It's not our town, Dallas. It's Mr. Esposito's and Larry Ladatta's town. Let's go see Larry at the Peppermint Lounge. He's probably there paying the beer delivery guy. If a fix can be arranged, Larry can put it in play."

I took a moment to throw on some clothes, and then drove while Dallas squirmed in the passenger seat. Intentionally driving slow to calm Dallas and ponder my options, I finally pulled into the back alley of the club. The stench of rotten garbage laced with rancid beer permeated the alley as we quickly made our way inside the Peppermint Lounge. Fortunately, Larry was there, paying the delivery guy. I hadn't taken the time to put on proper clothes, and neither had Dallas, so I could only image what Larry would say when he saw us.

Relying on my unspoken bond with Larry, I brushed off the dried grape jelly from my flannel shirt and pranced in like Cassius Clay.

Larry looked up and asked, "What's up Rocky … Dallas? What brings you night owls out so early?"

Placing my hand up in front of Dallas to stop him from speaking first, I said, "Larry, this is your town and we could use your influence."

Larry replied with a big grin, "Who exactly do you want me to kill this time?"

I laughed and added, "Just a nobody, so it shouldn't cost me much—right?"

"Seriously," Larry said. "What brings you out?"

"Bobby Starr fucked up and got himself arrested—took on two cops and lost. Charges include assault on two nigger police officers, drunk and disorderly, and drug possession. When he fucks up, he really fucks up. Bobby's sitting in the city jail and scheduled for transfer to the Ohio State Penitentiary sometime this morning. I assume you can put a call in and get this taken care of—right?"

Larry flipped on a mischievous smile, flickin' his nose at the same time; an acknowledgement of our unspoken bond. In his gracious nature, Larry brought Dallas into the conversation by saying, "As I remember, we had to do something like this for Bobby when you guys played the Kato Club. At that time, Bobby was guilty of everything you just mentioned except drug possession. Right? We got him out of jail in an hour, though drug possession changes the game. What if we teach Bobby Starr a lesson and let him suit up in orange and break rocks a night or two with real criminals. Do you think that will sober him up and teach him a lesson?"

Flickin' my nose, I knew what needed to be said, but it had already been communicated—mind to mind. I enjoyed Larry's humor. Perverted, often dark, we always ended in a laugh.

"Sounds good to me, Larry," I replied. "As for tonight's performance, we can get by just fine without Bobby, being that it's Wednesday. What time do you want us to meet you tomorrow morning to drive out and get Bobby? By the way, we can post bail and juice money."

"I assumed you would. I'll set everything up. Be here at 10, and we'll save Bobby's ass. I hope this humbles Bobby. On second thought, it probably won't."

As I turned to leave, Larry jerked on my shirt, asking, "What was in the envelope?"

"Don't know yet. I left it on the counter last night. Venus and the envelope were gone this morning. Expect I'll find out when I get home."

"Wiseguys play rough, Rocky. Stay out of their line of fire. You could get hurt—or worse."

When I arrived at the trailer, Venus was there, exceedingly anxious, obviously terrified by whatever was in the envelope. She scratched her arms violently, like a dope addict in desperate need of a fix. Avoiding eye contact and cowering like a whipped puppy dog, she resembled a rabbit caught in a snare. Suddenly, she bolted past and landed on the patio. As I stepped down to the patio, she rushed back inside, closing the door behind her.

Bewildered, I backed off, stunned by her off-the-wall behavior. Distancing myself from the scene seemed prudent, I stood next to the door and said calmly, "I'll be back around supper time."

"Don't hurry. I need lots of space to work through this."

Lunch with Smoke was almost refreshing. Conspiracy theories and visions of grandeur in Vegas spanned much of our time together. As was our custom, he did most of the talking, while I nodded and occasionally said, "Uh-hum." The more he talked, the more my thoughts wandered to the envelope and the wacky person rattling around in my tin can.

What have I gotten myself into? Am I going to be drawn into her situation—whatever that is? What price will I pay for my folly? Is judgment day closing in on me? Am I strong enough to control this or will events suck me in?

I dropped off Smoke at his bat cave, drove to the country, and sat by a stream. I had a lot more questions than answers. Watching the sun set, I realized that I hadn't answered any of my questions over the past hour, in large part because I needed more information. I finally drove back to the trailer. Before getting out of the car I reminded myself how Venus and I got here. Knocking lightly, I announced myself and entered. Fortunately, a .45 Derringer did not greet me.

Somewhat composed, Venus smiled and said, "Thanks for coming back to me. You did the right thing—giving me space to think this through. I know you have plenty of questions, but you have to shower, get dressed and go to work. Tomorrow, can we go to that beautiful place in the country? I'll explain everything tomorrow in the wheat field."

"Perhaps tomorrow afternoon. I have to meet Larry Ladatta in the morning and get Bobby out of jail."

"Anything you say, my love. Anything you say...."

The Carousels played Wednesday night without Bobby. We simply cut his vocals and the tunes he played drums—making a decent showing for ourselves. For one night, it was okay, but none of us wanted to do without our struttin' peacock. That night, Larry and I never mentioned Bobby Starr.

Thursday, Dallas banged my door at 8:30 a.m. "Time to go, Rocky," he yelled.

I didn't even open the door, yelling back, "Come back in an hour."

Venus consumed much of that hour, leading us through a spectacular love-making interlude.

Dallas returned at 9:30, and we met Larry at the Peppermint Lounge just before 10. This time Dallas and I were dressed in slacks and starched white shirts.

The fix was in.

During the entire 40-mile drive to the state penitentiary, Dallas squirmed in the back seat. It was raining cats and dogs when we drove up to the gates. We dodged raindrops as Larry led us into the penitentiary to sign for Bobby's release. Within an hour, a humbled Bobby Starr walked the long walk from the penitentiary gate to my '59 Cadillac Coupe de Ville. Without a word, he climbed in the back seat, soaking wet and shabbily dressed in his Monday night, robin-egg blue tuxedo, now filthy from the scuffle. He looked like a beaten wet dog and smelled like one, too.

Perhaps he learned something—perhaps not.

Neither Larry nor I showed interest in discussing Bobby's adventures—before, during, or after jail. However, Dallas wanted to know everything, asking five questions at once. Bobby didn't want to talk at all. But Dallas pressed, mostly out of youthful curiosity. Wet and sticky, Bobby slumped in my rear seat, cowering from embarrassment and unspeakable events that occurred inside the walls of that prison.

Finally, Bobby mustered a mumble, barely intelligible from the front seat. The highlights involved an orange jump suit, a crazed drug-addict cellmate, and instructions from a belligerent prison guard on how to "break that boulder down into small rocks by sundown."

I partially overheard fragments of Bobby's tale involving a cold shower, a bar of soap, and five gorillas. I could see Dallas' eyes widen like saucers in my rear view mirror. Feeling much like being part of the gawking crowd attending a disembowelment, I turned away, canceling out my curiosity of the lurid tales relayed in the back seat. Best not to know—yet, instinctively, I knew. I drove directly to Bobby's trailer and let him out to remake himself into a struttin' peacock before show time at the Peppermint Lounge. Dallas also exited.

Driving to the Peppermint Lounge to drop Larry off, I wondered if our peacock would be capable of strutting. However Larry had something else on his mind.

"What was in the envelope, Rock?"

"I'll know everything this afternoon. For now, I'm in the dark."

"Are you serious about Barbie Doll or is she just another split-tail?"

I knew Larry to be an honorable man, sensing he needed my permission before hitting on Venus. Unusual for me, I provided Larry a straight answer.

"Actually, the mystery excites me. She's different—and dangerous. She's definitely more than a band-aid—still Venus scares the hell out of me."

The suave Italian straightened up, brushed back his long black hair into its proper pompadour look and said, "Well, if you step aside, let me be the first to know. She's one of the most beautiful creatures I've ever seen. I fantasize about … well, you know. Hope I haven't offended you, but that's an incredible woman."

"Haven't offended me. To be candid, I'm like the frog in a pot of hot water. You know the story: If you bring a pot of water to a vigorous boil and toss in a frog, it immediately jumps out. On the contrary if you place a frog in a pot of cold water and gradually turn the heat up, the frog will remain there and the frog will cook. I'm identifying with that frog in cold water being slowly brought to a boil. Venus is a master at controlling heat."

Larry was undeterred. "I'd like to be the frog in the pot for just one long afternoon. But, since you are the main course in the chef's pot, you might as well lay back and enjoy her spicy recipes."

Larry flicked his nose and we both snickered.

Chapter 46

1964
SETTING THE SNARE

enus's ass replaced Larry's in the Cadillac later that afternoon. I drove to the country for answers. This time I brought a heavy quilt to soften the wheat shafts. Wildlife welcomed us—reminiscent of our first excursion into paradise. Cardinals, cedar waxwings, and yellow warblers sang a chorus of celebration, acknowledging our arrival. Ground squirrels foraged for nuts, fearlessly chirping away as we passed. Wild scarlet carnations bloomed, offering up an intoxicating perfume.

"I really love you, Rocky," Venus said as we walked through the woods. "You've changed everything. I only think good thoughts, dream happy dreams—clean and clear. Rocky Strong is my narcotic. I'm addicted to you. We can make it, Rocky. My body, mind, and soul are yours—only you. Life is so good with you."

"The envelope, Venus?"

"Not so good. Mike Gillich sent me the envelope, through Luca Esposito."

"Who is Mike Gillich?"

"Mike Gillich is a kingpin in the Dixie Mafia. He developed the Gulf Coast strip, owns a string of motels, nightclubs, strip joints, gambling dens—and me. He owns me, Rocky!"

"What does that mean, 'He owns you'?"

"I signed a personal management contract with him—I told you all about that in Louisville. The only way I can get out is to buy out my contract or find another goodfella to take me over. Either way, Mike gets his money … and he's all about money."

"So, what exactly was in the envelope?"

"A letter from Mike and a copy of our contract. He demands I pay him $10,000 or come back to Club Capri—now. I have to give him my answer by tomorrow."

"What are you going to do?"

"It's more complicated than that. When he finds out that I'm pregnant, he won't want me back on stage or doing tricks, at least until the baby is born."

"What baby?" I asked, my eyes widening and my stomach beginning to churn.

"Your baby is growing inside me, Rocky."

Trying to remain calm, I asked, "When did you find this out?"

"For sure—yesterday. The test came back positive, but I knew it before I went to the doctor."

"This does complicate things," I said, my biggest understatement to date. "What are you going to do?"

"Well, abortion is out of the question. I was Christened Catholic and believe abortion is murder—a mortal sin. I'd never have an abortion."

"Other options?"

"Paying Mike Gillich off or get Merrill Saks to take over my contract."

Somewhat bewildered, I asked the pivotal question: "What do you want from me?"

"Marry me, Rocky. I want to be your wife and raise your children. You can talk to Merrill and strike a deal to get Mike Gillich off my back. I'm done with that life. You are Merrill's golden boy, and the Carousels have been his biggest draw. Use your relationship with Merrill and all this will disappear. Marry me Rock, and everything will be okay."

"Other options?"

"You've seen my final option—in Louisville. I will never go back to Biloxi. I'd rather end it all right here."

"You serious?"

"I was never more serious. Although that's my last option, my final solution. Besides, you are the love of my life, and I know you love me. Your moral code won't allow you to abandon me or your responsibilities. I've always known that you'll do the right thing because you are a really good man. You have a good heart."

"You sure about that?"

"I'm sure I will make you the happiest man on earth. Isn't that enough?"

"Wow. Give me some time to think this over."

"I have until tomorrow to give Mike our answer."

Well, there it is. I have 24 hours to make the most important decision of my life. Br'er Rabbit's stuck hard to da Tar-Baby and Br'er Fox ain't lettin' go. Br'er Rabbit's tangled in da snare. Does I has da stuff to scape dis trap? Does I has da guts to knaw off my foot en scape?

The sun was bright and warm in the Ohio wheat field. I lay on the quilt and pondered—and pondered—and pondered.

A triple summersault without a net just might work. Except if I miss the catcher . . .

Back on stage that night, Bobby captured much of his previous strut, but not all. Dallas and I sensed veiled insecurities and embarrassment, although neither the guys nor the audience knew the depths of Bobby's abyss. His orange jump suit was never mentioned again, freeing Bobby to play the role of a master deceiver, hiding the foibles of an average human being. Bobby Starr was almost back, creating fantasy, selling illusion, and projecting God Power.

Chapter 47

1964
GARGOYLES WHEEZED

"Hi Mom. It's Dean."

"Dean—it's so good to hear your voice. When are you coming home?"

"Actually, we'll be in Shreveport late Sunday or early Monday."

"We?"

"Yes. Someone will be with me, Mom."

"Who?"

"Venus Cruz is coming with me. We want to get married in Shreveport next week."

The long silence spoke volumes. Finally Mom said, "Who is this woman … and do you love her?"

"She's Venus Cruz from New Orleans—an entertainer. And yes, I love her."

"The uncertainty in your voice gives you away, Dean. Something's not right. What's going on?"

"Nothing, Mom. When I get home we'll have a long talk, on the backyard swing."

"Something's not right …"

Venus and I left Toledo Sunday morning at 1:30 a.m., trailer in tow behind the Caddy. Driving straight through, we switched off driving every three hours. Pushing hard, we cleared the Shreveport city limit sign within 20 hours. Mom had warm milk and cake waiting and the bed turned down for our guest. The couch was made up for me. Mom welcomed Venus with skepticism, yet displayed grace. The hour was late, so we said our good nights, postponing the predictable conversation.

Monday morning Mom went to work and I snuck into my all-time favorite featherbed, next to Venus.

Mom came home from work at 6 that evening and immediately went to work fixing spaghetti with meat sauce. Venus fixed a green salad while I set the table. When dinner was over, Venus offered to wash dishes. Mom readily accepted, unusual for the most accommodating hostess I'd known. I poured two cups of black coffee and motioned toward the back door, leading to the swing hanging from a large oak tree in the backyard.

At dusk the canopy of large oaks sheltered the elements from those lucky enough to sit below. Mom settled into the cypress swing Dad built 25 years earlier and sighed. Sipping hot coffee, she managed a forced smile, but did not speak. I settled into the swing next to her. Mom planted her feet on the ground and pushed gently. She rocked me with unconditional love, like I was a baby in a crib. I touched her shoulder and found her pensive, on edge. The most important person in my life needed answers, many I couldn't or wouldn't provide.

"I know you have questions. Fire away," I told her.

"What are you doing with your life? Have you abandoned your father's dream for your future?"

"No. Just a little side trip."

"Your side trips have squandered the past five years—so far. When are you going to come to your senses?"

My shoulders shrugged like a scolded child.

Mothers see everything. It's futile to pretend with Mom.

"Venus and I got our blood test and applied for a marriage license today. Our plan is to get married this week because I have to be in Nashville by Sunday at noon. I'll stop by the First Presbyterian Church and see if we can book space in the chapel. Mom, I need your blessing on this. Can you take off work Friday afternoon?"

"Why are you in such a big hurry to get married?"

"There is a good reason."

"Well?"

"You raised me to follow God's laws, be a good person and take responsibility for my actions."

"What have you done?

"Venus is pregnant. It's mine."

"Are you absolutely sure?"

"As sure as I can be."

"Did it ever cross your mind that this woman is tricking you into marrying her?"

"I feel honor bound to marry her. Besides, she's beautiful and I love her."

"You only see the outside. I see inside."

"I can't turn my back on responsibility."

Mom looked away, starring at Mrs. Ray's house across the way. The swing stopped swinging, so I stood up to release my burden of guilt.

It seemed like an eternity before she said, "I had a long talk with Mrs. Ray, who raised four boys and a girl. After Mrs. Ray heard my concerns about you drifting further and further away from your future and our God-fearing moral beliefs, she advised me to be patient. She said, 'Eventually he'll come home to his roots and be the man you raised him to be. Eventually they all come home to roost.' I know she's right, but you are testing my patience."

"I have to admit," I replied, "I'm caught up in the chase to make it big in the entertainment business. We have a chance to get a hit record, play Vegas, be on TV and may even be in a movie. Wouldn't you be proud of me if we did that?"

"You are blinded by glitter. The price you are paying is too great. You've sold your soul to the devil. Don't you see what's happening?"

"I haven't sold my soul to the devil. I'm marrying Venus and trying to be the honorable man you raised. I'll make a go of this."

Mom stood, reaching for the chain of the swing to provide stability. Staring off into that private reservoir only accessible by Moms, she seemed to find answers to her tough questions.

"I've done this all wrong. Dean, I spoiled you rotten because you were all I had left, after your father died. Over-protective. I never scolded you or allowed anyone to correct your self-centered behavior. You turned out to be a selfish man. I sacrificed myself to protect you from bad people. In spite my shielding, you are attracted to them, drawn like a moth to a flame. I was wrong. I apologize, son. I am very sorry."

"Mom. I'm simply growing up."

"No. You are being led down a fool's path. You are blind to what's really happening here."

"Can you find it in your heart to give Venus and me your blessing?"

"Do you know what you're asking? I've had to endure the deaths of your father, your sister and your brother. Since then I've put all my love and faith in you. Then you abandon your father's wishes and drop out of Tech. And now you are marrying a woman I know nothing about. What do you expect me to say?"

"I need your blessing, Mom."

"I know you better than you know yourself. Venus is a huge mistake. The odds of you returning to Tech and making your father and the Masons proud are simply ..." she paused. "Please reconsider. Is there anything I can do or say to stop this marriage?"

"I need your blessing, Mom."

"You ask too much, testing a mother's unconditional love so you can get your way. You are all I've got, and you're asking me to bless what I don't believe is in your best interest."

"Mom, I need your blessing."

Following a long pause and many tears, Mom sighed and said, "With a heavy heart, you have my blessing."

Tuesday morning I asked Venus about her children, whom I'd never met and she rarely mentioned. At first, she didn't respond, though I could see her mind cycling through an emotional roller coaster, fraught with guilt and self-condemnation. I had the presence of mind to give her plenty of space and didn't pursue the matter. After a half-hour of ups and downs, Venus corralled her emotions and asked her question.

"Rocky, are you willing to take another risk—a big gamble on me? I'd like to drive to New Orleans and get Alicia and Ricky. I'll spend a couple of days with my sister and meet you in Nashville. It's my one and only chance to have a normal life, as a mother and wife. Can we take this extra risk? Will you do this for me—for us, Rocky?"

I'm on a very slippery slope. What have I done? Where is this going? When will I reach my limit? Can I walk away from my responsibilities? Too late. I'm stuck to the Tar-Baby."

"Okay, go get your kids and meet me in Nashville."

What else could I say?

In anticipation of our marriage and the immediate addition of two kids, we went shopping for a two-bedroom trailer, selecting a 40-footer with bath, living room, fully equipped kitchen, and a washer and dryer setup. The bedrooms were on opposite ends, allowing privacy for the newlyweds. To tow the big trailer, a used International Harvester bobtail half-ton truck was purchased cheap. My local bank financed the trailer and I paid cash for the old truck.

I parked our new home on Virginia Avenue, in front of Mom's large corner lot. Neighborly curiosity peaked, several requesting a tour of the trailer and an introduction to Venus. Our Shreveport relatives, the Bettingfield's and Starr's, came over to meet Venus and inspect our aluminum house on wheels. They were very nice, but transparent, offering obligatory compliments, yet failing to disguise their true feelings. An army of God-fearing Presbyterians had assembled, all aligned with Mom's displeasure with her only son.

Offering my 18-foot trailer to Dallas and Mary at the same bargain price I'd paid was met with enthusiasm. Dallas and Mary jumped at the opportunity and delivered cash in exchange for title to the trailer.

There was much more to do. I called Stan Zuckerman's secretary to coordinate the Nashville ETA. Then I called each of the Carousels to schedule a meeting Sunday afternoon in my new digs. They were curious about the meeting agenda, but I withheld the Stan Zuckerman audition announcement. Business completed, and Mom home from work, we enjoyed dinner together and conversation surrounding the planned wedding Friday afternoon.

At Venus's prodding, I met up with Merrill Saks to discuss buying out Mike Gillich's contract on Venus for $10,000. Merrill said he'd have to talk to Mike and Carlos before making any commitments. Then he put the skunk on the table: "What have you got to offer in return for my 10 G's?"

"We both know you'll drive a hard bargain," I replied. "Let me simply say I'm prepared to negotiate in good faith. See what Mike and Carlos say and then we'll talk."

Friday finally arrived, and the 1 p.m. wedding began on time in the chapel of the First Presbyterian Church of Shreveport, which featured ornate wood carvings and a pipe organ tucked away in a corner. It was not as I'd envisioned. Mom cried as Uncle Ed stood by her side, a perpetual scowl on his face—directed at me, of course. Gargoyles wheezed in harmony with leaks erupting from an old organ played by an emaciated skeleton of a man. His first musical selection was J.S. Bach's *Toccata and Fugue in D Minor*.

Venus was dressed in white, a surprise to all. The brief service bordered on sterile, led by a minister who didn't know us and vice versa. What should have been one of the happiest days of my life proved disappointing. However, Venus beamed with joy, the only bright light in an otherwise dark and unsettling ceremony.

Venus made sure our honeymoon at the Holiday Inn fashioned a much different outcome. She got her way as we found pleasure together.

At the end of the day, I pondered: Can I pull this off? If so, I'll be a very happy man.

Early Saturday morning, Venus pointed the Caddy toward New Orleans while I pulled the big rig north, bound for Nashville. A hundred miles later, I came to grips with my big mistake: gambling on an old International Harvester half-ton truck to successfully tow a 40-foot trailer. I lost the bet. Vapor lock and a leaking radiator precipitated 20 unplanned stops and a frustratingly late arrival in Nashville. Nerves frazzled, I pulled into the mobile home park at 5:30 Sunday morning, parked the rig in front of the office, turned off the truck's engine and went to sleep in the trailer's master bedroom.

When the office opened at 9, I checked in, found my spot and began setting up the rig for the first time. Exhausted, angry and irritable, I finished set up at 1:30, showered, had a sandwich and tried to compose myself for a motivational meeting with the Carousels— one tough assignment.

Cheshire Cat purred as I ate my sandwich, *"Meta-Essence is the life-force of Wonderland. That of your enemies is especially potent. Collect what you can. Use it wisely."*

Chapter 48

1964
PITCHING ZUCKERMAN

B obby arrived first, with Lance and Smoke following close behind. Dallas was next, and Big Joe last. Each offered varying degrees of congratulations, related to our marriage in Shreveport and our new abode. Finally, they settled into an overstuffed sofa and two chairs in anticipation of some great announcement. Before beginning, I served iced tea and soft drinks.

Accepting that I was not at my best, I took three deep breaths before speaking.

"Stan Zuckerman flies in from Los Angeles to review the Carousels this Friday at the Black Poodle," I told them. "In my judgment the possibility of inking a personal management agreement with Zuckerman represents our best opportunity to achieve stardom and fortune. If we dedicate ourselves to delivering a stunning performance Friday night, I'm reasonably confident we can strike a deal with Mr. Z.

"Questions?"

Big Joe barked, "How much of our bread does he get?"

I said, "Ten percent—standard fee. Of course, that's over and above the ten percent for the booking agent."

Again, Big Joe barked, "For what? Zuckerman guaranteein' fame and fortun'?"

"No guarantees," I answered.

Bobby posed the next question.

"What has Stan Zuckerman promised you? Can he get us a record deal with a major label, Vegas, national television or movies? What can he do that Carlos Marcello can't?"

I paused, realizing this was not going as well as I'd hoped. Time to regroup.

"First of all, Marcello is off our radar screen for the time being—too busy covering his ass in the alleged involvement in the JFK assassination. I talked with Merrill Saks last week and confirmed that negotiations with Carlos Marcello are suspended indefinitely. On the other hand, Mr. Z is the personal manager for some of the biggest stars in America, many of whom have record deals, Vegas appearances, guest spots on television, their own television show, and star in movies."

Bobby wanted to know what big names he handled, and I had the list memorized.

"Andy Williams, Perry Como, the Beach Boys, Pat Boone, Bobby Darin, Danny Thomas, Tony Bennett, and Ricky Nelson, among others. The Bobbie and Billy duo at the Black Poodle are one of only two lesser known names Mr. Z. represents."

Lance asked, "Why Zuckerman? Why not some other personal manager?"

I said, "In my opinion, Mr. Z's representation of our band will break the glass ceiling we've banged our heads against. He's in LA, the entertainment capital of America. He's got contacts we don't. Mr. Z's track record for catapulting artists to fame and fortune is exemplary. I think he's our passport to fulfilling our dreams."

"Where did this idea come from? Who provided Zuckerman's contact information?" Lance asked with a challenge in his voice.

"The contact information came from Bobbie and Billy, the duo at the Black Poodle."

Then Lance threw his big punch: "Did Venus have anything to do with this?"

Sensing the weight of a stacked deck against me, I mustered a politically safe answer, "We can't afford to make critical decisions based on opinions of six guys plus four or five women. That's the definition of anarchy. It's not the women's band—it's ours."

Lance said, "Venus's Tar-Baby fingerprints are all over this one."

With a bewildered look, Bobby asked, "What's with the Tar-Baby comment?"

Lance said, "Never mind, jus' somethin' between Rock and me."

Dallas was ready to back me up, saying, "Hey, guys. Rocky has done a great job as leader. When we leave Nashville he's already booked us into upstate New York, Louisville, Peoria and Chicago. I trust Rocky's judgment, and we should give this Zuckerman guy a shot."

In his southern accent Smoke added, "Personally, I want to play Vegas, get a hit record, become a television idol, and do something special with my life. If Mr. Zuckerman can get us closer to that, I'm all for it. But first we need to impress him—right? We can discuss whether we want to sign with him after he shows interest in us. What do we have to lose? Let's knock his socks off with a great performance Friday night—right?"

Building on the positive comments of Dallas and Smoke, I jumped back in.

"Yep. Friday night—probably the second and third sets."

"What ya thinkin'? Ya know, what'll impress dis Zuckerman dude?" Big Joe grunted.

Having carefully thought this through, I replied, "Second set we'll feature our eclectic genres with lots of horns and passing instruments around. Third set, deliver a knockout stage show. How's that sound?"

Bobby spoke for all. "Good plan. Let's clear the decks and focus on knocking Stan Zuckerman's socks off."

Finally, I sensed attitudes were turning positive, the beginnings of embracing opportunity. The fragile brotherhood aligned on a common mission: impress Stan Zuckerman. Four Carousels rose and left my trailer. Dallas lingered, asking, "Where's Venus?"

Posting my first smile of my day, I said, "Thanks for asking, Dallas. She's driving up from New Orleans and arrives Tuesday evening. She's visiting her sister and bringing her two pre-school kids to live with us. To be candid, I don't know what to expect, having never been around children. In some ways I'm turning into an old married man with rug rats."

"You'll adapt, Rocky," Dallas replied. "As for being an old married man with rug rats, that's exactly what Mary and I are praying for. Every day we pray to God to bless us with kids. You're lucky to have what you've got—a great wife and two kids."

"Thanks Dallas. Then again, as far as praying every day to God for kids, the recommended method is fornicating on a regular basis. I assume you two are holding up that end of your devotion."

"Mary and I are double-timing that part of our worship. In fact, I'm late for our Sunday afternoon prayer session, if you know what I mean."

Dallas cleared my trailer door, walking at a brisk pace toward my old tin can, ready to light Mary's firecracker passions during afternoon prayers.

Venus, Alicia and Ricky arrived Tuesday around suppertime. Awaiting them was a big pot of vermicelli boiling on the stove and Ragu sauce with ground chuck bubbling in a cast-iron skillet. Exiting the Caddy, Alicia and Ricky cowered like scared little animals, not knowing what to make of me, the trailer, Nashville or taking orders from their paternal mother—a foreigner issuing commands like a prison warden.

Following dinner, I offered to show Alicia and Ricky their bedroom at the front of the trailer. Venus nodded in agreement, providing me the opportunity to privately extend a warm welcome to two little aliens. The calmer I spoke, the more they defrosted.

Still this was their first night. We'd have plenty of time to become a family. I kissed each of them on the forehead before tucking them in.

Smiling Alicia said, "Thank you, Daddy Rocky."

I was surprised, but pleased.

Venus was exhausted, so I recommended a hot shower and early retirement while I went to the club. After dressing in my Mohair gray tux, I drove the Cadillac to Printers Alley, brushing away McDonald wrappers and picking up squashed French fries off previously pristine fabric seats.

Oh well. We all have a lot to learn … On the other hand, we're together, for the first time as a family.

Wednesday morning, Venus was well rested after the long drive, so I filled her in about preparations for the Zuckerman visit. She was pleased with my report, but decided not to attend Thursday's dress rehearsal.

"I'm staying home with Alicia and Ricky."

Anxious to know how the dress rehearsal went, she stayed up that night, waiting for my report.

"How did it go?" she asked the moment I stepped in the door. "Did Gert, Angelle, or Mary offer any constructive criticisms?"

"In my opinion, we're well prepared for Mr. Z," I answered. "According to the guys, their main squeezes babbled superlatives, adding nothing substantive to our polish. Their support for their men pumped up egos, just what they needed for an extra boost of confidence. Bet they'll get laid tonight and transform into giants tomorrow."

Venus's face lit up with a devilish smile.

"I guarantee you'll feel like Jack the giant killer for the next two days—in complete control of your meeting with Stan Zuckerman Friday afternoon. You'll be like a god on stage Friday night and then negotiate a big contract with Mr. Z Saturday morning. Now lay back. You're in for the ride of your life. You're about to become Jack the giant killer!"

Leading me to our rear bedroom, the light from 30 candles flickered on our naked bodies and her magic box of sex toys. My wife unselfishly guided me through an incredible journey. As dawn broke I yelled, "Uncle! Uncle! Uncle!"

Chapter 49

1964
THE BALL'S IN MY COURT

Friday afternoon I met Mr. Zuckerman at the Nashville Airport as planned and chauffeured him to the Marriott Hotel in my recently washed and waxed Cadillac—no traces of McDonald's food.

Mr. Zuckerman was all California and impeccably dressed. Gracious in every way, he personified class; a man of success and wealth. My initial impression was that we would get along famously. I immediately thanked him for accepting my invitation to audition the Carousels.

He politely thanked me for arranging—and paying for—the trip. Then, he added, "Had my brother not lived in Nashville, I probably wouldn't be here. However, I am here, and I confess, I'm curious."

As we lounged in overstuffed chairs at the Marriott, it was time to deliver my pitch, with just the right tone, pacing and eye contact.

"The Carousels have done well," I began. "We're the highest-paid band on our cabaret circuit—that is, without a hit record. If level one represents rank amateurs; level two, excellent entertainers moving up; and level three is megastar, the Carousels are stuck at the upper end of level two. I could give you a long story, but the bottom line is simple. Our success has largely been confined to packing nightclubs and working 50 weeks a year at good money. Our record deals haven't produced hit records, and our nightclub circuit has been intentionally limited to Central and Eastern U.S.—primarily due to a one-day travel requirement."

Mr. Zuckerman seemed to be paying attention, so I took a big breath and continued, hoping that I wouldn't bore him with my assessment of our current musical culture.

"The Beatles changed everything. In fact, I refer to them as assassins. The Beatles, English bands, and psychedelic rock bands have killed off great musicianship. Given the traumatic events over the past three years, America's culture and musical taste dramatically changed. Patrons are leaving nightclubs and moving to television, movies and Vegas. Music mirrors cultural taste. And American society has irreversibly changed. Therefore, if the Carousels fail to embrace change, we won't make our way into the music history footnotes. On our current cabaret circuit, our price tag, devoted audiences and music styles are rapidly coming to an end, soon to be replaced by long-haired, dope-smokin' guitar bands playing to long-haired, dope-smokin' audiences."

Pausing for another breath, I asked, "Do you agree?"

Zuckerman answered almost immediately.

"The Beatles certainly have changed the entertainment industry. And, you've grasped the changes under way in our country. What do you plan to do about it, Rocky?"

I was ready with an answer.

"Reinvent the Carousels into a fresh new sound, produce hit records, deliver a Las Vegas review second-to-none and position us for television and film. In short, transition the Carousels from a cabaret band into a stage show entertainment group that will appeal to television audiences. A hit record with a major record label is crucial. We have the talent and tenacity to make the leap into stardom and fame. However we need your guidance and contacts to achieve our goal."

Mr. Zuckerman leaned forward, so I sat back in my chair and kept on talking.

"Long ago, I accepted the importance of securing professional help to smash through the glass ceiling. I've been dancing with one of America's biggest Mob bosses. We got very close to signing an agreement, but the JFK assassination abruptly ended our discussions, along with his involvement in exploiting the legitimate entertainment industry. Since then I've been looking for the right relationship. That's why you're here. Within a couple of days we'll know if there's chemistry between us. If the answer is yes, we'll strike a deal. If not, the Carousels will keep looking."

Mr. Z scratched his chin with perfectly manicured nails, finally saying, "I like the way you think, Rocky. With your brains, what are you doing in this business? No, don't answer that now. There'll be time to talk about your education and personal goals later. Right now I need to rest before tonight's performance. Incidentally, you won't know I'm in the house tonight. Only Bobbie and Billy know me, and I'll keep a very low profile. You and I will have breakfast tomorrow morning, 8 o'clock sharp in the Marriott restaurant. By 9 we'll know if the chemistry is right. Okay?"

Rising to shake his hand, I confirmed, "Okay. However, I recommend you catch our second and third sets. The second set will demonstrate our musicianship and genre versatility. The third set will feature our stage show. I'll respect your request to remain incognito. I'll see you for breakfast tomorrow morning. Thanks for sharing your valuable time with me and the Carousels."

And with that brief conversation, I left him to rest while my heart was pumping with dreams of a megastar future.

Friday night, the second set was tight—musically flawless, generating an air of top-flight professionalism. On five occasions the audience rose in sustained applause. At the break we came off stage and mingled with the patrons. Privately, I was pleased with our second set delivery. Next up, the stage show.

Before kicking off the stage show set, I said, "Create fantasy—sell illusion—project your God Power."

THIRD SET STAGE SHOW LINEUP—THE BLACK POODLE				
SONG	ORIG'L ARTIST	GENRE	ENSEMBLE	FEATURE
West Side Story Overture & Stage Show	Leonard Bernstein	Broadway	Dance + Serial Solo's	All Carousels
Orange Blossom Special	Ervin and Gordon Rouse	Country	Fiddle, Banjo & Guitar	Big Joe & Smoke
Jolé Blon	Clifton Chenier	Zydeco	Cajun Accordion, Fiddle & Frottoir	Big Joe—Vocal, Dallas, Smoke & Rocky
Mule Train (Comedy Pantomime)	Frankie Laine (Pantomime)	Comedy	Dark Stage Peanut Spot	Dallas in Pantomime
Stand By Your Man (Comedy)	Tammy Wynette (Parody)	Country Comedy	Standard Ensemble	Bobby in Falsetto
Who's On First (Comedy Excerpts)	Abbott and Costello	Comedy Routine	Dark Stage Peanut Spot	Big Joe & Dallas
Slow Motion Baseball (Comedy) Excerpts from Casey at the Bat	Strobe Light—Slow Motion Comedy of Baseball Game	Comedy Routine	Dallas—poem reader & Baseball Stadium Organ	Bobby, Lance, Smoke, Rocky & Big Joe
West Side Story—Medley: When You're a Jet, Officer Krumpke, Tonight, Maria, America, Somewhere	Leonard Bernstein	Broadway	Standard Ensemble	Bobby, Dallas, Big Joe & Lance—Vocals

As the last set ended, we congratulated ourselves on delivering a first-class performance. However, Bobby, Big Joe, and Lance were angry.

"I'm pissed," Bobby said. "We busted our asses for this Zuckerman dude. He wasn't man enough to shake my hand and compliment us on a great show? Why?"

"*Cho! Cho!*" Big Joe grunted. "*Écoute!* Fer as I'm concerned, he's *la charogne*. Ga lee! He *se dégoûter* me."

Lance added, "That son of a bitch shunned us. What an arrogant bastard."

I could have played this differently, but in the end I felt my approach was right, resolving to accept Bobby, Big Joe, and Lance's slings and arrows, absent retort.

Hopefully, I'll be able to report positive results Saturday afternoon, diffusing their insecurities and hyper egos.

Saturday morning I met Stan Zuckerman for breakfast promptly at 8. He selected fruit, yogurt and green tea. From the buffet, I piled on ham, scrambled eggs and sausage gravy over an open-faced biscuit. Following a cordial exchange, Mr. Z began his review of our chemistry and the Carousels.

"Rocky, I like your ideas and vision that you presented the other day. Unfortunately, your brain is ahead of your band. Yes, the Carousels are an excellent cabaret band, and the stage show was highly entertaining. But you need more to achieve stardom—a complete makeover. Otherwise, you'll remain a copy band in a changing market—a market in rapid decline. In short, change or perish."

Following my sip of black coffee, I responded.

"What does your gut tell you about our chemistry and your representation of the Carousels under a personal management agreement?"

"Your band has a distance to go, and I can help you achieve your goals. Your journey will not be as rapid as you imagine. In my judgment, you'll be ready in a year—perhaps two. A hit record, professional coaches and my connections can get you there. However, remaking yourselves will involve travel to the West Coast and a financial investment for theatrical staging experts, choreographers, and musicality specialists. Don't expect quick dividends. Think of this as a long-term investment in a blue chip stock.

"Furthermore, there are no guarantees in the entertainment business. The buying public could reject your new music. Some of your musicians might get homesick and leave the band. Some could get into drugs or create a scandal, plus a thousand other things could potentially sidetrack or dead-end your dreams. Entertainment is a high-risk business. The odds of making it to the big time are lousy, but it can be done."

Now I was leaning forward, elbows on the table. Stan Zuckerman was in total control, leaning back in his chair, daintily wiping his mouth with a Marriott-engraved linen napkin.

Here comes his punch line. Listen up.

"You have two options. First: I'll accept representation under a ten-percent personal management contract and begin your journey to the big leagues. I'll guide you through the transition, greatly improving your odds of success. A recording contract with a major label can be secured, although you'll have the responsibility to develop a unique sound that will appeal to the masses. The Beatles, English bands, and psychedelic bands have made your job exceedingly difficult. However, a hit record can still be achieved. In the meantime, you'll play LA, downtown Vegas, and appear on local television stations until you get the elusive hit record. Think of this as going into training for a world champion boxing match. You have to be in peak condition before stepping into a championship ring—or you'll get killed."

He paused a moment and then presented Option Two: "Defer our agreement until you're ready to make the leap. You'll save ten percent. Then again, you'll be without benefit of my guidance, contacts and leverage. That said, you already know what needs to be done and can lead the Carousels pretty far down that path on your own. The price you'll pay is protraction of your time line to achieve fame and fortune.

"It's your decision, Rocky. Give me a call when you're ready. We'll move our relationship forward accordingly. Before I go, let me thank you for the opportunity to visit my brother and see the Carousels perform. Call me when you're ready."

I picked up the check, made nice with Stan Zuckerman, wished him a pleasant weekend with his brother, promised a call within a week and walked out of the Marriott. Then I drove to a city park and walked around the lake, weighing the pros and cons.

It is my decision. This is a puzzlement. The real question is where do I really want to be in ten years? Who do I want to be? Who is Rocky Strong?

Recounting the Zuckerman conversation with Venus back at the trailer, I hardly finished before she jumped up, yelling, "Option One! This is your big break! How soon can you sign the contract with Mr. Zuckerman?"

"I wish it were that simple," I replied. "I've scheduled a 2:30 meeting with the guys to discuss Mr. Z's options."

"This is your call—not theirs," she said. "You're the leader of the Carousels. You own the corporation, copyrights, logo, organ, instrument trailer, tuxedos, five months of bookings, and the bank account. It's your call, Rocky—not theirs."

"It's a band of brothers, Venus."

"No. It's a business. The brotherhood only exists in your mind. That's a fantasy. Any dreams of brotherhood died when Big Joe and Lance betrayed you guys with their back-door Nashville recording session. Run the Carousels like a business. Your pot of gold is right there for the taking, and you don't need their permission. Think of yourself. Think of us. Your family comes first, right?"

"You do have a point," I said.

Venus looked straight into my eyes with laser sharpness.

"Your last chance is Stan Zuckerman. Don't screw this up. Get this deal done—whatever it takes. Get tough with the guys. Turn ruthless if necessary. You have to win this battle and the war."

Like a ball peen hammer to my forehead, a quote from Ayn Rand surfaced, *"The question isn't who is going to let me; it's who is going to stop me."*

Chapter 50

1964
TWO OPTIONS

Later that afternoon Venus took the kids to a Disney movie. At 2:30, five Carousels arrived in my living room. Their body language telegraphed anxiety. The offer of drinks, sodas and coffee fell on deaf ears. They wanted action and answers.

"Quit stallin'," Big Joe snarled. "What did Zuckerman offer us?"

Before I could answer, Bobby jumped in. "You and Zuckerman shut us out of the business meetings. He insulted us last night. Why you changin' the game, Rocky?"

Lance also took a shot. "Is Venus making the decisions for the Carousels? I thought this was our band."

I pushed back sternly, saying, "Unless you guys are clairvoyant, you won't get answers until you shut up and listen."

Dallas raised his hand in a halting motion, saying, "Geeze, guys. Rocky has the information and is willing to share. Give him space."

"Rock's been responsible for bookings, agents, contracts, unions, money, and strategic planning," Smoke added. "He's dammed good at this. Shut up and listen."

Forgive me God for all those times I considered killing Smoke. He just saved my ass.

I looked from one Carousel to the other, saying, "Allow me the courtesy of telling the whole story. Then, I'll answer your questions."

Heads nodded in agreement.

"I met Stan Zuckerman Friday afternoon and Saturday morning," I began. "Each meeting lasted about 30 minutes—very businesslike. At his request, only Bobbie and Billy saw him at the Black Poodle Friday night. He wanted to remain incognito. I agreed to honor his request. Based on his comments over breakfast this morning, he saw most or all of our second and third sets."

Bobby and Lance stared at the carpet. Big Joe's arms crossed over his chest in open rejection. But, I continued in a somewhat upbeat tone.

"Overall, Mr. Zuckerman's assessment of the Carousels was complementary. However, he said we'd never make it big until we get a hit record. Records and television are today's medium of choice, at the expense of night clubs and copy bands."

After pausing to allow time for absorption, I explained Mr. Zuckerman's advice.

"In short, we have to reinvent ourselves. Under his guidance, we can accelerate our transition and achieve our goals faster than trying to go it alone. However he also issued a caution: our journey may take a year, perhaps two. It will involve travel to the West Coast and a financial investment in coaches, choreographers, and musicality specialists. Our investment will not pay quick dividends."

Finally, I came to the choice we had to make.

"Mr. Zuckerman offered the Carousels two options. Option One: He accepts the Carousels under a ten-percent personal management agreement. He'll secure a recording contract, although we'll be responsible for creating original material. Initially we'll play LA, downtown Vegas, and appear on local television with a canned stage show until we achieve a hit record. Mr. Z recommends we think of this as going into training for a world champion boxing match. We have to get in shape before stepping into the ring or we'll get knocked out in the first round.

"Then there's Option Two: We defer signing until we're ready to make a quantum leap. That'll save us ten percent, but we lose access to Mr. Z's contacts, coaches, and leverage. He complimented us on our strategic vision. According to him, we are blessed with abundant raw talent and good instincts. He perceives himself as an accelerator, increasing our odds of reaching our goals faster than if we go it alone."

Following a momentary pause, I asked, "One or two? I'll give Mr. Zuckerman a call next Friday with our answer. The ball is in our court. Each of you choose an option and let me know."

Standing up, I concluded my speech.

"That's it, guys. I have to throw a wicked piss. When I get back, I'll answer all your questions."

When I returned, the furrows on their brows had deepened. I sensed trepidation. Bobby asked, "Share your impressions of this Zuckerman guy. Do you trust him?"

"Great question," I responded. "Mr. Zuckerman is classy, tailored, pepper-gray hair, with the manner of a foreign diplomat. As to trusting him—yes, I do."

Lance asked, "Are Zuckerman's views the same as the club owners and frontmen we've been working for?"

I said, "Yep—right down the line. Unfortunately, what made us successful between 1959 and 1962 is no longer in style. Over the past year frontmen shared with me their frustrations about the pressures they're getting from Mob bosses to expand their markets to a younger audience. With the exception of traveling salesmen, conventioneers, and high-end businessmen who entertain clients, nightclub marks are disappearing. Television has robbed the Mob of their steady flow of marks. Pressure is being applied on frontmen to replace the traditional formula with a new type of mark—the under-30 group. They'll piss money away on drugs, shylocks, and bookies in nightclubs that offer Beatles bands.

"And here's an alarming statistic: the money they're paying us is equivalent to what they pay two or even three Beatles, English, or psychedelic bands. Those longhaired, out-of-tune, nose-pickin', dirty, no-talent punks in street clothes will work for nothin'. Clubs can rotate multiple Beatles bands for six or seven continuous hours, without breaks. For the Mob, it's a marriage made in heaven, allowing them to push pot, white powder, H, LSD, shylocks, and bookies on the younger audiences. With the emergence of free love, the Mob has relocated the best workin' girls to escort services and a telephone madam. It's all about the money, guys."

I went on to explain that a few clubs will hold out, reject the drug scene, and remain focused on delivering quality entertainment and fine dining. However those clubs and their audiences are shrinking rapidly.

"If we don't change with the times, the Carousels will perish."

Big Joe snarled, "I hate givin' da guy ten percent, on top of ten percent to da booking agent. Scabs. I hate paying for coaches telling us how to play, perform, and dance. We're takin' all da risks and dis Zuckerman guy is getting all da rewards. What risk is he takin'? What if dis Zuckerman guy is dead wrong and we don't make it? It's a trap and I hate it!"

"We've always taken risks," I replied. "Since that day at the Dixie, we accepted risks and the commitment required to make it to stardom. Zuckerman could be our next step to fame and fortune, but the risks remain ours. Some of you might get homesick and leave the band. One or more of us could be killed on the road, get hooked on drugs, create a scandal, or a thousand other maladies could sidetrack or dead end the Carousels."

I tried to hammer home the point.

"Entertainment is high risk. Keep in mind we've been on the road for five years—six if you count our first year as a college dance band and the Carousel Club. For six average guys from Louisiana, the odds of making it to stardom were lousy, but it still can be done. Stan Zuckerman guided some of the great artists of our times through these risks, achieving impressive success. No guarantees—none—nada."

Lance wondered why we had to be on the West Coast.

"That's three thousand miles from Louisiana. I'm exhausted. Getting' home will be impossible. Do we have an option?"

"Nope. That's where rich entertainment venues, records, television, and movies are. They won't come to us, so we have to go to them. That's not an option."

Dallas asked, "Are you sure we can choose the option we want with no penalty for choosing the second option?"

Quickly, I said, "In a word—yes. That decision is ours."

"Why does dis smell like Venus?" Big Joe asked. "Der's a skunk in dis. She's found dis dude in California dat's promised to get her back to Vegas, hasn't she?"

I glared at Big Joe and said, "You're way out of line. Put a lid on it."

Big Joe swung again, "Clever, Rock. Be true; is Venus running da show? She's got Vegas in her sights—frontin' the Carousels. She's taking over dis band—isn't she?"

Furious, I said, "Strike two, asshole. You're attacking my integrity and my wife. Venus isn't your problem. I'm not your problem. I'm the solution. Open your eyes and see the road to fame and fortune. Gert's jealousies of Venus and her fear of losing you to a Vegas show girl are tragically transparent. That's driving Gert's opposition to this move. Open your eyes."

"Unfortunately, Rocky, you're the one who's blind to what's happening," Lance replied. "My two biggest obstacles to the Zuckerman deal are traveling to the West Coast and Venus's involvement. We want assurances Venus isn't taking over the Carousels. Is she or isn't she?"

I can't bullshit Lance.

"All Venus wants is to be my wife and mother to her kids. As far as Venus fronting or leading the Carousels, she's retired—her chapter as an entertainer ended at the altar in Shreveport. She'll never be on stage with the Carousels again. Enough said. Besides, Venus, Mary, Gert, Angelle, and Betty don't have a voice in this. Lance, I'm practicing the wisdom Professor Kenny Livingston shared with us in Bossier. Can you say the same?"

Dallas leaned forward and asked, "I'd like to know more."

"Dallas, I'll tell you a true story. Before you joined the Carousels, we did a recording session in Tyler, Texas. A promoter funded the session, wrote the lyrics and melody line. He also invited Barry Gordy to attend the session and review our cuts. Gordy was not impressed—'No unique sound,' he said. After rejecting us, he auditioned a little blind kid in Detroit 'with a unique sound.' The kid's name was Little Stevie Wonder—the rest is history. In one form or another, that story played out over twenty-seven recording sessions—always ending in disappointment."

Dallas nodded and others followed in tacit agreement.

"For the next few months we'll play out our contracts to pay bills, mirroring the current set lineups," I said. "Second, I've studied the Beatles and determined that they're spending all their time in the studio. So should we. We'll exchange our rehearsal time at clubs for creating new original material—fresh and unique. We'll use our Roberts tape recorder and the clubs as our studio, experimenting with sounds and cutting demos.

"The third ingredient involves a jaw-dropping stage show, worthy of Vegas and national television. With a hit record we'll channel our stage show polish into a featured act on Ed Sullivan, Johnny Carson, Jackie Gleason, Steve Allen, and other prime time television shows. In summary, we'll refocus all our energies on creative time in the studio and polishing a knockout stage show."

Smoke asked, "What option do you prefer?"

I said, "Tough call. If pressed today, I'd sign with Stan Zuckerman. Now is our time to make a quantum leap, and Mr. Z's our guy. Any more questions?"

There being none, I said, "Make your choice and give me your answer by Thursday. I'll call Stan Zuckerman on Friday. Also, let's do each other a huge favor and keep this off the Black Poodle stage. Otherwise I'll be glad to talk with you privately or collectively any time except tomorrow. I'm taking Venus and the kids for a Sunday picnic in the park."

My front room cleared as five brothers shuffled their way back to their dwellings.

The skunk is out on the table, and it really stinks. A lot of anxiety, insecurities and anger sat in my living room today. I wonder...

Cheshire Cat's motor ran in my lap, *"Is our situation not dismal? Wonderland is so discombobulated that ladybugs have turned belligerent and enlisted in the queen's army! Punish their conversation!"*

Curled up on the couch, Hatter purred, *"Okay, he's as mad as a box of frogs."*

Chapter 51

1964
LINE IN THE SAND

Venus, Alicia and Ricky returned from the theater at 4 Saturday afternoon. The kids were happy, talking incessantly about Disney's *Mary Poppins*. I wanted to hear all about it, so they bubbled over with excitement in telling the story and acting out several parts. Sitting with Alicia on one knee and Ricky on the other, I looked at Venus and smiled; she smiled back. I was happy. She ushered the kids outside to play, then came over and sat on my lap.

I said with a grin, "Jealous?"

"You bet," she said. "But now I've got your handle, and I'm not letting go."

Sunday in Nashville was sunny, warm and clear, except for a few puffy clouds dancing in the blue sky. I ushered the Strong clan into the Cadillac and drove to the nearest grocery store, picking up ham, cheese, bread, condiments, potato salad, cold slaw and drinks.

The city park featured a large lake, which beckoned us to settle nearby in a shaded, grassy spot. The kids had never been on a picnic, and I had never been on a picnic with kids. Retrieving a Frisbee and an inflatable ball out of the Caddy's trunk, the kids gave both of us grownups a thorough workout. Then we ate our food, made small talk and walked around the lake, hand in hand.

The robins arrived by the hundreds. We escaped into a rare time warp; peace of mind. The Strong's were happy.

The Carousels didn't rehearse all week. I met one-on-one to discuss options and answer questions. On stage at the Black Poodle, we delivered our performance with professional panache. It was apparent, however, that Big Joe and Lance had galvanized against change. Bobby was flip-flopping, and Dallas and Smoke appeared to be in the reinvent camp—Zuckerman's camp, California camp, my camp.

By Thursday night, a consensus had not been reached on signing up with Zuckerman. It was clear to me that we would need to defer the signing decision until a later date. On Friday, a week following the meeting with Zuckerman, I called Mr. Z in California to convey our decision: defer a personal management contract at this time with the option to revisit in a few months.

Following our last set at the Black Poodle on Saturday night, I gathered the Carousels in Printers Alley and told them about my Friday afternoon conversation with Zuckerman. I quoted Mr. Z's response: "My door is always open to you and the Carousels. Call me when you're ready to initiate the business relationship we discussed. In the meantime, I wish you and the Carousels the best of success."

Then, I dropped the bomb I've been carrying around since my meetings with Mr. Z.

"Listen up, guys; you're either with us or against us. There's no middle ground here. Let me know where you stand by Monday noon. If you buy in, we'll begin our metamorphic journey together. If you don't buy in, I wish you the best of success—though not under the Carousel banner. Hopefully, we'll all sign up for a triumphant transformation, bound for super-stardom. However, if I don't hear from you by Monday noon, I'll understand that your decision is to leave the band. That possibility saddens me, but it's time we seized control of our destiny, chart a new course and realize our dreams of fame and fortune. Carpe diem."

As if choreographed, Big Joe, Lance, Bobby, Smoke, and Dallas stood stunned by my explosive announcement. Grunts, snorts, and fidgety body contortions emoted from Big Joe, although he said nothing that was intelligible. At one point I thought Big Joe was going to take a swing at me, though indecision won out. Lance shook his head in disbelief, as did Bobby.

Lance said, "Oh well," shrugging his broad shoulders as if accepting the reality of the moment. Incapable of completing a sentence, Bobby bounced and babbled, "But ... what if ... why ... shit ...!" Bewildered, Smoke and Dallas seemed to physically shrink before my eyes.

Without question, my line in the sand got their attention. I kept a smile on my face to soften the ultimatum, but they understood that the time for talking was over. Personal decisions were at hand. As they walked away, down Printers Alley, I pondered a bigger question.

Who will stay and who will go?' I'd better develop a contingency plan.

I returned to the trailer exhausted and tried not to awaken Venus and the kids. So it wasn't until breakfast that Venus noticed my concern.

"What's up Baby? You're stressed out," Venus said as she set the table.

I nodded. "Yep. For the first time, I'm stressed out. I delivered an ultimatum to the guys. Have to think this through ... consider all options, including the possibility of some or all leaving the band. Yeah. I'm stressed."

"Want to talk?"

"Sure."

Venus took two slow sips of CDM coffee before continuing.

"Rocky, remember our first week together in New Orleans?"

"How could I forget?"

"In spite of your many gifts, street smarts is not among them. You're naïve about your so-called band of brothers. If you want, I can offer my street smarts and, if necessary, ruthlessness. Interested?"

"I welcome your thoughts."

"First of all—up to this point, well done. You've always been the driving force behind the Carousels. They can't make it without you, and they know it."

"You sure?"

"Absolutely. They'll collapse without you. Change is hard. You've challenged the status quo. Your vision and passion intimidates them. You offer them a clear path to fame and fortune, yet the guys can't see beyond their personal insecurity and fear of failure. They'll never blame you. They love you. On the other hand, they have to blame someone. I'm it. They've made me their enemy. In their minds, I'm to blame for you reinventing the Carousels."

"Really?"

"Open your eyes. Big Joe and Lance are emotional pygmies. Experienced women like Gert and Angelle lead men around by their dicks. Expect Big Joe and Lance to do whatever their bitches demand."

Venus was opening my eyes to a reality I hadn't considered.

"Know what's really going on here?" Venus continued. "Gert and Angelle are terrified they'll lose their men if the Carousels go to California, Vegas, cut hit records, and get on national TV. They're desperate to hold on to their men at all costs. Have you taken a close look at Gert and Angelle lately? Scary. They've abandoned pride in their appearance and wallow in low self-esteem. Their vulvas and bitchin' are the only tools left. Scared to death they'll be tossed on the ash heap if the Carousels go west—and they will—they'll fight change with everything they've got. You're competing against desperation, treachery, and two super-sized tunnels of love."

"So what do I do?" I asked.

"Control the outcome. You're smarter than all of them put together. Be tough and never let them see you sweat—never retreat. Remember, you own the Carousels' assets and engagement contracts.

In the end, you can't lose—even if Big Joe and Lance leave the band. At the end of the day, where can they go without you? They'll crawl back to North Louisiana as beaten men—failures—blaming me for what happened to them. If Lance and Big Joe don't stand up to their women—right now—those bitches will make the rest of their lives miserable. Of that I am sure."

I said, "Venus, if you're right, I may be looking at a Pyrrhic victory."

"I don't understand. What's that?"

"A victory gained at too great a cost. I could win the battles with Big Joe and Lance and maybe Bobby, but lose our primary objective."

I remained silent for a few moments, trying to sort out all that Venus had laid on me.

"You do realize," I said as we finished breakfast, "that Big Joe and Lance might leave the band. After all, they've betrayed the brotherhood before. Bobby is on the fence, although I believe Smoke and Dallas are solid. So, just to be prepared, I've been thinking about placing an ad in the *Tennessean* Monday afternoon, following their response to my deadline. It would read something like: 'Open Auditions for the Fabulous Carousels Tuesday, Wednesday, and Thursday 2–4 p.m. at the Black Poodle—Printers Alley.' What do you think?"

Venus's eyes brightened.

"Brilliant. You couldn't pick a better town to replace band members than Nashville. The Fabulous Carousels will attract the best available talent—that's for sure. Who knows—you could end up with a superior stable of entertainers, better equipped for stardom. Absolutely brilliant, Rocky."

"I love you Venus. You are my true partner, in addition to my lover and wife. Speaking of that, let's get the kids and enjoy the day. The lover part will have to wait."

"It's a date, my love."

Chapter 52

1964
A BANKRUPT BROTHERHOOD

onday noon came and went. Stunned, not even one Carousel showed up in support of my plan. So much for my ultimatum. I rushed to the *Tennessean* and placed the ad, instructing the classified sales person to run it for ten days.

As of noon today, fulfilling our dreams just transformed into whimsical folly. I've lost my way. Where is my moral compass ... character ... inner strength—my God Power? Fuck it. I have to deal with this, bitter as it is. Significant challenges await, perhaps bigger than I can handle. Starting over with a bunch of greenhorns isn't what I had in mind. Goddamn! I'm the only one to blame for this cluster fuck. And, I'm the only one that can turn this around. I have to get off my pity-party ass and be a man. Where did I misplace my God Power?

Venus was furious with five Carousels and their deceitful bitches. Like me, she never considered the possibility of mass resignation. Visibly shaken, Venus poured two three-finger neat Scotches. It required three to reach my click.

Oh well, the show must go on, at least for the next two weeks.

Although the Carousels' interaction on stage was cool, we did our jobs well, highly professional. No mention was made of the Monday noon deadline. Following Monday's gig I got Smoke's attention on my way to the car, asking, "Breakfast?"

"Sure, Rock. I'd love to."

We drove to the Country Kitchen, a favorite all-night diner catering to country and western performers. After we ordered, I asked, "What happened, Smoke?"

Smoke looked at me over the rim of his coffee cup, making a long and noisy slurping sound. An aggressive tic dominated a strained face. Finally, he spoke with a pronounced southern twang in his voice.

"Rock, Venus happened. The guys are convinced Venus will be fronting the Carousels. According to them, you're blinded by her powers over you. They think you're pussy whipped. Big Joe and Lance say they can no longer follow you or trust you, because they're convinced Venus is pulling all the strings. According to them, Venus is an angel of the devil—evil reincarnated."

I sipped my coffee, without slurping, asking, "What about you, Dallas and Bobby? Why did you three go along with Big Joe and Lance?"

Smoke answered in a low tone, "Because Big Joe and Lance believe this is the only way to bring you to your senses. Mass resignation is the only way to get your undivided attention. They are convinced you'll come around and reconsider. Bobby, Dallas, and I went along with them because … because you won't feel the sting unless your ultimatum is met with unanimous rejection. Everyone is suspended in limbo, waiting to see what happens."

I was furious.

"I've saved your ass many times. Without me, you'd be wearing cement boots at the bottom of the Mississippi River or packed inside a Spam can in Peoria. How long can you last without me to watch over you?"

Sheepishly, Smoke responded, "You've saved my ass at least three times I can think of. I owe you a lot. Still this situation is really fucked up. Confidentially, Bobby, Dallas and I wanted to go along with you and reinvent the Carousels. Using the Roberts tape recorder to come up with fresh original songs is just what the doctor ordered.

However, Big Joe and Lance worked hard to convince us to stick together. It's really fucked up—isn't it, Rock?"

Last bite of food down my gullet, I responded, "It's fucked up more than you can possibly imagine. First, it's ludicrous to think I'd dump Venus to appease Big Joe and Lance. She's my wife. Second, Venus has no intentions of fronting or controlling the Carousels— she's retired from show business. Big Joe's and Lance's premise is fundamentally flawed—perverted beyond belief. Venus wants the Carousels to remain intact and step up to the big show. She only wants us to be successful and happy."

My voice rising with tension and emotion, I looked straight at Smoke. "Y'all's error in judgment can be corrected. It's not too late to change minds, but time is runnin' out. Smoke, I have crystal clarity on this. I see the right path to achieving our goals. Reaching stardom is driving my actions. I can't deal rationally with irrational people. I leave Big Joe and Lance to fight out their twisted perversions. I am firmly fixated on success."

Smoke cowered, accentuated by his uncontrollable tic.

I continued, "There is a place for you, Bobby, and Dallas with the new Carousels. Believe me, you three are warmly invited to remain with the band. I'd love this to work out for us, but decide quick. This week and next I'll hire Nashville musicians to fill the holes. In fact, auditions begin tomorrow at 2 at the Black Poodle. Come back in and go with me to select the replacements. Are you in?"

Smoke paused, then said, "Rock, it breaks my heart, but I can't commit right now. I have to wait and see what happens. I'm torn apart over this. Either way, this is a fucked up mess, isn't it?"

"Yep," I said. "It's a certifiable cluster fuck."

At the Black Poodle Tuesday afternoon, two musicians showed up for the audition. I provided a 3x5 card for them to print name, phone numbers and their instruments. Recording my notes on the back provided audition summary and a grade for musicianship, voice quality, stage presence, and personality fitness with the new Carousels. I instructed each to go on stage and perform a solo, a cappella, covering every musical instrument they played and their best vocals. The hollowness of an a cappella performance without backup brought out the best and worst of their abilities.

Each audition ended the same, telling them that I'd be in touch when all the auditions were completed. A few questions were asked and answered, and then I wished them well in their careers. It was a process I used for all further auditions.

Wednesday morning, I decided it was time to confront Lance. I knocked on Lance's trailer door, immediately getting to the point when he answered the door.

"My blood pressure's up. I'd like to get your slant on what happened and your personal plans."

Lance stepped outside and we sat on his patio in brand new lawn chairs.

"When John Lennon recorded *I Want to Hold Your Hand,* I knew in my heart it was over," Lance said. "Then Lennon said, 'We're more famous than Jesus.' That son-of-a-bitch is right—goddamn him for being right. Traveling to California for two or three years with no guarantees of success is lunacy."

Pausing for a moment, Lance managed a smile, saying "On the other hand, getting' out my free pass card and gettin' my ticket punched by eager West Coast chickadees is very appealing. Believe me—I've thought about going with you—more than I care to admit. However, it's time for me to become responsible— I've got Angelle and a kid to support. We think another kid is on the way. She's pressing me hard to go back to Louisiana and get a straight's job. I might even marry Angelle if we go back. Have to get serious about stabilizing our financial situation and support my family."

Lance just spilled his guts, telling me all the reasons he's going back to Louisiana. Angelle wins.

"You've been a good friend Lance. I hope we'll remain friends."

"We will, but give this space and time, Rock."

"As my friend, any advice you care to share?"

Lance did a double take before answering, "Since we are friends, I'll say it straight out. You're so pussy whipped—she's taken over your soul. To the rest of us, neon warning signs are flashing. Still, love is blind—how well I know dat. Venus is gorgeous, cunning, ruthless and lethal. Br'er Fox's gots ya stuck hard to da Tar-Baby. She'll destroy you, Rock. I'd hate to see dat happen.…"

I replied, "Remember the professor—Kenny Livingston? His wisdom was spot on. We simply didn't follow it."

Lance nodded, grinned and said, "Goddamn women!"

I nodded, grinned and said, "Goddamn women!"

Wednesday afternoon attracted six musicians to the audition. Two had talent.

Thursday morning, I decided it was time to talk to Bobby. I walked to Bobby's trailer, and he greeted me with a fresh cup of French Market java. We sat on his patio, enjoying the cool weather.

"How's yo hammer hangin', Rocky?" he asked.

"Like a lollypop—wanna lick it?"

Ice broken with chuckles, I turned to the business at hand.

"Still want to be a superstar? Don't sell your mule to buy a plow. Crawling back to Monroe and starting over is nuts. Go with me to New York, Chicago, and the West Coast. We leave a week from Sunday. Get your ass in gear Bobby. Let's go for fame and fortune together. Isn't that what you want?"

"Rocky, for almost six years, we've shared dreams, breathed the same air, fucked the same women, and trusted each other with our lives. It's been finer than a frog's hair. But everything changed. Not sure what happened, but we're stuck at a crossroads."

"Okay," I said. "You'd better choose your path carefully. One leads to a dead end and the other points to fame and fortune. Resurrect your peacock strut of arrogance and go for the brass ring.

The road to fame and fortune leads through the West Coast—not Monroe. Wanna go?"

"Don't piss on my leg and tell me it's rainin'. I'm dying here. If I break with Big Joe and Lance, my future with you in California is fuzzy—no guarantees. If I stay with them, at least we'll preserve the band of brothers. I'm sober as a nun in church, but I'm trippin' out over this one. I've decided to wait and see what happens."

"Bobby," I said, looking him in the eye. "The brotherhood went bankrupt when Big Joe and Lance betrayed us in Peoria. The band of brothers became an empty illusion. I'm not waiting on them or anyone. Your opportunity door is closing—fast. Get on board or crawl back to Monroe as a failure. If you head south, you'll kiss your dreams goodbye. Big Joe's engine's runnin', except nobody's driving. He'll never be the leader of anything successful. Reconsider and let me know—quick."

"Bobby, I know it gals your ass for me to quote the classics. Admittedly, I do get carried away at times. But Ayn Rand summed up our situation perfectly, '*A creative man is motivated by the desire to achieve, not by the desire to beat others.*'"

Thursday's audition produced eight musicians. Three were good and one was great.

Friday morning, I knocked on Dallas's trailer door, my old tin can. He was surprised to see me, but bounded out with a smile, obviously eager to talk. Initially, Dallas had signaled he was searching for a way to remain with the Carousels and me.

I said, "I'm saving a spot for you in the new Carousels. Don't wait too long or your spot will fill up."

My best persuasive arguments mirrored my pitch to Smoke and Bobby, with embellishments relative to Dallas's extraordinary talent and rapid growth as a professional entertainer. However, my sterling pitch began to tarnish as I watched Dallas's face. His final position aligned with Smoke and Bobby: non-committal, waiting to see what happens. Dallas was probably coerced by Big Joe and Lance, fortifying their position of shocking me into submission.

Finally, I accepted reality: *I'm talking to a parrot.*

"Mary believes we need a sign from heaven before making our final decision. We prayed all week to Jesus on our knees, two hours a day. So far, Jesus hasn't revealed his answer. His will be done."

Unless Jesus Christ parts the heavens and delivers a revelation directly to Dallas and Mary, they are destined to follow the flock, like lambs being led to slaughter.

Accepting the inevitable, I posted my Smilin' Jack façade and wrapped up our chat.

"Venus and I will miss you and Mary. My hope is you have a wonderful marriage and long lives filled with happiness and lots of rug rats. Goodbye, my friend."

We hugged and tears rolled down Dallas's cheeks. I turned and slowly walked away, listening to Dallas sob.

On a whim, I knocked on Big Joe's trailer door. Gert answered, sipping from her mysterious back cup.

"Is Big Joe here?"

"He is, but don't want ta see ya. He's made up his mind. No one wants to be told what to do, especially not by Venus. She's evil. She's responsible for breaking up da Carousels. Big Joe has all da talent and carries dis band. He'll never take orders from Venus. We were doin' fine before she got here. Come back to us, Rocky—to your brothers and sisters. Dump Venus."

"Nuts," I replied. "You're certifiably nuts. Whatever you're drinking out of that cup has fucked up your head. The only human stupid enough to follow your advice is Big Joe and that's because you serve him arsenic on a pussy platter three times a day. You two are jumping out of a perfectly good airplane without a parachute. There's not enough drugs in this world to break your suicide fall. You two deserve everything you're about to get—self-administered euthanasia. Don't count on me to attend your funerals."

Turning quickly, I walked toward my trailer as Gert yelled obscenities at the top of her lungs.

Well, if our relationship wasn't fucked before, it's fucked now.

Over lunch, I shared notes with Venus about the new group.

"From this week's auditions, three or four could become Carousels. However, three audition days are scheduled next week. Looks like recruiting in Nashville is the positive part of this crisis. Facing reality, Bobby, Dallas and Smoke may leave the band. Hopefully, resignations will be limited to Big Joe and Lance, but it might be all five of 'em. By the way, you were right about Angelle and Gert. They're terrified they'll lose their men to Vegas show girls or California beach bunnies."

Curled in the corner, The Mad Hatter meowed, *"Have I gone mad?"*

From my lap, Cheshire's motor ran, *"Meta-Essence is the life force of Wonderland. That of your enemies is especially potent. Collect what you can. Use it wisely."*

Chapter 53

SHOWDOWN IN PRINTERS ALLEY

Over the weekend, I sold the International truck and purchased a three-year-old, baby blue, 5-ton Ford F-650 bobtail, specifically designed for long-distance towing. It had a 5-speed transmission with a dual rear axle; 10 speeds in all. A custom-built, 400-gallon gas tank would carry us 3,000 miles between fill-ups. This truck would end my concerns about the long tow to Lake George in upstate New York.

The 5-ton Ford was great, except everything else in my life was falling apart.

That week in Nashville was surreal. Reminiscent of the dysfunctional Four Seasons, six Carousels performed on the Black Poodle stage as a cohesive unit, as though nothing had happened. Unbelievably, the uncertainty of our future together never surfaced on stage or on breaks.

Displaying optimum God Power, I remained cordial and normal, providing no sign of weakness. I found no comfort in knowing I was the only one on the Black Poodle stage who knew what the future held. In spite of my daunting journey ahead, my previous band of brothers faced an ambiguous future—crawling back to Monroe in defeat. They had set themselves adrift, without a rudder, waiting to see what happens.

If Dallas, Smoke or Bobby come forward on their own, I'll accept them back, cutting out one or more newbies who otherwise would have a job in the new Carousels. However, at this point they must take the first step. I must remain strong-willed and committed to reinventing the Carousels.

The audition process continued throughout the fourth and final week in Nashville. In all, 25 professional musicians registered for three days of auditions. Five were good, two were very good, one keyboardist displayed an operatic voice, and one was fantastic—a virtuoso superstar looking for a stage. To my disappointment, Dallas, Smoke and Bobby remained silent.

Perhaps they'd have a last minute change of heart.

Following auditions on Thursday afternoon, I reviewed my notes, organized, prioritized and contacted the top contenders until I filled five positions in the new Carousels. Scheduling rehearsals for Friday and Saturday at the Black Poodle, I challenged each new Carousel to come prepared to orchestrate five ensemble arrangements of their best material. My objective was simple: create a minimum of two sets, but hopefully three, comprised of the newbies' finest. We had to make a good showing in upstate New York—opening in just four days.

Preparing breakfast Friday morning, Venus beat the flapjack batter like a punching bag, slapped a dollop in the frying pan, circled plates on the kitchen table like out-of-balance spinning tops, slammed cabinet doors and cursed the curtains hanging over the sink.

"Goddamn my rotten luck," she said as she plastered flapjacks— burned on one side and runny on the other—on my plate. "I told you not to screw this up, Rocky. Be the man I thought you were. Make this right—today. Don't disappoint me."

Strike one. The way I see it, there are two choices: pick a fight with my only remaining ally or pass up what is sure to become a caustic confrontation.

I'd best bite my tongue, swallow my pride, ignore her verbal abuses and keep my mouth shut. The last thing I need is an enemy for a wife.

Following the Friday afternoon newbie rehearsal, I longed for a reassuring hug and a double Scotch. Venus was way ahead of me regarding the Scotch, lying comatose on the couch. Not acknowledging my arrival, her glassy pupils starred at the ceiling. Tongue-tied gibberish spilled through pursed lips. A nasty stink rose out of the carpet, the telltale sign of spilled Scotch.

Approaching for my hug, Venus stood up, stepped around me and stumbled toward the bathroom, shunning the compassion we both needed. Returning, she angrily slurred, "You're no God! You're a snake oil salesman! Had me believin' ya could pull dis off. Fraud! Fake! And royally fucked!"

Strike two. Fortunately I know the rules: can't rationalize with an irrational person. Venus is depressed, disillusioned, out of control, staggering her way through a drunken stupor. Let it go. Focus what energy I have left on outwitting Big Joe's and Lance's insecurities and the perverted blood feud at hand. Focus on luring Dallas, Smoke and Bobby back into the band.

Friday night at the Black Poodle I marshaled all my strength, presenting a cool and confident façade to the guys.

Pitting mental state of the self-condemned against my granite constitution, I'm winning this psychological battle, but at what price? I'm facing off with a Pyrrhic victory.

Desperately in need of some lovin' after our gig, I returned to the trailer at two in the morning and crawled in the sack with my beautiful Barbie Doll, hoping she had banished the demons from Friday. While my eyes gazed for several moments at her wistful golden hair, my nostrils inhaled Venus' unique scent of jasmine, stirring my passion. Gently caressing her silky-smooth shoulder, I seemed to elicit a welcoming response. Pheromones sent out a familiar bouquet, prologue to fulfilling carnal desires. My open palm eased under the sheet, tenderly caressing a luscious breast and transforming nipples into stones. Her honey hole went wet as my neatly manicured fingers did what they'd done many times.

She sighed a satisfying moan as I waltzed my index finger and thumb in circular patterns over ruby red lips of her vulva. She rolled over to face me. Short gasps of joy synchronized with my finger manipulations. Her whimpers of pleasure were music to my ears.

In our nimble dance of love, we set spontaneous tempo, rhythm, and harmony, usually beginning quietly in adagio, progressively building over time to crescendo in a triple forte finale. Patiently, tenderly, lovingly we navigated the tango of lovers.

Unselfishly giving one's self to one another unlocked a duet of uninhibited foreplay, a prelude to the main event. Her porcelain hands found the object of her affection, rhythmically stroking me with the feather touch of a Japanese geisha

I whispered, "Oooh yea. Ooooooooooh yeah."

The world may be against me, but I'll make it through with Venus's lovin'. I worship her. Foreplay is wonderful, but I'm ready for the main event—we'll fuck like minks 'til dawn.

Suddenly, Venus sat straight up in bed, pushed me away and yelled, "Hands off! You won't get what you want until I get what I want. Understand? Get those guys back on the bus or I'll … Don't screw up a good thing, Rocky!"

Her outburst over, Venus turned her body to the wall, pulling the sheet over her, squelching passion, rejecting love, abandoning me. I collapsed on my back and stared at the ceiling.

Strike three—I'm out. What happened? Venus never denied me— always eager. What's going on? Have I been played like a fiddle? Made a fool of myself? The sharks are circling. I'm way out on this gangplank, and Venus isn't there for me. In fact, she's pushing me overboard. Where's my God Power now? It's time I faced reality. My God Power is folly.

Summoning up what was left of my confidence at our next show, I gave an Academy Award-winning performance as a charming

southern gentleman, smiling and laughing with the brothers during breaks. Reliving stories about the rental house in Monroe, Jean Val's in the Quarter and the toilet with a bar in Toledo brought back great times on the road. All my barriers down, I expected a reversal of fortune, led by Smoke, Dallas and Bobby. Lance might even change his mind. I looked for a chink in their armor. As yet, none appeared. Although I nailed the psychological strategy, progress appeared frozen in *"Wait and see what happens."*

Too late to make a final one-on-one appeal. All I can do is welcome them back into the nest if the opportunity presents itself. Smile and be open—that's the best course of action at this late stage. Be available.

On stage, Big Joe seemed possessed by mystical forces, precipitated by massive internal insecurities and an unknown future. He assumed center stage supremacy. Although designed as ensemble acts, Big Joe dominated *Orange Blossom Special, Jole' Blon, Who's on First* and *Slow Motion Baseball.* Body contortions and rubbery facial expressions captured eyeballs, but at a price.

His desire to feel needed, by the audience, the Carousels, and me, morphed from capturing a magical allure to that of a bad actor in a B-movie. The deeper he dove, the shallower he swam. Desperation radiated like an abhorrent odor of dead fish. Resembling a child frantically seeking attention, approval and love, Big Joe's charade tragically dominated Friday night at the Black Poodle.

The next day, I rehearsed with the newbies, then went over our travel plans for the trip to New York, to commence early Sunday morning. I distributed AAA maps, emergency instructions and sequencing of vehicles. With a roll of cash in my pocket, I'd follow the caravan in my F-650 and trailer. Four would pile into my Cadillac and tow the instrument trailer. Chris Birdsong, our reed man and virtuoso superstar, preferred to drive his own car and meet us in New York, following a quick trip to Miami.

Feeling smug, I congratulated myself.

I successfully replaced five members of the band with high-quality musicians, all within a two-week period. Remarkable!

With little time to spare, I rushed home, hooked the Carousel instrument trailer to my Cadillac, ate dinner, shaved, shit, showered, dressed, and shagged ass back to Printers Alley, just in time to kick off our final performance. Every Carousel was at his best on stage at the Black Poodle. What was reality was lost in creating illusion. During breaks, Smoke, then Dallas, and finally Bobby approached me. With each, I searched for nuance, an opening to reel them back into a future with the new Carousels. Overtures to rethink their positions never materialized, at least overtly, although in each case, I sensed a burning desire to reverse course and embrace change. Their gut instincts spoke in whispers as peer pressure shouted, *"Wait and see what happens."*

As we walked back on stage, I violated my strategy, commenting to Dallas, "Why don't you and Mary join Venus and me on the adventure of a lifetime? Wouldn't you like to see New York, Chicago, and, ultimately, LA and Vegas? This is the beginning of an incredible journey and you're invited."

Dallas smiled and nodded, saying nothing.

When the final Black Poodle set ended, the red-tuxedoed Carousels loaded instruments into the Carousel trailer, just like always. Fortunately, the issue of ownership never came up. Abruptly, normalcy ended. Trailer doors buttoned up tight, I slid the key into my tux pocket. Standing at the rear of the trailer I stared, unflinching, into five sets of curious eyes. Their faces radiated the universal question, *"What will happen next?"*

I said nothing. They said nothing. Following a protracted awkward silence, five grown men began to cower under the pressure of the moment. Waiting to see what happens, they lost focus and eye contact. No one spoke. Only beating hearts broke the silence, now racing with anticipation of what happens next.

Five men stood in a semi-circle with slumped shoulders and blinking eyes. I displayed an ear-to-ear grin. Following one final round of piercing eye contact with each, I nodded my final goodbye, waived a James Dean hand gesture across my waistline, turned slowly, climbed into my Cadillac, started the engine, powered up the windows and turned the air conditioner to full blast.

Immediately, my coolness evaporated. An overwhelming, child-like protest replaced rationale. At that moment, madness consumed me. Shifting into drive, I slowly maneuvered the big Caddy away from the Black Poodle's front door, Carousel trailer in tow. Five yards down Printers Alley, my rear view mirrors reflected the images of five bewildered men, dressed in beautiful red tuxedos—pallbearers witnessing their own tragic death and the finale of the Fabulous Carousel band of brothers—at least as they knew it.

Hands clammy, I exploded in profuse sweat. Shallow breathing made me light-headed, so I took three deep breaths and touched my forehead to the steering wheel of the Cadillac. What I did next was sick—obscene. Tapping the Caddy brake pedal at 120 beats per minute, mimicking the tempo of a passionate fuck, the Caddy's four bullet-like taillights broadcast my enraged statement of defiance, repeatedly flashing on and off, accompanied by synchronized yelling: "FUCK! FUCK! FUCK! FUCK!

Tonight's Pyrrhic victory carries devastating costs. I find no joy in my victory, revealing the fountainhead of my undoing—the triumph of individualism over collectivism. Who is Rocky Strong? Who is Rocky Strong?

Chapter 54

1964
MOUNTAIN HIGH–VALLEY LOW

Sunday morning at 8, four eager greenhorn Carousels showed up at my trailer, ready to make the trip to Lake George, New York, in my Caddy. They left with the instrument trailer, AAA maps, emergency instructions and a Monday ETA at the club. I pulled out an hour later in my baby blue truck with domicile in tow. Venus, two kids and I squeezed into space designed for two. At first, the five-speed stick shift and dual rear axle proved challenging. Two hundred miles out of Nashville, I finally got the hang of the dual rear axle. Wind pressures radiating off passing trucks weaved the trailer like a snake.

Given my lack of sleep, rejection from five brothers, unknowns of starting a new band and Venus' unhappiness, I was stressed out. Venus turned up her bitch meter, barking at the kids for bothering Daddy Rocky. She ordered Alicia and Ricky to sit on the floorboard, where they cowered like beaten animals. After harassing the kids, she turned her anger on me, presenting a personality I hadn't seen before. Feebly, I tried to ease the tension, without success. Even my silly singing didn't work. We had begun a thousand-mile trip of misery, trapped in the crowded confines of my truck.

Sunday night, following an early dinner at a truck stop, I parked near some big rigs and announced we were going to bed down in the trailer for the night. Everyone was relieved. Our torturous day was at an end, at least for now, only to begin again early Monday morning.

I offered to walk the kids around the truck stop, and Venus readily agreed. Alicia, Ricky and I walked the parameter, three times. Not much was said, though we shared the freedom of being out of the cramped, hot truck. A large field on one side of the truck stop provided an opportunity for the kids to run. I told Alicia and Ricky to run as fast as they could up to one of the big trees and then back. They flew away like birds freed from a cage. So I told them to do it again, and they did. A great deal of pent-up energy was released. Returning to the trailer, I put Alicia and Ricky to bed and kissed them on their foreheads. Alicia smiled at me and said, "Good night Daddy Rocky. I love you."

Venus had one remaining finger showing on her neat three-finger Scotch glass. Slouched on the couch like a rag doll, she obviously had uncorked my bottle of 18-year-old Glenlivet Scotch, the one I'd saved for a celebration that never came. She didn't offer, so I poured myself three fingers.

Without electricity, our tin can was sporadically illuminated by truck lights flashing across walls and ceiling, forming ominous patterns. Feeling like prisoners in a dungeon, we poured down our fourth triple Scotch formula, like infants sucking on a bottle.

Finally, I got my click.

Following half an hour of staring off in space, Venus turned to me, slurring her words.

"I'm not happy wit da way dis is goin'," she said. "Not turning out da way we planned. We're startin' over. Been der too many times in my rotten life, and I don't know if I can do dis again. Today wuz horrible. Self-destructive feelings are back—trapped like a bird in a cage. Wanted to fly away from you and da kids. You have no idea what dis pressure does to my head. I'm not happy, and dat's a dangerous place. Change dis, Rocky. Make dis right."

Staggering to our bedroom, Venus fell spread eagle on our bed and passed out. I collapsed beside her. The last thing I remember was thanking God for providing the wonderful, 18-year-old Glenlivet Single Malt Scotch and the click.

Monday's sunlight streamed through the trailer window, waking me. I dressed and gathered up the Strong's and ordered breakfast at the truck stop. For a moment, we were tolerable to each other.

Climbing in the F-650, I set down new rules for the rest of our trip. We played games all the way to Lake George. The kids loved I Spy, stamping mules, and spotting different states on license plates. We began telling stories and passed another hour. Jokes came last. Alicia and Ricky didn't know any jokes, so Venus and I challenged ourselves to tell children jokes, with minimal success. The skyline of New York City came into view, and then passed as we headed north.

Finally, we began to enjoy our adventure, in part because the trip was coming to an end.

Pulling into the club at Lake George, I spotted my Cadillac, four greenhorn Carousels, and one Chevy Impala and driver. The newbies were all smiles in anticipation of achieving entertainment greatness.

Mark Rubio, the frontman, boomed out a hero's welcome as we stepped inside his club. Mr. Rubio relayed the great things he'd heard about us. The newbies and I unloaded instruments, set up, did a quick sound check and started to leave.

Without warning, Mr. Rubio stopped us, saying, "Hey, guys. I've arranged for all of you to stay at a place on the lake—a hundred-year-old mansion that is vacant for the next month. Call it a fringe benefit. I want you to be happy at Lake George and my club."

We nodded and smiled, following him to the mansion. It was old and elegant, but had not been occupied for some time. Dust was everywhere, even after we removed the sheets covering the furniture and chandeliers. Venus and I got first choice of bedrooms, selecting the master suite on the first floor. In turn, each greenhorn made his selection from the remaining eight bedrooms, all upstairs. We settled into our collective domiciles in Lake George for the next month.

I took the guys to a clothier and fitted them in red jackets. Before we left Nashville, I had instructed them to bring black pants, tux shirt, bow tie, and patent leather shoes. We quickly returned to the club and kicked off opening night. I called the tunes and did all the emcee work.

The band was not tight—loose as shit running through a goose. Fortunately, individual raw talent carried the evening. Chris, the reed man, was our best musician, playing six different instruments and covering many genres. Jimmy Johnson, our trumpet player, doubled on valve trombone and sang a bit. The keyboardist had previously sung with Fred Waring, and his voice approached operatic quality.

The guitarist was straight rock, blues and sang all the R&R hits. Bassist was a jolly fat man who smiled all the time and had a rubber face that compelled people to notice. First night completed, I called rehearsals for Tuesday, Wednesday, and Thursday.

However, I couldn't help noticing Mark Rubio's furrowed brow. I was in a race to make Rubio smile again or we would be out of here.

At rehearsal Tuesday, Mr. Rubio pulled me aside and said we would be backing up The Angels on Friday and Saturday night, informing me to rehearse their hit records Friday afternoon. I attempted to convey confidence.

Although the performances went well, the band was not coming together.

Staying at the mansion was great for the newbies, but didn't provide much relaxation for me. Our superstar reed man got into a daily morning habit of standing on the dock with slalom water ski and towrope in hand. Within 10 minutes, he was making waves, skiing behind some generous soul who gave him a tow. The other musicians were wide eyed, soaking up the adventure.

However, Venus and I were not happy. With two kids sleeping in our bedroom, we didn't make love for a week. Irritability and snippy attitudes sliced through the tenderness we had once known and loved. Pressures from Venus' unhappiness, Alicia's and Ricky's cowering under their mother's chronic barking, and a mediocre band proved debilitating. This was not going well.

At the end of the second week, Mark Rubio approached with his booking agent, the one who split the ten-percent agent's commission with Dottie LaSalle. With Carousel brochure in hand, Rubio pointed out the obvious.

"You are the only Carousel pictured in this brochure. You used me to form a new band, made up of greenhorns. I'm pissed, particularly about paying you top dollar and getting quiet cash registers in return."

The booking agent made his living from commissions earned off Mr. Rubio, so his position morphed into the heavy, saying, "You're out of here in one week, through next Saturday. That's the earliest I can get another band on that stage. I don't care what the contract says; you're gone in a week. Got it?"

We headed out of upstate New York with a week off and a Monday opening date in Louisville. Venus refused to get back in the F-650, so she and the kids rode with Chris in his Impala. I reluctantly agreed to that arrangement. Besides, I needed time to think through our situation. The brass man was ecstatic to ride with me, soliciting my counsel throughout the trip. I provided the stories and the trip was pleasant, particularly having someone to help drive the F-650 and speak only of positive subject matter.

I set up the trailer in Louisville with Jimmy's help. The rest of the band checked into a Holiday Inn. Venus, the kids, and Chris arrived hours earlier and were sunning out by the pool as the others straggled in. I dropped off Jimmy and picked up Venus and the kids.

She was not happy to see me. Making matters worse, Monday dragged by as 96-degree temperatures beat down on our tin can sauna—no air-conditioning.

Although the trailer park had a modest swimming pool, Venus said, "I want to be in air-conditioning and enjoy the nice pool at the Holiday Inn. Let's give our relationship some space this week. I'll be back at suppertime every day."

True to her word, she commandeered the Cadillac and made her way, with kids in tow, to and from the Holiday Inn, leaving our trailer at 8 a.m. and returning at 6 for cocktails and dinner.

Following dinner on Tuesday, in a quieter moment, I said, "You're snippy with the kids and me. What's up?"

"Nothin'. Give me space. Back off. Stop hovering over me. Can't stand your pressure."

Wednesday and Thursday, Venus returned at 7:30 p.m., irritable and repulsed by my amorous overtures.

Something is terribly wrong.

Chapter 55

1964
NAUSEATING PAISLEY

Friday morning, Venus dragged Ricky and Alicia to the Caddy before breakfast, presumably headed for another day at the Holiday Inn. As I stood in the doorway, I watched my car jerk violently as the right rear wheel bounced over a curb and culvert. Driving erratically, Venus zigzagged through the trailer park and finally disappeared onto the busy, four-lane highway. Car horns and loud cursing from angry drivers could be heard over the rooftops of trailers. Surprisingly, the crash of metal did not follow.

A few hours later, I drove the F–650 truck to the Holiday Inn and knocked on Chris Birdsong's door, announcing myself by name. Although I could hear voices and movement inside, no one answered the door.

Bounding down the stairs, I searched for Alicia and Ricky, finding them in the restaurant eating sandwiches.

"Where is your mother, and what are you doing eating alone?" I asked Alicia.

"Mom told us to have lunch then go to the pool and swim."

"How long since she told you?

"I can't tell time Daddy Rocky—we just got our sandwich."

"How often does this happen … your mother sending you and Ricky out alone to eat or play by the pool?"

"Every day, Daddy Rocky. Sometimes we don't see her 'til it's time to come home."

To hide my pain I crumpled a cotton napkin over my eyes, turning away from the kids as tears rained down from harsh reality—betrayal. Finally regaining composure, I looked at them, forced a smile, and said, "Do exactly what your mother said. I'll see you after you finish your sandwich."

Leaving the restaurant I looked for the motel's manager. Relying on my celebrity hero influence with the guy, who knew me from the Carousels' previous appearance at the Office Lounge, I fabricated what I hoped would be a persuasive lie.

"The kids are locked in the hotel room and can't get out. Give me your pass keys and I'll return them in a couple of minutes."

He handed over a ring of keys. Running up the stairs, I tried several keys until one finally fit the lock and flung open the motel room door.

I caught a glimpse of Chris's naked leg disappearing into the bathroom, the door closing behind him. Framed on a nauseatingly ugly paisley bedspread, Venus's nude body squirmed like a night crawling worm, desperately searching for a hole to crawl into. Dumbstruck, I said nothing.

Venus said nothing, but her dilated eyes said everything. Obviously fucked up on drugs, her unspoken, but all-consuming question screamed, *'Are you gonna kill me?'*

Putting a bullet in Venus consumed me, along with anticipating the satisfaction I'd feel from splattering her fuckin' brains all over that ugly paisley bedspread. Looking around the room I spotted a smorgasbord of drugs on the bureau: grass, blow, LSD sugar cubes, and several prescription bottles. The room smelled of sex, blended with Venus' unique scent of jasmine. Her bouquet turned rancid for me.

With crystal clarity, I reflected on Luis Cruz's words, spoken in the middle of Bourbon Street: "Venus will break your heart, just like she broke mine—many times. Suddenly, Venus goes crazy—totally nuts. No warnin'—jus flips out."

Luis didn't have the balls, but I do. I'll kill this bitch.

Reaching for Roscoe I came up empty.

Motherfucker. I left Roscoe on the nightstand by my bed.

Strangling Venus seemed a tantalizingly delicious alternative, but the sight of a naked Medusa turned me to stone. The souls of my feet scorched from the hellish inferno I'd wandered into. Nostrils flared like a raging bull, and foamy spittle oozed from my lips. My eyes fixated on a demonic creature framed in paisley. Frozen between rage and rationale, acquiescing to ineptness, I short-circuited. Overwhelmed, I wheeled and stormed out, leaving the door wide open for the whole world to see.

Running down the stairs, I forced a sober face, returned the master key ring to a clueless motel manager, picked up Alicia and Ricky, and drove to the trailer park. Ricky fondled cigarettes in the ashtray, while Alicia's green eyes starred at me.

She knows. Alicia's has seen this scene play out before. She knows I'm broken—and so is she.

I filled my flask with Scotch and took Alicia and Ricky to the trailer park pool. Sitting in the 99-degree Louisville sunshine, my thoughts raced out of control.

I want to kill something or someone; Mata Hari, Chris Birdsong, myself, or all of us at the same time. It really doesn't matter who dies, but someone has to pay for my pain and agony. The more hurt I inflict the better. Excruciating mental pain is driving me insane, deeper and deeper into a schizophrenic hell, with no hope of ever returning to normalcy. My will to live suffocates.

Panic-stricken, my mind switched off—going catatonic for the next three hours. Thankfully, just before I went over the edge, I heard the thin voice of sanity: "What's for dinner, Daddy Rocky?"

McDonald's always works with kids. Feeling much like a child myself, I loved McDonald's, too. Hand-in-hand, we walked three blocks, ordered burgers, fries, and milk shakes. Apple pies for desert topped off their day with big smiles. Alicia and Ricky were tired, but happy to be away from their barking Mom.

Meanwhile, my guts were churning from torturous self-persecution and the Big Mac and fries. Walking the three blocks back to the trailer was good exercise. I swore to take a long walk the following morning, or swim laps, or do something active. The kids took much-needed baths, got into their pajamas, switched on the TV and settled in for an evening with *Bugs Bunny and Friends*. I started to pour a Scotch, but stopped short.

As painful as this is, I must do whatever it takes to get a grip on sanity. Getting drunk won't help ... only hurt more in the morning.

Saturday morning, I found a pay phone in the trailer park and called the Holiday Inn, asking the operator to connect me with Chris Birdsong's room. Chris answered and I quickly said, "Tell Venus I have the kids and they're safe."

Hanging up the phone, I strolled back to my tin can sauna. Swimming sounded like a good idea, as this was going to be another blistering day in Louisville. The kids and I took a dip, spending all morning getting wrinkled as prunes. I served sandwiches, Fritos, and a big pitcher of Kool-Aid by the pool—no agenda beyond lunch.

Lying in the lounge chair, I snoozed for an hour, waking to recollections of an earlier time and place.

What was I thinking? My love affair with Venus was a long-odd's bet. Like the trapeze artist trying the triple somersault without a net, my naive ass is splattered all over the center ring of the big top—should have charged admission. SPLAT! SPLAT! SPLAT! I could see my epitaph: "Rocky was nuts for getting involved with Venus. Rocky was blind to Venus's demonic madness."

Wallowing in self-pity, madness moved in, taking up residence in my brain. Later that night, blurred vision, foggy thoughts and lack of balance forced me to the floor, spread out on a grimy carpet, praying just to survive another merciless night.

A knock at the door around 11 roused me from my pathetic state. Struggling to get off the floor, I finally made it to the door, my hand trembling around the knob.

Venus stood on the patio below, looking up with tears running down cherub cheeks. Neither of us spoke for several seconds.

At last she said, "Can I come in?"

I said nothing, but motioned with my hand and arm for Venus to enter.

Awkwardly, we stood in the living room, looking at each other, but saying nothing. She stared at the kids' bedroom door. Her body language appeared to be asking for permission to see them. I nodded and she entered their bedroom, stood nearby, and cried. Remaining in the living room, my emotions flip-flopped between numbness and rage.

The devil is here. She's booked me on a one-way trip, straight to Hell. I don't know if I have the strength to resist her, but if I can muster the gumption, I'll blow her brains out and break free. Tonight, madness is my ally. Welcome.

Venus took my hand and led me to our bedroom, seducing me with expert carnal knowledge. Emotionally bankrupt, I was easy prey for a seductress possessing Venus's talents. Like old times, we fucked like minks. Defenseless, I fell under Venus's spell—a dutiful slave.

But, her spell didn't last. Still engaged, I suddenly had an epiphany. Horrific images of a devil's underworld appeared. Venus's womb was sucking me deep into a hellish black hole—appropriating my essence in exchange for access to her carnal favors. Terrified, I abruptly broke her hold on my soul and rolled off the macabre fiend below. Instantly, my cock stopped crowing.

Scurrying out of the bedroom, I ended up at the refrigerator and drank from a quart of milk, most of it running down my chin and chest.

"Motherfucker!" I said as I spit out the sour liquid in the kitchen sink. Staggering to the bathroom, I knelt over the toilet, put two fingers down my throat, and heaved up the remaining spoiled milk. Then I removed my wedding ring and tossed it in the cesspool of vomit and flushed the swill into hell. To my surprise, Venus knelt beside me, caressing my back and neck with a wet washcloth.

Repeatedly, Venus said, "Don't kill yourself, Rocky—what poison did you take? Don't kill yourself, Rocky—what poison did you take?"

Crazy thoughts collided in my skull. Mentally deranged, I wanted Venus to suffer pain, too. She didn't realize I was upchucking fermented milk, not deadly pills. That moment presented inordinate pleasure; witnessing Venus suffer a heavy dose of guilt. Thinking to myself, she deserves pain, I withheld truth from a naked devil kneeling on the bathroom floor beside me.

Venus doesn't deserve truth—ever again. She's hurting—I'm happy.

With Venus twisting in the wind, I returned to the bedroom and lay down. She joined me, afraid to touch. With remorseful culpability on Venus' face and a big smile on mine, I rolled over and went to sleep.

Roscoe's at hand. Deliciously tempting … Oh well, I'll blow her brains out in the morning. Time to sleep.

I slept until 4:30, when Venus gently awakened me, whispering, "I'm leaving now. Chris is waiting in the car. Don't make a scene. This is the best thing for both of us."

As I struggled to clear my head, she continued.

"From the beginning, you were right. Your scorpion and frog story nailed me. Without realizing it, you challenged me to win you at all costs. I had to have you. You were my way out of everything wrong with my life. You should have trusted your instincts.

"When Mike Gillich finally caught up with me, I had to figure a way out fast. Then it came to me. Telling you and Mike I was pregnant accomplished two things at once. First, marrying you was my way out of that life. You'd protect me. Your good heart was easy prey. Second, you'd get Mike off my back by conning Merrill into buying out my contract. It was a brilliant lie, and it worked perfectly.

However my darling, just like the scorpion in your story—if you ask why, it is my nature to betray—you, my kids, and ultimately, myself. It's my nature."

With that, she packed up the kids, their clothes and carried them to Chris's Impala. The deep murmur of a Chevrolet V8 faded into the night. For an hour, I repeated, "SPLAT! SPLAT! SPLAT!"

Mad Hatter summed it up, *"Down with the bloody Red Queen!"*

Cheshire Cat purred, *"Of course, he's mad, too."*

CHAPTER 56

1964
DOWNWARD SPIRAL

S unday afternoon I called the Holiday Inn and asked the operator to connect me with Jimmy Johnson's room, our trumpet and valve trombone man. When he answered, I asked him to pass the word to the new Carousels that we'll unload the instrument trailer at the Office Lounge on Monday at 1:30.

"I'll be there early, so look for me inside," I added. "You guys drive the Cadillac and the trailer. We'll have a quick meeting and do a sound check."

"Okay Rocky," Jimmy replied. "I'll pass the word and see you at 1:30 Monday. Hey. Are you okay?"

"You bet," I lied and quickly hung up the phone.

The most ridiculous phrase in the entertainment business is, "The show must go on." Who am I kidding? My God Powers just walked out on me—left Sunday morning in a Chevy Impala. It could be months before I get my act together. On the other hand, I'm paid good money to create the illusion of desirability and fantasy. I have 24 hours to get my performance face on.

Reggio Greco, frontman for the Office Lounge, was waiting for me at 1 on Monday. Having prepared my spiel, rationalizing the reasons for the new faces and only five Carousels, we negotiated a reduced paycheck, pleasing Reggio. That month was one of the toughest of my life. It took me 20 hours a day to muster the four-hour stage persona required for the Office Lounge. I beat myself up with guilt and self-pity most of my off-stage hours.

Sex was out of the question, feeling unappealing and unworthy of pleasing a woman. I was fucked up, struggling to disguise it and failing in the process.

Rehearsing the greenhorns three days a week was insufficient, so we went to four rehearsals for the remaining three weeks. An acceptable sound finally emerged during the fourth week. However, this new band was a long way from matching up with the old Carousels. The operatic voice of the keyboardist raised us to above average status. Otherwise, starting from scratch, I began teaching stage presence, dance routines, personal grooming, and everything else a professional entertainer has to master.

At the end of the gig, Reggio was gracious, although he didn't invite me back for a return date or contract.

The new Carousels then opened at a show bar in Peoria, the third nightclub we played in that notorious Mob town. Hit men hung out at the bar like vultures, hungry for their next prey. I seized the opportunity to begin executing half my dream, reinventing the band into a show band. I pulled out some stock Carousel routines and began teaching.

The *West Side Story* dance routine was too advanced for the newbies, so I backed off the pressure, electing to feature each musician on his best solo material. Each Carousel really worked hard to perfect his featured spot. As self-appointed director, I laid out higher goals each week for the players.

In the middle of our last week in Peoria, the bass man informed me he would not be joining us in Chicago, going home to Nashville—homesick. Down to four Carousels.

As we packed up for Chicago, the Peoria club frontman called me aside and said he wanted us to stay. He was terrified that the next band booked at the club—a Beatles copy band—would be a disaster.

"I may lose my entire audience. Even so, my boss insists I bring in the English group he manages. If they don't draw, I'm out of a job. Why don't you stay on? We'll alternate your band with the longhairs."

Explaining that we were booked to open in Chicago at Club Laurel on Monday, we looked at a calendar and discussed a couple of available dates, mutually agreeing to get a contract in place soon. Privately, I didn't want to commit to a date because of the unpredictability of losing more musicians, jeopardizing our future and the survivability of this band. All the uncertainty made my guts swirl around like clothes in a washing machine. I struggled to contain my mental anguish, wrestling with misguided failures as a man.

When we arrived at Club Laurel in Chicago, Guido Marconi met us with a warm and gracious welcome. Sadly, our four-member version of the reinvented Carousels was a mere shadow of the original Carousels. We became little fish in a big pond; one more average band to grace the famous stage. Our saving grace once again was the operatic voice that turned on the ladies and Italian men. The unique horn sounds from Jimmy Johnson also was a big hit. As a result, I prominently featured the opera singer's Italian tunes and the slide trumpeter's showstoppers all four sets.

The narcotic of applause began to emerge, slowly, but surely—a feeling I'd missed for months. And the chickadees were all over the band members. I can't explain it, although I turned down so many band-aids that rumors got around that I was either queer or fucked up. If they had asked, I would have confessed that I was piecing Humpty Dumpty back together again from the big SPLAT.

The last night at Club Laurel our operatic voice announced he was going back to college, beginning his master's degree in voice. We were down to three musicians and headed for Orlando. Unfortunately, I couldn't sing worth a shit, and the two remaining musicians were the least talented of the original five hired in Nashville. However, Jimmy played trumpet and organ at the same time while Slim Simon played guitar or bass. Both sang a few songs. The downward spiral trajectory sucked me deeper into depression.

Success has a thousand fathers, but failure is an orphan. Trite, but true.

Jimmy and I drove my F-650 and trailer straight through, from Chicago to Orlando. Slim, the former guitar player, now bass player, drove my Cadillac with the instrument trailer in tow. Crossing the Florida State line, we were greeted by a raging hurricane, rocking the trailer all over the highway. I almost put the rig in the ditch five times fighting 110 mile-per-hour winds. Finally, we managed to pull in next to a large downtown Orlando hotel, parking on the leeward side of a tall building. Slim maneuvered my Caddy alongside.

The three of us rented one room for the night and weathered the hurricane at the bar, drinking and watching weather reports.

Jimmy, Slim, and I met for breakfast the next morning. I spun grandiose lies, leading the greenhorns to fictitious dreams of stardom. My word pictures involved reinventing ourselves into good then great entertainers, comedians, and a specialty act. They lapped up my bullshit, committing to work hard to fulfill the dreams I fed them, like babies eating pablum.

A major part of my plan entailed hiding out in Florida until we could polish an acceptable act. At that time, Florida was an entertainment wasteland, with the exception of Miami. If you wanted to be discovered, Florida was the last place on earth you'd want to be.

Interestingly, one of the biggest Mafia Dons—Santo Trafficante, Jr.—lived in Tampa, controlling the Tampa Bay area, Miami, the Bahamas, and devising a plan to get back into Cuba and the casinos. Trafficante and Marcello were still busy covering their tracks involving the JFK assassination, erasing all witnesses that could lead back to them.

Over time, perhaps I can return to a bigger stage. But, for now, Florida is my rehab center.

Sunday afternoon, I took a reality pill, facing truth straight up, no chaser.

My pride wrestles with practicality. Once brimming with savoir-faire, the realm of defeat reared its ugly head. Ego fell under relentless frontal attack, dinging my armor like a ball-peen hammer beating on cardboard. My guts were corroding from acidic poison of self-delusion. My once strong voice now quivers in insecurity. I'm living a dream that is turning into a nightmare.

During the next few months, we played an upscale supper club in Orlando, five weeks in Savannah, a month in Atlanta, a month in Tampa, the same in Cocoa Beach, even a bowling alley bar in Orlando, and six weeks in Melbourne Beach. While in Savannah, I drowned inside multiple bottles of Cuervo Gold Tequila, augmented by a case of limes and two boxes of Morton's salt. Regrettably, I missed out on one of America's most beautiful and historic cities—still a blur.

Adding a chick canary I picked up from auditions in Atlanta, the three-piece band expanded to four for three months. However the chick didn't have star quality, at least not on stage. Jimmy and Slim swore her remarkable talents lay in the bedroom. Reportedly, she could suck the chrome right off a trailer hitch ball while loosening your lug nuts.

I passed up the knob nibbler, knowing I'd fire her ass following the Tampa gig.

More the lap cat than ever, Cheshire Cat purred away, *"How fine you look when dressed in rage. Your enemies are fortunate your condition is not permanent. You're lucky, too. Red eyes suit so few."*

Chapter 57

1965
COCOA BEACH

At Cocoa Beach, I set up my rig at a trailer park near the main gate at Cape Canaveral. Engineers working at the Cape became neighbors, although they rarely spoke, rendering me incognito to daylight society. Frequently, I was awakened by early morning rocket launches. The park was so close to the Cape that the ground shook like an earthquake and ears ached from the sustained roars of rocket engines.

On one occasion, I was relaxing in a hot bath when a massive rocket exploded on a nearby launch pad. I was so sure the end of the world was upon us I offered my final prayer.

God, have your will with my life, give me the wisdom to know my mission and the courage to carry it out.

One Wednesday, I discovered a message taped to my trailer door: "Venus Strong called. Call 504-523-4169."

I called.

"Hello," the voice answered. It was the beautiful sound I had once loved—then hated.

"It's Rocky. You called?"

"Yes. Yes, I called. First, I really messed us up in Louisville—the drugs … I've come to my senses and want to be with you in Cocoa Beach. That's near Cape Canaveral, isn't it? Is that okay?"

Thinking of a million caustic answers at once, the only sentence that came out of my mouth was, "Yes."

"Great. I'll be there Sunday—our favorite day. Rocky, I love you and want to be with you."

Driving to the bus station, my shirt clung like glue to my chest and my asshole puckered with anxiety. My whole body became soaked in sweat because of a low Freon charge in the Caddy's A/C—no match for the blistering Florida heat.

Horrific flashbacks consumed my gray matter.

I reacted too fast—should have thought this through before agreeing to let Venus come back into my life. Can't undo what's done.

Perspiration beaded up on my face, sending a steady drip down my chin. A finger on my left hand mimicked a windshield wiper, skimming and slinging loads of sweat from brow to floorboard. Slippery hands skated over a plastic steering wheel.

This is a mistake.

Throat parched, I stopped at a gas station to buy a Coke. With plenty of time to meet the bus, I strolled to an adjoining park, sat in a child's swing, and sipped my sugar water.

What I really need is a stiff drink. Why am I doing this? I guess she's got nowhere else to go, so she's picked the first safe port in a storm—me. Am I that easy? Won't play her fool again. Pride is all I've got left, although my gauge is registering low. I'll hide my emotions behind an iron curtain, walling off her cunning schemes. On the other hand, she really is an Olympic lover. I'd be a fool to not lie back and enjoy her talents.

Once inside the bus terminal, my body began to dry out as I enjoyed the cold air being pumped through moldy vents. Her bus was late in arriving, and I watched as the driver hurriedly opened the door with flair, telling every departing passenger, "Thank you for choosin' Greyhound. Have a wonderful day in Cocoa Beach."

A couple of old ladies with canes exited first, then a bum with a bottle of wine staggered out, then a bag lady, followed by a man with a gray beard down to his waist. Three army guys and five fellows who appeared to be space engineers emerged, then stood off to one side and stared back at the open door of the bus.

Venus appeared, hair perfectly quaffed, makeup in place, and boobs jiggling like jell-o as they spilled over her low-cut sundress. The army guys and engineers stood and gawked at the beautiful creature floating off the bus.

Ignoring the stares, she looked around, but did not see me, not at first. Moving through the terminal double doors, I stood on the tarmac in plain view. Finally, her eyes met mine, transforming her haughty face into a gleaming smile. Rapidly approaching, almost at a run, Venus delivered the best French kiss I'd had in months.

Eyes of every swingin' dick were on Venus. A familiar aroma of jasmine filled my senses. As we walked out of the bus station, she pecked my cheek with liquid lips five times before we reached the Caddy. Once inside the De Ville, she went straight for object of her affection, prologue to doing what she came to do.

Inside the trailer, we fucked for six straight days, breaking only for sustenance and my nightly gig. Words had been held to absolute minimum, preferring to replenish our vacuous souls with passionate lovemaking. Living completely in the moment, Venus and my smiles returned.

My gorgeous Barbie Doll is back in my bed. As long as we blot out history, fuckin' like minks is all we need. Living life in one dimension makes life really simple.

It didn't last. On the afternoon of the seventh day, an unspoken, unavoidable tension surfaced. For a long time, Venus stared out of the living room window, apparently watching palm trees dodge the morning sea breeze. I approached with a fresh cup of coffee I'd poured for her. She didn't turn around, simply pointing toward the coffee table. After a while, she retrieved her coffee, now cold, mumbled obscenities, and meandered toward the sink.

Tripping over a throw rug, Venus fell to the floor, the cup and saucer shattering on the linoleum. Ass sprawled out next to the broken china, bleeding, bruised and bitchy, Venus growled, "Get your filthy hands of me!" when I rushed over to help.

Postponement of the obvious discussion had been easier than one might imagine. Swimming in shallow water for a week was safe. Diving into deep water could prove fatal. Instinctively, we accepted that our time had come.

That afternoon, with Venus somewhat calmer, we strolled barefoot on the sugar sands of Cocoa Beach. Onshore winds were up, and the sun warmed our bodies. Cumulus clouds danced above the Gulf Stream as children laughed and played with their families, building sand castles that mimicked fantasies. Waves beginning life off the coast of Africa crashed on Cocoa Beach in four-second intervals, sustaining a thunderous roar. Laughing gulls scurried on the beach, barking their boisterous disapproval of human intruders.

Without notice, Venus's demonic nature surfaced.

"You haven't asked about Alicia, Ricky, or Chris," she said.

My asshole puckered several times in quick succession.

"Venus," I said, "I really care about Alicia and Ricky—more than you know. They're precious kids, and I miss them. Are they with Chris? Is he still alive? He's a committed druggie—a dead man walkin'. And just so we're clear, if Chris Birdsong were doused with gasoline, I'd volunteer to light the match and roast the bastard. I wouldn't dishonor my dick by pissing on the son-of-a-bitch to put out the fire."

Her face twisted around pursed lips. Eyes blinking rapidly, her body coiled in preparation for spitting her venomous poison, aimed straight at my heart.

"Chris is built like a thoroughbred race horse … huge cock … great lover," she snarled back, eyes shooting daggers as her muscles tensed.

At that exact moment, the ocean breeze blew sand in her golden hair and blue eyes. Rubbing eyes, she wiped sweat from her face and chest, sending droplets inching down through exposed cleavage.

"I'm glad that mule made you happy in bed," I responded. "If that's true, why are you here fucking me in Cocoa Beach?"

Stunned, she had never heard my sharp tongue lash back, particularly at her. Head tilted with gaping mouth, she stammered, babbled, "But that's … You're … I'm …"

I took a step toward Venus. She stepped back, forcing a smile, then grimace, then smile, then grimace, shaking her head in bewilderment. My hands clinched into taut fists. Her eyes darted in fear, seeking an escape route from my pent-up wrath.

Suddenly, I grabbed her shoulders, my thumbs digging deep into soft tissue. She squirmed to get away and I dug deeper, producing a wince and a pleading whine. Her eyes begged for mercy. I was in no mood to relent.

In the blink of an eye, I wrapped my two open palms around her face, squeezing until her cheeks oozed like dough between my fingers. Drawing her in, her face less than a foot away, I forced her to see, hear and feel me drop a nuclear bomb on our marriage.

"You're a common whore, a certifiable cunt. You definitely love dick. In your perverted world, love is a sword used to destroy, leaving a wake of horror. You're drowning in a morass of madness, and I refuse to go down with you. Our marriage was flushed down the toilet in Louisville, along with my wedding ring. This relationship is forever broken, shattered, washed up, dead, finished, terminated, annihilated, and royally fucked. From now on, you are simply a bad memory. Anyway, it's just a matter of time before you put a bullet through your brain. And no one will be there to save you."

I released my hands from her face and head, leaving white imprints of my fingers. Speechless, she trembled, staggered back, but did not reach out for support. I stood motionless, smiling. Venus spun and walked over glistening white sand, toward the trailer park, sobbing like a baby. For the first time I noticed—Venus is pigeon-toed, evidenced by her footprints in the sugar sand. I did not follow.

Jack Kerouac said it best: *"We turned at a dozen paces, for love is a duel, and looked at each other for the last time."*

When I returned from that night's gig, Venus was ready with her demands. In summary, she wanted the '59 Cadillac, the Hoover vacuum cleaner—and out of the marriage. I agreed to her demands, although I insisted she sign a release, witnessed by a Notary.

The following morning I placed the Underwood on the kitchen table and typed up two agreements. One released me from "any and all financial responsibility for Venus Strong from this day forward." The second released me from "any and all personal or property liability arising out of an auto accident involving a 1959 Cadillac," and listing the VIN number. Venus was furious, but wanted the Cadillac more than her pride, so she signed both agreements in the presence of a Notary at the trailer park office. I then signed over title to the Caddy.

Standing outside in the shade, waiting for Venus to pack, I smoked a Pall Mall and smiled broadly. Taut muscles relaxed for the first time in months. Three pelicans flew over palm trees in formation, headed for the Atlantic Ocean. A squirrel sat on haunches pealing his breakfast, chirping a happy song.

Venus stormed out of the trailer, her suitcase spilling over with bits of panties, a bra strap and partial pant leg that hadn't made it inside. Hair mussed, sweat soaking through her stained Cocoa Beach tourist T-shirt, she threw the vacuum cleaner and suitcase in the trunk of the Caddy.

Turning, Venus looked at me with a curious stare, not knowing what to say or do. Leaning against a palm tree with right knee bent, my tennis shoe rested two feet above the ground. A long drag from my Pall Mall preceded a wink at Venus, accompanied by a huge Cheshire Cat grin. Mimicking the coolness of James Dean, I slowly waived my hand across my waistline, signaling a final goodbye.

Venus opened the heavy Caddy door, dropped car keys in the sand, retrieved them, climbed in, started the engine and backed out of the parking space. My last vision of Venus was appropriately symbolic as she drove the white pearlescent Cadillac Coupe de Ville out of the trailer park, its four phallic-shaped taillights flickering.

Relieved that this painful chapter had ended, my sense was that I got the better of the deal. Venus got a thoroughly worn-out Cadillac with 195,000 miles and I was free of Venus and her demonic influence—at least for now.

Another formation of pelicans flew toward the Atlantic, followed by several snowy egrets headed in the opposite direction, toward the inland waterway. The sea breeze was fresh and cool. The world looked different—very different.

Stepping back inside my tin can, the repugnant odor of a torture chamber made me gag. Too many horrific memories lurked in the crevices of a once idyllic place. The following week I sold the trailer and the F-650 truck and purchased a 1958 Lincoln Continental coupe, paying cash for the car and depositing $500 in my Shreveport checking account.

I selected the Lincoln because it had the largest trunk of any American car. My stereo, record collection, pots and pans, kitchen utensils, small appliances, clothes, and all the stuff from the trailer went in the trunk. A trailer hitch was installed to pull the instrument trailer. All my worldly possessions were contained either in the Lincoln or the trailer. With almost six years invested on the road, all I had to show for my efforts was a used Lincoln and some musical instruments.

Jack Kerouac's *On the Road: The Original Scroll*, noted, *"My whole wretched life swam before my weary eyes, and I realized no matter what you do it's bound to be a waste of time in the end so you might as well go mad."*

Over breakfast, I read the newspaper, cover to cover: President Lyndon B. Johnson proclaims his "Great Society" during his State of the Union Address; Some 200 Alabama State Troopers clash with 525 civil rights demonstrators in Selma, Alabama; Martin Luther King, Jr. and 25,000 civil rights activists successfully end the 4-day march from Selma to Montgomery; and, Some 3,500 Marines arrive in South Vietnam, becoming the first American combat troops. Given my state of mind, I could find no good news.

I actually enjoyed the short drive from Cocoa Beach to Orlando. The Lincoln's A/C worked great, but I put all the windows down anyway. My sandy blond hair danced wildly in the wind, twisting and turning till my scalp hurt. Silently, my head exploded in creative thought: *I'm free of the garbage that littered my psyche—cast aside on the sandy shores of Coco Beach. Time to have fun. Time to get my ticket punched.*

As if competing with a deafening airstream, I sang as loud as possible the Shirley and Lee R&B hit, *C'mon Baby Let the Good Times Roll.*

C'mon baby, let the good times roll
C'mon baby, let me thrill your soul
C'mon baby you're the best there is,
Roll all night long.

C'mon baby, let's close the door,
C'mon baby, let's ride some more,
C'mon baby, let the good times roll,
Roll all night long.

I feel so good when you're home.
Come on baby, let's ride some more
C'mon baby, rock me all night long!

...

C'mon baby, let the good times roll
C'mon baby, let me thrill your soul

C'mon baby you're the best there is,
Roll all night long.

...

Roll all night long,
Roll all night long.
Roll on, roll on, roll on
Roll on, roll on, roll on
Roll on, roll on, roll on
Yeah, roll all night long.

Chapter 58

1965
ANN-MARGRET VS. GHOST CRAB

An Atlanta booking agent talked me into accepting a month's gig at an Orlando bar adjoining a bowling alley. From the sublime to ridiculous, our rise to fame had turned into rapid descent into the abyss.

Slim said it best, "What a dump. Never thought I'd be playin' to bowlin' balls."

The stage sagged, forcing us to place beer boxes on the dance floor to support one end of the organ, barely making room for our instruments. Rancid stench from too much sour beer and cigarettes emanated from dirty black carpets, bringing tears to my eyes. A dense haze of smoke hung just over the heads of blue collar workers braggin' 'bout their strikes.

Our tuxes were absurdly out of place, given the bowling-shirt audience who came there to talk loud, laugh loud, chug-a-lug beers and ignore the goofballs on stage. Bright stage lights mounted behind a drop curtain on a low ceiling trapped 110-degree heat, soaking our tuxes to the bone. We had to smear on suntan lotion to protect our faces.

The postage-stamp dance floor attracted lovers and fighters. On many occasions, we were glad to have at least a foot-high advantage over the brawlers. Everything associated with achieving entertainment dreams of grandeur were on hold, at least for the next four weeks.

Jimmy and Slim located cheap lodging, a dollar a night in advance. Cheshire, Hatter and I moved into a 6x9-foot room with a single bed, nightstand, lamp, and bureau. The walls were papered with a jungle theme that pictured flora and fauna during the day and turned into a forbidding forest at night.

If my dollar was on the bureau in the morning the room was mine that night. No dollar, no room. My life was running day-to-day; why shouldn't my lodging be the same. The flophouse was clean, although little more than a buoy marker on the route to skid row—an old wooden two-story house located in an earthen depression behind a Royal Castle. How appropriate. I actually walked up a hill to purchase my Royal Castle burgers. I was so far down, the Royal Castle was up.

The first day in the flophouse I experienced a revelation, discovering Khalil Gibran's *The Prophet*. The little hardcover book was the only personal object in the room, in plain view on the bureau. I couldn't image who left it there. But, I quickly took possession of it, reading from cover to cover, several times, savoring the wisdom of Gibran's poetry each night before placing my dollar on the bureau and turning off the lamp. One of my more deeply felt poems was *Love*—the last verse particularly impactful:

… To know the pain of too much tenderness.

To be wounded by your own understanding of love;

And to bleed willingly and joyfully.

To wake at dawn with a winged heart and give thanks for another day of loving …

Sensing that a guardian angel led me to Gibran's *Prophet*, the powerful book left Orlando in my pocket.

The Driftwood Bar and Grill was a casual place, located right on the Atlantic Ocean, nestled in the laidback community of Melbourne Beach. Thatched roof and driftwood siding washed up from exotic places around the world set a distinct architectural style: dilapidated. Down A1A, just 25 miles south of the hustle and bustle of Cape Canaveral and Cocoa Beach, Melbourne Beach was a magnet for dropouts, sun worshipers, and habitual marijane suckers.

Inside the Driftwood, I sized up the small triangular bandstand situated in a corner, glass walled on two sides, windows opening to the beach at night to lure in Gulf Stream breezes. For the second gig in a row, we barely got the Wurlitzer organ, Leslie, tubs, amps, and PA on the tiny stage, raised only six inches off the dance floor. I couldn't set up my vibes, bone or the double bass, giving them a well-deserved rest in the instrument trailer.

The Driftwood's wiry Italian owner weighed no more than 140 pounds, sported a wiseguy attitude much like a Mustache Pete—a wannabe big man. In truth, he was a nobody.

The audience was local beach community: flip-flop wearing flower children and tie-dyed T-shirted beatnik carryovers from Jack Kerouac's era. By all appearances, pot had been legalized in Melbourne Beach—everyone openly lit up. At best, the women were Grade D skanks. That didn't deter Jimmy or Slim. They never culled nuthin'.

At one of our infrequent rehearsals, Jimmy told me, "Rocky, you really need to get laid—and quick. We've watched the sap rising in your eyes and it's gonna spill over. Go screw some chick's brains out. Life's too short to pass up good pussy."

My high standards for selecting primo bed partners were a distant memory. Reaching a place where quantity exceeded quality, my manly needs stood at attention, ready to salute the first beaver that pranced by. While laying a skank on Melbourne Beach one night, I damn near sand-papered my pecker down to a pencil point. The sand in her Schlitz was painful for me. On the contrary, remarkably, it gave her pleasure.

As I pumped away, she yelled, "Dump ya cum. Dump ya cum. Dumped cum yet?" Then she rolled me over and over in the sugar sand, all the way down to the Atlantic Ocean. The salt water felt good, although nothing could wash away my self-contempt.

Whatever pride I'd accumulated over my life just got washed away in the ocean.

"Buy ya breakfast, den do dis again," she said.

"No thanks. Got to get my rest," was the most gracious utterance I could muster. Mortified by her invitation to join her for breakfast, the answer I should have given was, "My life will be over if anyone sees me in public with a Grade F pothead blob like you."

Temporarily buoyed the next morning, I prepared an outline and rehearsed my spiel for delivery to Stan Zuckerman. It went something like this: "I'm in Florida with a stripped-down group doing comedy and stage show material. I've been thinking about your option and may be ready to move forward in a couple of months. However, I need to augment the group with some fresh talent, preferably a couple of beautiful women—you know … bookends. Any ideas?"

When I was satisfied with my presentation, I made the call, and his secretary forwarded the call to Stan's desk.

Ever gracious, Stan replied, "I'm delighted you called, Rocky. There is a group out here in California that needs strong leadership. I already have them under contract. Collectively, they have what it takes to achieve stardom, including two, uh … beautiful bookends, as you cleverly call them. We can put them on the fast track if they secure direction and discipline. Are you interested in leading this group? I think it may be tailor-made for you. We can even rename the group the Fabulous Carousels if you want."

Elated to hear his vote of confidence, I replied, "I'm definitely interested Mr. Zuckerman. What kind of fast track do you have in mind?"

"As you know, I make no guarantees. However, as a favor to me, some of my friends will book your new group while you polish the act. Early on, we can secure coaches in Los Angeles, fresh material for recordings and stage presentation. The money will not be great at first, primarily because you'll spend most of it on creating new material, performance coaches and outfits. If this group comes together, I'll book you in the better clubs in LA and downtown Vegas. When you're ready, I'll place you on regional television shows, then national television. Danny Thomas, Jackie Gleason, and Ed Sullivan owe me favors. I'll leverage them to book you on their shows.

"Oh yeah. In case I didn't mention it, we'll need a hit record out of you, Rocky. I have contacts with major record labels and can secure a deal—with the right material. Your job is to come up with creative hit music that appeals to the masses. All this should take about six months to a year on what you called the fast track. Interested?"

"Yes," I said. "I'm booked here in Florida for the next six weeks. When do you want to put this deal together?"

"Think about this for a few days and call me back with your answer. If you want to move forward, we'll put agreements in place. You can be in California in six weeks, leading the new group. Okay?"

"I'll give you a call next week with my answer, Mr. Zuckerman."

Hanging up the pay phone, I felt challenged to make the right decision this time. Second chances don't come along often. The potential for rising from the ashes of the Phoenix was appealing—very appealing.

Following good sex with a petite chick who worked at the local dry cleaners, I showered in her bathroom. While toweling off, I saw a distorted shape reflected in her K-mart full-length mirror. I felt as if I was in a carnival fun house, except there was nothing funny about the way I looked, especially my protruding belly.

Shit. I've let myself go to pot. Got to get in shape, mentally and physically.

My 24-hour clock changed, and I began hitting the sack mid-morning and sleeping til 5. Following each show, I read books and newspapers till 4:30 a.m., driving to an isolated beach two miles south of the Driftwood Bar and Grill. I discovered a special peace while witnessing inspirational sunrises over the Atlantic Ocean. Going to this spot became part of my daily ritual, augmented with a good run on the beach, beach chair, fresh coffee, morning paper, swim suit, and a fresh change of clothes.

My constant companion was an osprey, feeding her young chicks from the bounty of the Atlantic. She and the chicks sang happy songs of life and wonderment.

Following a two-mile run just before sunrise, I sipped black coffee from a thermos and relaxed in my lounger. Within a week, I was running four miles on the sandy beach. My body and mind were getting stronger every day.

The blissful beach routine continued with runs, coffee, and an increased determination to do something right for a change. Laughing gulls made fun of me, at least they seemed to. Considering all my options, I made a commitment to end my death spiral.

What do I do with the rest of my life?

I wrote down my options:

- Accept Stan Zuckerman's offer; go to California, remain a professional entertainer and leader.
- Call the dude in New York, play the pit in *Hello Dolly* and cut an album for Blue Note.
- Become a studio musician in Nashville, sign on with one of the big recording and touring stars or become a classical percussionist in a major orchestra.
- Go to Shreveport and get a straight's job and play music on the side.
- Go back to Louisiana Tech and finish my degree.

Much to think about. Luckily, no one was around to witness my indecision except graceful pelicans riding wind currents ten feet above surf's edge. They see my weaknesses, but aren't laughing—yet. Above, a flock of terns soared in perfect formation before chirping unanimous agreement on the perfect spot to pick up a tasty breakfast.

The pressure of the Zuckerman decision within two days began to loom large. I knew the option I picked would likely determine where I'd spend the rest of my life.

I'd better be right this time.

By 9 a.m. most days, the blistering heat of the Florida sun ran me off the beach and into the air-conditioned coolness of a local blue-plate diner for a quick breakfast. Then it was back to the rented apartment, shower and sleep til 5 or 6. After dressing for the gig, I'd stop by a tasty eatery and then amble over to the Driftwood Bar and Grill. I completely dropped out of daytime life, preferring sunrises over the Atlantic Ocean.

One morning, after completing a pre-dawn, five-mile run on the beach, I collapsed in the beach chair, my running clothes thoroughly soaked and clinging to my body. Tired, but serenely content, I slowly sipped French Market Pure Coffee while watching the emerging sun's rays reflect off clouds above the Atlantic and admiring the beautiful hues of blue, purple, orange, and gold radiating across the sky—a promise of another beautiful day. The crashing of Atlantic waves added a tympanic accompaniment to the sunrise, repeating their rhythmic sounds every few seconds. Sandpipers raced through the sand as the tide rolled back and forth, munching on coquinas for breakfast. A welcomed peace filled my soul, seducing me into a trance-like state.

Two puffy clouds parted, freeing the sun's rays to splash their colors on the beach. The sunbeams seemed to spotlight a woman riding a white bicycle down through the clouds, headed for the water's edge, pedaling slowly, moving fast, and coming my way. She was wearing a white flowing gown of sheer chiffon, which could not hide her breathtaking figure. Flaming red hair topped her angelic face.

She looks like Ann-Margret—my all-time fantasy lover. Ann-Margret bicycling down to be with me, Rocky Strong—could it be? That's a heavenly thought. It's also madness. Perhaps she's an angel; perhaps a devil.

Appearing to glide effortlessly above the sugar sands of Melbourne Beach, the bicycle and its redhead beauty came directly at me, stopping five feet from my chair.

"Good morning, Rocky," said my mysterious bike rider. "I've been sent to get you. Come with me."

Stunned, I sat speechless, bewildered.

"It's time you return to your roots," she continued. "Come home. I'll make it easy. Leave this place. It's a condemned life, filled with disappointments. You've had quite enough pain, Rocky. Leave it behind and come with me."

Struggling to speak, I found I could not. Desperately wanting to ask questions and get answers, nothing came out of sealed lips. The red-haired angel of my fantasies was inviting me to join her in some sort of moment of revelation. Unable to talk and powerless to embrace her beauty, I sat paralyzed.

What happened next was even more bizarre.

Ann knelt next to me, as a ghost crab suddenly crawled out of a hole in the sand and began speaking to me.

"Rocky, don't trust her," the crab said. "She's a woman, and you know what pain they inflict on men. Remember what Eve did to Adam? She's a figment of your imagination—a sexual fantasy. To prove my point, caress her breast and check out her reaction. Ann's a frigid witch, dressed up to lure you into her web, seize control over your soul. You just went through all that with Venus. Didn't you learn anything from the experience? You paid one hell of a price for the lesson."

As dreams go, this has turned into a nightmare. I'm watching a crab debating a beautiful redhead. Powerless to speak or move, I'm reduced to little more than a paralyzed spectator as the crab and Ann bargain for control over my soul.

The crab turned to me, offering a deal right out of a Faustian play.

"Rocky, I can open your mind to a vast source of divine knowledge and wisdom. Leave the Holy Scriptures at the public library; reject the theology of *'turning the other cheek'* and *'the meek will inherit the earth'*. Those are silly myths. I'll make you an intellectual giant. Your grandest desires will be granted. Abundant pleasures will befall you from this day forward. Dream it and I will make it happen. Join me for a journey to eternal ecstasy for the rest of your physical and spiritual days."

As the strange crab was speaking, Ann-Margret moved closer. Speaking in a soft, yet confident voice, she offered a rebuttal.

"He's offering you a deal with the devil, Rocky. The unquenchable thirst for knowledge he speaks of is bitter, ultimately self-destructive. According to the Holy Scriptures, giving up your soul in exchange for the devil's pleasures condemns you to burn in Hell. That is a heavy price to pay for a few moments of self-indulgence and guiltless pleasure. It's a false promise of happiness."

Her eyes dissolved all remaining resistance as she whispered, "The divine knowledge I offer is peace of mind, guaranteed by a deal with God. You are in the midst of a fierce tug-a-war between good and evil—between the physical world and the spiritual world. Within that battle your unquenchable thirst for knowledge will lead you to divine understanding. If you seek love, peace, self-esteem, pride, dignity, integrity, and knowledge of God, the path is clear. This all has to do with the destiny of your soul."

Suddenly, the ghost crab was animated, dancing wildly on the sand to re-capture my attention, squeaking, "She lies! She can't be trusted! That red-haired witch will lead you in the *'paths of righteousness for his namesake'* and walk out on you in the end, just like Venus. Don't fall for a woman's seduction ever again. Reject her lies. Come with me. I'll give you more beautiful women than you can possibly imagine. If you want Venus back, to use for your carnal pleasures, I'll get her with a snap of my claw. When you grow tired of Venus, I'll replace her with ever-increasing beautiful and seductive creatures—women like Venus, all beautiful and eager to please you. If it feels good, you can do it. I'm offering a lifetime of endless free love and guiltless pleasures."

I remained frozen in my nightmare of madness, as Ann leaned in so close I could feel her moist breath caress my ear.

"You've abandoned your mother's and father's respect in exchange for selfish pleasure. If you believe in *'God's will be done,'* you will forever reject Satan and follow me, back to your roots. God has a special plan for you Dean 'Rocky' Strong—return to your roots now."

A sea breeze blew Ann-Margret and the ghost crab from view, leaving only the busy sandpipers digging for coquinas at water's edge. Dolphins rolled beyond the surf line, while skimmers skimmed the waters to snatch unsuspecting fry. Seven roseate spoonbills elegantly set a westerly course toward the Intercostal Waterway. My dream—or nightmare—had ended.

On the contrary, another nightmare was about to begin. As I began clearing my head from the strange dream of Ann-Margret and a ghost crab, an uneasy feeling took hold. I knew something was wrong. What came next was an epiphany of sorts—something inside of me saying that I had to call Mom—right now.

Rushing to a pay phone, I nervously dialed her home number, getting no answer. With sweaty fingers, I hung up and called my Uncle Ed.

"Your mother is in Highland Hospital," he told me. "She has a bleeding duodenal ulcer. It's serious. She may not make it."

No time for small talk, I hung up on Uncle Ed, called information for the number of the hospital, and spent an eternity waiting to be connected to Mom's hospital room. A very frail voice finally answered the phone.

"Mom!" I cried out, then launched into a babbling series of questions. "How are you? What happened? Are you okay? When did this happen?"

Realizing I was repeating myself over and over again without giving Mom time to answer, I finally asked the right question: "Do you need me at home?"

A frail, one-word response crept through the phone line: "Yes."

Gasping for oxygen to refuel my brain, the receiver almost slipped out of my sweaty hand.

"I love you more than life itself," I said, pushing aside commitments to the Carousels, Florida or California. They no longer mattered.

"Hold on Mom. I'll make everything right. I'll be there in three days."

I shut down the Carousels and pointed the Lincoln and instrument trailer northwest, toward Shreveport.

Straight man for 20 years and bent for six, what's next? Make Mom and Dad proud. How? How?"

Curled up on the passenger seat of the Lincoln, Hatter groused, *"Okay, he's as mad as a box of frogs."*

Snuggled in my lap, Cheshire Cat meowed, *"Oh, but it's loads of fun!"*

Chapter59

1965-1966
I APOLOGIZE

Anxious, my guts churned and head throbbed on the long drive to Shreveport. Like a recurring nightmare, I couldn't shake the parable of the Prodigal Son, worrying if I would be shunned or welcomed.

Uncle Ed met me in the lobby of Highland Hospital with grim news.

"Your mother is close to death. I think she's given up. You have no idea how worried she's been about you. Dean, you broke her heart."

My knees buckled as I collapsed into a washed-out couch in the reception area. Head in hands, I wept like a baby, gasping for air in the process. Almost passing out from hyperventilating, I lowered my head between my knees. Regaining my equilibrium, I stood up to face Uncle Ed's pent-up anger at my lifestyle and how I've hurt my mother over the past six years.

He spared no words about my behavior and lifestyle.

"You had everything going for you: total respect from your father's good name, unconditional love of a giving mother, abundant natural talents, and education," my uncle began. "We were so proud of you. Suddenly, without warning, you threw everything away, dropped out of Louisiana Tech, ran all over the country with questionable characters, knocked up a divorcee with two kids, and then married her. And now I understand your band and the marriage failed. You've come crawling home to beg your mother's forgiveness. Upstairs, your mother is dying of a broken heart. You are to blame for my sister's situation!"

Uncle Ed towered over me like a drill sergeant, puffing aggressively on his stubby cigar. Pointing toward the elevators, he led the Prodigal Son to his sister like a jailer leading a condemned prisoner to the gallows.

As we reached Mom's hospital room, Uncle Ed turned to me and said, "For once in your life, be kind to your mother. At least for now, put your self-absorbed nature on hold. This is not about you. It's all about your mother in what could be her final hours."

A barely audible "Dean?" escaped from the frail figure on the hospital bed, shrouded in white cotton. Only her head was visible, face appearing nearly as white as the bed sheet. Shades were drawn, and an untouched lunch sat idle on the bed table. The room smelled of death.

I leaned over the bed and gently hugged her, saying, "Mom. I love you and I'm here to take care of you—for a change. I'm here when you need me."

"Ummmm. Ohhh, don't squeeze so hard. I love you too."

Uncle Ed stood at the foot of the bed, watching the scene and ready to pounce on me or anyone else who threatened his sister. His critical eye judged my every move. He blamed me for her condition, and he made sure I knew it.

I held Mom's right hand for what seemed like an hour, until she patted my hand with her left hand and said, "Go home and get some rest."

"No Mom. There's something I have to say and now's the time to say it—been too long in coming. You up for a good dose of the truth?"

"Always," she whispered.

Continuing to hold her frail hand, I said, "You devoted your entire life to me and my happiness. Too many times I've taken advantage of your boundless love. I'm a self-centered coward."

"You were my life—I had no choice. I loved you more than life itself," she replied, pausing after every third word to catch her breath.

"It's my turn to apologize," I continued, "for all the things I've knowingly or unknowingly done to hurt you. For the past six years, I've nourished my indulgences while starving your boundless love. It's been a one-way street—all about me. I'll confess: my adventures exceeded my wildest expectations, carrying me to the tops of mountains. Standing up there, I began to believe that I was invincible; never thought judgment day would come. However, the price I paid was with your blood, sweat and tears. For all the pain and disappointment I've inflicted, I humbly apologize. I am so truly sorry."

I managed to hold back the tears forming at the corners of my eyes so I could finish what I wanted to say.

"I'm here for you, and I'm going to stay with you for as long as it takes to get you back on your feet. It's my turn to do the giving for a change. "

A smile appeared on chapped lips, but she was too weak to speak. Mom squeezed my hand in loving appreciation that only a mother can convey. Closing her eyes, she rested.

Within an hour, her doctor made rounds. Following his exam we spoke in the hallway.

"Your mother is very weak," he said. "She has a duodenal ulcer. Unfortunately, she didn't come in until it reached an advanced stage. These ulcers are usually caused by an infection with a bacterium called *H. pylori*. A 4 to 8-week course of acid-suppressing medication may allow the ulcer to heal. In addition, a one-week course of two antibiotics plus an acid-suppressing medicine may clear the *H. pylori* infection. This usually prevents the ulcer from coming back.

"However, your mother is at a crucial stage. At this point, she and God are in control. If she gives up, expect the worse. However, she could fight her way back. We'll just have to observe her and see how much fight she has left."

With the exception of going home to shower and get some clothes out of my car, I didn't leave her side for seven days. Occasionally, I fed her and ate the leftovers. The hospital cafeteria provided me with two meals a day. Otherwise, I remained with Mom day and night. For the first time in my life, she was the center of my attention, not me.

"How long you going to be home?" she asked one day.

"For as long as it takes to get you up and going again."

"Then what?"

"I've been thinking about that all week. Don't know exactly what's next. Right now, you are all that's important to me. I'm here to help you get back on your feet, for as long as that takes. You're sick and I'm a broken man. Together, we'll lean on each other and make it back. Besides, I need time to put Humpty Dumpty back together again. Ya know, this week with you gave me time to think. I decided that I'm not going back on the road. That life is behind me."

"Thank God."

"It's time I gave back some of the love you've given me—all your life."

"Son. You've succeeded in everything you put your mind to."

"That might have been true before I dropped out of Tech. Since then, I've failed as a bandleader and failed at marriage. My batting average for the past six years is lousy."

"You will succeed at anything you put your mind to. I know you'll make the right choice this time. I can feel it in my bones."

"You gonna be here to cheer me on?"

"You bet."

"I'm going to hold you to that. Now get up and try to walk with me."

From that moment on, she got better by the day. Even Uncle Ed was amazed at her recovery, and cut me a little slack—just a little. Truth be known, I was recovering, too. Humpty Dumpty was getting reassembled, piece-by-piece.

Happy to be home with Mom the following week, I began rebuilding my life and helping Mom rebuild her health. She gave me hope, and I gave her a reason to live. I got a job selling stereos and televisions, augmented by one-night sideman gigs. Not much money, but enough to get by. I knew my career was going nowhere, although being home with Mom was satisfaction enough, for now. I was doing the giving, and it felt good.

Absorbed as I was taking care of Mom, I was caught off-guard by the unexpected phone call from my long-time booking agent, Abie Goldstein.

"I have a Friday and Saturday night gig at the Shreveport Elks Club—want it?" he asked.

On a lark, I accepted. Mom was recovering and didn't need me as much. So I became leader of a dynamic duo playing ricky-ticky music with a recovering alcoholic who sang like Peggy Lee and played a Hammond B-3 organ. We opened on Friday at the Elks Club, the lowest-priced private dinner club in Shreveport. We must have done something right because they liked us—all 300 of 'em.

Midnight Saturday, Abie approached to collect his commission and discuss business, saying, "If you pay me double to make up for commissions you cheated me out of at Saks, I'll keep you in this Elks gig for as long as you want."

Abie was right about stiffin' him on Saks commissions, sort of, so I said, "Sign me up."

Then, I made another decision. On Monday I drove to Ruston and enrolled in the School of Business Administration. The same prim and proper born-again registration counselor from six years earlier, the one with a puffy lacquered bouffant hairdo, squeaked, "Weeellllll, we can transfer your engineering math credits and you'll graduate with a math minor if you add three statistics classes. Aaaaaaaand, beginning this semester, Tech is offering a brand new computer science curriculum. We're soooooooo excited. Tech just got our own IBM 360 computer and a professor with a PhD in Computer Science from the University of Alabama. Wanna sign up?"

"You bet. Sign me up for statistics and computer classes. Guess I'll need some business classes thrown in. What books will I need?"

Stuffing the requisite books in my attaché, I went off in search of a place to live, finally renting an apartment over the bus station. No need for a clock as the Greyhound buses roused me on schedule every day—10:42 p.m., 2:28 a.m., 3:19 a.m. and 5:34 a.m.—accompanied by the stench of diesel fumes and the roar of the belching engines.

The apartment featured a bedroom with a sagging mattress on a cast-iron double bed, a kitchen with a porcelain-topped metal table and two vinyl-covered chairs, and a bathroom down a long hallway. A large drafting table completed the appointments. No air conditioning. The pre-war brown vinyl floors and dismal gray walls set a new low for decorum. I managed to erase most of the depressed atmosphere with a fresh coat of honey-mustard yellow splashed on walls and a 12x12-foot rug imported from Shreveport. Goodwill had a sale on Michelangelo, Picasso, Wang Ximeng, and Monet prints, transporting a touch of culture onto unsullied walls. The stereo got assembled and record albums organized.

Standing by the drafting table, I swore to do whatever it takes to graduate from Louisiana Tech.

Opening the terse *Computer Fundamentals* textbook, I began my campaign toward victory.

I attended my first class Wednesday morning, an alien sitting next to pale-skinned, born-again Christian virgins and momma's boys displaying boners.

I made the best of it. Classes on Mondays, Wednesdays, and Fridays, studies and fly-fishing Tuesdays and Thursdays, playing the Elks' gig Friday and Saturday nights and bartending Sunday mornings for passionately dedicated Elks. I even found time to open a small music school in a Ruston radio station—five drum and bass students signed up for classes. However, my schedule included time with Mom every weekend. We both got stronger by the day.

I settled into a routine and made it work. Ready for a treat, the Lincoln got a "For Sale" sign and I bought a 1963 Buick Rivera with a brilliant gold flake paint job.

The courses at Tech were intellectually challenging. My computer science professor knew his stuff, requiring determined effort to grasp technical concepts at warp speed. Statistics classes proved fascinating. That said the big surprise was Dr. Frank Edens, professor of Modern Organization Management Theory and other business courses. Reserved, ultra-conservative, eloquent, and published, Dr. Edens and I were polar opposites. Nonetheless, he became a lot more than a great teacher. He provided new dimensions to my thinking during our office visits.

I spun a lot of positives about my adventures to elevate my stature in his eyes. Inadvertently, I revealed how much I made as leader of the Carousels.

"That's more than I make as a college professor," he replied. "If you were that successful, why did you quit the road and return to Louisiana Tech? What demons are you running away from?"

That was the question, wasn't it? The man had cut to the core. It was time to abandon my cocky façade and reveal all my sins from my decadent adventure on the road.

I confessed God Power, the Venus saga, the brotherhood breakup and the downward spiral that followed. I even mentioned my mystical dream on Melbourne Beach—starring Ann-Margret and a ghost crab—that ultimately led me back to Louisiana Tech. The mask was removed and the truth was exposed.

My ultra-conservative professor listened to every bizarre tale, a look of shock on his face. At the end of my true confession, he finally spoke.

"You've squandered your God-given talents, turned your back on decency, moral standards, good taste and propriety. In life's class on character, you clearly get an 'F'. As I look at you today, I have to wonder about your true character."

Pausing for a moment, Dr. Edens seemed to reach a conclusion.

"Are you the Prodigal Son, returning home after living in sin and wasteful extravagance?" he asked. "The Prodigal Son realized the depths he had sunk, crawled back home, and was embraced by a loving father. You've come home and been welcomed by your loving mother. The big question is have you really changed? Can you climb out of the demonic pit you've dug for yourself?"

That was as much as either of us could handle that afternoon. We concluded our talk, but agreed to meet the following afternoon.

Am I really a Prodigal Son? Can I overcome my demons and be the man my parents want me to be? Can Dr. Edens show me the way?

Chapter 60

1966
ABRACADABRA

I wasn't sure I could handle another session with Dr. Edens, but I managed to force myself to knock on the door of his office for our next appointment. Whether he was surprised that I came back, I couldn't tell.

We sat facing each other as he began probing deeper into my soul.

"Tell me more about this God Power you spoke of, and how you used it to control your audiences. Does it really work, or are you dancing on the cusp of self-delusion and madness?"

"God Power is the Holy Grail of the entertainer," I said. "While leading the Carousels, my God Powers focused on spiritual conversations, compelling adoring fans to worship the Carousels. With practiced techniques, concentration, and tenacity, audiences transformed into disciples. I discovered ways to control human thoughts and attitudes, leveraging God Power to expedite opportunity. God Power armed me to achieve supreme control over others."

Dr. Edens frowned.

"Who's sitting with me today, Rocky or Dean? Whoever you are, you scare the hell out of me … a paranoid schizophrenic. You need professional help."

We spoke for a few more minutes, although I was in no condition to continue and said I'd be back the next day.

I felt humiliated. My professor thinks I'm nuts. What's the use of going back?

Body bent in shame as I walked back to my apartment. I encountered a pair of barking dogs finding easy prey. They smelled my weakness.

The next day turned out to be a surprise. Rather than continuing his endless litany of my sins, Dr. Edens made his confession. He also had demons.

He began his confession by telling me about a 12-year career at Dow Chemical, working with punch cards in the IBM unit record department and processing payroll and accounts receivables. By his own admission, he wasn't good at it. However, while with Dow, he earned an MBA and began thinking about a PhD. That's when he concocted a scheme where he would be laid off or fired and use the generous Dow severance pay to complete his doctorate. He even convinced his boss to go along with the ruse. Somehow, the scheme succeeded.

When the momentous date arrived, the boss delivered the termination notice with a straight face, smiling at the end. Dr. Edens was stunned, realizing his boss had out-foxed him—the boss was looking for a way to fire him all along.

As he talked, I realized that his job failure and termination from Dow still torments him. He's bitter with himself.

There was more. While he was earning a PhD from the University of Texas as a graduate student and adjunct professor, one of his students, an ex-Marine by the name of Charles Joseph Whitman, armed himself with a sniper rifle, climbed to the top of the university's bell tower and killed 14 people and wounded 32 during a shooting rampage. The massacre affected everyone, particularly Dr. Edens. In one day, he lost 40 percent of his students, including Charles Joseph Whitman—gone forever.

Emotionally bankrupt, Dr. Edens said he struggled to finish his PhD. Wrestling with disillusion and gruesome demons, he ran away by accepting a tenured professorship at Louisiana Tech.

Synchronicity? Indeed. Dr. Edens and I were desperately searching for a handle on a planet spinning out of control. Peer professors at Louisiana Tech were inculcated in North Louisiana narrow-mindedness. Apparently, my out-of-the-box thinking attracted Dr. Edens to me, and his enormous intellect and wisdom attracted me to him. A fragile friendship emerged.

Dr. Edens confessed that the Dow termination and the Texas massacre still haunt him.

"I'm emotionally distraught, preoccupied with the 'whys,'" he told me. "Those two events killed my optimism and faith in mankind. I can't teach anyone anything—not until I wrestle my debilitating demons into submission. Find another teacher. You're on your own.'"

Angry at his defeatist attitude, I shot back.

"I came back to Tech out of fear of failure as a man. Failure is not an option. I have to learn, right here, right now. It's your job to teach me. Don't squander your responsibilities by hiding behind false demons. I can't afford to wait for you to get your head straight. Unlock that big brain of yours and teach me important things. I have to have it—right now. Get your head out of your ass and teach me. I demand you teach me!"

He looked at me, speechless. I was the first to challenge his demons. With nothing else to say, I rose and left him to wrestle away the afternoon with dragons. Only time would tell if he was up to teaching me anything.

The following day, Dr. Edens displayed a metamorphic transformation, becoming the great teacher I had demanded. At that seminal moment, we realized we desperately needed each other. During the rest of my time at Tech, I spent many hours in his office discussing the meaning of life with him.

At one of those meetings, Dr. Edens paid me the supreme compliment, saying, "My name is Frank. Yours is Dean. Let's be friends."

At another meeting, Frank moved a heavy urn from his credenza to the center of his desk and took a sheaf of paper from a desk drawer.

"Take these 20 pieces of paper," he said, "and write down the stuff you're ashamed of—sins, shortcomings, hatred, flaws, guilt—limit yourself to the top 20."

I did what he asked and noticed he also was scribbling. Frank placed his 20 sheets in the urn and motioned for me to follow his example. Then he lit a match and touched it to the slips of paper, saying, "Abracadabra. Abracadabra. By the powers vested in Dean and Frank, we hereby send our guilt, sins, selfishness, embarrassments, grudges and anger up in smoke, freeing us forever from these heavy burdens. We cast off our guilt, never to embrace self-persecution again. I forgive Dean—Dean forgives Frank. And, most importantly, we forgive ourselves. We are free to live our lives as we choose— in pursuit of happiness, love and self-esteem—emboldened by self-forgiveness."

The pieces of paper blazed away in the urn and gray smoke rose, carrying away the very essence of our guilt. Frank and I never mentioned our past again or the heavy burdens we wrote down on those sheets of paper. Self-forgiveness is potent magic.

Abracadabra.

Over the following months Frank and I explored many subjects. Tracts from Plato, Socrates, Aristotle, Archimedes, Pythagoras, Galileo, Michelangelo, Newton, Da Vinci, Pascal, Locke, Darwin, and Einstein served as discussion guides. Enlightened, we traveled light years beyond the city limits of provincial Ruston.

Frank and I debated disparate views on Vietnam, Civil Rights, the Kennedys, President Johnson, and protesters.

"We're living in a divided nation," Frank said during one of our sessions. "Black against white, Democrats against Republicans, and militant protesters against our government, courts, religion and cultural norms. Over time, President Johnson's Great Society is destined to bankrupt America. It's chaos out there, and it's getting worse by the day. America is spinning out of control."

I asked him to explain.

"America's got 250,000 troops in Vietnam," he said. "When you graduate you'll probably be drafted and sent off to war—you'll die. U.S. planes are bombing Hanoi and Haiphong. Thousands of dissidents are demonstrating across the United States against the Vietnam War. Some 20,000 South Vietnam Buddhists marched in demonstrations against the policies of their and our governments. Tens of thousands of anti-war demonstrators are picketing the White House and the Washington Monument.

"Civil Rights activist James Meredith was shot while trying to march across Mississippi. Meanwhile, Bobby Seale and Huey Newton founded the Black Panther Party and boasted of their license to kill. This country is at war with itself. Everyone's the enemy, and no one trusts anyone. We're rushing into chaos. Love of mankind is out of vogue. As a nation, we've lost our moral compass. We're at the beginning of the end. America's future is bleak."

"If that's so," I replied, "where am I in this world of upheaval?"

"You caught a music wave just before it crashed hard on the beach. About three years ago your wave crested, ending the golden era of music, replaced by a new wave—Beatlemania, Rolling Stones, Jimmy Hendrix, Bob Dylan, and acid rockers. That's life— eventually all good things hit the beach, suffering a predictable, but agonizing end. Look around. You're lying next to music legends, also abandoned on the scorched sands of time. There's Cole Porter, Harold Arlen, Miles Davis, Oscar Peterson, Gerry Mulligan, The Four Freshman, Bill Haley, The Platters, Otis Redding, Etta James, Fats Domino, Andy Williams, Woody Herman, Stan Kenton, Al Hirt, Pete Fountain, and hundreds of yesterday's music legends. They simply fell out of favor—victims of life's natural cycle. Catch a fresh wave forming over the horizon, way out at sea. Catch it early and you'll ride the crest to a rewarding career."

"Okay friend," I said. "Which wave do I catch?"

"First, reread Ayn Rand's *Atlas Shrugged*. You'll learn more about the free market economy and strategic thinking in there than you'll get out of an MBA at Louisiana Tech. To prove my point, name the dominant symbol as the book ends. It's the U.S. dollar sign. Objectivism works. Visualize your private heaven in Galt's Gulch. That said, you'll pay a price—suffering through Rand's dystopian society, objectivism, ultimate inversion, and antichrist caricatures. Separate the wheat from the chaff. On your second reading, you'll emerge with illuminated horizons.

"Secondly, avoid getting embroiled in an immoral war or dissident movements against our government. Johnny Mercer and Harold Arlen said it best in *Accentuate the Positive*. In 1945 it was No. 1 on Billboard and remains the guidepost for a life well lived.

"Fortunately, Dean Strong has choices. Your math scores were in the upper 10 percentile on the Graduate Record Examinations. That alone qualifies you to apply for a master's program—avoiding the draft. You've shown interest and aptitude for computer science. I don't know if that's a real profession yet. On the other hand, with your brains, computers could hold promise. And Tech's new PhD in computer science is among the best computer guys in the South. He'll prepare you intellectually for the computer industry—a new wave forming over the horizon. After all, it's in your nature to embrace risks."

This was a lot to absorb. Frank was filling the dual roles of surrogate father and oracle—leading me away from self-destruction, toward positive possibilities. A roadmap for living a worthwhile life. Frank gave me permission to forgive myself, although his biggest gift was permission to become a straight. As my teacher and friend, Frank equipped me to achieve peace of mind as a straight. Once again, I recalled 'Alice's Adventures in Wonderland.'

"Would you tell me, please, which way I ought to go from here?"

"That depends a good deal on where you want to get to," said the Cat.

"I don't much care where—" said Alice.

"Then it doesn't matter which way you go," said the Cat.

"—so long as I get SOMEWHERE," Alice added as an explanation.

"Oh, you're sure to do that," said the Cat, "if you only walk long enough."

Curled up two seats away, Mad Hatter groused, *"Do you know 'Twinkle Twinkle Little Star?'"*

Chapter 61

1967
HERE COMES THE SUN

That was my story. It took a few hours, but Daryl listened to every word without interruption as we sat in the varsity gym that night.

Finally, he asked, "Will you ever go back on the road as a professional musician?"

"Nope. I'm out of time with changing times. During my time, a trailing generation became disenfranchised, betrayed by the hypocrisy of their parents and national leaders. They turned to acid, blow, bongs, angel dust, amp, applejacks, aunt mary, and auntiemma, opening thoroughfares to faux intellectual freedom, escape from reality, and rebellion against everything establishment. Veiled in ambiguity, the hippie generation was born, searching for the meaning of life, channeling a spaced-out communion with an imaginary god.

"Overnight, old school became passé. The Summer of Love was held in San Francisco's Height-Ashbury District. Hippie school was in, creating a demand for amped music to accompany space cadet hallucinations. *Sgt. Pepper's Lonely Hearts Club Band* engulfed the looking glass, transforming musical taste forever.

"Impregnated by psychedelia, the fallaciously idiotic perceived brilliance—garrulously gushing out of Lennon, McCartney, and

Harrison's lyrics—linked up with a stoned audience—accelerating America's cultural revolution to warp speed. *Lucy in the Sky with Diamonds* speaks volumes … a personal testimonial to LSD. Everything we need know about that battery acid generation is right there, compacted into one song. Just four years my junior, that stoned generation un-plugged from the grid, seeking enlightenment by altering cognition and perception inside a hallucinatory haze. Music tailored to hippie philosophies and subculture precipitated a whimsical marriage made in druggie heaven."

"On the contrary, weren't you chasing the dragon?" Daryl responded. "You certainly had access and opportunity."

Following a long pause, I chose to answer by quoting from Jack Kerouac, *The Scripture of the Golden Eternity*: "*Roaring dreams take place in a perfectly silent mind. Now that we know this, throw the raft away.*"

"I know it sounds square, almost puritanical, but I abstained from heavy drugs, with the exception of my beloved Scotch. Clearheaded, I captured enlightened observations in indelible detail. Even though I'm sober as a Presbyterian minister, my gray matter chases dragons nonstop. The elusive pursuit of the ultimate high is ever-present in me, living large in dimensions of John Locke's empiricism experience. Stone cold sober, I'm tap-dancing on the edge of a straight razor, struggling to maintain balance."

Looking straight into Daryl's eyes, I confessed, "I'm terrified of tripping over the razor's edge and never righting myself. Right now, I'm standing tall on my hill and can see Valhalla, the same Valhalla the psychedelic generation is misguidedly searching for in their valley. In spite of our common goals, our conduits are spectacularly different. At 27, I'm a dinosaur—relegated to old-school square—desperately searching for a handle on a world spinning out of control. Druggies never search for handles."

Slouched in the gymnasium chair, feet draped over the seat below, my mind drifted aimlessly toward a peaceful state, forgetting for a moment that Daryl was occupying space on that row, just two seats away.

Reconnecting with Daryl, I tried to explain my feelings at this moment.

"I'm emancipated. Released from self-imposed imprisonment. I'm free to pick up the next wave forming over the horizon. It'll carry me in new directions—new career—cresting on the beach long after I pass into the spirit world. Yes, I'll miss applause and adoration—desperately. However, the music I love was abandoned on forgotten beaches. My Linus blanket will always be a good single-malt Scotch and my vintage vinyl classical and jazz record collection."

The sun was beginning to make an appearance, sending multi-layered shades of purple through the windows and across the gymnasium ceiling.

"So, here we are Daryl—my big day. I'm pleased Mom and Uncle Ed are driving over from Shreveport. I'll wave to them when I receive my sheepskin. Finally, they'll be proud of something I do—see me walk across that stage and receive a Bachelor of Science in Business Administration. Gosh, I hope they're proud of me, at least this morning. The Mason's set a very high bar: 'Make your father proud.' I'm finally getting there."

I've probably lived higher highs and lower lows than anyone my age—probably exceeding the guy delivering the commencement address this morning. So far, life's been one hell of a ride, in spite of my madness. One question remains: Who is Rocky Strong; or should I be asking, Who is Dean Strong?

"*Oh, you can't help that,*" purred Cheshire Cat, curled in my lap. "*We're all mad here. I'm mad. You're mad.*"

Stretched out the balcony ledge, Mad Hatter purred, "*Okay, he's as mad as a box of frogs … I rest my case! … I think our luck is finally changing … Follow me; I'm getting us out of here.*"

As if on cue, the sun's rays erupted, washing away shades of purple and splashing eye-squinting brilliant orange everywhere. Daryl extended his hand, saying, "Rocky, thanks for sharing your story. Congratulations on graduating this morning … quite a journey."

Nodding, I shook Daryl's hand, replying, "Good luck as a novelist. Perhaps tonight's tale will turn into your first of many best sellers."

The irony of it all. Today, I realize that the Carousels' demise was brought on by revolutionary changes in America, not by the Beatles. I'm beginning to see reality. Guess I'll try to play in time with changing times.

A tune penned by a spaced-out George Harrison in Eric Clapton's garden came to mind, summing up everything. Humming the melody line as I reached the top of the stairs, I turned and headed for the green Exit sign on the south end of the gymnasium. All constraints abandoned, I bellowed out *Here Comes the Sun.*

> *Here comes the sun*
> *Here comes the sun, and I say it's all right*
>
> ...
>
> *Little darling the smiles returning to the faces*
> *Little darling it seems like years since it's been here*

My eyes squinted from the radiance of a new day and Mad Hatter grimaced, leading our way. Cheshire Cat followed with a broad smile. Satisfied at last, my gait fell into time with changin' times. Peace enveloped me.

> *Here comes the sun*
> *Here comes the sun, and I say it's all right*

Before passing under the Exit light, I looked back. Daryl was shaking his head as he turned away. "Well, at least Rocky was honest about one thing. He really can't sing."

The looking glass never lies. Surviving the American Cultural Revolution, the most tumultuous decade of the 20th Century, Dean "Rocky" Strong stepped through the looking glass and experienced life to its fullest: youthful dreams, hopes, fears, free love, subterraneans, drugs, mobsters, conspiracies, assassinations, eroticism, betrayal, and, ultimately, self-actualization.

It was lunacy.

Yet, on Dean's deathbed, he's certain to display a massive smile— reveling in having had the guts to exploit madness. After all, it was in his nature to do so.

THE END

Epilogue
What Happened to the
Cast of Characters?

PRINCIPAL CAST OF CHARACTERS

Bobby Starr died in 1969 at 2:30a.m. on a desolate highway, 12 miles south of Monroe. Bobby was high on drugs when he stopped to change a flat tire. Two spades drove up to help, Bobby smarted off, a tussle ensued, the blacks wrestled Bobby's tire iron away and bludgeoned him to death. Bobby's squeeze and enabler, Ana-Mae Mobley, described the shines to police and to Bobby's father. According to the grape vine, Bobby's father and five Klan members bludgeoned the two blacks to death in their beds, wielding Bobby's very own tire iron. No one has ever been charged with the murders.

Norman "Smoke" Van Dyke continued to blow smoke, particularly about the Carousels and his insider knowledge of JFK's assassination. Remaining a professional musician without distinction, Smoke suffered from alcoholism and over-indulgence in weed and multiple hard drugs. He filed for bankruptcy and died at 34, absent friends or family. Smoke was buried with his only remaining possession, a cherry red ES-345 Thinline Semi-Hollow Electric Archtop Gibson guitar.

Lance Love married Angelle Devero shortly after the birth of their second child. Following the Carousel breakup in Nashville, Lance and Angelle moved back to Monroe, became born-again Christians and pillars of the community. He cursed John Lennon and women for destroying the Carousel brotherhood. Rocky and Lance commiserated by phone shortly before Lance died of cancer in 2012. Angelle and two loving children were at his side.

Joseph "Big Joe" Robecheaux remained a full-time musician, moved to Dallas, and worked part time as a contractor for Bell Helicopter in the numeric controls division. Big Joe divorced Gert after more than 30 years of tortuous hell. In 1995, Rocky saw Big Joe in Dallas playing at a downtown casual bar and grill. Big Joe weighed over 300 pounds, sported a full grey beard down to his waist, but played and sang great Ray Charles songs as the alpha dog of the band. His life ended in 2004, caused by the widow maker, a massive heart attack.

Marion "Rooster" Badcock disappeared from the commercial music scene, mandated by his born-again Pentecostal wife. Rooster became an inside sales representative for an electrical wholesale distributor. As the story goes, Rooster was speaking in tongues, living out the literal interpretation of Scripture, preaching evangelism, and tickling the ivories at a Pentecostal Church in Shreveport. Rooster and his Holy Roller wife spawned seven warm-blooded disciples. He died on December 31, 2000, from the widow maker.

Mathew "Dallas" Fingers remained a professional musician, limiting his realm to Shreveport and Bossier. He fronted several upscale restaurants and bars with his own band and nightclub management abilities. However, over time, all his business ventures failed. But in the process, Dallas received a bachelor's degree in Business Administration from Centenary College, ran for Mayor of Shreveport, but received less than 1 percent of the vote. At this writing, Mary and Dallas remain happily married with five offspring. Dallas is a Deacon in the First Baptist church of Shreveport.

Dean "Rocky" Strong graduated from Louisiana Tech with a B.S. in Business Administration at 11:30a.m. on May 29, 1967. Dean extended the Elks Club gig and enrolled in Tech's newly created Master's of Computer Science program. He caught the new computer wave at exactly the right time and spent the next four decades building a successful career and loving family. Dean serves as an Ordained Elder in the Presbyterian Church, achieving stature as a straight while skillfully disguising madness—most of the time. At long last, Dean made his father, mother and the Mason's proud.

SUPPORTING CAST OF CHARACTERS

Venus Cruz Strong received final divorce papers from Dean's lawyer in the fall of 1967. Preceding the final divorce decree, she made a pilgrimage to Shreveport. Venus and Dean fucked like minks all day, but Dean got up, washed up and walked out on the femme fatale—never speaking with her again. A month later, Venus put a .45 caliber bullet through her Barbie Doll brain.

Angelle Devero Love—Following the birth of her second son and marriage to Lance, they settled into an unpretentious life in Monroe. Angelle went on a diet, recaptured her youthful beauty and dedicated her life to Lance, two children and church.

Gertrude "Gert" Brown Robecheaux was finally served with divorce papers from Joseph "Big Joe" Robecheaux. According to Big Joe, Gert became a slobbering alcoholic, homeless derelict, and died in a Dallas alley from a drug overdose. Big Joe loved Gert, all the way to her bitter end. Big Joe never revealed the essence of the mysterious elixir in Gert's black coffee cup.

Mary Fingers remains happily married to Mathew "Dallas" Fingers. They attend the First Baptist Church and have five well-balanced rug rats. Last time Rocky saw Mary, she thanked him for serving as bridesmaid in her wedding. Mary and Dallas Fingers still live in Shreveport.

Goldie's trademark remained her solid-gold tooth in the middle of a glistening smile, wider than a '52 Buick Roadmaster's grill. During Dean's return to Tech, he and a friend ate lunch at the Nanking Restaurant, orders taken by Goldie. Although Goldie was married, she still had the urge and made it known she was available for the afternoon. Dean's lunch buddy looked at him with a scowl, reminiscent of Pappy Morgan's disapproval from years past. Graciously declining her invitation, Dean resumed his conversation with his buddy and consumed Mu Shu Pork, served by Goldie.

Barbara Banks delivered a boy in Phoenix, Arizona, facilitated by a Catholic adoption agency. Although Barbara and Dean stayed in touch, they never discussed the obvious. Following Rocky's graduation, Barbara moved to Oklahoma and worked in state government until her retirement in 2010. Had the timing and events differed slightly …

Finn chose Airborne, Ranger, and Officer Candidate School, completed his third tour in Vietnam and retired from the Army with a government-funded undergraduate and master's degrees in business and finance. Happily married for 46 years, Finn epitomizes the warrior's warrior, quietly wrestling with demons, sleepless nights, and madness.

Dr. Frank Edens retired a full-tenured professor from Louisiana Tech and lived peacefully in Ruston. For many years, Dr. Edens and

Dean met to discuss the world situation, secrets of life, universal truths, God, and the hereafter. Dr. Frank Edens died with Dean at his bedside in 2007. Thanks, Frank, for giving Dean permission to be a straight!

Mom Strong finally had something to be proud of in her only remaining child: Dean's graduation from college, marriage to a Cajun Catholic, two grandchildren, and Dean's stature in the Tampa community. Dean moved Mom Strong from Shreveport to Tampa, arranged for residency in a nearby retirement community and immersed her into a loving family environment. At 83, she passed peacefully with a smile on her face. Dean was at her side.

Cheshire Cat and **Mad Hatter** remained with Dean for the duration of their nine lives, purring away with *Alice's Adventures in Wonderland* philosophies that only Dean could hear.

Final Thoughts

Transitioning from the Carousels, back to Louisiana Tech, into the computer industry, locating in New Orleans then Tampa, Dean put distance between his bent Carousel years and life as a straight. Dean often savors the rich memories of the subterraneans and the glorious times on the road with the Fabulous Carousels. In the November of his years, what better way to exit stage left than with a satisfying smile? That, too, is in his nature.

Author Resume

John L. Nelson graduated from Louisiana Polythnic Institute and served 40 years in the computer industry, 35 as a senior executive. He launched Nelson Consulting, Inc., (www.NelsonConsultingInc.com) in 2000, delivering merger, acquisition and investment banking services. Married with two grown children and two grandchildren, John lives in Tampa, Florida with his wife of 45 years. Although John has written countless business and techincal documents, this is his first novel.